DREAMS *of* REVOLUTION

A Novel

Linda J. Collins

Linda J. Collins

Dreams of Revolution. Copyright 2021 by Linda J. Collins

573 Coleman Road
Mansfield, Ohio, 44903
www.lindacollinsauthor.com

Print ISBN: 978-1-09838-879-9
eBook ISBN: 978-1-09838-880-5

First Edition: September 2021

~ CHAPTER 1 ~

September 1777, Hopewell Village, Berks County, Pennsylvania

Fifteen-year-old Rachel Palsgrove slunk along the side of the rough stone building, hugging her body so close to it that the sandstone scoured the skin on her face and arms. The new crescent moon was barely visible tonight. The silhouettes of trees and buildings were hardly discernible, and this side of the furnace building was dark and deep in shadow. She moved slowly, her feet whispering in the tall, sweet-smelling grass. There were no trees nearby, so no dry leaves crackled underfoot. Her heart thudded, and bile rose in her throat, but curiosity drove her forward to the one small window. Her booted feet felt the ground tentatively. A soft spot or rabbit hole might twist an ankle. Reaching the window in the middle of the long wall, she peeped around its corner, spat on her fingers to wipe the caked-on dirt from the glass, and then rubbed her grimy fingers on her pants.

What is happening inside, she wondered. A brilliant glow illuminated the interior of the building. Red-hot liquid iron poured from the giant ladle hung from the pulley overhead. Sparks flew everywhere. Men scurried with their sand-filled mold boxes, positioning them under the river of metal. Near them, a team of workers struggled with a much larger mold box several feet high. Fascinating. She had never seen a mold that size. Usually, the furnace cast stove parts or iron pots. Furtively, she glanced down the wall to make sure no one was coming. Yells from inside made her turn back to the window. Her father, the furnace founder, shouted and gestured for more men to help support the large mold box as a heavy load of iron filled it.

A rustling at the far end of the building startled her. She could see nothing in the darkness, but the sound of someone approaching was unmistakable. She slithered as quickly as she could in the opposite direction. Before she turned the corner, she glanced back to see someone outlined by the glow of the window. *Who else is here?*

As Rachel backed around the corner, strong arms encircled her, squeezing her tight. Hot, rancid breath filled her ears. "I warned you yesterday evening to stay away, and here you are again," George Coggins growled.

She struggled in his grasp. "Let me go!" she squealed. "You're hurting me."

A teamster loading his wagon across the way looked up at the commotion. His cream-colored team stamped their feet. "Do you need help, Miss?" he called.

"Mind your own business, Jesse," George retorted. "She knows she shouldn't be here."

The teamster looked away and continued his loading.

"What did you see in the window?"

"Nothing," she lied. "I never got that far."

He relaxed his grip, then grabbed her arm and jerked her away from the building. She stumbled behind him.

"Go home," he commanded, flinging her forward, "and don't come back."

"Please don't tell my father I was here," she begged, rubbing her bruised arm.

"I must. You've left me no choice. Now go."

She sniffed back tears, then hurried down the lane toward home, glancing over her shoulder once. He was still glaring at her, a greasy lock of black hair draped over his forehead and burly arms crossed over his chest. *Father is going to whip me when he finds out.*

Rachel crossed the little wooden bridge spanning French Creek that carried runoff from the waterwheel at the furnace. A short distance later, she turned onto the path to her house, then peered in the window. The keeping room was empty. The structure was dark, just as she had left it several hours ago.

She lifted the latch and entered the kitchen. The smell of freshly baked bread in the pie safe permeated the room. As she turned to tiptoe up the stairs, a stern voice from the keeping room commanded, "Come here, Rachel."

Now I'm caught again, she thought as she slunk into the room. "Oh, Mother, I thought you were in bed."

"Sit down."

Rachel crossed the room to the chair. Her mother struck a match, and the candle on the table beside her flickered to life. Silhouettes of Rachel and her mother danced on the walls. On the settee, Rachel saw the shirt her mother had been sewing earlier beside the sewing basket. Her mother sighed at the sight of her daughter crumpled in the chair.

"I've been waiting a long time for you to return. Where have you been? I've warned you over and over about going out at night."

Rachel's leg jigged. "I get so restless, Mother. I can't stay inside."

"Running around the village in the middle of the night is shameful behavior for a young woman. We've been through this before. Why don't you listen?"

"Hopewell is so different at night, Mother. Everything seems to come alive. The creatures roaming around—skunks and possums and deer. There are the nighttime sounds of crickets and katydids in the meadow and the people bustling at the furnace. I want to see it all."

"There's no time to explore every night. Your curiosity will get you in trouble. You should be in bed, especially tonight. You must prepare for the dance tomorrow evening. There are lots of chores to be done before then."

"Must I go to the dance?" Rachel whined.

"Yes, your schooling will be done soon, and you need to find a beau. You'll never meet one spending all your time in that smelly barn with horses or with your nose in a book."

"But I don't want a beau, Mother."

"You can't stay with Father and me the rest of your life. You need to start wearing dresses and not breeches all the time. They're not ladylike. You don't want to end up a spinster with no means of support. Now go to bed."

"Yes, Mother." She knew further discussion about dresses, the dance, and marriage was hopeless, but she wasn't about to give up her late-night excursions. Hopewell bared its secrets at night, and she yearned to discover them, no matter what the consequences. *You can't stop me!*

~ CHAPTER 2 ~

In the parlor of the Big House, Rachel sat beside Susanna Sterling at a wooden card table inlaid with fancy scrolls and cherubs. Rachel marveled at the opulent furnishings of the room. There was a wide fireplace, with ornately carved woodwork and brass andirons, below the almost life-sized, gilt-framed portrait of Daniel Sterling's father staring from above the mantle. A colorful wool rug lay on the gleaming hardwood floor. Heavy floor-to-ceiling, green velvet drapes graced the large multi-paned windows, leather-bound tomes overflowed the bookcases, and a flint-lock musket hung over the doorway. A massive map on the wall showed, in shaded red areas, the Sterlings' land holdings, and the pigeonholes in the ironmaster's mahogany desk were bursting with papers. A small fire crackled and popped in the grate, taking the autumn chill off the room.

The girls were here for their lessons in math, classical poetry and literature, and writing. Mr. Elliott, their tutor, was a lanky man with soft, brown eyes topped by a high forehead. At the nape of his neck lay a wild shock of curly, shoulder-length, dark hair. His simple suit was well-worn and a little frayed at the edges. He handed their papers to them.

"Rachel, would you please read your review of *Robinson Crusoe?*"

She stood and read her prose with enthusiasm, describing the plot and her favorite characters. Susanna, slouched in her chair, played with the cuff of her sleeve.

Rachel sat down and looked expectantly at her teacher. He said, "That was a marvelous report. It sounds like you immensely enjoyed Daniel Defoe's novel."

"Yes, I barely put it down long enough to do my chores. I would love to read similar books if you have them."

"I'll drop one at your house sometime this week. Susanna, let's hear your essay on *Gulliver's Travels*."

Susanna reluctantly rose, holding her paper in front of her. "Oh, I don't understand why it's necessary to read these stories and write about them. That's not going to help me run a household or catch a man," she lamented.

"A well-rounded lady in society has to be able to converse intelligently about the popular novels of our time."

"Well, I can understand the need for reading books, but writing about them ruins the book for me."

"Writing a composition is my way of making sure you finish the assigned work."

"My essays aren't as exciting as Rachel's and never will be," she protested. "How can I compete with her? She could be a writer herself."

"We are not competing. By composing essays, you sharpen your letter writing skills too."

"But the people to whom I'll send letters won't judge my grammar, punctuation, and penmanship like you do. There's too much work to do it perfectly."

"I'm sure at times you will correspond with influential people. They may not know you personally, and they'll judge you by how well you write. It *is* important," he insisted.

Susanna sighed, defeated again. She began to read haltingly. Rachel sat patiently, her drifting mind wondering what book the tutor would choose for her. *Why does Susanna always make such a fuss?* She supposed part of it was being a spoiled rich girl being bested in academic matters by a mere founder's daughter.

The Palsgroves paid for the tutor's services since schooling was neither mandatory nor free. Mr. Elliott thought Susanna might enjoy her education more if she had a companion close in age studying with her. But age was where their similarities ended. Susanna's interests were fashion and hair, boys and city life. Rachel dressed like a tomboy, usually didn't check her hair after combing it once in the morning, and wasn't very interested in the opposite sex. As for life in the city, Rachel had never even seen a city. Susanna delighted in accompanying her parents to Philadelphia to go shopping and to visit friends. Intellectually, Susanna was bright, but Mr. Elliott's best pupil was Rachel, who was constantly questioning and eager to learn.

Susanna finished her report and slumped in her chair. "You did a fine job," the teacher praised. When he glanced at the clock behind him, Susanna stuck out her tongue at Rachel.

"This new assignment is for the next time we meet. I want you to imagine what you want to accomplish in the future. What will you be doing in five years? Ten years? What are your dreams? I'll expect at least one written page with good grammar and penmanship, so don't dash it off the night before. Give it some thought, scribble your ideas, make a rough draft, and write a perfected final copy. Any questions? This will be our last requirement for our time together."

"I understand," said Susanna. "Thank goodness we aren't writing about a book. That will make it easier. I can make it up from my head."

Rachel nodded in agreement as Mr. Elliott gathered his books. "Meet here next Tuesday."

The following week, the girls sat primly on the chairs around the table, holding their final essays. Rachel wore a simple, floral frock, and Susanna wore a yellow ruffled dress that accentuated her blonde curls. The stately tall case clock in the corner ticked loudly as they waited for their tutor to get settled.

"Who wants to read their composition first?"

"I'll go first," volunteered Susanna. Both Mr. Elliott and Rachel looked surprised since Susanna never volunteered to share first.

She stood, smoothed down her petticoats, and coughed daintily. "My Future. Within the next five years, I will be living in Philadelphia in a mansion with lovely, manicured gardens filled with topiary plants shaped like exotic animals. In front, there will be a broad porch where guests can relax on wicker furniture on hot summer days. Six bedrooms will enable my friends and family to stay over anytime they visit. A cook, a maid, and another servant will tend the house and grounds.

"The carriage house in the back will stable two sleek, black horses and a black chaise with gilt accents and red leather cushions. I'll use it to attend parties and theater engagements with my friends. My clothes will be the latest fashions from Paris, and I won't wear the same dress more than twice. Ostrich feather plumes and fresh flowers will adorn my hats, and I'll own a set of gloves to match each outfit.

"To accompany me to social events, I'll choose from several suitors, each one more handsome than the other.

"In ten years, I picture myself happily married with two small children. My husband, a successful businessman, will be tall, with dark wavy hair and a mustache. He'll adore me and will be a doting father who roughhouses with our healthy, freckle-faced boy, and reads nursery rhymes to our blonde, curly-haired little girl.

"Every month, we'll host elaborate parties, attended by all the important people in Philadelphia. My husband's many business contacts will bring their lovely wives to view our richly decorated home. Everyone will eagerly attend our lavish fêtes.

"My days will be filled with running the household, pampering my children, and planning our social engagements. I'll be an envied pillar of the community."

Susanna sat down with a grin. Mr. Elliott was speechless. Susanna envisioned a life dreamed about by many women, but such a life was possible for her. He would never achieve such riches. He was a poor tutor, relegated to teaching the wealthy, not to experience being one of them.

Recovering from his initial shock, he said, "You did a fantastic job on your paper, Susanna. You gave the assignment a lot of thought and added some excellent details. That's your best work this year. Well done."

"Yes, I found this assignment easy." Her face glowed with pride.

"Rachel, could you read us your essay?"

Rachel now was the dismayed student. Her aspirations weren't anything like Susanna's, and they would probably both laugh. But if she were to achieve her goals, she had to acknowledge them to herself and everyone.

Rachel stood and said, "My dreams are quite different from hers. We have dissimilar personalities and stations in life, but these goals are as real to me as Susanna's are to her. I hope you won't think them odd or unachievable." She glanced nervously at their faces.

"I'm sure whatever you have written is fine, Rachel," Mr. Elliott encouraged. "There are no right or wrong ideas." Susanna smirked and gazed into space.

Rachel began. "My goal is to become a teacher, like Mr. Elliott. I admire the work he does, educating young people, and expanding their knowledge of the world. Learning is my greatest passion, and I want to not only know more facts and skills but learn how to instruct others.

"I want to attend the university in Philadelphia. When I graduate, I hope to find a teaching job in the city or a village like ours. By teaching scientific principles, perhaps students will invent products to make our lives easier. I want to enrich their days by exposing them to novels and newspapers that describe events here and elsewhere. They will learn mathematics, so unscrupulous people will be unable to cheat them. I want them to delight in music and dance and art to relieve the drudgery of everyday life.

"In ten years, I hope to have established a class of youngsters of various ages whom I have taught for several years. I'll add new young students each year, and as the older children mature, I'll feel fulfilled in having been a part of their development into productive young adults."

Rachel sat down. Susanna looked puzzled. "You didn't say anything about what kind of house you'd live in or your husband or children."

"The house where I live is not important, as long as it's adequate. I won't want a husband or children because I'll be too busy. I won't be responsible for cooking and cleaning and taking care of others since too many other exciting pursuits will occupy my time."

"I'm flattered you want to become a teacher, but Rachel, you know most young ladies desire a family and need to run a household. There are no female tutors for that reason."

"Don't you think I would be a good instructor, Mr. Elliott?" implored Rachel.

"Yes, I think you would be a great teacher, but it would be difficult to tend to a family and teach too."

"I realize a career and a busy home life aren't very compatible, though some women here at Hopewell have both. Look at Sally, who mines iron. She's doing a man's job and earning money. Then there's Tacy, who cuts wood for the colliers."

"Yes, but those mothers work due to necessity. Their husbands died young, and they need to support their children. You must admit, most women do not work outside their homes."

"But they do extra chores at home to earn money. They harvest excess food in their gardens to sell to the store, raise chickens or livestock for eggs or meat, spin yarn and weave cloth to sew clothes, or dip more candles than they need. Women are constantly working to make additional funds to help support their family. The only difference is men's jobs are valued more and pay more than women's work. I prefer a job I love and get paid decently for it than to do jobs around the house I don't enjoy."

"How will you be able to go to the university? I don't believe they allow ladies to attend, and even if they did, can your family pay the tuition?"

Rachel sighed. "That's the main problem with my dreams. My parents don't have the money, and they think further schooling for a girl is foolish. I'm not sure how I can go." She stared at the floor.

"Your goals are admirable," said Mr. Elliott, "but I can understand your family's reluctance to send you for more schooling. It's a big commitment of resources, and most young women find fulfillment with a husband and family."

"I'm not like most people," Rachel wailed. "I'm confident I can do the college work, but no one will give me a chance to prove myself."

He patted her on the shoulder. "You must trust everything will turn out for you."

Rachel, close to tears, sniffed and gathered her papers together. "Are we finished today?"

"Yes, we're done, not only for today but with your schooling from me. Here is a certificate of achievement for both of you. Congratulations."

Susanna eagerly looked at the parchment written in beautiful calligraphy and lightly hopped to her feet. "Thank you, Mr. Elliott. I'll run and show this to my mother."

"Yes, yes, go show her."

Susanna paused. "I'm sorry if I caused you aggravation over the years. You know how stubborn I can be."

"You are a delightful young lady, Susanna, and I enjoyed teaching you." She smiled and floated out of the room, calling for her mother.

"Aren't you excited about your certificate, Rachel?"

"I am, but I'm also sad because it signifies the end of my schooling with you."

"Your education always goes on. You can read books and newspapers, debate with your parents about events in the world, and continue to write. You have an excellent foundation of skills."

"It won't be the same," Rachel grumbled. "But I'll try to accept it and do the things you suggested. I find your teaching inspiring, sir."

"And you are one of my favorite students. You've made our time very enjoyable."

Rachel smiled weakly and went out the door onto the porch of the house. Holding her skirts aloft with one hand while holding her certificate in the other, she went down the steps and walked toward her house. *I'll find some way to achieve my goals, no matter what it takes,* she vowed.

~ CHAPTER 3 ~

As Tom McCauley's sweating, heaving body ebbed and flowed toward her, Rachel plastered a smile on her face. He locked his right arm with hers and swung her around, then hooked left arms and whirled in the other direction. Dizzy and nauseous from his exuberant twirling, she hardly kept her feet. Her bruised toes slammed back and forth in the oversized shoes she had borrowed from her older sister.

"Having a good time, Rachel?" shouted Tom over the din of the music. Twenty years older than her, his plump body and red face revealed his lack of physical prowess. As the store clerk, the most taxing job he performed daily was lifting his quill pen to scratch in his ledgers. The buttons on his casual shirt that fit him better twenty pounds ago strained and threatened to pop at any moment.

"Yes, Mr. McCauley, I'm enjoying the melodies."

"How old are you now, Rachel?"

"I turned fifteen last month."

"Please, call me Tom. Now that you're grown up, we can use first names."

"All right... Tom."

The caller's strong, clear voice belted out the steps to the dance. After what seemed like an eternity of swinging and foot-tapping and promenading, the music stopped.

"May I have the next dance?" Tom's flushed red cheeks and panting breaths made her wonder if he could survive another dance without collapsing.

"I think I'll sit awhile and get some cider. You're wearing me out."

"Why don't you sit there?" He motioned to a bale of straw off to one side. "I'll get us some drink."

"Don't you want to ask someone else to dance awhile?"

"No, I welcome a brief rest too. Would you like something to eat? A cookie perhaps, to go with some cider?"

"A pumpkin cookie would be fine if they have them." She knew they did because her sister had made them earlier.

Tom strode to the refreshment table, and Rachel glanced around. She fidgeted, wiggling her aching toes. The pins holding her dark shoulder-length hair on top of her head were digging into her scalp, and her ears were ringing from the loudness of the band in the confines of the hay-filled barn. The band played at all Hopewell's gatherings and alternated the tempo between rollicking tunes and slower-paced melodies. Through the dust motes flying, she craned her neck, hoping Nate Kirst, a suitor of her sister's with whom Rachel was slightly infatuated, would rescue her. She spied other boys and girls her age from the village, but there was no sign of Nate.

The dancers began to form groups for the next dance, and the band started playing again. Nimbly performing the steps to the frolicking quick step, the dancers tapped and floated around effortlessly. Rachel didn't have experience with this dance step, so she gladly sat this one out. She watched Tom weave his way back through the crowded sidelines. As he balanced the drinks and cookies, he kept well away from the twirling men and women.

"Thanks, Mr. McCauley... er, Tom." Rachel reached for the cookie and cider.

She nibbled on the morsel, and her stomach stopped churning so much. Tom stood sentry by her chair, silently proclaiming her as his territory.

"The cookies are tasty. I wonder who made them?" he asked.

"I must confess, my sister, Phebe, baked them. We weren't allowed to eat any at home, and my mouth watered all afternoon."

Tom laughed. "Your sister's a fine cook," he said, wiping crumbs from his mouth. "Did you have a good crop of pumpkins from your garden this year?"

"Yes, plenty for the root cellar. We set them out in the sun for two weeks to harden before storing them."

"I don't see your mother and father or your sister here tonight. I hope they are well."

"Father had night duty at the furnace, and Mother didn't want to leave Phebe alone at home with my brother, Nick. My sister isn't able to dance because of her heart, and she tired herself baking this afternoon. Sometimes Nick's seizures are more than Phebe can handle by herself."

Tom munched his cookie while Rachel sipped her drink. They had little besides pleasantries to discuss. She only socialized with him when visiting the company store to buy sugar or flour or calico for the family. The store was the only source of goods for the village, and anything not stocked was ordered from Philadelphia and arrived on the return trip from shipping Hopewell's iron products to the city. Being so much younger than Mr. McCauley, Rachel never thought of him romantically and was repulsed by his constant attention tonight.

The band announced a short break, and a crowd gathered at the refreshment table.

"Good thing we got our food before the rush," Tom said. People stood around the barn, relaxing on bales of straw and chatting, while Rachel and Tom sat in awkward silence.

Eventually, the musicians took up their instruments. "The band is getting ready to start again. Shall we dance?" asked Tom.

She glanced at the open barn door, and her hopes leaped when she saw Nate's face, scanning the crowd. *At last, a rescuer!* But to her dismay, he caught her eye, then turned and disappeared outside. *Why didn't he come in?*

After a moment, she looked at Tom's eager face and said, "Yes, I can dance another." She rose and shook out her skirts.

They took their positions, and the music began. The dancers had just started moving when the toe of Rachel's shoe caught on a nail. She lurched headlong toward Tom, who attempted to catch her, but she hit the floor hard. The music halted, and everyone gathered around.

"Are you hurt?" asked Tom, as he extended his hand.

"No," she replied, ignoring his hand. She heard tittering and girlish laughter at her misfortune. She got up by herself, her dress torn where she had stepped on it. After brushing off the loose dirt and straw covering her hands and clothing, Rachel reassured everyone she was not hurt and headed for the door.

"Are you sure you're all right?" Tom hurried after her, trying to hold her elbow.

She jerked her elbow from his grasp. "Yes, I'll be fine, but I need some air." Her hair now spilled across her face, and the edge of the torn frock trailed the ground. "I'll come back shortly," she lied as she picked up the dragging fabric.

"I'll be waiting for you," he said as he turned and rejoined the dancers reorganizing themselves.

Tears stung her eyes, and one trickled down her face as she hurried out the door. Why had she come? *I don't belong here,* she thought and ran outside into the crisp night air.

Outlines of farm wagons and carriages loomed along the lane, parked outside for the night instead of in the barn. As she walked down the sloped road between the ironmaster's big house and the barn, she skirted couples standing around. Occasional bursts of laughter punctuated their whispering. Other couples lingered in deeper shadows of the building, engaged in more passionate romance.

She hurried past them all, averting her eyes to avoid noticing who was with whom. After removing the remaining pins from her hair, she shook her head, and her locks cascaded to her shoulders. The muted roar of the furnace at the cast house hung over the village, the bright sparks from its chimney lighting up the night sky.

When she neared the end of the barn, the lane forked. The right path veered up the hill to the charcoal shed and the roads to Reading or Philadelphia. The left trail descended toward the cast house and tenant houses beyond. But before she reached either fork, Rachel turned onto the footpath leading to the barn's lower level's stable door. Upon entering, she paused a minute for her eyes to adjust to the dim interior lit by a single lantern in the middle of the walkway. Long shadows played on the walls. A row of tie-up stalls lined the left side, where each stall held a horse or cow, secured at its head and separated from its neighbor by a rough board wall. Box stalls were on the right side. Occasionally an animal stomped a foot or shook its head, but muffled music and footfalls from above interrupted the peaceful silence. The rumps of the massive draft horses towered over Rachel's head as she walked down the aisle. Aromas of sweet hay and pungent manure mingled together in a mish-mash of scents.

Each box stall had a door outside to the fenced pasture. She passed a sleek chestnut gelding lying in a bed of straw, and in the last stall, a palomino mare with delicate features poked her nose over the top rail and nickered.

"Hello, Missy," Rachel cooed. She rubbed the palomino's face and ears, and the horse lowered its head, enjoying her touch.

Rachel continued up the aisle to where the lantern hung outside the tack room.

"Greetings, Ben," she called to the tall, white-haired gent sitting on a sawhorse.

"Welcome, Rachel," he replied.

She watched him apply a lather of soap to a fine English saddle. He worked the bubbles with a soft rag, rubbing with a circular motion, rinsing the material in a bucket of water, wringing it, then wiping off the dirt and suds. On another cloth, he tipped a bit of neat's-foot oil from a bottle and finished polishing the leather to a warm, buttery glow.

"They're making enough racket overhead to keep every animal awake tonight," said Ben. "Why aren't you up there enjoying yourself?"

"I was there for a while, but the only one who danced with me was Mr. McCauley. During the last dance, I tripped and ripped my dress. I feel so embarrassed."

"Are you all right?"

"Yes, only my pride is bruised."

"Weren't there any young lads your age dancing?"

"A couple of boys with whom I'm acquainted, but they danced with the pretty girls and didn't pay any attention to me. I didn't feel I belonged at all." Ben's non-judgmental attitude and mutual love of animals made him one of the few adults with whom she felt comfortable sharing her feelings.

"Don't let yourself believe they're prettier than you. You can hold your own with any girl when it comes to beauty."

She sighed, grateful for his encouragement. "Thanks for the compliment, Ben, but the boys only think of me as the teacher's pet. Mr. Elliott always tells them, 'Rachel knows this or Rachel knows that,' to shame them into studying more. They don't want much to do with me."

"Their attitudes will change over time, don't worry. What about that collier lad you spoke about yesterday, Nate Kirst? Did he come?"

Rachel blushed, glad for the darkness so Ben couldn't see. "He wasn't there," she lied. "I suppose he was in the woods, tending his charcoal pits with his boss, Henry Zerbey."

"Yes, I'm sure every pile of charcoal he can produce will build his credit at the store. He'll need as much as he can get before winter arrives. They can't burn wood into charcoal when the temperature drops."

"Are you staying here all night, Ben?"

"No, no, only until the festivities are over. The animals will settle down, and I can go home. The dance gave me the chance to do this neglected cleaning."

"I'll be over after church tomorrow to ride Missy, so she won't be so gingery for Susanna in the afternoon. I'll clean the stall, too."

"Susanna will appreciate a calm mount. Last week that palomino was so wild, she almost threw her off. Missy knows Susanna's a little afraid and takes advantage, like when she ran under the low tree limb, trying to scrape her off. If Susanna rode her more often, she wouldn't be so hard to handle. I hope Missy lives up to the good meaning of her name—Miss Behaving."

"She needs a firm hand and to be reminded who's boss. I'll work with her tomorrow so she'll be tired and will mind better. It won't do for Missy to throw off the ironmaster's daughter. I'm going home now after I visit Father at the cast house."

"Be sure to hold your dress up out of the manure on your way out. Your ma will be mad enough that it's torn. A barn full of animals is no place for a girl in pretty clothing."

Rachel raised the hem and picked her way out, then closed and latched the barn door. Avoiding the wet ground around the pump near the watering trough, she crossed the grassy area to the cast house on the other side of the path. *Maybe I can find out what's been going on at the furnace.* Usually, the activity there was rather mundane as the molders made their molds in the sand-filled wooden frames, or the men dug troughs in the dirt floor in front of the stone furnace to pour pig iron bars. But lately, there was a lot more going on at the furnace at night. *What were they making in that big mold? Who was the other night visitor to the furnace, and why were they interested?*

~ CHAPTER 4 ~

As Rachel approached the cast house's open doorway, the bell in the tower clanged, signaling time for an iron pour. *Funny,* she thought, *workers usually poured in the early morning or evening, never this late, but I don't remember hearing the bell earlier.*

Apparently, George Coggins had not told Father about her visit to the furnace last night since he had not confronted her earlier, so she decided to say hello to him before heading home. Her father usually worked the daytime shift, but for some reason, he was here again tonight.

Her father, Lewis Palsgrove, was the founder at Hopewell Furnace and held the crucial responsibility of making the metal the right consistency and determining when to tap the molten mass into the forms. For each pour, a worker at the top of the furnace stack shoveled four hundred pounds of iron ore, fifteen bushels of charcoal, and three shovels full of limestone into the furnace. Carbon from the burning charcoal combined with the ore and strengthened it, and impurities bonded with the limestone to form slag, which floated to the top in the crucible. Lewis directed the addition of various ingredients every half hour to make the perfect mix. Before Hopewell, he had been a well-respected founder at the Colebrookdale Furnace about ten miles away. Daniel Sterling, the ironmaster, had recruited him for his new furnace at Hopewell in 1771.

When the iron concoction reached its peak, Lewis directed a gutterman to tap out the clay plug near the top of the furnace, draw off the slag, and discard it onto a pile outside. Then the lower clay stopper was released, which allowed the iron to flow into the giant ladle.

Tipping the ladle, workers directed the iron either into pig beds on the dirt floor or into box molds. The pig beds were shallow connected troughs resembling a sow nursing her young. After cooling, each metal "piglet" was broken away. The furnace shipped the bars to England, where craftsmen transformed them into iron wares to be delivered back to the colonies. To keep English workers employed and the colonies dependent, English law forbade colonial furnaces to make wares, but Hopewell made iron products anyway, defying the law.

The wooden box molds contained damp sand with a hollowed-out imprint of the item being made. After the iron cooled, the molders knocked away the sand leaving the iron product. The furnace ran day and night for months, so the molders were always busy making new molds. But today, Saturday, the workers typically only poured pig iron.

As she approached the doorway to the furnace, burly George Coggins stepped in front of her, blocking her way again.

"You still can't come in here tonight, Miss Palsgrove."

"I came to visit Father, George. I appreciate that you didn't tell him I was here last night." She tried to push past him.

George planted himself in front of her, standing as mighty as the trunk of an oak. "I'm sorry, you can't go inside tonight, and I *did* tell him you were here last night. You'll see him tomorrow."

"What's going on?" Rachel asked as she peeked around him. Like last night, she spied the outline of a large upright mold in front of the furnace.

"I can't tell you. Ask your father later. Please–leave–now," George commanded. "Stop coming back!"

What's the big mystery? She set her jaw and stomped off toward home. *I hope Father comes home soon. I have to know what's going on!*

~ CHAPTER 5 ~

Rachel walked toward her house—a white, two-story cottage with powder blue trim, rented from the ironmaster. The "Big House," where Susanna lived with the other Sterling family members, was a three-story mansion across the lane from the red-and-white bank barn and the furnace. Daniel Sterling's holdings were vast, spanning over eight thousand acres of woods and fields and three iron ore mines. The ironmaster governed every aspect of the village, which would not exist without the production of iron. Miners dug the ore, wood choppers cut the trees, colliers burned the timber into charcoal, and teamsters drove the goods to market. Every activity, such as feeding, clothing, and housing the men, supported those operations.

Rachel passed the blacksmith shop on her right, dark and silent now. It would clang to life Monday morning when the smithy started hammering the iron pigs into horseshoes, wagon wheel rims, and tools. Pausing on the wooden bridge over the creek, she leaned over the rail to listen to the water burbling in its banks. Music from the dance wafted in the air, and her ears caught the lilt of one of her favorite tunes, *Billy Boy*. Rachel sang the lyrics under her breath while tapping her foot.

> *Oh, where have you been, Billy Boy, Billy Boy?*
> *Oh, where have you been, charming Billy?*
> *I have been to seek a wife, she's the joy of my life,*
> *She's a young thing and cannot leave her mother.*

Her visit to Ben had calmed her distress from the fall, but now her curiosity was even more piqued about the unusual activity at the cast house. She could hardly wait until morning to ask her father about it, although she would probably receive a scolding for her late-night outings. He and Rachel shared a special bond. She loved his gentle but authoritative nature and was proud of his position at Hopewell. He was very astute about political events in the colonies, and he often discussed with the family the articles from newspapers the teamsters brought back from Philadelphia. Rachel took an avid interest and asked many questions.

The music stopped. The dance was over. Soon the villagers would be taking this same route to their homes, so she quickly gathered her skirt and resumed her walk home. Her house wasn't far and was a privilege afforded her family because of her father's standing.

She turned off the lane onto the short path leading to her house. Suddenly the dense weeds beside her shook violently, and a dark, furry form darted out to clasp her ankle with its paws. Rachel shrieked. "Jack, you frightened me!" She bent to pick up the gray and white tiger cat and petted him. "Did you find any mice tonight?" As she stroked his side, he nuzzled her chin, purring. Abruptly the cat squirmed free from her arms and ran into the tall grass again after new quarry.

Rachel reached her door and lifted the latch. "It's me, Mother," she whispered as she tiptoed into the cottage, not wanting to awaken her sleeping brother and sister upstairs. The large hearth in the kitchen still held a few glowing embers.

"A biscuit left from supper is in the pie safe," her mother said quietly. "You must be hungry from dancing."

Rachel grabbed the biscuit then turned into the keeping room where her mother mended a man's shirt by candlelight. She flopped into a chair, her dress trailing the floor.

"What happened to your dress?"

"Oh..." She held her hand under her chin to catch any falling crumbs as she nibbled the biscuit, then finished swallowing. "I'm sorry to cause you more mending. I tripped on a nail and fell at the dance."

"Well, you tore it, so you can mend it. I've got too much sewing to do. You know I'm trying to finish these five linsey-woolsey shirts before winter comes."

"But you sew so much better than I do. It'll take me twice as long to mend."

"How do you think I got to be a fast seamstress? It takes practice. You don't learn how to sew faster by having someone else do it," she admonished.

"But it's so tedious," Rachel whined. "Almost any other chore is better, even cleaning out a horse stall."

"Shush, keep your voice lowered," Martha cautioned. "You don't like to sew and cook, but in the future, your family will need you to do those chores, so you'd better learn to like them."

"I don't want a family if I have to do all those things for them," Rachel fumed. "I can't spend time reading and learning about the world if I spend every waking moment doing mundane tasks. I want to do important things in my life."

They sat silently for a minute after Rachel's outburst. Women's work was a topic on which they often disagreed. Martha said, "Everyday chores *are* important. No, they aren't as exciting as imagining far-off places or learning about other cultures, but if you don't do them, who will?"

More silence.

"On a different subject, how was the dance?"

"Mr. McCauley was the only one who asked me to dance, and I couldn't get rid of him."

"Tom McCauley? He's old enough to be your father. Weren't any women his age there?"

"No, not many single ladies attended without their beaus. I didn't have any other offers. No boys my age asked me."

"I hope you were polite. We can't afford to be on his bad side."

"Yes, I was nice to him. He even asked me to call him 'Tom'."

"Well, be careful around that kind of man. Even though we know him well from the store, old bachelors like him sometimes get ideas around young, naïve girls."

"Oh, he's harmless, but I wish Nate had come so I could dance with him. He would have asked me if he were there. I guess he must have been in the woods tending his charcoal pits." Rachel didn't want to admit Nate had ignored her at the dance.

A look of dismay crossed Martha's face as she looked up from her sewing. "Nate was here tonight, Rachel."

"Looking for me? Did you tell him I was at the dance?"

"He asked about you, but he came to see Phebe."

"Phebe?"

"Yes, he had gone to the dance, and when he didn't see Phebe, he came here. He wanted to make sure she was feeling all right. You remember he doted on her last year when she came down with scarlet fever."

"I don't understand why he's interested in her. I can ride a horse and chop wood better than Phebe any day."

"Rachel, young men don't court women who can do the things they can do. They're looking for women who can tend a household and children while they're working."

"He only likes her because she's prettier than me."

"Now, Rachel, remember Nate is older than you. He's a year older than Phebe, so that would make him four years older than you. No doubt he's thinking about taking a wife soon. You're too young."

Rachel pouted. After a minute, she sighed and asked, "Can I borrow a needle and thread? I'll sew the dress tomorrow when the light is better."

Her mother dug in her basket and handed Rachel a needle and a wooden spool of thread matching her dress.

"Tomorrow after church, I'm riding Missy because Susanna Sterling plans to ride her later. I'll clean her stall, come home and start mending the dress."

"Sounds like a busy day. You can help me in the kitchen in the morning too. Your father will be tired when he gets home."

"Oh, what was happening at the furnace tonight? I went to visit Father, and George Coggins wouldn't let me in. He said to ask Father about it."

"Yes, dear, you'll need to ask him." She put her sewing away and stood. "It's late, and I'm going to bed. I wanted to wait up and ask how you got along." She gave Rachel a gentle kiss on her cheek and a pat on the head as she passed her chair. "Don't read too late tonight." She picked up the candlestick to light her way upstairs.

"Yes, Mother. I'll only read a chapter or two. *Gulliver's Travels* is a hard book to put down, but I'll try."

Rachel rose from the chair, tucked up her dress, and carrying the other candlestick, followed her mother upstairs. Martha walked through the first bedroom and opened the door to the bedroom beyond. Rachel's bed stood by the wall at the top of the stairs. She was careful not to bump her head on the sloping ceiling, as she had grown taller the past year and one time had gotten a nasty bruise.

The soft snoring of her sister, Phebe, emanated from the bed on the other side of the room. Rachel saw the faint outline of her back as she slept on her side, facing the wall. Her six-year-old brother, Nick, slept at the other end of the room behind the screen separating the boy from the girls. Rachel tiptoed around the screen to gaze at his angelic-looking face. She marveled at how such an innocent face at the oddest moments could contort with the terrible epileptic seizures he suffered. Thank goodness he felt dizzy before a spell so he could lie down before one started. She smiled and pulled the covers up around his ears to ward off the chill.

She placed the candlestick on the table beside her bed. *Good, the light won't bother them if I read awhile.* She pulled the dress off over her head, slipped on her flannel nightgown, and hung the dress on the peg on the wall. After kicking off her sister's too-large shoes, she placed her knee-high wool hosiery inside the shoes and pushed them under the bed. Sitting gingerly on the rope bed, she massaged her bruised toes before shoving her feet under the sheets.

In the next bedroom, she heard her mother moving around. Soon, the bed creaked, and the light seeping under the door went out. Rachel grabbed her book from the bedside table and eagerly turned the pages to the bookmark. Mr. Elliott had loaned the book from his library since Susanna had finished reading it. She read a little, then her mind wandered. *I'd like to visit other places,* she thought. *I wonder what Philadelphia is like? There would be more exciting things to do than around here. We have chores and more chores—cooking, cleaning, mending—always the same thing day after day.* She imagined libraries, concerts, art exhibits, and outings with her friends to explore the city. *Friends,* she pondered. *I don't have friends here, and certainly, no time to socialize if I did have any.* She looked back at the book, but after a few more moments of reading, her eyelids grew heavy. Tucking the precious book under her pillow, she blew out the candle, turned a few times to find a comfortable spot, and sank into deep slumber.

~ CHAPTER 6 ~

The following day, Lewis dragged himself home from the furnace and wearily climbed the house's steps. He gave Martha a hug and a gentle tap on her rear. "Ummm… that bacon smells delicious." He looked around. "Where are the children?"

"Rachel took Nick to gather eggs for breakfast and Phebe's in the keeping room."

With its fire in the hearth, the kitchen warmed the house after the cool temperatures the night before. Oregano, bay, and parsley, used to flavor soups and stews, hung from the rafters with other herbs to dry. Money plant and dusty miller would make pretty dried flower arrangements, while lavender would fragrance soap and potpourri. Their sweet scents perfumed the air.

Nick burst through the door carrying the egg basket, and Rachel came in behind him. "Gently, Nick." Martha scooped the basket from him and began cracking eggs into a bowl.

"Nick was careful in the chicken pen, Mother," Rachel said. "He didn't step on any today."

The boy beamed with pride as his father ruffled his hair.

"You two wash up," Martha commanded. "Breakfast is almost ready."

Phebe joined them, and the family began their usual Sunday morning breakfast. Nick fidgeted and squirmed in his seat.

"Nick, sit still and finish at least half the food on your plate. Then you can go outside and play until we leave for church."

He gulped his milk and ate a few bites. "Is that enough?" he implored his father as his mother frowned.

"Yes, you may go."

As he scampered out the door, Martha called, "Don't get your clothes dirty."

Phebe sat quietly, pushing eggs around on her plate.

"Phebe, you need to eat more too," her mother said. "You'll have to take in that dress if you don't regain the weight you lost last winter. It's hanging on you like clothes on a half-stuffed scarecrow."

Scarlet fever had left Phebe's heart weakened, but her luxurious reddish-brown hair had finally regained its luster. Beautiful, green eyes sparkled in a face with skin as delicate as fine-grained porcelain. She was lucky to have survived.

Lewis's black-stubbled chin almost dropped into his plate several times as his head drooped, and after the second near miss, he said, "I'll not be going to church this morning, Mother. I'm going to bed."

"We'll be fine by ourselves, Lewis. You get some rest." She patted his arm.

"Thanks, Martha. I don't know when I've been so tired." He pushed away from the table and started up the stairs.

Rachel bit her tongue—she wanted to ask him about the cast house last night, but she knew the time wasn't right. *Maybe later.*

The sisters helped their mother wash the dishes and tidy the kitchen. "We better leave now if we're to arrive on time."

The three of them removed their aprons covering their Sunday dresses, gathered their Bibles, and stepped outside into the warm autumn sunshine. The blue sky was cloudless. When they reached the lane, they called Nick to join them from the field where he had been playing.

He ran to Phebe and shoved his treasure close to her face. "Look what I found."

Phebe squealed. "Nick, put the toad down. You can't take it with us."

"But look, he can do tricks. If you pet him on his side, he leans over." Nick placed the creature on the ground and stroked one side then the other. Amazingly, the toad leaned toward one side then the next, like it was ticklish. They laughed.

"He *is* mighty fine, Nick," observed Rachel. "I don't think I've ever seen a toad so big or so talented."

"You still can't take it with us," commented Martha. "Now, come along."

Nick scooped up the creature and put it behind a nearby rock. "I'll see you later, Toady."

As they walked, tenant houses loomed ahead, and they soon passed the large boarding house where many of the single men slept at night. Grazing cows and horses in the pasture cropped grass, and shocks of corn stalks dotted the fields. Each house had a scruffy fenced area beside it where the remnants of a garden lay—tomato, potato, and pumpkin vines pulled up and plucked of their fruit.

Many trees stood naked, but others still blazed in vivid oranges, reds, and yellows. Crunching the dry leaves underfoot, they strolled under a towering buckeye with large spreading limbs. Nick stopped to pick up some of the nuts popping out of their dried green pods littering the ground. Rachel watched him sneak the smooth brown and tan buckeyes into his pockets that held who knows what other treasures.

Neighbors on the road walked in the same direction—to the Lloyd Meeting House. As the Palsgroves approached them, they exchanged pleasantries and caught up on village news, stopping when Phebe needed to catch her breath. Much of the talk was about the dance last night, and a few sympathized with Rachel about her fall, but she wondered why no one mentioned the strange happenings at the furnace. *Hadn't they noticed?*

They reached the new clapboard church built last year. Already three gravestones punctuated the long green grass in the adjacent cemetery. Ezekiel Crosby had died from being kicked in the head by a horse, and two young children last winter perished from dysentery, the "bloody flux," as the villagers called it.

The whitewashed structure was simple inside, and the parishioners were milling about. Unlike many churches, there were no assigned pews. The people of Hopewell simply paid a fee for the privilege of attending. Rachel, her mother, sister, and brother found seats toward the back, in case Nick felt a seizure coming.

The first hymn was *Little Marlborough*, and though Rachel loved the song's words, the mournful tune was depressing. *Shouldn't church songs be joyous*, she wondered.

Announcements were made: Mrs. Kirkpatrick's burned arm was healing, baptisms at the pond would be postponed until warmer weather in the spring, each of the ladies of the church was asked to contribute a fabric block to be sewn into a quilt for a poor family for the winter, the minister from St. Gabriel's Episcopal Church in Douglasville would be the speaker next Sunday. Rachel's mind wandered, ticking off all the chores waiting for her—cleaning Missy's stall, mending the dress, helping prepare supper. She chafed at the thought of wasting time here when she could be finishing chores so she could get back to reading her book.

Rev. Clements's sermon ranted about the perils of bad behavior, and he chided parents for not raising their children carefully enough. Nothing was soothing about his message. Was his intent to make his audience as uncomfortable as possible? By the end, everyone was squirming in their seats, except Nick, who dozed peacefully through it. Rachel had tuned out the minister's voice long ago as she speculated about what secretive thing the men could be making at the furnace? *A new stove part wouldn't be a big secret, nor would a new farm implement. Perhaps something for the war? That might explain the secrecy.*

The service concluded with a rousing rendition of *Amazing Grace*, the melody lifting everyone's spirits.

After the final prayer, the congregants chatted with each other and slowly filed out, congratulating Rev. Clements on his fine sermon as they passed him at the door. Bored by the small talk, Rachel could hardly wait to escape to the barn and excused herself to skip home.

At the cottage, Rachel put on a pair of old breeches that ended just below her knees. She was still young enough to get away with wearing them, certainly when riding a horse.

Martha, Phebe, and Nick arrived home. "Eat this bread and butter before you run off, Rachel," Mother directed. "It's a long time until supper."

Impatient to leave, Rachel ate while standing, and she quickly drank the cup of cider her mother offered.

"Be careful riding that ornery horse. I worry about you. It's dangerous."

"Don't worry, Mother. I'll be fine."

Free at last, she ran down the lane to the barn.

~ CHAPTER 7 ~

The bridled and saddled palomino stamped her feet and shook her head as she stood at the hitching post. Rachel arrived at the barn and patted Missy's neck.

Ben greeted her. "She's ready to ride but be sure to tighten the cinch before you mount." Rachel pulled the buckles on the girth with all her strength, then slid her hand between it and the horse's belly to check the tightness.

"Do you want the crop today?" He held it out to her.

"Yes, I better take it. Sometimes just knowing I have a switch in my hand is enough for her to behave. Can you give me a leg up?"

Ben lifted Rachel by her knee, boosting her into the saddle. "Where are you riding today?"

"I think I'll go toward Valley Forge. When she starts to settle down, I'll come back. I don't want her exhausted for Susanna's ride later. I won't be gone long."

She clucked softly to the horse, who eagerly leaped forward. Riding on the lane between the Big House and the furnace, Rachel headed up the hill and soon reached the road at the top. The crudely painted sign indicated Reading left, seventeen miles, and Valley Forge right, twenty-five miles. She loved the feel of the powerful horse's body between her legs, the creaking of the saddle leather, and the smell of the fresh autumn air. Being a confident horsewoman, the freedom and thrill of riding was pure joy.

Out on the level road, Missy strained at the bit, anxious to gallop, but Rachel held tight and only let her trot. She had a smooth trot compared to most horses, which was why she was an excellent mount for Susanna. The palomino shook her head and danced sideways to go faster, but every time she tried that trick, Rachel made her turn in circles. Missy disliked circles even more than going slow, so she soon accepted the jogging pace. When the mare settled down, Rachel let her ease into an easy, loping canter, as smooth as a rocking chair. After a mile, the mare's breathing became labored, and she slowed to a walk.

Suddenly, from the bushes on the left, a rabbit darted across the road. Startled, Missy shied to the right. Rachel's left foot popped out of the stirrup at the sudden move, and the horse, sensing Rachel's shifted weight, gave a hop, dislodging her. "Oh!" she cried as she fell to the ground, the wind knocked out of her. As Rachel lay gasping for air, she saw Missy cantering down the road heading back to the barn.

A few minutes later, Rachel recovered her breath and clambered to her feet, patting her clothes in a cloud of dust. She rubbed her backside, which had taken the brunt of the fall. There were no broken bones, but she was sure there'd be bruises tomorrow. She searched the bushes until she found the crop. The walk back to Hopewell would be a long one.

Halfway home, she saw Ben riding bareback on the big chestnut, Chester, and leading Missy.

He pulled up beside her and handed over the reins. "When the horse came back, I figured she threw you off. Are you all right?"

"Yes, I'm fine. A rabbit ran into the road and scared her. She zigged, and I zagged. Thanks for bringing her, so I don't have to walk all the way."

"I couldn't leave her all sweaty with no one to walk her out and thought you'd need a ride back."

Rachel straightened Missy's crooked saddle and retightened the cinch. Putting her foot in the irons, she hopped stiffly aboard. "Good thing she's not as tall as Chester, or I'd never get on."

"Missy will be good and tired for Susanna's ride. We'd better walk back and cool her down."

As they approached the barn, Susanna came out of the Big House and fell in step. Her bouncy, blonde curls spilled from under her straw hat adorned with feathers, and her fashionable riding habit emphasized her hourglass figure. "David will be coming soon. He's going to ride along today. Has Missy been good?"

"She got spooked by a hare, but she's calm now. She should be fine for your ride," Rachel said.

"Thanks for exercising her, Rachel. She's too much for me when she's fresh."

"She can be a handful, but once she settles down, she's a pleasure to ride, isn't she? I bet as she gets older, she won't be so energetic."

"I hope you're right. Otherwise, I might need to trade for a less lively horse." Susanna stroked Missy's neck. "I would hate to do that. She's so pretty with her golden coat and white mane and tail. Here comes David now."

David Sterling, Susanna's older brother, was six feet tall and towered over his sister, his height further increased by the tri-cornered felt hat covering his brown hair braided down the back of his neck. He wore spotless white breeches and black leather knee-high boots with gold buckles. Under his cape, bright brass buttons accented his navy blue waistcoat. Rachel thought he looked very dashing and handsome.

Rachel saddled Chester for David at the barn, and Ben replaced Missy's saddle with Susanna's sidesaddle, then boosted Susanna onto it. *What an awkward and uncomfortable way to ride*, thought Rachel. David mounted Chester, adjusted his clothing, and settled his hat.

"Have a nice ride," Rachel called, as Susanna and David headed out.

On the way home, Rachel saw Nick playing with some boys, running after a rolling hoop they pushed on the rim using a short stick. He was having such fun that he barely glanced up when she called his name.

At home, she didn't tell her family, particularly her mother, about her spill. Rachel ran upstairs, taking the steps two at a time, and retrieved her torn dress. In the keeping room, she dug the needle and thread from her mother's sewing box and sat by the window to start her mending. Martha was preparing supper in the kitchen, and Phebe sat in the other chair, reading her Bible.

Phebe looked up and exclaimed, "Whoa, Rachel, you stink like a barn."

"I'll wash up as soon as I finish mending my dress."

"You better also wash that dress. It'll smell too, by the time you get it mended."

"I need to wash it anyway since part of it trailed on the ground coming home."

"Mother told me you had an accident last night."

"Yes, and she mentioned you had a visitor. Were you going to tell me Nate came to see you?"

"I probably would have if I thought you wouldn't be jealous."

"Do you like him?"

"Well, yes, he's always been kind to me. He's good-looking, too. What do you think?"

"I think he's handsome and rugged looking. I dreamed he would come and dance with me and save me from Mr. McCauley. Mother says Nate's too old for me though."

Mr. Palsgrove clumped down the stairs and settled into a chair, running a rough hand over his stubble. "Who's too old, Rachel?"

Phebe shot Rachel a warning look. "Oh, Mr. McCauley danced with me several times last night," Rachel said. "Mother thought he should have been dancing with the older ladies."

"Well, that's for sure," her father replied. "I hope he's not getting ideas."

"No, I don't think so, Father. He was very polite. On my way home from the dance, I stopped to see you at the furnace, but George Coggins wouldn't let me in. What was going on?"

Lewis pensively rubbed the back of his neck, hesitating before he spoke. "Well, I guess it's time I told you and Phebe about a few things. You're old enough to hear them. But you both must promise you won't talk to anyone else besides your mother and me. It's important."

"We promise, don't we, Phebe?" said Rachel, eager for the mysterious news. Phebe looked up from her reading and nodded her head.

"Daniel Sterling is involved with the colonists opposing the British. The Iron Act is oppressive for his business since it keeps us from casting products to sell to markets in Philadelphia. They want us to produce only pig iron, ship it to England, and they will make iron goods to sell to us. It's a ridiculous plan. We can make those products here at a fraction of the cost and keep our workers busy.

"Daniel has joined the Sons of Liberty. Our soldiers in war need cannons and balls, and he decided Hopewell will make them. The last several nights, we cast cannon. Although most people at Hopewell agree with his ideas, not everyone does. We must be careful who knows about these activities, so Mr. Sterling and the rest of us don't get in serious trouble."

The girls took in the gravity of this secret.

"We won't tell anyone, Father," Phebe whispered.

"No, we won't breathe a word," concurred Rachel, her eyes wide.

"And, Rachel," he continued, "George told me you were sneaking around the cast house. You must stop doing that."

"Yes, Father. What kind of trouble might you get into if someone discovers this?" She thought of the person watching through the window the first night she was there.

"Our lives and the future of the furnace could be in danger."

"I saw someone at the window of the cast house the first night I was there."

"Do you know who it was?"

"No, I didn't see their face."

"Did you see in the window?"

"Yes, and I'm sure they did too, but I couldn't tell what you were making."

"Don't worry," he said. "I'll take care of that and cover the window. I'm glad you told me. You're my eyes and ears when I'm busy at the furnace. Let me know if you see anything else suspicious."

"You can count on me, Father. I can keep a secret. Our lives depend on it."

~ CHAPTER 8 ~

The following Monday, Rachel and her mother were in their back-yard, stirring the contents of three large, steaming kettles hanging over a fire. Even though most autumn days were chilly now and many of the leaves had gone off the trees, the Indian summer had made its appearance, warming the air to summery temperatures. Rachel rolled her sleeves up to her elbows and tied her hair on top of her head. Beads of sweat stood out on her forehead and upper lip.

In the first kettle, they boiled old ashes from the fireplace with water from the rain barrel. When the liquid lye rose to the top, they skimmed it off into the second pot. They simmered the lye until an egg would float. In the third pot, they cooked meat fat and lard left over from their meals all summer. When the pure fat had risen, they poured it into the lye mixture, careful not to splash the caustic liquid. The pot required constant stirring, and the soap was finally becoming thicker.

"Rachel, don't forget to wax the bottoms and sides of those wooden mold boxes so we'll be able to get the soap out after it hardens."

Rachel had helped make soap many times before, but one time she forgot to coat the molds. They had almost destroyed the boxes trying to release the stubborn mixture. Her mother would never let her forget that mistake, not that she was likely to forget it either. She wasn't accustomed to making mistakes and took to heart any reminders about the few errors she did make.

She dutifully prepared all the molds and laid them out side by side on a level area of grass.

"The molds are ready, Mother."

"Good. A few more minutes, and it will be the right consistency for pouring." Martha held up the wooden stirring spoon and let a dollop of soap drop off into the kettle.

Rachel readied the large iron ladles used to scoop out the hot mixture to pour into the molds. Suddenly, her teacher appeared around the corner of the house, startling them.

Rachel said, "Oh, Mr. Elliott. I didn't see you come. We're just about ready to pour the soap."

"Phebe told me I would find you back here. I can see this is a bad time to talk. Will you be home after supper?"

"Yes, we'll be home. Can you come back then?"

"I'll be back later," he called, as he sauntered off across the grass, his battered knapsack of books slung over his shoulder.

"I wonder what he wants," Rachel's mother said. As she held up the wooden spoon again, she motioned for Rachel to quickly bring the ladle.

"Be careful scooping it out. We don't want to get burned." She scooped a dipperful of steaming soap and poured the liquid into the innermost rows of molds. Rachel came behind to gather soap in her spoon and filled the next row of molds. Their repeated movements were like a dance orchestrated for maximum efficiency and safety.

When the kettle was empty, Martha doused the fire with water. "We'll let those molds cool until evening, then bring them in the house to cure. Later we can box the soap with the lavender we've been drying. I hope Mr. Elliott doesn't stay too long this evening. I'm exhausted from making soap all day, and the days are growing so short. Let's get washed and see what Phebe has prepared for dinner. Your father should be home soon."

"I'm famished," exclaimed Rachel, as she wiped her hands on her apron and went into the house. *I wish I could have spent today doing anything else,* she thought.

After supper, while the girls were putting away the last of the dishes, Rachel's teacher arrived. "Would you like a cup of tea, Mr. Elliott?" Phebe asked. "There's some left from dinner." She handed him a cup and saucer.

"Thanks, that will be good," he said, as he inhaled the pungent aroma. "I've been running around all day and haven't had any since morning. This smells strong the way I like it."

"Let's go into the sitting room," suggested Martha. She and Rachel went first, and Lewis and Mr. Elliott followed. Phebe and Nick stayed in the kitchen to play a game of checkers.

Martha and Lewis sat on the sofa, and the tutor took the upholstered chair. The sun was beginning to set, and the light was fading fast in the cottage.

Lewis said, "Jonathan, Mrs. Palsgrove and I are very pleased with the education Rachel received with you. We realize she can be a challenging young lady. Are we all square with what we owe you?"

"Oh, yes, that's not why I came. Thank you for your kind compliment. It's always good to hear that parents are satisfied with their child's education. I enjoyed teaching both Phebe and Rachel. I look forward to when Nick will start with me."

"He'll probably begin next fall. He needs more time before he's ready. We've been working with him on his alphabet and numbers, but you know how boys sometimes take longer to catch on," stated Martha. "He'd rather be outside playing."

"And how is Phebe's health? I hope she continues to improve from her sickness last year?"

"Yes, she still feels weak occasionally, but she's much better," replied Lewis.

"Her color looks good," Mr. Elliott said. "Well, I suppose you're curious as to why I'm here. I have a proposition for you concerning Rachel."

"Oh?" said Lewis.

"Rachel expressed in a paper written for our last class that she dreams of going to the university to learn to become a teacher. I think that is an admirable goal for a young lady of her talents, and I would like to encourage her in that endeavor."

"We can't afford to send her to college," interrupted Lewis.

"Yes, who around here except the Sterlings could afford such a thing? Speaking of them, Susanna will be going to boarding school in Philadelphia soon, and Daniel Sterling would like someone available to help her with her studies and act as a companion for her while she's there. Rachel's name came up as a possibility since the two girls know each other and have had their classes together.

"His proposal is this: in exchange for helping Susanna, the Sterlings would pay for college for Rachel. While Susanna takes instruction during the day, Rachel could be getting her schooling too. They would also arrange Rachel's room and board. The one condition is that Rachel comes back to Hopewell when her education is finished and teaches the children whose parents don't have the money to hire me. What do you think?"

Martha gasped, and all the Palsgroves looked stunned, especially Rachel. Here was her opportunity! She squirmed in her seat with excitement but knew better than to say anything until her father had spoken.

"That's a very generous offer," Lewis said. "However, I don't think we want to accept his charity." Rachel's mother nodded her head in agreement.

"Don't think of it as charity. Rachel would be performing a valuable service for Daniel by helping his daughter, and think of all the youth at Hopewell who would benefit from a good education when she returns."

"But what if Rachel fails to complete her studies or decides not to teach? Then we would be indebted to the Sterlings beyond what we would be able to repay," Lewis objected.

"Of course, everyone would want a document spelling out all the details. They don't want any misunderstandings. Will you at least give it some thought?"

Lewis looked at Rachel, who was holding her breath. "I know Rachel would make a good teacher, and I'm proud of her abilities. But I don't know what we would do without her help around the house. We would miss her terribly." He paused, thoughtful. "Martha and I appreciate the offer and will think about it. Can you come back the day after tomorrow, and we'll discuss any questions we have and give you our answer?" He stood and extended his hand to Jonathan.

Jonathan heartily shook his hand, smiling at Rachel and her mother. "Yes, I'll see you in two days. Shall I bring Mr. Sterling?"

"Yes, please do."

"I'll arrange a meeting."

Mr. Elliott nodded goodbye to the Palsgroves, and Rachel escorted him to the door. "Oh, Mr. Elliott, thank you for your help," she squealed, dancing a little jig. "I hope they will accept the offer. I've been praying for an opportunity like this."

"You deserve the chance, Rachel. I'll do my best to make it happen for you."

~ CHAPTER 9 ~

In the woods near Hopewell, two days later

"Nate, go out there right now and jump on that pit like I told you to!" barked Henry Zerbey, master collier, as he warmed some tea in a pot while frying eggs and bacon in a cast-iron skillet over the tiny wood stove in the hut. The sizzling meat filled the small enclosure with a tantalizing smell.

"Isn't it Jacob's turn this morning? I jumped the far one yesterday evening," replied Nate. Jacob stirred slightly in his bunk at the sound of his name but continued snoring, feigning sleep until Henry sorted out the situation.

"No, I want you to do it, so get going. The boy will have a pit to jump soon enough after breakfast." Henry's voice became louder still. "Don't argue with me."

"All right, all right, I'm going. You don't have to yell." Nate stiffly rose from his bed inside the small conical wood structure, rubbing his face and eyes vigorously and stretching his muscles as much as the cramped space would allow. Jumping the pit was the part of a collier's job he detested the most. It was a hazardous procedure any time and especially when you were half asleep and not yet quick-witted. He felt scared every time he did it.

The word "pit" was misleading. There was no hole in the ground but rather a high mound. After clearing away the vegetation to make a hearth thirty to forty feet in diameter, the men precisely stacked twenty-five to fifty cords of logs in upright tiers with a chimney through the middle and a covering of leaves and dirt on the surface. Set afire through the top of the hole, the wood gradually burnt down for up to two weeks until reduced to the high carbon charcoal used to fuel the iron furnace at Hopewell.

If a fire broke through the top layer of foliage and earth and burned the wood quickly instead of charring it, their days of hard work would be fruitless. The collier jumping the pit checked for any hot spots close to burning through. The danger came if you jumped into a soft spot and fell into the sizzling embers below. Your shovel, held mid-body horizontally, would prevent falling lower than waist-deep in the heap, but even then, the potential for injury or death was great.

Nate put on his jacket and heavy boots and turned sideways to squeeze out the narrow door. He picked up the long-handled spade leaning against the hut and headed toward the pit a short distance away. He found some consolation in the fact that the mound of wood was close by, not a half-mile distant like some, although a hike might have sharpened his senses. He scaled the sturdy log ladder stretching up the sloping side, carefully balancing each foot on the cut notches. At the pinnacle, he gingerly stepped off the ladder, holding his shovel level for balance, and trod cautiously around the head of the pit and over the bridge covering the peak of the chimney. As moisture and gases vaporized from the logs, they charred and shrank, forming gaps underneath. With the toe of his boot, he tested for any soft spots or "mulls" and didn't shift his weight until the footing felt firm. If he found a mull, he jumped up and down on the surface's firmer parts, which moved the solid wood into the voids. Any low areas were "dressed." They were dug out a little and refilled with new timber, leaves, and dust to restore the pit's original shape.

Nate gingerly worked his way around the top and only needed to jump twice to fill in mulls. Henry and his two helpers, Jacob and Nate, had just started this pit yesterday, so it hadn't had much time to burn through anywhere. Nate breathed a sigh of relief—there had been few mulls and little repair work to be done. He climbed back down the ladder, and before he went back to the hut, he inspected the draft holes, bored into the sides of the pit about two feet up from the bottom.

He noticed a slight blue smoke emanating from the draft holes. Blue smoke signaled that the fire was charring well and slowly. White wisps meant fast burning and was a sign a collier hated to see.

His job done, Nate returned to the hut. As he arrived, Henry shoveled portions of eggs, bacon, and cornmeal biscuits onto the tin plates. Jacob had roused himself for the meal and reached for his plate and cup.

"Food sure smells good. I'm mighty hungry," Nate said as he gathered his plate and cup of tea. "The pit looks good so far, Henry. Nice blue smoke puffing out."

"Those fumes give a man an appetite. It must be the pitch tar smell that causes it," remarked Henry. "Eat hearty this morning. If the fourth pit is ready today, we'll coal it out." Nate scowled at this news. They were in for a dirty, tedious day of hard work. When a pit had charred down to the foot after two weeks of slow burning, the fire presumably was burned out. The workers would remove the dust and charcoal in small amounts at a time. Often, when exposed to the air, a flame would rekindle, and the area had to be recovered and allowed to cool. Then they shoveled the charcoal into a wagon for the trip to the furnace.

"Will we start another pit after that one is done?" asked Jacob.

"We'll build one last one there. It's getting too late in the year to start any more. By the time we finish these eight and one more new one, we'll almost be in the middle of November." Henry reached for the last biscuit. "Will you fellows be chopping timber this winter when work is done here?"

Jacob, fourteen years old, said, "My father and I are planning to work together. He knows the woods better than me, and with me helping, he can cut more cords."

"I hope to chop wood this winter too," Nate said, "but I'll have to buy an ax with my wages from you. Will Mr. McCauley tell me the areas needing lumbering?"

"Yes, Tom will tell you what tracts are available. You'll probably be assigned one farther out since you're new this year. Maybe he can set you up with another lone chopper too. It's always better to work in pairs when you're out in the forest in the winter. Ride along with Isaac when the next load of charcoal goes to the furnace and talk with McCauley. I don't know why you didn't see him when you went in Saturday," Henry said disapprovingly.

Jacob smirked. "Yes, Nate, how was the dance? Did you twirl around that young lady you like?"

"No, she didn't feel well enough to go. I went to her house instead and visited with her and her mother."

"Visiting with her parents, eh? It must be serious," Jacob teased as he cornered a bit of egg with his biscuit.

Nate blushed. "No, she's just a good friend."

"Well, from the amount of time you spent with her during her sickness and since then, it seems you want more than friendship."

Henry piped in, "Stop talking, Jacob, and leave him alone. We'll be going out soon, and you're still in your long johns. Get dressed. I'm not your mother."

Nate was glad Henry changed the subject. He *did* like Phebe and thought about her constantly. *She's the stuff of every man's dreams. Her voice is soft and melodious, and her face, pure and angelic.* He longed to touch her coppery hair heaped on top of her head with a few inviting stragglers flowing down her creamy neck. Even when ill, she looked beautiful to him. He loved being around her family too. Nate's father and mother were both dead going on three years. His father died when his wagon overturned with a runaway horse, and his mother passed of cholera the following year.

With no means of support, Nate apprenticed with Henry, who took him into his household in exchange for his help. He was grateful for a place to live, but Henry's brood of ten children caused constant chaos in the house. Phebe's house was a stark contrast, peaceful, clean, uncluttered. It didn't hurt either that her father was the founder of the furnace. He hoped a marriage into her family would guarantee an improvement in his future job outlook since he would prefer furnace tasks to being in the hazardous woods in all kinds of weather. Phebe's epileptic brother, Nick, wouldn't be following in his father's footsteps, so there might be room for a son-in-law to take Nick's rightful place at the furnace. Phebe's sister, Rachel, also amused him. She was not as pretty as Phebe, with a long, plain face, but she wasn't bad to look at either. He enjoyed her tomboyishness, and her flirtatious comments boosted his male ego.

"Finish up, and let's go," urged Henry, gathering their plates as they crammed in the last bites of food. He put the tinware and spoons in a bucket of water to soak and wiped out the heavy iron skillet with a damp rag. "Time's a-wastin'."

The men gathered their shovels and baskets and headed toward pit number four.

~ CHAPTER 10 ~

Jesse Quinter prepared for his weekly trek from Hopewell to Philadelphia to deliver iron. He pulled the brim of his tricorn hat snugly down over his forehead. His thinning, brown hair didn't give much cover from the burning sun. A smattering of freckles across the bridge of his nose gave him a youthful appearance, even though he was twenty-three years old. At times, those freckles and his exuberant nature caused people to treat him more like a boy than a man, but he could be authoritative and stubborn when the situation demanded. In times of crisis, he was a quick thinker and kept a level head.

Since dawn, he had been hitching his team of four draft horses to the wagon and loading oats for them for the six-day round trip. The evening before, men had stacked the heavy load of pig iron in the wagon on a bed of straw.

Jesse's American Cream draft horses were the love of his life. The matched set of massive equines stood six feet high at the shoulder. Their creamy white, champagne-colored coats had a gold tint, and their manes and tails shone dazzling white in the sunlight. Jesse adored these horses. They were so powerful yet docile and easy to handle. The older two stood hitched in the front, and the back two were green and needed to follow the lead of the more experienced animals. Jesse had worked them since they were foals and knew all their quirks. Everyone around Hopewell and Philadelphia knew when they saw the distinctive horses that Jesse would be on the wagon seat driving them.

He inspected the wagon and harnesses. The sixteen-foot vehicle's seat was a hard plank with a short back, iron arms, and a spring-type shock absorber underneath that did a poor job softening the bumps. Iron strips rimmed the wooden wheels. His first stop for the night would be at Churches' farm near Valley Forge, where he would water, feed and corral the team, eat a meal, then bed down in the barn for the night. The Churches always were glad to see him and welcomed his news of the outside world. Sometimes he brought them supplies from the city on his return trip, and he was sure the money the furnace paid for his lodging bought necessities the family otherwise couldn't afford.

Ready to depart, Jesse sprang to the seat, took up the reins, and clucked to the team. They easily pulled the heavy burden up the hill. After he turned the corner from Hopewell onto the Reading-Valley Forge road, he could see several miles ahead until the road disappeared over a rise, which was the end of Hopewell's acres. Beyond that lay private lands with a few scattered farms. The countryside was gently rolling with lush green pastures and woods. Virgin growth timber, giant oaks, elms, maples, and hickories, stretched for miles on this side of Hopewell, as yet uncut for charcoal making.

The blue sky held a few puffy cumulus clouds but no sign of rain. Jesse's senses were acutely attuned to weather conditions. Nothing was worse than driving a slow wagon in the pouring rain. There were places along the road where he could hole up under an outcropping of trees if a severe storm approached. Of course, with winter coming soon, he worried about blizzards and deep drifts. Light snow and cold temperatures didn't bother him much. The road froze hard, and the horses' thick hairy coats kept them warm. Summer months were the most torturous, with biting bugs and stifling hot temperatures.

There was little traffic. A single horse chaise carrying a young man sped around him at a trot, no doubt on his way to the city too. Around midday, he came to a little shaded spring near the road where he scooped buckets of cool water for the animals and a dipperful for himself. It felt good to stretch and get a break from the endless road ahead. He put a little grain in the horses' feed bags, and while they munched, he unwrapped his lunch of bread with jam and a hunk of beef jerky. Soon he was back on the road.

As he passed one farm, Jesse whistled and waved to the farmer's wife, who was hanging wash on the lines strung beside the house. About dusk, he arrived at the Churches' farm, one-third the way to Philadelphia. The days were getting shorter, so he was relieved to reach his destination before nightfall, although the horses had been there many times before and could instinctively find their way. He always felt better after securing the animals for the night. The woods after dark teemed with dangerous creatures: bears, bobcats, and coyotes, that would possibly attack horses if hungry enough, especially in winter when snow made finding a meal more difficult.

As Jesse pulled in, two boys and a girl ran out to meet him. Their father, Levi Church, came out of the stable after them, raising his hand in greeting.

"We wondered if you'd be joining us for supper tonight, Jesse," he said. "How was your trip?"

"Uneventful, just one chaise passed me today. Beautiful day, though. I hope we'll still have another good month before the snow flies."

"The woolly bears are predicting a snowy winter this year. Their middles are barely brown," Levi observed.

"Do you believe those old folk tales?"

"My father always watched the animal signs, and that's one of them. I guess we don't have much choice of weather, no matter what the woollies say."

"I pray they're wrong this year," said Jesse. "I don't look forward to a lot of snow."

"Let's unhitch your horses and put them in the paddock. Supper's about ready."

Jesse had parked the team and wagon parallel to the barn. He tied the front two horses while he unhitched the rear two. One by one, he haltered the horses, heaved the collars and harnesses over their heads, and led them into the corral. He rewarded each with an apple from the stash he kept under the buckboard seat. Levi pitched in a large pile of hay, and his boys made sure the water trough was full. Jesse hung the harnesses on pegs in the barn to dry off the sweat and protect them from any overnight frost.

Jesse said, "After supper, I'll come out and give the horses some grain. They'll cool down by then. Let's see what's cooking. I'm hungry." Levi's daughter, Polly, swept up Jesse's calloused hand in her tiny one and pulled him to the house, skipping along the path.

They crossed the barnyard to the log cabin where tantalizing aromas swirled on the air. Levi's wife, Hannah, greeted Jesse. "Wash up and sit down. Supper's ready. Glad you got here while the food's hot."

"I could smell that delicious pot roast and pie all the way to the barn," he said. Hannah blushed.

The family washed at the basin on the washstand in the corner, then Levi took his place at the table's head, and Hannah sat at the foot. Jesse and the children filled in the sides.

After they loaded their plates with steaming food, everyone quieted down, intent on eating. "The meat is delicious," commented Jesse as he took another helping. "What is it? Venison?"

"Yes," replied Hannah. "Levi shot a large buck last week. It should help keep us in meat for a good part of the winter. We'll butcher one more hog when the weather gets a bit colder. Then we'll be sure to have enough."

Mashed potatoes and giblet gravy, cooked carrots, and warm biscuits were followed by apple pie with a lattice crust. The adults drank cider, the children, milk.

"You sure can set a delicious table of food, Hannah," Jesse exclaimed as he sat back and loosened his belt a notch. "I'd be fat if I ate here all the time."

"We don't dine like this every day," Levi said. "When you're coming, she always tries to make something special."

"I appreciate that. The meals along the road can be monotonous. It's great to eat something different in good company."

Levi said, "You probably have some good meals in Philadelphia, don't you?"

"Yes, but I'm only there one dinner a week and one breakfast the next morning before I'm traveling again. However, I guess that's more variety than most people have. I'm grateful Mr. Sterling pays for these meals. I couldn't bear the expense."

"But, Jesse, you indirectly pay for them by not being home with your family," Hannah pointed out.

"Right now, I'm young and unmarried, so I like the adventure of different places and new people. I'm always happy to return home though."

Jesse ate the last bites on his plate and polished off his drink. He rose from the table, dishes in hand.

Hannah stood and took the dishes from him. "I'll wash those. You've still got chores to do. Don't forget your blanket in the chest for your bed."

"Thanks," he said. "I'll go feed the team and bed down for the night. I want an early start in the morning."

"Come in for breakfast anytime. I'm usually up before dawn."

"Thanks, Hannah." Walking by the children, Jesse tousled the boys' hair and squeezed Polly's shoulder affectionately. "Goodnight, everyone."

After feeding the horses, Jesse burrowed a nest for his bed in the haymow. He slept fitfully though, his brain chewing on the idea of whether or not he wanted to continue this life on the road forever.

~ CHAPTER 11 ~

Jesse and the Church family rose early the next morning for a quick breakfast. In the cool air before dawn, Jesse hitched the animals and proceeded down the road. The weather was holding nicely and probably would stay clear until he reached Philadelphia tomorrow.

Once up, the sun warmed Jesse's back pleasantly, and his thoughts turned to his future. Hannah's observations the night before about his sacrifice of family time by being away so much had set him thinking. Where did he see himself in five years? Would he still be doing this job? Probably, since he liked working outdoors and driving the team. Although the trip was monotonous, the weather always added a challenge of uncertainty.

In five years, would he be married and have children? He didn't see how that would happen. He never was at Hopewell for any length of time to meet young women, and traveling six days a week wouldn't make for a pleasant family life at home. He'd be a good provider with a steady income, but most wives wanted and needed their men home. Sometimes he met young ladies on his travels, but the situation would be the same no matter where he set down roots. Local hauling jobs were available in Philadelphia, but he didn't like the idea of being away from his mother and siblings at Hopewell.

As he approached the toll house, his musings were interrupted. Many of the roads he traveled were privately owned and required a fee to use them. He dug three pence out of his pocket and flipped the coins to Owen, the gatekeeper, who deftly caught the money and raised the log across the path so Jesse and the wagon could pass. Owen waved an envelope.

"Could you take this letter to Philadelphia with you, Jesse? The missus is worried about her sick mother and wants to know if she needs help."

"Sure, I can take it. Where does it go?"

"Drop it at the address on Spruce Street. I think that's close to where you unload the iron, isn't it?"

"Yes, it's on my way. Should I wait for an answer?"

"We'd appreciate one if it doesn't take too long. Her mother had a fit of apoplexy and was still unconscious the last we heard."

"Sounds serious," said Jesse. "I should be back in two days."

"Next time you come through, there'll be no charge to compensate you for your trouble."

"I'm happy to help." Jesse tucked the envelope inside his shirt and drove through.

At dusk, Jesse pulled the wagon into Berry's Tavern between Valley Forge and Philadelphia. The fieldstone and log structure rose two stories high with sleeping rooms upstairs for travelers. Downstairs, patrons could order a meal and alcohol if they wished. Jesse tied the horses to the hitching post.

"Hello, Jimmy," he called to the owner, Jimmy Berry, who was sweeping the entrance floor. "Can I settle the horses and come in for supper and a room?"

"Of course, Jesse. What would you like to eat? Mary's got beef stew and biscuits on the stove."

"That sounds great. I'll be back shortly."

Soon Jesse returned and wormed his way across the crowded dining room to a table by the window. Quite a few travelers were eating while others lined up at the bar chatting and drinking.

Jimmy brought a steaming bowl of stew with six biscuits for dipping. "What'll you have to drink? Your usual beer?"

"You know me too well," Jesse chuckled.

While he tackled the chunks of tender beef and potatoes and carrots, a stranger entered and scanned the room. Jesse knew many of the inn's usual guests, but didn't recognize this one. He was a middle-aged, short, thin man, no taller than Jesse's shoulder and about half his weight. His suit of clothes was well-worn but serviceable. Perhaps he was a store merchant somewhere because he certainly wasn't dressed for farming. The man spied Jesse and made his way over to the table. "Is that your fine team of yeller horses in the corral?" he questioned with a broad smile. "I saw you drive in."

Jesse motioned him to sit down. "Yes, it is."

"Well, my name's Roy Dickenson," he said, as he pulled out a chair. "Tell me about them."

Jesse proudly described their glowing attributes.

"They sure look wonderful. Can I make you an offer for them?" Dickenson flashed a roll of money from his money pouch. "I can pay handsomely."

"No, they're not for sale at any price. They're my livelihood, and I trained them from foals. It would be like selling my family."

"One doesn't often encounter such fine horses. You can't blame me for trying to buy them," said Roy. "Where are you headed?"

"I'm taking a load of iron to Philadelphia from Hopewell Furnace. I make a trip about once a week. How about you?"

"Lancaster. I have a small farm there. I had business in Philadelphia, and I'm on my way back. Do you mind if I eat with you? There don't seem to be any other open tables."

"No, I don't mind. I'd be happy for some company. A long day traveling can be lonesome."

Roy waved his hand to attract Jimmy's attention. "Can I have the same as he's having?" He pointed to Jesse's plate.

Soon Roy was devouring stew and biscuits and drinking a beer, too. After some pleasantries about the weather and such, the men fell into an awkward silence while they ate. Although Jesse wasn't usually much of a talker, he loosened up after a few beers and chatted freely with this gap-toothed stranger. Roy asked a lot of questions about Hopewell and listened attentively. Jesse guessed Roy didn't have much male company at his farm and was eager to share a few pints, dinner, and conversation.

Jesse scoured his plate with his last biscuit, wiped his mouth with his napkin, and pushed back his chair. "I've got to start early in the morning. Nice talking to you."

Roy got up also. "I better head to bed too."

They went to the bar where Jimmy was polishing glasses. "Which room do you want me to take?" Jesse asked.

"I need a room too," said Roy.

"Do you two mind sharing a room? There's one left with two beds. All my other rooms are occupied."

Jesse looked at Roy. "I don't mind if Roy doesn't."

"That would be fine with me," Roy replied. "Better than sleeping in the barn."

Jimmy reached under the counter and handed Jesse the key. "Room three at the end of the hall. That'll be fifty pence each for the meals and room. That includes breakfast in the morning."

The men paid their money and climbed the stairs. Room three held two single beds, a washstand with a pitcher of water and a bowl, a small chest of drawers, and a chair. The plank floor was rough but clean. A single window overlooked the road in front of the tavern.

"You can use the chest, Roy," Jesse said. "I'll put my clothes on the chair over here."

"Thanks. Where's the key for the door?"

Jesse rose and fished it out of his pants pocket. He tossed it to Roy. Roy said, "I'll lock it and put the key in the lock from this side. I don't want to disturb you if I rise before you do."

Jesse pulled off his boots and stripped to his long johns. At the washstand, he splashed water on his face and dried his hands with the coarse towel hung over the rack on the back, then with a yawn, stretched out on the bed. He ran his hands through his hair. "It feels good to lie down. My eyes got mighty heavy after that meal."

Roy took off his outer clothes and laid them carefully in the drawers. He looked out the window at the darkness settling over the countryside. "Sure gets dark quickly these days. There's a flock of geese flying in a V headed south." He walked over to the lighted oil lamp on the chest. "You ready for lights out, Jesse?"

Jesse didn't reply, and his snoring told Roy he was already asleep.

Roy blew out the lamp and settled into the sagging rope bed. He lay awake awhile, listening to Jesse's snoring, then smiled to himself and closed his eyes.

~ CHAPTER 12 ~

Daylight streaming in through the window woke Jesse. He yawned and stretched his arms toward the ceiling, shrugged his shoulders to his ears, and rotated his crackling stiff neck. He hadn't intended to sleep this late, but he could still reach Philadelphia easily today if he wolfed breakfast. Glancing over at the empty bed, he guessed Roy had gotten an early start like he wished he would have.

As he put on his shirt, he noticed the letter he was carrying from Owen's wife lying on the floor and bent to pick it up. *I mustn't be careless. I need the address on that letter. It must have slipped out of my pocket when I got the key for Roy last night.* After replacing it in his pocket, he made sure to button the flap.

He dressed, smoothed down his hair with water from the pitcher, removed the key from the unlocked door, and hurried down to breakfast. He scanned the dining room for Roy, but he wasn't there.

"Your friend took off early," said Jimmy, as he plunked down a heaping plate of scrambled eggs and sausage. "He seemed anxious to leave." The innkeeper pocketed the room key Jesse handed him.

"I should have been up early too, but it's too late now to worry about that. Thanks for breakfast. I'll be off as soon as I eat. See you in a couple of days."

Jesse arrived in Philadelphia mid-afternoon and went first to Spruce Street to deliver the letter. To his dismay, Owen's wife's mother had died that morning, having never regained consciousness. Jesse didn't relish being the one to give Owen's wife that news.

"Tell her the funeral will be Friday. We hope she can come," Owen's sister-in-law informed him.

"I'll give her the message first thing the day after tomorrow. I don't know if that will give her enough time to come."

"We'll understand if she can't."

He clambered to his seat on the buckboard, clucked to the team, and headed toward the docks of Philadelphia. Soon he arrived on Water Street and parked where an enormous three-masted ship lay docked. He went into the small log cabin onshore next to the wharf.

"Hello, Jesse," welcomed Theuben Bailey, in a thick Liverpudlian accent. He laid down his quill and corked the ink bottle beside the manifest book in which he had been writing.

"Greetings, Theuben."

"I'm glad you got here before the ship left for England tomorrow. We've got room for more cargo. Hate for her to sail half empty." Theuben's massive arms bulged in his short-sleeved shirt, and his skin was tanned a leathery nut brown from hours in the sun.

Jesse took papers from his pocket and gave them to Theuben. "Here's the inventory list. Lots of pigs in the wagon."

Theuben glanced over the papers, uncorked the ink bottle, added some lines and numbers to the ship's manifest, and wrote a receipt. "Let's unload that iron before the lads decide the day is over and head to the pub for their last night in port."

Going out the door, Theuben called to some men on the dock. "Lower that block and tackle over the side with a crate so we can lift this load up. Then two of you come down and help unload."

The four men on the dock formed a bucket brigade to pass the iron from the wagon and stack it in the crate. Jesse pulled out the four-foot bars and passed them along to the next man. Theuben deftly stacked the iron in the container at the other end, so the load wouldn't shift and fall when raised to the deck of the schooner. The men worked swiftly, and the process took less than an hour. Even though the day was cool with a slight breeze, sweat rolled off the workers by the time they finished lifting the heavy loads.

"That's the last of it, Theuben," said Jesse. He latched the tailgate of the wagon.

Theuben came to the wagon and shook Jesse's hand. "Are you sure that's all? Your wagon's still sitting a mite low in the front."

"Yes, I'm sure." Jesse winked at him.

Theuben leaned in close. "Someday, you'll get in trouble selling that stuff to the stores. What is it? Stove parts?"

"I won't tell anyone if you don't," replied Jesse.

"Well, lad, as long as you keep shipping the pigs with me, your secret is safe."

Jesse climbed up, and the team moved off. He doffed his hat to Theuben as the wagon rumbled away.

Two blocks from the dock, Jesse pulled up to the side of a warehouse. He rang the bell on the door, and soon a clerk appeared.

"I'm delivering iron parts for the store," he said.

The worker nodded and slid open a large door on the warehouse. Jesse drove the team inside, and the man closed the door. Together they unloaded the iron stove parts from the front of the wagon. "The boss is anxious to stock these parts," the worker said. "We've lots of orders since winter will soon be here. When will you be able to deliver more?"

"I'll be in town again next week and will bring more then."

They finished unloading and completed the paperwork. Jesse handed the worker a paper. "Here's a list of the supplies we need. I'll pick them up tomorrow morning like usual."

"I'll make sure the boss gets it. They'll be ready for you."

"Thanks." Jesse got back on the seat while the worker reopened the door. He skillfully backed up the wagon and team into the street and headed for the livery stable to bed the horses for the night.

After stabling the horses, Jesse wearily headed for his overnight lodging place, Tun Tavern, a short walk from the stable. The sun had set, and darkness enveloped the city. He scolded himself. *I should have risen sooner this morning, especially since I had that extra stop for Owen.*

Tun Tavern sat on the waterfront, at the corner of Water Street and Tun Alley. As he approached, the three-story tavern loomed large out of the darkness. Bright lanterns on the covered porch threw sparkling light on the steps. Raucous laughter flowed out the door. The place was lively tonight. A fixture in the city since 1685, the tavern brewed fine beer and hosted the first meetings of the Masons in 1732. In the 1740s, an addition named Peggy Mullan's Red Hot Beef Steak Club opened, and its hearty food was instantly popular. Jesse's mouth began to water at the thought and smells of fine tender steak.

As he entered, he heard unusual music. A crowd gathered around a man playing a jaunty tune on a boxy wooden instrument in one corner of the room. He sat on a keg while his fingers danced over white and black keys. The sound was unlike any Jesse had ever heard. Amazingly, the player's fingers either floated lightly over the keys producing pleasant, soft tinkling notes, or pounded heavily for a loud, bold sound.

"What's that thing he's playing?" Jesse shouted to a slightly intoxicated man beside him, who alternately swayed or stomped as the music moved him.

"It's called a 'pianoforte'," the man said. "I haven't heard one since I left London. Some man named John Behrent here in Philadelphia is making them. Isn't it grand?" He began clapping with the beat. "They just got it yesterday, and that fellow playing sure is good. Wait 'til you hear Molly sing."

Jesse had to agree it was a mighty fine tune. A buxom, red-haired woman took her place beside the piano man as he got to the end of the song.

"Here's Molly now." The man beside Jesse excitedly grabbed his arm.

Molly smiled at the gathering crowd. Her dress was emerald green silk with a tightly laced corset top displaying her ample cleavage and tiny waist, below which her skirt puffed out with voluminous petticoats underneath. After a few opening bars of music, she began to sing. Her lusty, soprano voice rose in volume as she belted out the words to the patriotic *Pennsylvania Song*.

As Molly began the melody again, the crowd joined her, their voices growing louder and more enthusiastic. Jesse caught the infectious enthusiasm and began to sing too, with a rich tenor voice. But when they started the third stanza, Jesse, bone-tired, realized he needed to eat and go to his room.

He backed out of the crowd that had enveloped him and sauntered over to the registry desk. A pretty, petite woman appeared behind the counter and asked, "Need a room for the night, Jesse?"

Jessie tipped his hat to the woman. "Yes, Mrs. O'Neal, my usual room, number fourteen, if available." He pulled his money pouch from his jacket pocket.

"Yes, it's available," said Mrs. O'Neal as she placed the key on the counter.

Jesse opened the money pouch to pay. Empty! He couldn't believe his eyes.

"Is something wrong?" inquired Mrs. O'Neal, who looked alarmed at his sudden intake of breath and ashen color.

"Yes, I've been robbed!"

"Robbed? How can that be? You still have your pouch."

"I'm not sure. I put my money in here when I left Hopewell. But there's nothing in here now."

"Did you spend it in town and forget?"

"No, I last opened the pouch yesterday night at Berry's." Then it dawned on him. "I shared my room with a stranger from Lancaster there. He left the inn before I did this morning, and I guess he helped himself to my money."

"'Tis terrible, Jesse. What are you going to do? Shall I send for the constable?"

"No, the man is no doubt long gone to who knows where. He probably wasn't even from Lancaster. I'll try to trace him when I return to Berry's tomorrow night. Fortunately, I didn't lose a lot of money, just my traveling expenses. I'm sorry, I can't pay for my room and meal."

"Since you're here every week, I can give you the room on credit if you sign a voucher. I know you'll repay us next time you come through."

"You're very kind, ma'am. I'm very embarrassed but will accept your hospitality."

"I'm sure you'll find the man and get it back. Have you eaten supper yet?"

"No, I'll go hungry tonight."

"Don't be foolish. I'll advance you the money for your supper and breakfast too. Just tell Charley to put it on your bill."

Jesse scribbled his signature on the voucher. "Thank you, Mrs. O'Neal. I apologize for any inconvenience." Disgusted and fuming, he went to the dining room and sat down.

He was almost finished with his supper when a pretty young woman in a low-cut dress with petticoats and a beauty mark on her chin flounced down in the extra seat at his table. She batted her eyes at him coquettishly.

"Hello, Hetty," Jesse said. "How are you?"

"I'm fine, Jesse, but you don't look so good. Rough day on the trail?"

"I had the usual day of long, dusty roads and heavy unloading, but the worst part was a stranger I shared a room with last night stole my money."

"How did he do that?" Hetty asked.

Jesse explained the whole situation.

"Would you recognize him again if you saw him?"

"Yes, I'd know him. He told me his name was Roy Dickenson, and he was a farmer from Lancaster, but I doubt if anything he said is true."

"How did you pay for supper?" Hetty looked at his near-empty plate.

"Mrs. O'Neal advanced me money for the meal and my room."

"I guess you won't be buying me a drink tonight."

"No, and I can't afford anything else either," Jesse lamented.

"But, Jesse, I always save Wednesday nights for you. I'm so disappointed."

"I'm sorry, Hetty, I was looking forward to our time together too, but I don't have any money." She was a pleasant diversion at the end of his haul every week. Far away from Hopewell, he felt free to sow some wild oats.

Hetty rose and straightened her petticoats. "I'll be moving along. I'll see you next week."

Jesse watched her strut over to a patron leaning on the bar and begin working her charms on him. He drank his last sip of beer and crossed back to the tavern where Molly was still singing. As he plodded up the stairs to his room, he thought, *my bed will feel mighty cold without Hetty to warm things up.*

~ CHAPTER 13 ~

After a quarter-mile walk through woods and fields, Nate, Henry, and Jacob arrived at pit number four to see if it was ready to be coaled out. The mound had shrunk considerably from its original eight-foot height, signaling that the hardwood beneath the dirt had been reduced to charcoal.

"How long has it been since we started this pit?" Henry asked Nate, who pulled a small notebook out of his pocket.

"Twelve days."

Henry shoveled some of the soil off the base of the pit. No fire flared up, and the earth they had placed on top of the wood was very dusty, indicating the heat underneath had evaporated any moisture. Using his long, iron-toothed rake to pull out some of the charred wood, he watched again for any hint of flame. He continued around the mound, repeating the process. Everything seemed cool.

"It looks good," Henry said. "Jacob and Nate, you follow me with the baskets and scoop up the charcoal. Then rake that dust off to the side. I'll keep checking the foot. The wagon should be coming soon."

A rumbling noise echoing through the woods caught Nate's attention. "There's Isaac now." A six-mule team and high-sided vehicle passed the pit, then turned around in the field and pulled beside them, headed in the direction of the furnace. The short, wiry driver leaped down. He was filthy from head to toe and covered with black charcoal dust. His curly mop of hair might have been blond underneath the black. The brilliant whites of his eyes contrasted sharply with the rest of his blackened face, giving him a scary look. His shirt and pants were smudged black, as were his arms, hands, and neck. His dirtiness was his persona in the forest since he always looked that way. The few times Nate had seen him at church, he had failed to recognize the man until he spoke.

"About time you got here, Isaac," grumbled Henry.

"I got a late start this morning. That ornery white mule wouldn't come in from the field. After I caught him, I ate an extra breakfast 'cause I'd burnt off so much energy."

"You're always looking for an excuse to eat," joked Henry. "I'm surprised you don't weigh as much as a mule, eating the quantities you do."

"I never gain any weight, no matter how much I eat. Good thing the Sterlings feed me, or I would need another job just to buy my grub."

Henry turned to his helpers. "Start loading the charcoal, boys."

Henry resumed pulling the dirt and testing the charred wood. So far, there were no flare-ups. They had tried to coal out this pit two days ago, but it had been too hot and needed more time to burn itself out. He picked carefully around the edges, gradually digging out more and more charcoal until he reached the center.

By mid-morning, the wagon almost overflowed, and the pit was empty. Piles of dirt and dust lay in a ring at the edge of the hearth. Isaac had helped, making the work finish sooner.

When they loaded the last basketful into the vehicle, Henry said, "Nate, you can ride to Hopewell with Isaac and see Tom McCauley about getting a partner and a tract of land to lumber over the winter. Just be sure to be back here first thing in the morning. We'll be building that last pit tomorrow."

Nate handed his tools to Jacob. "Thanks, Henry. I'll be back as soon as I can."

Isaac and Nate hopped on the seat. The teamster took up the reins, clucked to the mules, and they lumbered off.

The first stop at Hopewell was at the furnace's upper level at the charcoal shed, which was open on three sides. Sometimes the charred wood arrived still smoldering, and this cooling area helped prevent fires in the shed or the covered walkway leading to the tunnel head at the top of the furnace.

Isaac pulled the mules through the building until the wagon was centered under the roof. After setting the brake, he and Nate unhitched the team, took them around to the back end of the wagon, and fastened them to the pull rings connected to the boards at the bottom of the vehicle. At Isaac's cluck, the animals lurched forward, the planks jerked out, and the charcoal fell to the ground. Then they unhitched the animals from the boards, refastened them to the front, pulled them forward, and restored the planks to the wagon floor. Isaac used a shovel to spread out the load, thoroughly picking through it to check for burning embers.

"I almost burned a wagon last week," Isaac said to Nate. "A hot coal in the load caught fire, and I lost a quarter of the charcoal by the time I got the floor pulled. McCauley docked me for only delivering part of a load. Lucky the whole thing didn't go up in flames. You can never be too careful. Sometimes those coals seem to wait for just the worst moment to flame up. Charcoal can carry fire for a long time, but I guess you know that."

Nate was anxious to leave. "I better go see McCauley. I hope he's still got a tract of land left for lumbering. Thanks for the ride, Isaac."

"Good luck and I appreciate your help."

It was a short walk down the slope from the shed to the store. Nate patiently waited while a woman ordered material and asked for five pounds of flour. The shop was small but was packed from floor to ceiling with a myriad of items. Along one wall stretched a counter, and behind it stood a desk with open ledger books where Tom McCauley recorded sales.

Nate drooled over the jars of stick candy and looked at the array of iron pots and lids, candles, brooms, decks of cards, and sewing kits and buttons. Children's playthings were displayed, a wooden ball on a string attached to a cup, dominoes, and checkers. One corner contained a hand mirror, a straight razor and strop, shaving soap and brushes, fine-toothed combs for battling head lice, hair dye, and medicinal products such as Epsom salts, castor oil, and worm syrup. Cooking supplies were in the backroom. Meat and fish, bacon, beef, and mackerel were on the lower level.

Nate perused the tools, found an ax, and noted the price. He hoped he had earned enough from charcoaling to purchase it.

"That's $1.25 off your account, Mrs. Dunlap." Tom McCauley showed her the entry under her name. He pointed to another figure in the book. "Here's your balance."

The clerk finished bundling Eliza Dunlap's goods in her basket, and she walked out the door.

"What can we do for you, Nate?"

"I have several things I need to ask you. How much money is in my account?"

Tom flipped some pages in the ledger. "Here's your credit as of the last time Henry Zerbey reported about a month ago. I imagine you'll be getting more when the charcoal season is over soon. Right?"

"Yes," said Nate as he looked at the figure. He felt relieved the amount was enough for the ax. "I also want to know if any areas of woods are available for cutting this winter. I want to try my hand at lumbering until charcoaling starts up again in the spring. Do you know anyone who needs a partner?"

"Let me get the map." Tom stepped over to the desk, pulled out a large chart, and unrolled it on the counter. "We're lumbering these tracts of land over to the east." He pointed to an area. "It's about two miles from here. Many of the plots have been spoken for by the men who cut wood each winter. You'll be assigned a tract at the farthest end. If you want, I can give you one today. I don't know any single cutters now, but I'm sure there will be some coming in who need a partner. Do you want to do that?"

"Yes, I better take an assignment today before the trees are even farther away."

"All right, I'll write your name on these ten acres, number eighty-eight. The numbers are painted on the trees at the corners. Just be sure to keep your cords stacked away from other choppers' wood, so they aren't mixed up. You'll be paid by the cord, thirty-five cents each. Does that sound acceptable?"

"Yes, it does. I'll come back in when the charcoal season ends and pick up supplies. Can you put back one of the axes for me to pick up later?"

"Sure, I can. And I'll ask around to see if anyone needs a partner. Inform me if you find one, too."

"Thanks, I'll be back." Nate walked out the door. He felt relieved to have enough money to buy the ax and to be assigned a lot, but he didn't relish a cold winter in the woods. *I'd rather be working at the warm furnace and be near my lovely Phebe.*

~ CHAPTER 14 ~

After leaving the store, Nate walked down the lane toward the tenants' houses. About a quarter-mile from the bridge crossing over French Creek stood the Zerbey house. He still had some daylight hours left and didn't need to be back in the woods until early morning, so he decided to clean up there. He could eat some supper and then call on Phebe, even though he had visited just a few days before. No one would expect him to visit again so soon, but she had been on his mind since he had seen her last, and he longed to see her again. He also wanted to tell her that after the charcoal season was over, he planned to cut timber and might be out of touch for several months. The long walk to his tract of land would be too much for him to go back and forth daily. He would build a hut to stay in the forest as long as the weather remained above freezing.

Before he reached the house, he heard youngsters in the yard playing and yelling. There was seldom a quiet moment in this household of ten children. There were continual conflicts. Older ones picking on younger ones, smaller offspring squealing for attention, and babies crying for food, a diaper change, or a cuddle. The oldest siblings had chores such as minding the infants, milking the cow, gathering eggs, weeding the garden, or hanging out laundry. The middle-aged children performed more menial labor such as bringing in firewood, carding the wool to be spun, or washing dishes. Toddlers learned to dress and feed themselves, often resulting in more clean-up tasks. Usually, the household ran smoothly, but Margaret Zerbey looked frazzled, trying to keep the peace, ensure everyone was fed and clothed, and referee the occasional fight. To complicate matters, she was perpetually pregnant, and her husband spent ninety percent of his time at the charcoal pits, earning money to sustain the burgeoning family. Despite the chaos, Margaret usually had a smile on her face and few harsh words for her brood. The only education her children received was what she had time to give them, rudimentary mathematics, and essential reading.

Nate entered the house and walked around the scattered toys and baskets of dirty clothes. Cooking and cleaning for the group was a gigantic task. He found Margaret in the kitchen, stirring a stew.

"Hello, Nate," she said. "I didn't expect to see you. Is Henry along?"

"No, I'm alone. I came to talk with Tom McCauley about lumbering for off-season money. I'm going back first thing tomorrow morning."

"Are the pits about done for the year?" she asked, as she gingerly slurped the hot slurry on her wooden spoon, then added more salt.

"About two weeks left at most. What is Henry planning for the winter?"

"I'm not sure whether he's going to be cutting wood. He's getting a bit old to be doing such a physical job. In the past, he's worked with a couple of different woodchoppers, so perhaps he can still work with them in an easier capacity. He's not a young man anymore."

"He hasn't talked to me about his plans. You know Henry. He's a man of few words. It's hard to tell what he might be thinking."

"Will you be joining us for supper tonight? I can throw in another potato or two. Perhaps afterward, you could help with some of the chores the older children can't quite manage, like splitting some logs for firewood. That would sure help me out."

"I'll split some now, before dinner, in exchange for some of that delicious smelling stew. Then I'm going to clean up and take a little walk."

"I'll bet you're taking a stroll to the Palsgroves, aren't you?" She grinned and winked at him. "I heard you paid Phebe Palsgrove a visit the night of the dance."

Nate's face turned red. "You've got me all figured out. Yes, that's the direction I'll be heading."

"Love's a wonderful thing. I haven't regretted for a minute marrying Henry, and look at our fantastic children. We may not have many possessions, but there's enough food and clothing for everyone, so what more does one need? Nothing compares to the love of family."

Margaret adored her life and thought it perfect. Who was he to disagree? But Nate didn't think it was for him. He liked a more peaceful, sedate way of life. Of course, if his birth family had been bigger, perhaps he wouldn't have felt so devastated when his parents died. If he had had siblings, he would still have people of his own to live with instead of the Zerbeys.

"I'll go start chopping that wood," Nate said.

"You know where the ax is," Margaret replied. "I'll send one of the children out when the meal is ready. The girls will help feed the youngsters first, and then maybe we adults can eat in peace."

By suppertime, a sizable pile of wood littered the yard. Nate's face gleamed with sweat. He picked up the shirt he had discarded and poked his supple arms into the sleeves. It felt good to stretch different muscles than usual. He quickly stacked the wood at the back of the house. After washing at the pump, he gathered an armful of kindling to fill the box in the kitchen. The older children and Margaret encircled the worn table and were digging in. Nate sat down and started eating the stew and a slab of buttered bread on his plate, washing it down with a mug of tea. Margaret had portioned out the food so there was enough to go around. Leftovers didn't exist with all these mouths to feed.

"Your cooking sure beats our poor grub at the hut," he exclaimed.

"Henry never claimed to be a cook, now did he?" she laughed.

"Often we're so hungry, we'll devour almost anything,"

After eating, he washed up more thoroughly, scrubbing his hands and face to remove the caked-on charcoal dust streaked by rivulets of sweat. "Do I still have fresh clothes upstairs?"

"Yes, they're on the end peg in the boys' room. Bring your dirty ones down when you come, and the girls will wash and hang them out. They should be dry by the time you leave in the morning."

"They certainly need washing. They're so crusty they can stand up by themselves." Nate climbed the stairs. The first room to the right was the girls' room, where several beds they shared lined up along the walls. A long row of pegs by the door held nightclothes and extra outfits. In the corner stood a rickety chest of drawers containing underthings and socks.

The next room down the hall was the boys' room, a mirror image of the girls' room. He found a shirt and a pair of pants his size on the far end of the line of hooks. Fortunately, he was bigger than any of the boys, or one would probably be wearing his clothes. After closing the door, he stripped and redressed. He checked his appearance in the mirror over the chest, slicked down his hair with some spit, and made himself presentable enough to call on Phebe.

Back in the kitchen, Margaret motioned him to a washtub sitting in the corner. "Sarah filled it with some water and soap already. Toss your dirty clothes in and stir them with the stick."

He did as instructed. "I'm going now. I won't be gone too long."

"Some red chrysanthemums are blooming in the back of the house. Pick some for her if you like."

"That's a grand idea. I'll do that."

"Have a good time," cackled Mrs. Zerbey, as she folded clean clothes into a basket. "Don't do anything I wouldn't do!"

~ CHAPTER 15 ~

Rachel's face registered surprise when she answered Nate's knock on their door. "Nate, you're the last person I expected." She eyed the bouquet of red chrysanthemums in his hand.

"I don't suppose those are for me."

"Sorry, no, they're for your sister."

"I hoped to dance with you the other night," she chided. "I needed rescuing from Tom McCauley. He wanted every dance. Then I fell and tore my dress. It was a disaster."

"Sorry I couldn't help, but I'm sure you took care of yourself."

"I was so embarrassed. I couldn't leave quickly enough. I was happy I tripped so I had an excuse to go. Oh, I'm sorry. I've been rattling on instead of inviting you in."

Nate stomped the dust off his boots and came into the kitchen. "I can't stay long. Is your sister here?"

"Hello, Nate," called Phebe from the keeping room. "I'm here. Come in."

Nate entered the room and held out the flowers to Phebe. "These are for you."

"Thank you very much." She ducked her chin and blushed. "I'll get a vase for them."

Rachel rushed in carrying a container of water, spilling a few drops. "Here, Phebe, I got one for you already." She put in the mums, fluffed them apart, and placed the arrangement on the table beside her sister. She began to sit but saw Phebe's disapproving look and stood back up, and as she retreated to the kitchen, she said, "I'll ask Mother if she needs any help." She liked Nate and wanted to hear their conversation but knew he was there to see her sister, not her. Her disappointment morphed into happiness for her sister, who despite her beauty, had few suitors due to her illness.

Nate sat on the settee beside Phebe. Her light green dress was embellished with tiny embroidered flowers, and it accentuated her slender waist and perky small bosom. Lace draped under her chin and ruffled at her wrists. Her beautiful, red-burnished hair was gathered on top of her head, and three graceful curls cascaded down her creamy white neck. Her small, slightly upturned nose drew Nate's eyes to her full luscious lips. He caught his breath at her beauty.

The scent of bayberry from a lit candle on the mantle gently perfumed the air. In Nate's mind, Phebe was the image of the ideal woman. He had a strong desire to become part of this picture and make her his.

"Nice to see you again, Nate." The soft, pearly voice matched the rest of her. "What brings you to the village twice in one week?"

"I rode in with Isaac on the charcoal wagon this morning to ask Tom McCauley about wood chopping a tract of land this winter. Charcoaling season is almost over."

"Was any land available?"

"Yes, he assigned me an area. Now I hope to find someone to work with me."

"It can be dangerous working alone, and I don't know how one can stand to be out in the cold all day long."

"Once you start swinging the ax, you heat up fast. But the long walk to and from the woodlot can chill your blood."

"I'm thankful I can stay in my warm house."

She stowed her sewing into the basket to give him her full attention. Rachel came in bearing a piece of cake and a cup of tea for each of them. "I've completed school now, Nate," she said.

He broke his concentration on Phebe to glance her way. "How do you feel about that, Rachel? I know you loved school. I, myself, felt relieved when I finished."

"Oh, yes, I'm missing it."

"She had an offer from Mr. Sterling," her sister commented.

"What kind of offer?"

"He will send her to the university in Philadelphia if she chaperones Susanna at finishing school."

"Chaperone! That would be a tall order. I hear she can be pretty wild away from home."

"Well, not really chaperone, but help her with her studies and be a companion. Mr. Sterling wants to keep an eye on her as well as ensure she's not wasting his money there."

"The city is quite a bit different than Hopewell," Nate said. "Wouldn't you be afraid to be so far from home in a strange place?"

"Have you been to Philadelphia? What's it like?" asked Rachel.

"I only went once when I was trying to decide whether to apprentice with Henry as a collier or try some other trade. It's a chaotic town. There are scores of people scurrying around, carriages and wagons going up and down cobblestone streets, and it's noisy and dirty. It stinks, too. People dump their filthy, disgusting water out in the gutter, if you know what I mean. Down by the docks, the air smells like salt and rotten fish. Philadelphia isn't where I want to live or even visit. But if you want more education, the city is where you need to go."

"I'm sure it would take some time to adjust."

"We don't know if Father will let her go or not. He and Mother are thinking it over," Phebe said.

"Do you want to go, Rachel? You're probably yearning for a new adventure," Nate asked.

"Yes, I'd like to see the city." She sighed. "I want to learn how to teach, and I want to experience the world. Mother and Father have seen so much having crossed the ocean from England to Philadelphia to settle here. I haven't been anywhere but Hopewell."

"Well, it *would* be an adventure. Make sure you understand what is expected of you from Daniel Sterling and Susanna before you go. He seems like a fair man, but you don't want a misunderstanding," Nate advised. "Wouldn't you miss your family?"

"I would miss them, but I'd write letters and come back frequently. Since iron goes to the city every week, I could get correspondence often."

Phebe said, "I don't know what we would do here without her, but I guess we could manage somehow." She winked at Rachel.

"That's certainly an exciting proposition for you. I can see how the Sterlings would think of you for such a position. But the university? Can you handle that?"

"Mr. Elliott is the one who recommended me. He says he has more pupils than he can handle and wants me to help him. I would also instruct students whose parents can't afford to pay."

"I'm sure it will work out for the best." Nate's mind raced at this new development. If Rachel left, the Palsgroves might need his help more than ever around the house. She did many of the chores, and with her father at the furnace twelve hours a day, someone would need to assist. This was not only an excellent opportunity for Rachel but perhaps an even greater one for him.

"When does Henry require you back at the pits?" asked Phebe. "Can you stay in the village for several days?"

"No, I have to be back tomorrow morning. We're coaling a pit then. I'm going to sleep tonight at the Zerbeys, if I can find a bed, and head out before dawn. Speaking of turning in early, would you like to go for a short walk before I leave, Phebe?"

"I would love to," she replied. "I better put on my shawl. The evenings are so cool now."

Phebe covered her shoulders with the wrap hanging over the back of the chair.

Nate nodded toward Rachel. "Let me know if you're going to the city. I'll be hoping it goes your way."

"Thanks. I appreciate that."

The couple headed for the door. Passing through the kitchen, Phebe said to her mother and father seated at the table, "We're going for a walk. I'll be back soon."

"If Nick is out there, tell him to come in," Martha said.

Abruptly the door burst open, and the boy bounded in. "I'm here, Mother. You didn't have to call me. It started to get dark, and I knew to come in," he said proudly.

"Good boy, Nick. We're glad you're acting grown-up," said Lewis, nudging Martha with his knee. "Did your friends go home too?"

"Yes, they're responsible like me." Martha and Lewis laughed at his use of such an adult word.

"Go clean up, son, and put your nightclothes on," chuckled Lewis, and the boy scampered up the steps.

Nate held the door open for Phebe. They stepped off the stoop and walked down the narrow path to the road. "Ouch!" yowled Nate, as he kicked violently at the gray-and-white blur in the grass. Jack, the cat, went flying. "I hate that animal," he complained while inspecting his leg for claw marks.

Phebe, startled by his outburst, said, "I don't understand why he attacks you. He shouldn't think you're a stranger anymore."

Nate pulled down his pant leg and recovered his composure. It didn't look good to abuse the family pet, even though he was at odds with it. He never did like cats; dogs were more to his liking. If his plans to make Phebe his wife and move into the Palsgrove household were successful, Jack would have to go. The cat could 'conveniently' disappear.

Reaching the lane, Nate put his arm around Phebe's shoulders, and she leaned into him. Soon they neared the bridge. A frog hopped with a 'whump' into the water as they approached. They watched the creek meander along and listened to it gurgle when water splashed against the rocks.

As they stood and absorbed the myriad of night sounds, the rosy glow of sunset disappeared, and Phebe shivered against the cool air. Nate hugged her closer and held her hand. They watched the full moon gradually rise above the horizon. Darkness enveloped the countryside. They heard an occasional stamping of a hoof in the field where cows and horses grazed and the rustling of nocturnal predators on the hunt in the brush. The stars were visible now, and Nate pointed out the Big Dipper and the North Star.

They didn't talk much and were content to enjoy each other's company and the serene setting. Nate's thoughts wandered to his coming job. He dreaded the idea of chopping wood in the frigid forest, but that seemed to be his fate, at least for the moment. He needed work. A collier had some relaxing time while waiting for the fires to sufficiently char the wood to charcoal, but a chopper was either working a sweat up in the dangerous job of felling a tree or dodging 'widow-maker' limbs stuck in the treetops that could come crashing down at any time. Cutting the massive virgin timber logs into four-foot lengths, then splitting them and stacking cords four feet wide by four feet high by eight feet long was exhausting work. Then, after a long hard day of labor, men walked back home to fall wearily into bed.

He hoped Tom McCauley could find him a partner since working with someone more experienced removed some risks. Either way, by himself or not, he was not looking forward to the grueling work. The only bright spot would be that he could court Phebe more if he had any energy left. He had to find a way to ease his burden, make more money, and be home more often, all year round. His scheming thoughts turned to how to weasel his way into Phebe's family and get a job at the furnace. He'd have a beautiful wife to meet his needs as well as an easier job.

"May I continue to call on you, Phebe? After I'm finished charcoaling in two weeks, I may be around more."

"Yes, I'd like that." She gave his hand a gentle squeeze and gazed shyly into his eyes.

Suddenly, he bent his head to kiss Phebe's full moist lips. She reciprocated the pressure on his mouth and melted into the embrace. When he broke it off, she gazed longingly into his eyes, and then she kissed him again, this time with open lips. He tasted her peppermint breath and felt her breasts pressed against his chest.

He desired to continue kissing her, but he felt himself stirring below and moved away.

"Let's go back," he said, as he straightened up. They started toward the house. *I don't want to play my cards too soon. I'll leave her wanting more,* he thought.

Later in her bedroom, Phebe's thoughts swirled in her head. She had loved the feel of Nate's muscular arms around her and his soft kiss. Her feelings for him had deepened ever since he had visited so faithfully when she was ill. As his attentions continued over the months, it became more apparent he liked her, as further evidenced by the red chrysanthemums tonight, meaning 'I love' in flower etiquette.

What might a future with him be like? He knew and accepted her limitations caused by her illness. No other man had ever shown such attention and devotion to her. He was a hard worker and could provide for a family.

It seemed all her girlfriends were falling in love, getting betrothed, and beginning families. One married friend from church had a baby on the way, and another was engaged. The social pressure to not be the last single girl was enormous.

She imagined the style of her wedding gown, whom she would invite, where the ceremony would take place, and the honeymoon. Where would they live? They couldn't live with her parents in their two-bedroom cottage, but she couldn't envision herself living in a house alone with Nate gone to the woods all day, especially if he didn't come home evenings.

She was attracted to this man who was decisive, possessive, and strong. *Will Nate ask me to marry him?*

~ CHAPTER 16 ~

The day dawned rainy and gray in Philadelphia as Jesse Quinter drove the team and wagon to pick up supplies for Hopewell. At both the livery and the store, he explained why he didn't have money to pay. They were understanding, but he felt mortified that he had been so gullible. The worst part of the whole situation was that he would have to reimburse the funds he lost out of his own meager pocket. His wages allowed him to live comfortably with a few indulgences such as Hetty, but he had nothing saved back for emergencies. It was a hard lesson.

When he reached the highway to Berry's, the sky opened up. The wind blew at a brisk clip, and the cold, pelting rain pounded the backs of the animals and his slicker. After miles of soggy roads, the damp began to seep through his clothing, chilling him. Although discouraged by the weather, his angry thoughts kept him distracted. His brain continually played back the scenario of how the robbery happened and how he had stupidly trusted a total stranger. Upset at Roy Dickenson and himself, the weather seemed a fitting climax to a wretched trip. He was glad he had securely covered the merchandise in the wagon. Any ruined goods would come out of his salary too.

As he pulled into Berry's for the night, his anger softened at the sight of his bedraggled horses, who looked miserable. In the barn, he rubbed them down with handfuls of straw while they munched their hay. He scoured the harnesses with old burlap grain bags he found and hung them up to dry. Fortunately, he always kept the tack well-oiled, so any water wouldn't soak in and ruin the leather. While working, he contemplated what he would tell Jimmy Berry. He didn't blame Jimmy for what had happened. The innkeeper had no idea Dickenson was a crook when he paired them for the night. With not enough rooms for everyone, it had made sense to share the space. Jimmy would be apologetic, but perhaps he could give Jesse a lead to help him find the thief.

The downpour let up to a slight drizzle, but the lane to the tavern from the barn was sloppy. Jesse dodged puddles and tried not to fall on the slippery clay. He stomped onto the porch of the inn, scraped his muddy boots on the board edge, and shook out his oiled coat before entering.

"Nasty day out there, huh?" bantered the proprietor as he entered. "Hang your slicker on the peg there by the door. We've got venison pie tonight. I'll bring you some. I shot a big buck yesterday. The deer sure are stupid in autumn when they're after those does."

"Before you serve the food, Jimmy, can I speak to you privately?"

"Sure, let's go outside. Something bothering you?" he asked, as they went out on the porch.

"What do you know about Roy Dickenson, that traveler I ate dinner with the last time I stayed here? He and I shared a room."

"Well, I don't know much of anything about him. I never encountered him before and didn't talk to him much. We had so many customers that evening. You talked with him more than me. He said something about traveling to Lancaster."

"Do you remember which direction he went that morning he left?"

"No, I was busy serving breakfast when he departed."

"What horse did he ride?"

"A black gelding with a white sock on his left rear hock. Why all the questions about Dickenson?"

"When I got to Philadelphia after leaving your place, I discovered money missing from my purse. He had to be the one who took it while I slept."

"That's terrible. I never thought he could be a swindler. He looked a bit tattered, but he paid for his meal and the room."

"He's very clever. I never thought he might rob me either. He acted pleasant and well-mannered. That brings up another matter. I don't have money for my dinner and room. Can I reimburse you next time I'm back here?"

"Sure, you're good for it. I feel bad I set you two up in the same room."

"Not your fault. He saw an opportunity, and he took it. He fooled us both."

"Let's get out of this cold. Some supper will warm you up." Jimmy waved Jesse in the door ahead of him.

"Tell me if you think of any other details that might help me find him. He's got some payback coming."

The weather the following day cleared, and the wet road baked in the bright sun. Jesse rose before dawn, hurrying to Owen's toll house in case they might want to attend the funeral. The energetic horses were eager to be off. Having traveled this way many times before, they knew they were heading home.

Several hours later, Owen met him as he pulled in. "You're here early today, Jesse. The missus is anxious for news. What did you find out?"

"I tried to arrive as soon as I could. I'm sorry to tell you your wife's mother died the morning of the day I arrived with the letter. The burying is tomorrow."

Owen's hand flew to his mouth, and his head drooped. "Oh, I'm not surprised." He paused to take a breath. "Her mother's been poorly for several months, and it was just a matter of time, especially with this most recent spell of apoplexy. I'm relieved her suffering is over, but my wife will be inconsolable. Thanks for bringing the news. I'll put up the gate so you can drive through. Then I'll tell her. We may be heading to Philadelphia today."

"I regret the bad tidings." Jesse urged the team under the raised log, grateful for this free pass, so he didn't have to confide his penniless condition to Owen too.

Jesse debated how to pursue the robber. He couldn't go now with a busy schedule to keep. There weren't many clues anyway—just the description of Dickenson and his horse. Lancaster was probably a cover story. He decided to take his lumps for now until he formulated a plan. *I won't soon forget Roy Dickenson.*

~ CHAPTER 17 ~

A week later at Hopewell, Jesse loaded the last of the trunks into the wagon. The rig sat in front of the Big House, where stacks of luggage covered the veranda, topped with a half dozen hat boxes. This new assignment today for the trip to Philadelphia was one he didn't relish. He and Ben, the stable master, were taking two young ladies and all their baggage into the city for an extended stay. The ironmaster's daughter, Susanna Sterling, would ride in the one-horse chaise, and the other miss, whom he didn't know, would be riding with him. He hated the idea of making small talk all the way. He enjoyed his solitude. The girls would be sleeping in the house at Levi and Hannah Church's farm, the first stop for the night. Even his usual enjoyable meal there would be ruined with girl talk.

What could be in all those chests? Some were heavy, perhaps filled with books and shoes; others were light, probably containing frilly ladies' dresses and petticoats. He was uncertain as to the exact destination in Philadelphia. Ben would direct them once they arrived in town. He had never seen much of the city except Spruce Street, where Owen's relatives lived, and the dock area around Water Street.

Jesse tapped his toe and jingled a few coins in his pocket, waiting impatiently for everyone. Ben appeared from the barn's upper deck with the bay gelding and chaise, which he tied to the hitching block at the side of the lane.

"We'll be taking the palomino mare and sidesaddle too. We'll tie her to the back of your wagon."

"Do you need help?"

"No, she's ready to go. I just have to bring her up." He strode down the slope toward the lower level of the barn.

Jesse again was left waiting. He pulled on all the straps securing the cargo. He tightened the harness connections and confirmed the chaise and wagon wheels were securely pinned, and no cracks lurked in the frames. He checked his case of blacksmith tools he always carried in case a horse threw a shoe. The morning dragged on and on.

Eventually, Ben was back with Missy. "This one decided she didn't want to go anywhere," he exclaimed. "She can be a handful." Jesse fastened her halter to the tailgate.

Ben spotted a female form coming up the path from the tenant houses past the smithy. He nodded towards Jesse. "Here comes your passenger."

Rachel toted one bag of necessities. Her small trunk had been brought earlier by her father. As she approached the men, Jesse noticed her springy step and long, brown hair. Her simple, blue dress accentuated her bright blue eyes and a youthful figure. Her broad grin showed straight, white teeth. But he recognized her as the troublemaker at the furnace the night they cast the cannon.

"Hello, Ben," she greeted. "I can't wait to start."

"Rachel, this is Jesse Quinter. He'll be going with us and taking all the belongings in the wagon. You'll be traveling with him. Jesse, this is Rachel Palsgrove, Miss Sterling's companion."

Jesse removed his tricorn hat and nodded. "Nice to meet you. Let me take your bag." With some rearranging, he crammed it under the seat in the crowded wagon. "I'll warn you. It's a long way to Philadelphia."

Rachel stepped up to the team and stroked the faces of the cream draft horses, who nickered at her touch. "Oh, I love your animals. What are their names?"

Jesse was surprised. No woman had ever admired his team nor asked such a question.

"Well, Rubin and Mary are in front, and Yancy and Cap, in the back." He pointed to each horse as he said its name.

"I've seen them before in the field but didn't know to whom they belonged. They are so gentle and beautiful." Jesse blushed with pride at her praise for his most treasured possessions. "Are you gone a lot? I usually only see them on Sundays."

"I travel to town each week to deliver iron and pick up supplies. It takes six days, round trip."

"How exciting that must be," she gushed.

"I like it except when the weather is bad, like last Thursday. Then it can be downright miserable, but even then, I like it better than being cooped up inside."

"Rachel's father is the founder at the furnace," Ben added.

"That's a complicated job. I could never do that," replied Jesse.

"Yes, I suppose at first it's hard, but like anything, after a while, it isn't so difficult. I bet many people would find your travels too demanding," she said.

"I guess so, although I never thought of it that way." He found Rachel easy to talk to, unlike most of the young women in the village.

"Here comes Susanna," Rachel observed. "She's looking very pretty today."

Susanna flounced down the steps in a fancy gown with a long row of gilt buttons down the front, a tight bodice displaying her bosom, full petticoats underneath the long skirt, and a bonnet with a plumed feather jutting out from the brim. Jesse noted her bouncy, blonde curls and narrow, cinched-in waist but laughed to himself at the ridiculous outfit for traveling.

"Are you ready to go, Susanna?" asked Ben as her mother, Catherine, appeared on the porch, dotting her red-lidded eyes and tear-streaked face daintily with her handkerchief.

"Yes, I'm champing at the bit. Mother and I said our goodbyes. Let's get going before she breaks down again," she answered.

Ben held the chaise door for Susanna, who stepped nimbly in, arranged her dress, and sat down. He took the other seat and gathered the reins.

Rachel jumped on the wagon seat before Jesse had a chance to offer help. He climbed up. "Let's get started, Ben," he called.

Catherine waved her hanky. "Write to me as soon as you arrive, dear!"

"Yes, Mother, I will," Susanna said irritably. "You've told me that twice. Tell Father and David I love them. I adore you too." She fluttered her hand as the vehicle lurched forward.

Jesse clucked to his team, and the wagon followed the shay up the hill to the road to Philadelphia. *This will be an interesting trip,* he thought.

~ CHAPTER 18 ~

The first few miles, there was an awkward silence between Rachel and Jesse as she assessed the teamster's countenance and demeanor. He was the man who had tried to rescue her when George Coggins had her by the arm the night she had visited the furnace. He probably didn't recognize her in a dress. While he wasn't what a girl would call handsome, her first glimpse of him when she handed him her bag revealed an appealingly rugged look. She particularly liked his freckled face.

Sitting beside Jesse, the only parts of him she could observe without impolitely staring were his muscular thighs and his hands on the reins. The circumference of his legs looked the size of tree trunks, and the tanned backs of his hands ended in fingers, short and sinewy. She had trouble judging his age with those freckles. His handling of the team and the way he had leaped to the seat indicated youth to her. But how young?

She knew it wasn't proper to entertain such thoughts about strange men, but she met so few new people that she was excessively curious. She wished she had observed him more when they first met instead of gushing about the horses so much.

They didn't talk at all for several miles, the silence between them thick. Was he shy? Did he like quiet when driving? He was probably used to solitude with just the team to keep him company on his long hauls to town. If she were to discover more about him, she decided she would have to speak first. But about what? Phebe said men liked to talk about their work, so she hoped that line of questioning would lead to other, more personal, conversation.

"How long have you been going to Philadelphia?" she asked, breaking the stillness.

Jesse looked startled out of his musings. "Oh, I don't know, maybe about seven or eight years. It's been so long the years melt together."

"You must have started when you were very young?"

"I began when I was fifteen, assisting my father, who was also a teamster. He taught me everything I know. After he died, I took over since neither of my brothers wanted the job." She did some quick mental math to calculate his age to be around twenty-two.

"You have two brothers?"

"Yes. Both are older than me. They have families in Hopewell and didn't like being away so much."

"You don't mind being away?"

"No, I don't. I'm not married, so I can travel freely without feeling guilty about leaving a wife and children behind."

"Doesn't your mother miss you?"

"I'm sure she does, but my younger spinster sister lives with her. I'm home Sunday to visit them and do the heavy work around the house, and my brothers live close enough to help out during the week."

"Do you like traveling constantly?"

"At times, it can be boring, but the challenge is to keep the team healthy and deliver the iron on time. I stay at the same lodgings at night and meet the same people, so they take the place of my family when I'm traveling. The horses are my company the rest of the time. Infrequently, something unusual happens to break the monotony, but I don't like too much excitement."

"Your life is so different than mine. Now that my school is over, I only do chores and go to church on Sunday. It must be exciting to explore new places."

"So why are you going to Philadelphia?"

"Susanna Sterling, she's the one in the chaise, and I, are about the same age and were tutored together. Now she's off to a young women's school in town. Her father wants her to have a companion, and I was asked to go."

"Now that sounds like a tedious job," exclaimed Jesse. "No offense, but she strikes me as haughty. She didn't even glance at me so Ben could introduce us. She acted like I didn't exist, not that I care. I'm the hired help."

"She is rather arrogant, and I suppose she's not altogether happy I'm going along. I'm sure she would prefer to be in the city by herself, but she'll be on her own a lot."

"How so, with you being her 'companion'?"

"Well," she tried not to sound like she was bragging, "I'm also going to school in Philadelphia. I want to be a teacher, so I'm attending college to continue my education. I'll mainly aid Susanna with her studies when necessary."

"You must be bright to be going there. I can't imagine being cooped up in a room all day talking about philosophy and studying Latin or Greek and fancy mathematics and such. I never had much schooling myself. Oh, I can do basic figuring and reading and write my name, but I don't need any other skills."

"I like academics, and it's the only way I can learn to teach. I think college will be fun," Rachel replied.

"Better you than me."

They sat a minute in silence. "Is that your palomino tied to the back?"

"No, she's Susanna's horse, Missy, short for Miss Behaving. I ride her too though. Susanna thought she might ride in the city, and since I'll be staying at Mrs. Graydon's boardinghouse, I'll need transportation to travel where Susanna will be. Missy can be a handful, but when she's ridden regularly, she's a pleasure."

"How long will you be in Philadelphia?"

"I don't know how long it will take to finish our schooling, maybe several years."

"That's a long time to be gone. Will you come back to visit?"

"Oh, yes, I'm sure we'll be back for holidays and special occasions. I hope I'm not too homesick."

"I come to town every week, so I'll probably see you to pick up and deliver letters from home."

"I do hope so. It will be nice to see a familiar face."

"You'll make friends fast enough. Then you won't miss home at all."

Jesse eased the horses to the side of the roadway behind the stopped chaise. "Here's where we water the animals and eat a bite of lunch."

Ben had already hopped down and was helping Susanna out. She flounced her skirts and complained, "It will take us forever to get to Philadelphia at this rate. Can't we go faster?" She motioned to the wagon. "They can meet us there."

"No, miss, I had strict instructions from your father to stay together. Only I know the exact directions for our destination, and only Jesse knows the road and where to spend the night. We want you young ladies and your belongings to arrive safely."

Jesse piped up. "Just two weeks ago, I was robbed by a man who seemed perfectly respectable. You never can tell whom to trust away from home." He tipped his hat at Susanna. "By the way, my name is Jesse, Jesse Quinter. If you need anything Ben can't handle, just ask me." Ben frowned but grinned at the jab.

"All right, Jesse. My fate on this trip is in Ben's and your hands." She batted her eyes at him and smiled demurely.

Rachel silently ate her sandwich. *Great,* she thought, *there's too much competition when it comes to men—first my beautiful sister and now Susanna. But I'm going to the city for another purpose—to become a teacher. I won't have time for courting. I'll be too busy studying.*

~ CHAPTER 19 ~

Finally, the little procession of chaise and wagon pulled into 1685 Walnut Street, home of Mrs. Levering's School for Young Ladies. The School was an ivy-covered, four-story stone mansion sporting a sprawling veranda supported by stately columns. White wicker furniture littered the porch. Intricately carved walnut doors, each adorned with a shiny brass lion's head knocker, were flanked by spectacular stained glass windows.

Susanna alighted gracefully from the chaise and instructed everyone to remain at the street until she returned with instructions. She shook the dust off her dress and smoothed her skirts, ascended the majestic steps, and let the lion's head fall.

A young lady dressed in white answered Susanna's knock, and after a short conversation, Susanna went in, and the door closed.

"Welcome, Miss Sterling," said the headmistress, Mrs. Levering, who approached the vestibule from the inner reaches of the house. "We've been expecting you. How was your trip, dear?" Susanna observed four young women in the first room to the left of the great hall in the center of the house. They were diligently sewing with their heads down, watching their embroidery hoops but trying to peep unobtrusively at the new arrival. Their ears were cocked, listening to every word.

"I'm glad to meet you, Mrs. Levering. I must look a fright after three dusty days getting here. I'm so grateful the school has an opening and that I can satisfy your requirements. I hope I'll be worthy of your instruction here." Susanna curtsied to the headmistress, her voice light and airy.

"It was unfortunate our other girl left us due to some unpleasantness in the city, but we are excited such a fine candidate as yourself would choose our school. Where are your things, dear?"

"Outside on the wagon. If you will be so kind as to show me where you wish my men to deliver them, I'll instruct them to do so. They have other stops to make before dark."

"Certainly. Have them come to the lane beside the carriage house in the back. Drop your belongings there, and our servants can take them up to your room. Then I'll introduce you to the other ladies and show you your lodgings."

"I'll step outside a minute," Susanna said, moving toward the door. She directed Ben, Jesse, and Rachel to drive to the back of the house. "When you've finished unloading my trunks, you can leave," she instructed. "Mrs. Levering said they would take them to my room."

Rachel asked, "Do you want me to come tomorrow to see if you need help with anything?"

"No, why don't you come Saturday? That will give both of us some time to settle. I'm sure I can handle everything."

"I'll come Saturday afternoon then."

Ben piped up. "Jesse and I will be staying in the city tonight to rest the horses, but we'll stop back tomorrow morning on our return to Hopewell. If you write a letter to your parents, we can pick it up then."

"Yes, I'll compose one this evening. I'll have a lot to tell them, and Mother will worry if I don't write." She turned and flounced back into the house.

As Susanna entered, Mrs. Levering was waiting. The headmistress was the embodiment of a high society gentlewoman, with stick-straight posture, a ready smile, and a quiet, smooth voice oozing graciousness.

"Come, Susanna, let me introduce you to some of our other young ladies." As they walked into the room, their curious eyes met

Susanna's gaze. "I'm sure you won't remember everyone's name at first. There are forty-eight pupils, twenty-four of them are boarders, and twenty-four are day students who live in Philadelphia." She pointed around the room. "The miss in the yellow dress is Mary, in the green is Louise, next to her is Frances, and lastly, there's Karah. Say hello to Susanna, ladies."

They all murmured hellos.

"Karah, since you are sharing your room with our new arrival, would you please give Susanna a tour of the house and show her the bedroom and other facilities?"

"Yes, Mrs. Levering," replied Karah, as she stowed her embroidery in a basket and rose from her seat. "Come with me, Susanna."

"Thank you," Susanna said with a slight curtsy. She followed Karah, a slip of a girl who didn't weigh more than eighty pounds. Her pale blonde hair accentuated her pretty blue eyes. Susanna guessed her to be of Swedish heritage.

They stopped at the doorway of the room. Karah whispered, "This is the library, as I suppose you already inferred from the bookcases on the walls, but we often practice our sewing or art here." She pointed to the French doors on the side of the room. "Over there is another entrance to the porch and the covered driveway, so you don't get wet getting into the carriage on rainy days."

They crossed back into the great hall from the library's rear, where a ten-foot-wide staircase wound up to the second floor. "We do our exercises here when the weather is frightful outside, but normally we exercise in the garden. Sometimes we go for a walk first thing in the morning."

Entering a spacious room across from the library, Karah said, "This is the sitting room." Chairs dotted the edges of the room. A grand fireplace graced one wall, and the firebox opening was surrounded by beautiful delft-blue painted ceramic tiles and topped by a thick, carved oak mantle. "We sometimes take classes here during the day."

"Where is everyone?" inquired Susanna as she surveyed the empty room.

"The day girls went home—they leave about four—so it's just the boarding students here after that. Most of them are in their rooms, relaxing before dinner."

Behind the sitting room was a long dining hall, where three young women laid out place settings at the massive table. Karah introduced them to Susanna. "We each have dining room duty one day a week. A hostess must know the proper way to set an elegant formal table. You'll probably be assigned Tuesday since Ann, the girl you replaced, had been given that day. Mrs. Levering will confirm that for you. I imagine she will meet with you after dinner with your schedule."

A quick peek into the heat-filled kitchen at the far end of the dining hall showed several sweating women of color scurrying around, preparing the evening meal. "Fortunately, we don't need to learn cooking—just how to carve a roast or slice a pie. The back stairs to the maids' quarters and teacher's rooms are off the kitchen. There's also a stairway to the basement and the wine cellar. We never go there—just the servants and teachers."

Back through the dining room, they passed through a doorway leading to the rear of the central hall and the stairs. "I'll show you the main classroom on the fourth floor, the top level, and then we'll come back to our room."

Holding the banister, Karah began climbing the steps. When they reached the second landing, she said, "This area is for senior girls only. We juniors live one floor up."

They trudged on, and Susanna felt breathless and began to pant. "You'll get used to the climb in a week or so," chuckled Karah. "We all felt winded climbing the stairs when we first got here. Your room is on this floor, but we'll come back to it after seeing the classroom." They paused a minute as Susanna caught her breath before plodding up the final flight of stairs.

At the top of the house, Karah swung open a massive door to the attic. The rafters overhead were raw timbers, and huge dormer windows on the front and rear of the room flooded the area with light. At one end of the room desks and benches faced the near wall, the middle area held more desks turned the opposite direction, and stacks of trunks lined the far wall. "Your trunk will be coming up here when you've unpacked."

"I have several," Susanna announced.

"That might be a problem," Karah said. "You'll understand better when you see your room. The classes here are the ones everyone takes, such as literature and philosophy. While one group hears a lecture at one end of the room, the other students are studying at the opposite end."

"Isn't it hard to study with a lesson being taught in the same room?" asked Susanna.

"When I first came here, I got easily distracted, but now I can concentrate even when teaching is going on. Besides, we often write notes to each other instead of studying, as long as we're not caught. It can be a lot of fun!"

"I bet it's dreadfully hot up here in the summer."

"Oh, yes. That's why everyone goes home then. It's too stifling for lessons. We only attend from September to May." Karah and Susanna exited the room latching the door behind them.

They descended the stairs to a landing intersecting a hall. They took the left hallway, which turned down another long passage. "You can't lose your way. These halls form a big rectangle. Just keep going one way, and eventually, you'll reach the stairway. Our room is at the end."

Halfway down the hall, Karah stopped at an opened door. "Here's the washroom with a mirror and water and the washtub. When the door is open, you can come in, but you only get fifteen minutes at a time except for thirty minutes on bath nights. Everyone is assigned a different bath night and time, and our man brings up hot water. In the morning, we line up in the hall to wait for our turn in the bathroom. First come, first served. You're sharing with six other girls whose rooms are on this side of the house. The other side has another washroom for the rooms there."

They arrived where Susanna's baggage was stacked. Karah used her key to open the door. "Be sure to ask Mrs. Levering for a key tonight if she forgets to give you one. Are those all your trunks?"

"Yes, they are."

"Oh, dear!" exclaimed Karah.

Inside the room, Susanna was appalled at the two narrow beds each pushed up against a wall in the ten- by twelve-foot space. A window was opposite the door. Two small bureaus and two adjacent tiny desks stood underneath the window. Rows of pegs hung on the wall, and many held clothing, presumably Karah's. *This room is much smaller than my room at Hopewell,* Susanna thought, *and I don't share it with anyone else. There I have three floor-to-ceiling windows. In this tiny pigeonhole, where will I keep all my belongings? They certainly won't fit in that little bureau. And only fifteen minutes in the washroom at a time? Impossible.*

Karah saw Susanna's scowl as she looked around. "At least there's a window. The rooms on the other side of the hall have none."

"Where do you store all your clothes?"

"This cabinet and the pegs on that side of the room," she motioned to the left, "are yours. That is all the room there is," Karah sighed. "Since you brought a lot, you'll need to put some of it in your trunks in the attic classroom or send some of it home. There isn't much room in here."

"I'll stow it in the attic, I guess. I'm not sending things home. I'll have to rotate my clothes each week."

"I can help you decide which things you want here for now," Karah offered. "I like to see what kinds of clothes everyone brings."

"You can advise me what dresses would be most appropriate this week."

"Choose what you want, and the men can take the trunks up after dinner. Mrs. Levering doesn't like anything cluttering the halls."

Susanna pulled one trunk into the room, retrieved her key from around her neck under her clothes, and opened it. *How will I pick which garments to keep in my room,* she thought. *What have I gotten myself into?* Her first impulse was not to unpack at all and to head home tomorrow when Ben came, but she had been so insistent with her parents to come to Philadelphia she couldn't go home right away. She resolved to give it a try, although it would test every bit of her patience. *Is this the pathway to my dream?*

~ CHAPTER 20 ~

No more than a mile from Mrs. Levering's place, the wagon and chaise pulled up to Mrs. Graydon's boardinghouse on Mulberry Street. Rachel had never seen a whole block of connected houses. Row houses, they are called, Jesse said. A wide sidewalk of flagstones stretched from the row houses to the street with an occasional tree. Cobblestones paved the main city streets, but most side roads were dirt.

As they prepared to dismount from the wagon, a troop of musket-carrying Redcoats came marching around the corner. Their Captain barked orders, and the men hastened their pace. Jesse kept a firm grip on the reins and reassured the nervous horses that everything was all right. The troop soon passed. "These horses have seen Brits before, but they're wary of their shouts and loud stomping on the cobblestones," said Jesse.

"I've never seen so many soldiers before," replied Rachel. "They made me nervous too."

"Get used to it. They're marching everywhere in the city."

Jesse pulled Rachel's trunk from under the seat. "This isn't very far from Mrs. Levering's School. It should be easy walking or riding for you."

"I think the College is a block east of here," Ben added.

Rachel reached to grab her valise, but Jesse held on.

"I'll take it in for you." He waved his arm in a sweeping motion. "Ladies first. Ben will stay with the horses, won't you?"

Ben nodded as he exited the carriage, stretching his legs. "I'll leave taking that heavy trunk upstairs to a much younger and energetic person. I'm not used to riding all that way. I'm glad I had the carriage, not the wagon, or I'd be even more worn out."

Rachel ascended the steps and rang the bell. A short, squat woman with graying hair and a few wrinkles on her face answered, wiping her hands on a dishtowel.

"You must be Rachel!" she exclaimed. "We've been expecting you. Come in, come in. I'm Mrs. Graydon."

They entered the house, and the aromas of baking biscuits and simmering roast beef pleasantly assailed their noses. The stairway to the upper floors rose to their right, and to the left was the parlor. Straight back down a hallway, they could see the dining room. There were windows only in the front and back of the house. A burning whale oil lamp sat on a narrow table in the hall to light the gloomy interior.

"Mrs. Graydon, this is my friend, Jesse Quinter. Where should I put my belongings?" Rachel asked.

"Andrew!" she yelled to the back of the house. "Bring the key for room eighteen." She turned back to her new boarder. "Andrew's my son. He'll show you your room. Mr. Quinter may take your trunk to your room, but he can't stay. We don't allow single men on the same floor as the young ladies—only on the third floor. Excuse me. I must finish cooking dinner. Take some time to settle, then come down for supper in about a half-hour." She glanced at Jesse. "My apologies, but I don't have enough food to invite Mr. Quinter to stay."

Rachel said, "That's all right, Mrs. Graydon. Our other companion is waiting outside with the horses, and they have other business in the city."

A boy with tousled hair, about ten years old, appeared with a key. "Follow me, please." He started up the steps. Rachel and Jesse followed with the trunk.

Halfway down the hall, Andrew stopped, put the key in the lock, and opened the door. "Here's your room, miss." He handed her the key.

The room was small but tidy. A single bed occupied one corner, a bureau sat against the opposite wall, and a pitcher and bowl stood on a washstand beside it. "I'll bring your water and towel up shortly so you can clean up before dinner if you like," he said, as he grabbed the pitcher.

"Where is the carriage house to put her horse?" Jesse asked.

"It's the red barn directly behind the house. Go around the end of the block and up the alley. Take any stall. Help yourself to hay and grain."

"Thanks. Her horse is the palomino."

"I'll feed and water him in the morning with the others, but she'll need to tend him in the evening." Andrew turned and left.

Jesse placed the trunk beside the bed. "Not a bad room, except for no window. I suppose windows are at a premium in these row houses. But at least it's clean."

"It will be fine. We better bed down Missy before supper's ready."

Rachel locked the door, and they went downstairs to take the wagon to the barn. "Ben, you might as well stay here a few minutes more," Jesse said, as they reached the wagon. "We're going round to drop off Missy and her saddle."

"I'll be waiting right here," he said, smoking his pipe. "Take care, Rachel. Watch out for any shenanigans from that horse."

"Don't worry, Ben. I'll manage her."

At the barn, Jesse slid open the big, red door. Inside were eight stalls, but only three held horses. Rachel selected a stall and opened its door.

Jesse said, "Go bring Missy, and I'll put some straw down and find some feed."

Rachel led in the palomino, and the horse began devouring the oats in the feed box. Jesse pitched her two mounds of hay while Rachel filled the water bucket from the pump outside. "That should keep her busy awhile," he said.

They took the tack from the back of the wagon and put it in the tack room.

"There must be a back door to the house," Jesse said. "Think you can find it?"

"I'm sure I can," Rachel replied, unsure how to end the conversation. Over the last couple of days, she had grown to admire Jesse's talent for handling horses and his easy way of talking. It was intimidating to be on her own in the city, but she had to be strong to complete the task for which she had come.

Jesse stepped closer to her and gently held her shoulder. "Every Wednesday evening, when I come to town, I'll deliver any messages from home and pick up any letters you might have going back. I stay at Tun Tavern and head out Thursday morning. If you continue down Mulberry Street to the waterfront and turn left on Water Street, you're at the Tavern if you need me for anything else. Is that all right with you?"

"Oh, yes," smiled Rachel, disconcerted by his closeness. His musky scent rose to her nose, and she was startled by the earnestness and caring in his green eyes. "I'll look forward to seeing you again."

"Next Wednesday, then." Smiling, he gave a final squeeze to her arm and exited the barn. He leaped to the wagon seat and clucked to the team. Rachel watched as they rumbled down the alley. When they reached the corner, Jesse looked back and waved. She waved back, watching until he disappeared.

Jesse and Ben went to the livery stable near Tun's and bedded the horses. Jesse settled his bill with the owner from the last time he boarded there.

"Any sign of a black horse with a left rear white sock?"

"No," replied Caleb, the livery owner.

"Let me know if you see one. I've got a score to settle with its owner."

They headed toward Tun's.

"What was that all about?" inquired Ben.

"I was robbed two weeks ago at Berry's. The thief shared a room with me, then stole my money while I was sleeping. Jimmy Berry described his horse. It's a remote chance, but I search for that animal wherever I go. The scoundrel said he was from Lancaster, but I think he could be anywhere."

"That's terrible. I'll keep my eyes peeled too."

The men continued their walk to the tavern in silence.

Ben said, "The city has grown since I was here five years ago. The cobbled streets look cleaner. I'm amazed at all the shops. I suppose you can buy anything you want within several blocks of here."

"Would you like to live here, Ben?"

"No, no, I'm too old for that. I'm content to be at Hopewell and look after the horses. The city's too busy for my liking. How about you?"

"I enjoy visiting, but I wouldn't want to stay here. Too many people around. I like the peace and tranquility of the country best."

"I think the girls will find Philadelphia intimidating at first, particularly Rachel since she's never been here before. But I'm sure they'll adapt in time. They're young and adventurous. You know, that Rachel's a fine horsewoman. She can handle Missy a lot better than Susanna. I doubt Susanna will ride much. She's more the carriage type."

"I noticed Rachel has a way with horses," Jesse said. "My team certainly responded to her attentions."

"I think you liked her attentions too," kidded Ben.

Jesse blushed. "She seems very nice."

"She's a great girl. Smart, with good judgment and manners too, unlike that haughty Susanna Sterling who couldn't wait to be shed of us. You could do worse, my boy."

"I'm not looking for a wife, Ben. My job keeps me on the road too much to think about a relationship."

"When the right girl comes along, all that will change," Ben quipped, with a twinkle in his eyes.

Jesse was unsure what he thought about Rachel. She had stirred some ideas he previously thought impossible. He liked her slim build, long, brown hair, and blue eyes. She was easy to talk with too. Perhaps she *could* better his life. What might the following weeks bring?

~ CHAPTER 21 ~

Rachel rose early since she had many tasks planned for the day. She wanted to enroll in the college and obtain her schedule. Although the idea of college was intimidating, she felt excited to start on her path to independence. Many new subjects would be foreign to her, but she was confident she could master them.

From the few dresses in the wardrobe, she picked a blue print one with tiny flowers on it. She pulled back her hair and fastened it with a matching blue ribbon; everyone told her she appeared more mature with it worn that way. After scrubbing her face and patting it dry with the coarse linen towel, she drew on her socks then laced the shoes her mother had ordered specially for her trip. Turning her head left and right while glancing in the mirror hanging over the washstand, she tucked a few stray strands of hair behind her ears, straightened her collar, and was at last satisfied with her appearance. Into her handbag she put her pencil, a small notebook, and several pence. The rest of her meager funds were stowed in the hidden compartment in her trunk. She locked it, then placed the string of keys around her neck.

Once outside her room, she stooped over to lock the door since the cord holding the keys was short. She dropped the keys down her neckline under her clothes for safekeeping.

"Hello, Rachel," said the thin woman coming down the stairs from the couple's floor above. They had met at dinner the previous evening. A mop of curly, strawberry blonde hair covered her fore-head above her slightly pock-marked, pale face. Her sharp, blue eyes accented her pointy nose. A generous smile revealed two rows of crowded teeth.

"Good morning, Mrs. Brown. How are you today?"

"Call me Sarah. We'll be seeing a lot of each other since we're the only lady boarders. I'll walk down to breakfast with you."

Two female and four male lodgers occupied the house. Mr. Brown, Sarah's husband, had been missing from the introductions the night before. He was a traveling salesman and only stayed in the city on weekends to visit his wife and replenish his supplies.

The boardinghouse had four rooms on each of the three floors. On the second level, Mrs. Graydon and her son, Andrew, occupied the front room with a view overlooking the street. The next room was empty, followed by Rachel's room. Widow Hartman resided in the back bedroom, but she wasn't a boarder. She helped with cooking and cleaning to earn her keep. The four single men on the third floor consisted of two college students, who shared a room, and two businessmen. Mr. and Mrs. Brown occupied the fourth room. Rachel had asked the students about their studies at school but hadn't told them about her intentions of attending for fear of shocking everyone. She didn't want to start that kind of conversation on her first night. One businessman was a silversmith with a shop close by, and the other, Mr. Morris, was a scrivener. After she asked what his job entailed, he explained that he read and interpreted legal documents for people with limited or no reading ability.

Only Mr. Morris dined this morning with Sarah and Rachel. After the ladies settled at the table, he passed them steaming platters of hash browns, scrapple, scrambled eggs, and biscuits. Widow Hartman and Mrs. Graydon scurried around the kitchen while Andrew ate at a separate small table in the corner.

"Are the students already at classes today?" asked Rachel between passes of food.

"They're not early risers," said Mrs. Graydon, as she filled water glasses and teacups. "We usually don't see them until after nine. The boys don't seem to mind cold victuals for breakfast. I'm not going to fix the meal twice. It runs too near luncheon if you serve all hours in the morning."

Rachel turned to Mr. Morris. "Where is your office located?" she asked.

"It's about three blocks away, on High Street near the bank." Impeccably dressed, his frock coat was made of fine navy cloth, his wound cravat hugged his neck, and the white cuffs of his shirt poked out of his sleeves. A bow at the back of his neck gathered the tail of his dark hair. Rachel guessed his age to be over thirty. His nails were clean and trimmed. She assumed a scrivener's hands never saw any manual labor. They certainly didn't show it if they did.

"Where do you find your clients?"

"People come into port who don't read or write English, particularly those involved in the shipping trade from Africa and Asia."

"Where did you learn the law, Mr. Morris?"

"I studied at Cambridge University and came from London three years ago."

"Why did you decide to locate here?"

"In the colonies, there are more opportunities for an inexperienced barrister than in England. I didn't feel like competing with all the old codgers there who have been practicing for decades."

"I'm in the city for a new beginning too," Rachel said.

"Where do you call home?" he asked. "You seemed to have traveled a long way here."

"Well, I didn't travel as far as you. My home is a small village called Hopewell, forty miles northwest."

"And what is Hopewell like?"

"Hopewell is centered around iron making. My father is the founder. He controls the combination of iron, charcoal, and limestone in the furnace to produce a high-quality product."

"That sounds like an important position. What endeavor brings you here?"

"I'm here to continue my education."

"An admirable goal," Mr. Morris observed. "I'm always in favor of people bettering themselves."

Rachel finished her breakfast. Unsure when she might return from her errands, she ate heartily although more than what was ladylike, she thought. When finished, she rose to take her dishes to the kitchen.

"We'll clear your plate, dearie. The kitchen's too small for a lot of people traipsing through," said Mrs. Graydon, coming out.

"Ma'am, I'm not certain whether I'll be here for lunch, but I'll arrive for dinner. Last evening's repast tasted delightful."

"Be careful walking around town," she warned. "Always carry your pocketbook near you in front. Don't let it dangle at your side or thieves can easily grab it and run. You never know who might be sizing you up."

Mr. Morris said, "A young lady in the city can never be too cautious. I would be happy to show you around sometime, Rachel."

"Thank you for your kind offer, sir. I may take advantage another day. Philadelphia seems like such a big place. Sarah, I'll talk to you later."

Sarah nodded, her mouth full of food.

Reaching for the shawl she had draped over a chair in the parlor, Rachel settled it over her shoulders and stepped out the door into a whole new world. The day dawned fresh and crisp with an azure sky and a few puffy clouds. Horses and loaded wagons clopped along on the cobblestone streets.

She knew the College of Pennsylvania was on Mulberry Street toward the wharf not too far from where she was now, so she began walking in that direction past more row houses until she arrived at the end of the block. She dodged across the intersection, skirting around mud puddles and mindful of passing carriages. The next block's buildings held businesses at street level with residences above. Fascinated by the variety of shops, Rachel stopped to look in the windows.

A grocer's store displayed an assortment of fruits and vegetables. She had never seen some of the food, such as a long, curved, yellow fruit in bunches or prickly looking, oblong shapes crested with a crown of spiky green leaves. In a bakery next door, a worker pulled trays from an oven while another kneaded a clot of dough on a table. A clothier's store exhibited women's hats imported from Europe sporting pheasant and ostrich feathers. Gentlemen's headwear featured the typical tricornes as well as more formal hats and wigs. A group of people gathered in front of the print shop window, reading newly printed notices.

In the next block, she strolled by a Quaker church and cemetery and a stonecutter's establishment beside it, handy for bereaved relatives needing a tombstone. The next entrance advertised a physician. Rachel mused that the patients whose treatments were unsuccessful didn't have far to go.

Finally, she came to an enormous edifice at the corner of Mulberry and Fourth Streets that reminded her of a grand church. A sign proclaimed, 'College and Academy of Pennsylvania.' Beyond grassy lawns, the two-story building towered majestically with a steeple on one end and two chimneys near the center. An arched entryway sprouted from the middle of the structure, and numerous tall windows graced the building's walls.

Perpendicular to the College stood a three-story building identified as the Charity School and Dormitory. A grassy courtyard with walkways led to the entrances. An iron fence surrounded the yard terminating with two stone pillars topped by brass orbs.

Rachel felt small as she walked to the door of the College. Strangely though, there were no people anywhere. Perhaps they were all inside. She opened the door and entered a cavernous hallway. Each tap-tap of her heels echoed loudly. She approached a doorway with wooden benches on each side. Scattered on a table beside the door were pamphlets describing the school, its curriculum, and the teachers. She took these to study later and saw an application form. After digging in her purse for her pencil, she completed the questionnaire, outlining her prior schooling. She pondered the next question, which asked her to select the academy in which she was most interested: the Medical School, the English School, the Mathematics School, the Latin School, or the Philosophy School. Hesitant about which one to pick, she left the boxes blank. The deserted hall loomed eerily quiet. She tried the door marked 'Provost Office,' found it unlocked, and went in.

An extended counter ran down the center of the room, separating a line of seats from the rest of the office. At a desk behind the counter, a gray-haired woman busily shuffled papers. Rachel stood patiently waiting while the woman continued to work, oblivious to her presence. After a few moments, Rachel rustled her paper. Startled, the clerk glanced up.

"How can I help you, miss?" she inquired, as she came from behind the desk.

Rachel said, "I wish to apply for admission to the College."

The woman scanned Rachel's form, then handed it back. "We need the name of the student on the first line, not your name."

"I *am* the student."

"You must be mistaken. We don't admit women, only men. Besides that, the school has been closed indefinitely due to the British occupation of the city. We don't know when classes will resume."

Rachel's thoughts raced with confusion. *Didn't Mr. Elliott know they didn't admit women? What would she do now?* "But I've come a long way," she protested, "and my tutor told me I should come. I have tuition money and a place to stay in the city. I'm a good student. Won't you give me a chance?"

"No, miss, I'm sorry. We can't make exceptions."

Rachel felt a blackness creeping over her vision. She gripped the edge of the counter, but the darkness increased. With a gasp, she crumpled to the floor.

~ CHAPTER 22 ~

Since Rachel left for Philadelphia, Nate tried to ingratiate himself in the Palsgrove household. During his days off after charcoaling had ended and before woodchopping had begun, he made himself useful by completing her chores. The entire family seemed in mourning at Rachel's absence. They grieved her light laugh and lively spirit as well as her contributions to the daily duties.

Nate chopped firewood, kept the fires tended, carried out ashes, retrieved foodstuffs from the root cellar, and hauled water. To reward his efforts, the family often invited him to dinner. He continued his evening strolls with Phebe, and their caresses after the walks had become more fervent and harder to resist taking them further. It was apparent she was falling in love with him, and he was smitten with her. He loved her freshly scrubbed face and shiny hair, clean clothing, and sweet lavender smell. Although he often didn't appear his best, particularly after heavy work, she didn't seem to mind.

Then winter timbering started. It was hard labor, but he was relieved Tom McCauley had found him a partner. Elisha Cadwalader was a young man in similar circumstances. His parents were dead, and he was on his own, staying at the single men's boardinghouse and eating his meals in the community dining room in the basement of the ironmaster's house. He had chopped wood last year, so he knew the shortest ways to their wooded tract and the procedures for cutting and stacking the timber. In just a couple of weeks, they developed a bond of respect and camaraderie, and watched out for each other in the woods.

So far, the weather held with no early snows, just frost in the mornings. Even though the days stretched long, he still found time for walks and church services on Sunday. He was grateful to spend as little time as possible at the Zerbeys'. With Henry home now, Nate not only had to deal with all the children but him too. He much preferred the peaceful atmosphere at the Palsgrove house and the potential for better things to come.

Toward the end of November, during one of their evening outings, Phebe inquired, "Are you taking me to the Christmas dance at the Big House?"

"Yes, of course. I bet you have already sewn a new dress for the occasion. I know all the young ladies wear their finest clothes."

"Yes, I decided on an ensemble."

"I hope I have something suitable to wear. Most of my shirts and pants are tattered."

"I shouldn't tell you this, but I've made a shirt for you as a Christmas gift, so you needn't worry."

"I'll feign surprise when I open it. Describe your dress for me."

"I'm not going to tell you that too," she exclaimed. "Wait until you see it. It's a surprise."

"No doubt, it will be amazing. Perhaps we can also astonish everyone then with some news." He smiled mysteriously.

"What do you mean?"

"We could announce we're getting married."

"Married? Is that a proposal?" She gazed into his eyes and held her breath.

"It is. What's your answer?"

"My reply is yes!" She squealed as she kissed him and threw her arms around his neck. "I'm delighted you asked me."

"Don't tell your family yet. I want to ask your parents' permission first. Do you think they'll object?"

"No, I'm sure they won't. They think of you as a son already."

"I'll come tomorrow evening to talk with them after I get cleaned up from work. Can you be busy somewhere else?"

"Yes, the ladies are decorating the Big House for Christmas, so I can go help. Oh, I'm so excited! I can't wait to plan everything." She danced a little jig. "Perhaps Rachel can come home for the party. I'm anxious to tell her the news." She kissed him again as he held her tight.

~ CHAPTER 23 ~

"Miss, miss, are you all right?"
Rachel opened her eyes and saw the gray-haired woman and a man standing over her, the woman fanning papers in front of Rachel's face. Still groggy, she stared confusedly at their features. The man knelt beside her.

"What happened?" she asked.

"You fainted," replied the man. He was tall and thin with a shock of white hair and a deeply wrinkled face. She started to rise, but he gently held her down.

"Lay there awhile until you're feeling better." After a minute, she slowly sat up with his assistance.

"Take a sip of this water." He offered her a glass.

"Who are you? I don't remember seeing you."

"I am Provost William Smith, head of the College. Miss White summoned me from my office after you collapsed."

Rachel felt her head. "Oh, I've never swooned before. I feel so humiliated."

"Are you hurt?" he queried.

She shrugged her shoulders and stretched her legs. "I don't think so."

"Let's move you to one of these benches. Miss White, can you take the young lady's other arm?"

They helped her to her feet. "Here, take another drink of water," he said, once she was seated.

Rachel sipped the water. "Thank you. I'm better now."

"Should we call a physician?" inquired Smith. "There is one down the street."

"No, I'll be all right. It was just such a surprise that the College doesn't admit women. I wanted to attend and thought I could. Why aren't females permitted?" she challenged, although, with a fluttering heart, she knew what the answer would probably be.

"We don't think the education we offer here is appropriate for young ladies. In our Academy, we educate boys in history, geology, geography, and languages, which will help them in their careers or our College. We have six English School classes, four in the Mathematics School, and four in the Latin School. The last school I mentioned is a preparatory link between the Academy and the College. Only after a student has achieved mastery of all those courses and passed a rigorous examination can he apply to the College to earn a bachelor's degree.

"We are preparing gentlemen for professions in medicine, banking, navigation, surveying, law, or as schoolmasters. We do not take women pupils," he explained.

Rachel drew an envelope from her handbag. "Here are letters, one from my tutor detailing the topics I mastered, and the other from Mr. Daniel Sterling, guaranteeing my tuition money. My goal is to become a teacher. You told me you prepare students to become teachers. I don't see what difference it makes whether I am male or female if I am qualified."

"It doesn't matter what qualifications or sources of income you may have. We do not allow entry to women. If you want to write a letter of appeal to the Trustees, you can, but I doubt it will change our minds."

Rachel gathered her things. "I shall be writing that letter, Provost Smith," she declared. "I feel the policies are grossly unfair." She rose to go. "You will hear from me again shortly."

~ CHAPTER 24 ~

Rachel walked slowly back toward the boardinghouse feeling greatly disappointed. At the Quaker Church, she pulled on the massive doors and found them open. Entering the empty cavernous sanctuary, spartan in its furnishings, she sat in a pew towards the back, silently crying. *It's not fair,* she thought. *I can't give up and go home. I've worked so hard to get this far. I won't accept defeat without a fight!* She blew her nose on her hanky and dried her tears. But no solution came to mind.

After exiting the church, she wandered around the area, absent-mindedly looking at the shops that had been so intriguing before. She still had not decided what to do by the time she arrived back at Mrs. Graydon's.

Almost all the boarders were seated at the dinner table except Sarah's husband, Mr. Brown, who had not yet appeared. Rachel sat at the table and placed her napkin on her lap. Barely noticing the food on her plate, she pushed it around and around with her fork. She sat quietly while the others shared their adventures of the day.

Although she had just met her, Sarah perceived Rachel's mood. "How was your day, Rachel?" she asked. "I see you're not eating this delicious pork roast."

"No, I'm not hungry. I got some disturbing news today, and my appetite is gone."

"What happened?"

"Well, I came to Philadelphia to enroll in the College to learn to become a teacher, but Provost Smith told me they do not admit females under any circumstances. What am I to do? It's so unfair."

Timothy, one of the students, said, "She's correct about no women. No ladies at either the Academy or the College. I've attended the Latin School for almost three years, and the only place for both boys and girls is the Charity School next door. Some of my teachers instruct at both places, but the Charity School teaches poor children in the city, not instructors. We hope the College reopens soon."

Mr. Morris asked, "Did the Provost give you no options?"

"He said I could write a letter of appeal to the Trustees but implied it was a waste of time."

"At least it's an action you can try," he replied. "Inequities never change unless people protest to make injustices right."

"I'm unsure what evidence might sway them, and I'm too emotional to compose a convincing letter."

The scrivener sat still for a minute, his fork hovering mid-air. "I could help you with a letter. Business has been sparse at the shop, and I could spare some time for a friend." He smiled kindly at her.

"But I don't have money to pay you, and I couldn't impose upon your valuable time. Thank you, I *do* appreciate your offer."

"I don't expect any payment. I would be delighted to help. As I said this morning, I believe in education and people improving themselves."

Maybe I still have a chance, she thought. "I would be extremely grateful for your assistance, Mr. Morris."

"Good, that's settled. We'll meet in the parlor tomorrow morning and walk to my office. Now, don't worry and eat up."

After breakfast the next day, Rachel and Mr. Morris walked to his shop. Comfortable-looking walnut chairs with green velvet cushions furnished the small waiting area in front. "Let's go to the back where there's more room. I have ideas about some arguments we can make that might persuade them to grant you entrance."

He led her to a room lined with books. "Sit there at the table," he instructed. Morris skimmed his fingers along the law books on the shelves and selected several. Before he sat, he pulled the door closed. "I don't want anyone to disturb us."

He opened his writing portfolio and took a chair beside her.

"First, Rachel, tell me about yourself. Why do you want to be admitted to the College?"

She told her story, her studies at Hopewell, and her dreams of becoming a teacher. She elaborated on Daniel Sterling's generous proposition to send her to school in exchange for helping Susanna and her promise to return to Hopewell to instruct the village children.

Morris scribbled notes as she talked. "You have a great deal of backing from your parents and community for your continued schooling. You must be a very bright young lady."

Rachel beamed at the praise. "Here's a letter from my tutor, Mr. Elliott, detailing the subjects in which I'm proficient, and another one from Mr. Sterling affirming his financial guarantees." She handed the documents to him.

After several minutes of reading, he made more notes. "These letters will be beneficial. The missive from your instructor shows your hard work and proficiency in various difficult topics young ladies usually don't attempt. As for the ironmaster, I'm aware of his fine reputation. Now, tell me more about Hopewell."

She described the furnace's vast land holdings for charcoal production, the three ore mines, and the smelter for iron making.

"How many people are employed in the various operations?"

"Several hundred. Woodchoppers, colliers, teamsters, molders, furnace workers, farmers, and the people who provide meals, rooms, and clothing. All the workers' families live there and contribute to the community."

"What products are made at Hopewell? Do they only make pig iron?"

Wary of telling him they made items other than pig iron since she knew it was against the law to do so, she said, "Yes, they only make pig iron."

Mr. Morris smiled at her. "But Rachel, you told me that molders work at the furnace. They wouldn't be needed if the furnace only makes pigs."

Caught in a lie, she hesitated. "They make a few stove plates and pots for people in the village." She noticed him writing. "Don't record that."

He put his quill down. "You're right. We don't need to make any reference to those things since they are only for local use. Mr. Sterling's financial support is crucial for your schooling, both for your tuition and your accommodations during your studies. Tell me more about him."

"He learned to smelt in Shropshire, England, and when he came to the colonies, he worked with the ironmaster and my father at Colebrookdale near Boyertown. When he started Hopewell in 1771, he recruited my father to be his founder."

"Has Mr. Sterling done well?"

"Yes, he began with fewer than thirty workers, and now he employs many times that. The furnace expands each year and is prosperous."

"Are you aware Dr. Benjamin Franklin is one of the trustees of the College and Academy?"

"No."

"Do you know about Dr. Franklin?"

"I believe he is a printer and an intellectual. He's a trustee?"

"Dr. Franklin is a most influential person in Philadelphia. In fact, not only is he a Trustee but starting the College was his idea. He also began the Charity School. Are you aware of Dr. Franklin's political leanings?"

"Yes, I believe he has been outspoken about the injustices of some laws such as the Tea and Stamp Acts." Rachel didn't want to reveal that she knew all about his activities in the revolution. *Does Morris favor Great Britain or the colonies*, she wondered. Politics was dangerous ground. It was hard to tell if someone was a friend or an enemy.

"He is not only outspoken but is instrumental in fostering the unrest against England. He wants independence."

"I heard about that, but I don't know the details."

He patted her on the arm. "Don't worry, Rachel. I, too, am in favor of independence. As a scrivener, I must uphold England's laws, but I feel the colonists have been mistreated. I applaud their actions. Is Mr. Sterling an acquaintance of Dr. Franklin?"

"I think so. He comes to Philadelphia periodically."

"Perhaps we can use their friendship to your advantage. Dr. Franklin's policies for the Charity School, which admits both boys and girls, can also be a basis for changing the enrollment requirements for the College."

He pulled open the legal books. "Some precedents in English law for the education of women might strengthen your argument. Let's make a list of the points to cover."

Together they crafted an outline and constructed the letter. After several hours of work, they were finally satisfied. "I'll give my assistant this copy, and he can rewrite it on our official stationery. If the Trustees see you sought legal assistance, they will take you more seriously. He'll finish it today, and I'll bring it home to Mrs. Graydon's for your signature. On Monday, you can present it at the College."

Rachel gathered her papers and stood to leave. "Thank you so much for your help, Mr. Morris. Without it, I don't know what I would do."

"You're welcome. I'm glad we became better acquainted today. I understand why so many people are trying to make your dream come true." He patted her shoulder. "Let me show you to the door."

He escorted her out of the conference room, through the outer office, and out to the brick sidewalk. "Can you find your way home from here?"

"Yes, I'm sure I can. I'll see you at dinner," she said, as she began walking up the street. She felt heartened by their activities of the day. *I hope this letter works. Maybe after the college reopens, I can attend. They should at least let me try!*

~ CHAPTER 25 ~

Nate fidgeted on the settee in Phebe's living room while waiting for Lewis Palsgrove, crossing and uncrossing his legs and twiddling his thumbs. The man intimidated him. As founder at the Hopewell Furnace, Lewis was authoritative and known for his stern demeanor with workers under him. But Nate was willing to face his fear because he loved Phebe dearly, and in the back of his mind, he hoped as Lewis's son-in-law, he would be offered a job at the furnace. It was a typical procedure to grill a potential fiancé about how he would support the couple, where they would live, and his views on religion and fidelity. Nate pondered possible answers and hoped he could bluff his way through any tricky questions.

Lewis entered the room, his six-foot height dominating the space. He sat on a chair opposite and ran his hand over his face and rubbed his neck.

"How has wood chopping been going, Nate? Do you like it as well as being a collier?"

"It's very different from charcoaling, but I like being home every night."

"I'd thought you'd be staying in the forest while the weather is good rather than walking back and forth daily."

"I would, but I find the walk invigorating, and I like to help out around here with Rachel's chores since she's gone."

"You certainly have been a big help here."

Nate asked, "How was your day at the furnace?"

"Nothing out of the ordinary. What brings you here this evening? Phebe mentioned something about decorating the Big House for Christmas. I thought you would be there helping her."

"Well, sir, I wanted to speak to you about a serious matter." He hoped his voice wouldn't crack with nervousness. "I... I ...," he hesitated.

"Tell me what's on your mind, Nate."

"Well, I might as well say it. I want to ask permission to make Phebe my wife."

Lewis sat back in his chair and crossed his leg. He carefully packed his pipe full of tobacco from a pouch in his vest pocket, cupped the bowl with his gnarled hands, lit it with a match, and drew deeply on the stem. He puffed until wisps of smoke emanated. "I thought you might be heading that direction. You've been seeing quite a lot of her lately. I have a couple of concerns though."

After a few more draws, he said, "Phebe had some grave health problems last year. Scarlet fever has damaged her heart, and she may never regain all her strength. I am extremely protective of her, more so than I would be of a daughter who can better take care of herself, like Rachel. Are you sensitive to her limitations? You can't expect as much of her as you would a stronger person."

"I'm aware of her fragile constitution, and I would not expect her to work beyond her ability."

"She sometimes pushes herself too hard without realizing it. Are you willing to watch for signs of fatigue?"

"Yes, sir. I've been around her enough that I can tell when she's getting out of breath and should sit down and rest."

Lewis gazed at the suitor directly, his eyes piercing. "Nate, you were quite faithful visiting her when she was sick. I am grateful for that, as she looked forward to your visits. I think they gave her the motivation to get well."

"I am exceedingly loyal to her. I truly love her with her best interests at heart."

"I believe you do." Lewis relaxed his stare, inhaled on the pipe, and when it failed, relit it. "If I give my consent to marry, where would you live?"

"Unfortunately, I don't have much money to get us started. Tom McCauley said there is a small vacant cabin available about a half-mile down the road. But in summer, when I'm absent for weeks at a time, I think Phebe might be lonely not being near her family."

"That could be a problem, particularly with her condition. It might be more advantageous if she lived closer to us when you are gone."

Nate wished Lewis would come of his own accord to one of the solutions he had envisioned. Either build an addition to the Palsgroves' house so they could live rent-free with Phebe close to home or find a job for him at the furnace so he could be around in the evenings all year round.

"I'm not sure how else we can solve that," Nate replied.

Lewis didn't rise to the bait. "Well, I'm sure we can find a solution when the time comes. If I give my approval, when do you plan to wed?"

"We thought to announce the engagement at the Christmas party and be married in the spring."

"Won't it be difficult to keep the betrothal secret that long? Phebe and her mother will want to tell everyone before that. Women get so excited over these affairs. Why not proclaim the pact now and pledge at the holiday, or is that too soon?"

Nate had not dared hope for such a speedy progression of events. The winter had not turned brutally cold yet, and he hoped a furnace job would happen soon so he wouldn't have to cut trees in January. "That would suit me fine if it's all right with Phebe."

"We only have today, my boy. Pursue those things that will make us happy now, not months or years from now. Don't waste time waiting. You have my blessing for marriage whenever it works out best for the two of you."

Nate stood and eagerly extended his hand. "Thank you, Mr. Palsgrove."

"Call me Lewis since you're almost one of the family."

"Thank you, Lewis. I'll be sure to cherish your daughter. I'll head over to give her the news."

~ CHAPTER 26 ~

Rachel cleaned out Missy's stall, brushed her, and tacked her up. They had only brought the sidesaddle, thinking there wouldn't be room to store two saddles and that Rachel was getting too old to ride astride like a youngster. She would travel like a proper young lady.

Missy chomped hay from the bag dangling beside the mounting block at the back of the barn. Rachel hopped on the stone, placed her left foot in the stirrup, and after some fumbling, hooked her right knee around the saddle's horn. She felt unbalanced and awkward with both legs on one side of the horse and her bottom seated sideways.

Settling herself as much as possible, Rachel reined the horse's head toward the alley after the mare pulled a final wad of hay. Gingery from being in the stall for two days, Missy's prancing soon lessened. Rachel trotted through the alleyways, being careful not to lose her way in the tangle of lanes. Turning down Walnut Street, the Levering mansion appeared after a short distance. With its stately residences, spacious front lawns, and curving drives, this part of town was undoubtedly different from the block upon block of row houses near the boardinghouse.

At her destination, she unhooked her leg and stiffly jumped down. Rachel tied Missy to the black iron horsehead hitching post. After patting the dust off, Rachel strode up the walk, climbed the portico steps, and knocked on the massive doors.

Susanna appeared, but instead of inviting her into the house, she came outside, even though the air was cold. She steered Rachel to an area on the porch hidden from the sight of the mansion's windows.

"Oh, Rachel, I forgot you were coming today. I don't need your services. We haven't had any studies I couldn't understand on my own. Don't come back until next Saturday. I probably won't need your assistance much at all while we're here."

"Won't your parents expect me to help you more?"

"I don't care what they expect. I only agreed to this silly arrangement so they would allow me to come here. I don't need a chaperone. I want to see you as little as possible."

Rachel was surprised and hurt by Susanna's rebuff. "Will you want to ride Missy Sunday? I can bring her over if you like."

"No, no, that won't be necessary. We are having tea after church so I won't have time for that. Now that I have more interesting events to occupy my time, I won't need riding to break that day-to-day drudgery at Hopewell. Missy frightens me sometimes, so I won't miss riding her."

"I understand. Missy can be a handful. If you need anything, you can send a messenger. Do you know the address?"

"Yes, I do." Susanna stamped her feet and shrugged. "I'm freezing out here. You can go now." She turned and flounced in the door.

Rachel sighed with relief. If the ironmaster's daughter didn't want her assistance, she couldn't force her, but per her agreement with Mr. Sterling, she'd check back periodically. She mounted the mare and headed home. *I'll have more time for my studies if I can just get admitted.*

True to his word, Mr. Morris brought the finished letter home. It was enclosed in a beautiful envelope addressed to Provost Smith and impressively cited her qualifications and the legal precedents for her admittance.

Monday, she went to the College, armed with the document. Her chances were as good as she could make them. The secretary, Miss White, instantly recognized her, and not wishing a repeat performance of Rachel's fainting episode, showed her immediately into Provost Smith's office.

"Here's my letter of appeal," Rachel said, handing him the envelope.

He motioned to a chair in the corner. "Sit there while I read it."

The Provost sat behind his massive desk cluttered with papers, carefully opened the flap of the envelope, and began reading. After several minutes, he returned the letter to its envelope and placed it on the desk. He settled back and looked Rachel straight in the eye. "I can tell you're serious about your desire to enter the College, and I'm impressed with your arguments. I'll bring the matter up at the next trustee meeting."

"When will that be?" she asked, faintly smiling.

"As you already know, the College and Academy are temporarily closed. Since General Washington's defeat at Germantown, the British troops have overrun Philadelphia even more than before the battle. That's why we are closed. We don't want to put our students' lives at risk. Due to the trustees' political leanings, King George believes we are promoting subversive activities here, and his spies are closely watching us. When the occupation resolves, we will reopen.

"I can tell you though, the trustees meet weekly to assess the situation. I'll present your request at this Friday's meeting. Come back next Monday, and I may have a decision for you then."

"Thank you, Provost Smith. I will be anxiously awaiting their answer."

At dinner that night, there was an unfamiliar face at the table. Sarah introduced Rachel to her traveling salesman husband, Mr. Brown. He was a short, thin man with slicked-down dark hair and a gap-toothed smile.

"I've heard many fascinating things about you all afternoon." He grinned at her, looking at his wife. "I'm glad to put a face with the name."

"Thank you, sir, but I doubt Sarah's praise is fully justified. We thought you would arrive last Saturday."

"Call me Arthur. Coming back from New York, I made a few extra stops and sold most of my goods."

"What do you sell, Arthur?"

"I peddle cutlery such as cleavers, knives, scissors, whetstones, and so forth. Utensils that people on the farms need but can't obtain easily. It's a prosperous business, but I don't like being away so often. I miss Sarah." He beamed and squeezed his wife's arm.

"That must be hard on both of you. I imagine your wife misses you greatly."

"I certainly do," said Sarah, "but one must make a living."

Rachel looked around the table. "Where's Mr. Morris?" she asked. She wanted to share her news with him about her visit to the Provost.

Sarah replied, "He sometimes works late if he has an important case. He'll probably arrive later."

After the meal, Rachel announced, "I'm going out to feed my horse. Then I'll be retiring to my room. Goodnight, all."

In the barn, she filled Missy's pail with oats, refilled the water bucket, and pitched her two flakes of hay. While Missy ate, Rachel cleaned the stall and then groomed her with the big curry brush. On her way out, she noticed a new animal in the end stall, a sturdy black horse with a left white rear hock.

~ CHAPTER 27 ~

Later that evening, Rachel lay in bed reading a book by candlelight when she heard a soft tap at her door. "Who's there?" she called, wondering who would be calling at this time of night.

There was no reply, but a few seconds later, the knock sounded again. Rachel got out of bed, put on her robe, and strode to the door. She cracked it and peered into the darkness.

"Miss Palsgrove, may I come in?" whispered Mr. Morris.

"I don't think so," she answered apprehensively. "You shouldn't be here. Mrs. Graydon will be angry."

"I'm anxious to hear how well the University received your letter. Please, let me in for a moment. I don't want her to catch me on this floor."

Rachel reluctantly widened the door. "Just for a minute," she said, as he entered the room. He quickly shut the door and turned the key.

Seeing her alarm, he murmured, "Don't worry. I don't want any-one disturbing us. That busybody Graydon has a habit of poking her nose in matters none of her business," he asserted. "I just arrived from the office, and I've had an extremely long day. Do you mind if I sit?"

Before she objected, he sat on her bed and patted it next to him. "Come, tell me everything. Did you see the Provost? Did he read the letter?"

Rachel perched gingerly beside him, keeping some distance between them. "Yes, the Provost studied the paper and said he was impressed. I think he was surprised I came back and that I had talked to a lawyer. He said he could tell how serious I am about my request."

"How marvelous." Mr. Morris took her hand. "Did he say when they would make a decision?"

Staring at the large hand grasping hers, she was amazed at its strength and warmth. Long, smooth fingers clasped her slender ones. She gazed up into his warm, brown eyes.

"He said the Trustees meet every Friday, and he would read the letter to them. I'm to return Monday for an answer."

"That's good. I thought he might put you off with excuses." He grinned at her. "You did well for yourself, young lady." He moved closer, squeezed her hand, and rubbed her back lightly. She felt uncomfortable with him being so near but didn't want to insult him by pulling away.

"Yes, I did do well, didn't I?" She was pleased with herself.

"You challenged their inane rules and showed them you wouldn't be dismissed so easily. I'm proud of you." His enthusiasm was contagious, and pride swelled in her just as if her father were here praising her accomplishments.

"I knew you would do well, so I brought you something." He pulled a slim package out of his waistcoat pocket.

"A gift? You shouldn't have done that. It's I who owe you a debt of gratitude."

"It's nothing much. Open it."

As she caressed the wrapping, she wondered what it might be? No one other than family had ever given her anything. She pulled on the ends of the ribbon tied around it, discarded the paper covering, and opened the box. Nestled in tissue paper lay a lovely fountain pen. She picked it up and ran her finger along the grain of its polished mahogany wood, and the gold nib on the tip glittered in the candlelight. "It's beautiful," she gasped and flung her arms around him.

He held her embrace a few moments, gazed into her eyes, then bent his head to kiss her. His slightly prickly mustache tickled her mouth, but his lips were surprisingly soft. At first, she leaned into the kiss, but then his strong hands again enveloped her wrists. Alarmed at his grasp, she began to struggle half-heartedly, but his grip tightened. When their mouths unlocked, his hot breath warmed her face, and his eyes searched hers longingly. The pen clattered to the floor.

"Oh, Mr. Morris, you must go," she implored.

"Is that any way to repay me for all I've done for you?" he muttered, not to be put off. "You know what I want."

She attempted to rise from the bed, but he pulled her down. He kissed her anew, more forcefully, and she whimpered. His sharp fingers dug in. She tried to pry herself from his grasp, but his size and power pinned her. "Please don't!" she cried, as she twisted her wrists. "You're hurting me. Let me go!"

She squirmed mightily, but he held her even tighter. He silenced her protests by covering her mouth with his. She tried to scream but felt smothered, the breath going out of her. She realized there was no escape. He pulled his face an inch away from hers, whispered, "You're mine now," and leaned over to blow out the candle.

She felt her nightgown pushed up. Tears flooded her eyes as her shame washed over her.

He lay silently atop her until his breathing calmed, then rolled off. He stood, buttoned his breeches, and combed his fingers through his hair. "Now that's a thank you," he said and walked out.

As soon as he was gone, she fled to the door and locked it. Her foot accidentally kicked the fountain pen that had fallen to the floor. She picked it up and threw it with all her might, shattering it against the wall. Then she collapsed face down on the mattress, trembling, and sobbed into her pillow.

~ CHAPTER 28 ~

Rachel cried until the sun's rays peeped in her window around the edges of the shade. Curled in a ball, she finally succumbed to a fitful sleep, racked by dreams of terror. She puzzled over how a person she trusted could do such a thing to her. Mourning her lost virginity, she realized her foolishness in confiding in a man who was essentially a stranger. How would she face him again?

She slept until mid-afternoon until a gentle tapping at her door startled her. "Rachel, it's Sarah. I've brought some lunch. Are you ill? Can I come in?"

Rachel crawled out of bed. "Wait a minute, please." She rearranged her nightgown and robe and patted down her hair, then shuffled to the door, mindful of the tenderness between her legs. Unlocking the door, she opened it a crack and saw her friend carrying a plate of food.

"I'm not too well, Sarah."

"Can I come in? I noticed you didn't come down to breakfast or lunch, so I fetched you a meal."

"You're very thoughtful," Rachel said as she let her in. "I *am* hungry."

She sat gingerly on the bed, and Sarah handed her the plate and a fork. Her friend pulled the chair over. "What kind of sick are you?"

"Oh, just that usual female malady," Rachel replied. "It hit me hard this month."

"I understand. Sometimes I get it so bad I can hardly bear it."

"I'm a little better now."

"Mrs. Graydon may have a stoneware container for hot water if you think that will help."

"Yes, after I eat, that would feel nice." She ate a few bites. "Did your husband leave this morning?"

"He got an early start at sun up. He can't sell anything sitting around here all day. Guess what? Mrs. Graydon said Edmund Morris packed up his room and left late last night. Isn't that odd?"

Rachel almost choked on her food. "Yes, that's surprising," she said, feeling an enormous weight lifted. "Does she think he's gone for good?"

"She said he owed her quite a lot of money, so she doubts he'll be back. I'm surprised you didn't hear her shouting at breakfast about what a ninny she was to have given him credit. He had everyone fooled."

"Yes, he certainly did," Rachel muttered bitterly. She breathed a sigh of relief at his exit, not knowing how she would have faced him.

Sarah rose. "Are you finished eating? I'll take your plate downstairs."

"Yes, I feel better now." Both the food and word of Morris's departure brightened her mood.

"I'll see you at dinner?"

"Yes, I'll be there. Don't bother asking about the hot water container. I don't think I need it after all. Thanks for your concern."

"We women have to look out for each other," Sarah said as she left.

Rachel pondered her circumstances. *I wish Phebe were here so I could ask her what to do. I've been here less than a week and am already a victim. Both Jesse and even Morris warned me about trusting people. My dream of a college education is fading away. Susanna doesn't need or want me. I miss my family! There's no one here to tell my woes, no shoulder on which to cry.* She blew her nose, then pursed her lips, her resolve strengthening. *I'm not defeated yet. That letter was good, and it might change the Trustees' minds. I'm not giving up so easily.*

Tomorrow Jesse would arrive in Philadelphia. She longed to see a familiar face and hoped he'd bring a letter from home. She felt safe in his presence. *He's someone with whom I could talk about the University; he'll be sympathetic.*

Pulling herself together, she decided to seek solace with Missy. She donned her riding clothes and headed to the barn.

"Hello, Missy," she cooed to the horse, who nickered upon seeing her. "Are you homesick too? I bet you miss all your stable mates from Hopewell." She stroked the mare's face gently, and the animal pushed back on her hand, demanding a more vigorous rub.

Rachel saddled her, and for once, was grateful for a sidesaddle.

She rode down the alley, looking to explore new territory. *I might not be here much longer.*

~ CHAPTER 29 ~

Jesse backed the team of cream horses beside the dock. This was not his usual stop at Theuben Bailey's on Water Street, but a dock several blocks away. He had to deliver this precious cargo first.

He entered the run-down shack that stood onshore next to the pier. The building appeared uninhabited, and there was no ship anchored nearby. When no one answered his knock on the door, he debated what to do next. As he turned to leave, a man ran down the boards from shore and pulled up, panting. "Sorry, mate, I was getting a bite to eat. I'm Frederick. Are you Anthony?"

"Yes, I'm Anthony. I have a delivery for you, but we'll need help—they're heavy." 'Frederick' had spoken the code names previously arranged for the meeting, so Jesse aka 'Anthony' knew he was at the correct place.

"Here come some lads back from their meal who can help us." He beckoned the men coming across the street.

"Where are we taking them?" Jesse asked.

"Let me show you," the man said, opening the door to the shack with his key. Inside the building, ropes, chains, blocks and tackles littered the floor. "Help me push some of these out of the way."

Jesse and Frederick shoved some things to the side, revealing a trap door in the floor. "We'll stow them below until the ship docks tonight to pick them up. We don't want any prying eyes seeing what we're loading. It'll be safer at night."

They went to the rear of the wagon, where the other men lingered.

"Let's unload the freight as quickly as possible, boys," Frederick instructed.

"Use this tarp to cover the cargo," Jesse said.

The deckhands draped the tarp over the first of the cannon. These cannons were not large battlefield size but were smaller ships' artillery destined for the revolution's infant navy. The workers heaved the first one out and strained under the heavy load. Once inside the shack, the tarpaulin was removed to be draped over the second gun on their next trip.

After they finished stowing the last cannon and had replaced the trap door, Frederick said, "Well done, men." He handed the tarp to Jesse while the crew respread the equipment over the floor. "We'll meet you again next week, Anthony?"

"Yes, that's the plan," Jesse replied. The men shook hands, and Jesse walked down the dock and jumped to the wagon seat. He clucked to the team and arrived shortly at Theuben Bailey's.

After greeting Jesse, Theuben helped him unload the pig iron. He noticed the empty end of the wagon. "Been making some other deliveries, Jesse?"

Jesse knew Theuben didn't believe Hopewell only made pig iron to sell to England. Seldom did he completely discharge his haul at Theuben's—he often went to the store warehouse to deliver other products. He hoped Theuben would assume that was the case today.

"No, I'm just delivering to you," lied Jesse.

"Seems like a long way to come with only half a load." The big man winked at him.

"I only drive the wagon. I don't analyze how much is in it."

After unloading, Jesse drove to the stable, where he unhitched the horses and settled them in their stalls. He headed over to Tun's.

Hetty greeted him as he stepped inside the front door. "Hey, Jesse, you've got a visitor." She pointed her head to the booth by the window. "Been waiting for you all day."

"Thanks, Hetty," he said, as he slyly patted her rump. "I'll see you later." He strode to the table.

His face broke into a smile when he saw Rachel. She looked beautiful with the late afternoon light streaming in the window and shining on her glistening hair. She glanced up at him with her azure eyes, and his heart leaped in his chest. But something about her seemed off, different somehow. Her mouth didn't have its usual smile.

"Rachel, what a surprise." He slid into the other side of the booth. "I planned to stop at your place this evening. Here's a letter from your folks." He pulled an envelope from his pocket.

Her face lit up at the sight of the letter. She eagerly opened it and scanned the contents. "My sister's getting married," she exclaimed.

"To whom?" Jesse motioned the barkeep to pour him a beer. "Do you want anything to drink?"

"No, thanks. I had tea earlier. She's marrying Nate Kirst. Have you met him?"

"I don't think so. Does he work in the village?"

"I'm not surprised you don't know him. He's an apprentice collier under Henry Zerbey and spends most of his time in the woods. When my sister was sick last winter, he often visited since they don't make charcoal when it's cold. The Zerbeys took him in after his parents died."

"Does she love him?"

"I'm sure she does. I liked him too for a while, but he's closer to her age. I'm happy for her."

Rachel reread the letter, folded the paper, and put it in her handbag. "There's not much else new at Hopewell. I miss them so much."

Jesse's drink arrived, and he took a sip. "I'm amazed you're here. Guess you found the place all right."

"You gave good instructions. There are distressing things to tell you, and I didn't want to discuss them at the boardinghouse."

Jesse was alarmed. "Oh? Tell me what happened."

She opened with a report of Susanna's rebuff.

Jesse said, "I'm not surprised. That's good for you. You won't need to see her very often. That should free up time for your studies."

"Yes, but there may not be any studies." Rachel frowned. "First, the university is closed at the moment, and second, women aren't admitted."

He sat back in his chair, stunned. "I thought your enrollment was all arranged. What are you going to do? Come back to Hopewell with me?"

"No, not yet. A scrivener at Mrs. Graydon's helped me write a letter of appeal. Now I'm waiting for the Trustees of the College to determine whether or not to admit me."

"When will they decide?"

"Next Monday at the earliest, but perhaps a lot longer. I think the more time they take to make their decision, the better my chances. A quick ruling probably means no."

"How likely is it they will change their minds?"

"The letter was well-written. Provost Smith read it and said he was impressed. But I don't know if he was sincere."

"That was generous of that scrivener to assist you. His help will give you the best chance possible to enroll."

"Yes, it was good of him to aid me, but..." Her voice cracked, and her eyes lowered.

Jesse scrutinized her face. "What happened?"

Rachel sat still, trying to calm her raw emotions. She was embarrassed to tell him the whole story. How would he react? Should she reveal this secret? Could she trust him?

"He... he..." she stuttered. A tear ran down her cheek, and she shielded her face with trembling hands.

Jesse came out of his seat, around the table, and sat beside her. He gently held her hand and lifted her face. "Rachel, you can tell me anything. We may not be friends long, but I care about you. I worried about you all week."

"I feel so stupid, Jesse. You warned me about not trusting people, and I didn't listen." She lowered her voice to a whisper. "He assaulted me." She paused, softly crying. "He violated me in the worst way."

Jesse sat stunned for a moment, then tenderly pulled her toward him and wrapped his arm around her. He could feel her racing heart and trembling body. He held her tight, then bowed his head on hers and whispered, "Oh, Rachel, I'm so sorry."

After a few minutes, she calmed. He raised her sleeve, saw the bruises on her arm, and felt rage grow in him. *How dare anyone harm her?* "What's his name?" he growled. "I won't let anyone who has hurt you go unpunished."

Rachel's weepy eyes searched his fiery ones. "Morris. Edmund Morris. He was a boarder at Mrs. Graydon's but left in the night with his bills unpaid. He seemed nice at first, but I was wrong."

Jesse leaned back in the seat, thinking. "We need to inform the constable. This Morris can't avoid prosecution for assaulting a woman."

"No, I don't want the law involved. I want to keep it quiet. I won't be able to face anyone if they know what happened. Telling people can't undo what's been done."

Jesse balled his fist and clenched his jaw in frustration.

"For some reason, that name 'Morris' sounds familiar. Did he say where he's from?"

"He said he came from England about three years ago and lives in Philadelphia, mostly working on various shipping contracts. His office is on High Street, near the bank."

"Did you go there?" he asked.

She sighed. "Yes, I went there. He seemed so respectable. He asked a lot of questions about Hopewell and me. I thought he was genuinely interested in helping."

"Since he has a place of business, he can be found. I want to talk to him."

"No, Jesse, what's done is done."

"But he must be punished," he persisted.

"It won't change anything," she implored. "I want to forget it ever happened."

Jesse sat perplexed. He glanced up, and a man seated near the door caught his eye. "Rachel, I need to consult with that fellow, but I'll be back shortly. Wait right here for me. We'll order dinner and talk more."

She nodded and blew her nose into her handkerchief.

Jesse walked across the room and sat opposite the man.

The stranger spoke. "Was the package delivered safely?"

"Yes, Frederick received it with no problems."

"Good. We'll arrange another delivery next week if that's all right."

"I'll plan on it."

The man stood. Jesse said, "Before you go, do you know a man by the name of Morris?"

The man sat cautiously back down. "Yes, we have identified a man with that name," he said haltingly.

"What can you tell me about him?"

"We suspect he is spying for the British here in Philadelphia."

Jesse's face clouded. "Is he dangerous?"

"Yes, he could jeopardize our whole operation. Why do you ask?"

"I think we may have a problem. My lady friend from Hopewell encountered him on another matter. I want to find him."

"I don't recommend that idea. He's treacherous. Stay away from him," he cautioned.

"All right, I'll leave it alone. She doesn't want me to confront him anyway."

"There are more people to protect than just one."

"I understand," Jesse said. They shook hands, and the liaison left. Jesse crossed back to Rachel's table.

"Rachel, tell me everything you told Morris. He may be a spy."

Rachel gasped. "He wanted information about Hopewell for background for my letter. I let it slip that we had molders, but of course, I didn't tell him about the cannon." She barely breathed the last word, looking left and right, ensuring no one overheard.

"You know about them?" he asked, shocked.

"Yes, I stumbled upon the molders casting them one night, and my father told me. I swear, I didn't tell Morris. I presume you deliver them to the city."

"But Morris may reveal to someone else that Hopewell makes more than pig iron. The furnace might be at risk for doing that, but if soldiers go there, they could find a lot more than some pots and stove plates."

"We've got to warn them," said Rachel in a panic.

"I can tell them when I return," said Jesse, "but with the team, I won't arrive for three days."

"If I go on horseback, I can be there much sooner. I'll start at dawn."

"I can't let you do that; it's too perilous. You might meet soldiers on the way, or even worse, you might encounter—" he spit the name out, "Morris. It's too long a trip for you alone."

The idea of confronting soldiers or Morris frightened her. She would be defenseless against them. Maybe Jesse was right. It was too risky to go by herself.

"Then come with me," she blurted. "I can't sit by and do nothing. If the British go to Hopewell and discover what they're making, the furnace might be shut down or burned, and people like Mr. Sterling and my father might be imprisoned."

"You're right. Hopewell might lose everything, as well as the revolutionists who are depending on us for weapons." He thought about the severe consequences that could befall the village. "But I can't come with you. I've got the team to care for, and I don't have a good riding horse. Besides, I haven't ridden in years. I drive horses, not ride them."

"You never forget how to ride a horse, and perhaps the stable has one for rent. The creams will be safe here. We must go," Rachel implored. "If something terrible happens that I could have prevented, I will never forgive myself. I have to warn them!"

~ CHAPTER 30 ~

They ate a hasty meal, then Jesse rented a stocky, bay gelding at the stable and retrieved his emergency kit from the wagon. He mounted and pulled Rachel up behind him. Fortunately, the horse wasn't a tall, spindly nag. It wouldn't be the fastest animal available, but it looked durable enough for the long trip.

So Mrs. Graydon wouldn't think another boarder had run out on her, they stopped at the boardinghouse, and Rachel left a note explaining she would be gone a few days. She changed to her breeches, so if the sidesaddle became too unbearable, she could ride bareback. Then they saddled Missy and at dusk took off, riding at a slow trot through the streets to not attract unnecessary attention. Once they reached the outskirts of town, they cantered awhile. The horses were fresh and eager to go in the crisp night air. The sky was clear, and the moon was high, illuminating the road. They couldn't have chosen a better night to travel.

"I wish we would have borrowed a horse with a smooth trot," said Jesse. "This one feels like a rough wagon seat without a spring. I'm going to be sore tomorrow." Alternating between walking, trotting, and loping, they made the best time possible.

After about four hours, they paused at a creek to water the horses and stretch their legs. When Jesse jumped off his horse, he crashed to the ground—his rubbery legs unable to bear his weight. Rachel helped him up, and he limped around, shaking his feet to get his circulation going and work the kinks out. After a short while, they mounted again and walked to prevent overheating the animals after their drink of cool water.

More hours passed, and the horses' heads drooped with weariness. So far, they had seen no one. As dawn began to break over the horizon, they saw Berry's Inn in the distance. Jesse pulled to a stop to confer with Rachel about their next move.

"Let's inquire here if any soldiers have come through. We should also eat some breakfast and let the horses rest. If the Redcoats haven't passed by, we might be able to sleep a few hours."

"What if they have already come?" Rachel replied.

"Depending on when they were here, we may be too late."

"I hope not."

"We'll have to find out and decide then what to do."

They walked on to Berry's and tethered their mounts to the rail. When they went in, the dining area was empty, except for Jimmy Berry, cleaning off tables and preparing for the morning meal.

Jimmy looked at them with a start. "Hello, Jesse. I didn't expect you until evening. And I see you've got Rachel with you."

"Jimmy, have any British soldiers come through here lately?"

"Why, are you running from the law?" he teased.

"No, I'm serious. Have you seen anyone?"

"I guess you didn't look out back. There are twenty footmen camped behind my barn. They marched in late yesterday evening."

Jesse and Rachel ran to the window and viewed a sea of tents. No one was stirring yet. No campfires burned to cook breakfast.

"Jimmy, can you fix some sandwiches we can take with us? We need to start moving."

"Sure, I can do that. Hang on a minute."

Rachel pulled her companion away. "What are we going to do?"

"I think we should try to pass the soldiers and beat them to Hopewell. They won't be able to move as fast as we can. Maybe Jimmy has some horses we can borrow since ours are pretty tired. Let me ask." Jesse disappeared into the kitchen.

Soon he came back with the food. "Bad news. Jimmy doesn't have any riding horses to loan us, so we'll have to use the ones we've got. I asked him to stall those men as long as possible if anyone comes inside."

They watered their animals while devouring their sandwiches, then mounted. "Let's walk past the soldiers and not act like we're in any hurry. We're just out for a pleasant day of riding. We can ride a few miles ahead of them by the time they awaken, eat breakfast, and get organized," said Jesse.

No one observed them travel past the soldiers' camp, and when out of sight, Jesse and Rachel loped again for a while. The brief rest at Berry's had revived the horses a little, but they were not anxious to keep up a fast pace any longer. The riders weren't faring much better.

Rachel sleepily listed to one side of the saddle and awoke with a start. "Jesse, I don't know how much farther I can go on without some rest. I almost fell off just now."

"When we arrive at Owen's toll house, maybe we can catch several hours of sleep. We'll be a couple of miles farther along by that point. Owen can watch for the soldiers and wake us if they come. I doubt he has any horses we can borrow, but I'm sure when we reach Levi Church's farm, we can grab two fresh ones."

"How far is the toll-house?"

"Another two miles."

In another hour, they reached Owen's place. They explained their situation, and he allowed them to stable the horses, pitch them a flake of hay, and rest in the barn. He promised to keep a lookout.

After only three hours, Owen woke them. "I see a huge cloud of dust down the road kicked up by those Redcoats. You'd better leave out of here."

"Don't bother saddling the palomino," said Rachel. "I'll ride bareback. I'm sick of that sidesaddle."

She bridled Missy and hopped on. "Go on out, and I'll catch up," called Jesse.

He hurriedly saddled the bay, strapped on the emergency kit, and stiffly climbed on. "If you can think of a way to delay them, Owen, do so."

"I think the wife baked a cake this morning. We could offer them some. That might buy you a few minutes."

"Thanks, Owen, we would appreciate it." Riding out of the barn, he barely discerned Missy's golden form far away and urged the bay forward with his heels.

Rachel was still rubbing the sleep out of her eyes when he approached. "My head hurts worse after that nap than before," she exclaimed.

"You may feel terrible at first, but you'll be glad later you got some rest. The horses seem perkier now."

They crested a rise and couldn't see the dust cloud anymore. Jesse constantly looked back. "We need to put more distance between the soldiers and us."

They rode in silence for several miles. Rachel nervously fretted about whether they would reach Hopewell in time for the workers to hide any incriminating items. She felt like a little child on a trip, thinking every mile, 'are we there yet?' but knowing they still had a long way to go.

A quarter-mile from Church's farm, Missy's head began to bob. "Stop, Rachel. Your horse is limping," Jesse commanded. Rachel dismounted while he ran his hands down the mare's legs and inspected her hooves. He got the hoof pick out of the kit and dislodged a pebble that had wedged itself partially under her shoe. "It's only a stone bruise, but we'd better walk the rest of the way. We don't want to make it any worse."

It felt good to be off the backs of the horses and stretching their legs, but progress was painfully slow. They tried to walk briskly, but their tired legs wouldn't go as fast as their minds wanted. The desperate sense of being chased and not being able to get away quickly enough hung like a heavy coat upon them, dragging them down.

"Ouch, these boots are terrible for walking," Jesse said. "My feet are throbbing, and I can feel blisters rising on my heels."

Finally, they reached the Churches' home and explained their predicament to Levi. He and his oldest son, Samuel, rounded up two horses from the corral and transferred Jesse's saddle. Rachel still preferred to ride bareback and declined Levi's offer of a saddle. They now progressed at a much faster speed with the fresh animals. Even though bone-tired, they now had hope they could reach Hopewell in time.

About two hours from the furnace, ominous black clouds rolled across the sky. The air hung dank and heavy. They were walking the horses after an extended canter that helped open up the miles between them and the soldiers. "Looks like we're in for some rain," Jesse said. He fumbled with the latch on his kit and extracted a slicker. "Put this on. At least one of us will be dry."

Rachel didn't argue. She dropped her reins while the horse continued to walk and pulled the oilcloth coat on.

"I feel guilty about taking your slicker."

"I'll turn up my collar. My hat will help keep me dry too. For all we know, the soldiers won't stop at Hopewell. They may be pursuing Washington's army and not turn off."

Suddenly, a sharp flash of lightning followed by a loud crack of thunder spooked the horses. Rachel's horse reared, and she clung desperately to its mane and clamped her legs around its belly, but she couldn't hold on and slipped off. The frightened beast ran down the road a short distance with Jesse in pursuit, then doubled back and headed full speed toward Levi's barn. Rachel thought to stop the animal, but when she spotted the terrified look in its eyes, she stepped out of its way and let it tear past.

Jesse returned, gave her the stirrup and an arm, and boosted her up behind him. Fat, cold raindrops began to fall and peppered the ground. She opened the front of the slicker so Jesse could wrap it around himself, too. The rain fell faster and harder each minute, and lightning and thunder crashed around them. Jesse patted the horse reassuringly, and the animal restrained its fear under his expert touch. The sunny day had turned black, and rivulets of water ran in the road's ruts and turned to mud.

Rachel tightly held Jesse's belt to maintain her seat and pulled in close to him so the slicker would cover them both as much as possible. She tucked her head down, so the rain ran off his hat and splattered on the coat rather than on her head. His muscular shoulders rippled under her head, and her hands felt his lean sides as she grasped his belt. His strong body felt safe and warm. There was no possibility of conversation with the storm roaring around them. The muddy road sucked at the horse's hooves.

Jesse bowed his head into the stinging wind to keep the rain out of his eyes. His chest was soaked from the cold torrent hitting him, but at least his back was relatively dry. Rachel's body against his kept him from shivering. The weather was brutal on them, but it would be even more challenging for the British foot soldiers slogging through the mud.

After a while, the rain let up, but the sky still threatened. Jesse walked his horse since the animal was carrying double weight. Plodding on for miles, they finally topped a rise and saw Hopewell laid out below them. They breathed a sigh of relief.

Jesse kicked the bedraggled animal to go a little faster, and they pulled up to the cast house. Rachel dashed inside to talk with her father while Jesse sprinted to ring the bell to call the workers. The clanging alarm in midday meant trouble. Soon men ran from all corners of the village: Valentine from the blacksmith shop, Tom McCauley from the store, Daniel Sterling from the Big House, and Ben from the barn. Rachel's father directed the molders to dig a pit beside the slag pile outside the cast house, and shortly they brought out three cannon and several dozen cannonballs that had been hidden behind the waterwheel. They buried the contraband and covered the freshly turned earth with slag. Other workers destroyed any molds and hid other iron goods as best they could.

Two frantic hours later, Lewis Palsgrove called the men together inside. "British soldiers are heading this way, and we don't know if they will stop here or not. We need to go about our usual routine, but we'll only pour pig iron. Any hot slag we have, we'll pour over the pile. Go about your work as you normally would."

Everyone chatted with relief that they had hidden the illicit items, but they also realized the actual test might come later if the soldiers stopped to search. They resumed the tasks they had been doing before the bell had rung, but instead of making molds, they dug trenches to prepare for a pig iron pour.

Lewis briefly supervised, then turned and said to Rachel, "Take your friend back to our house and rest. I'll talk to you later."

At Rachel's house, her mother and sister peppered them with questions. "Mother, I'm so tired I can't think straight. I'll answer all your questions after I get some rest."

Martha saw the haggard look on their faces. "He can sleep in Nick's bed," she said, nodding at Jesse. "Do you want something to eat first?"

"No, Mother, we just want to collapse somewhere. Bed sounds delightful. We can talk and eat later." She led Jesse up the stairs, and he crawled into the boy's bed after shedding his wet hat, shirt, and muddy boots. Rachel took note of his hairy chest and muscular arms. His head burrowed into the pillow, and his legs hung over the side of the too-short bed. With a deep sigh, he fell asleep.

Rachel snuggled into her old bed. Within minutes she was snoring too.

~ CHAPTER 31 ~

The clatter of dishes downstairs and her father's booming voice awakened Rachel. Her arrival had caused panic and chaos, and she expected him to be angry with her. She was ashamed of her carelessness in revealing to Morris that Hopewell Furnace poured more than pig iron.

Crossing the room to Nick's bed where Jesse slept, she gazed at his stubbly face. She would have never made it back in time to warn the village without his help. Jesse could have been upset with her stupidity, called her a silly fool, and let her come by herself, but he hadn't. He became part of the solution at a time when she desperately needed help. While initially shocked and outraged at Morris's assault on her, he didn't accuse her of any wrongdoing. She admired his rugged face and sinewy hands. *He looks so peaceful.* Her heart fluttered in her chest, a feeling of warmth came over her, and she smiled to herself.

As she watched him, Jesse opened his eyes and woke with a start in the strange surroundings. He blinked and put his hand out to her. "How did you sleep?" he asked.

"Like a bear in hibernation. Father is home. We should go down and explain everything."

"How much are you going to tell him about Morris?"

"I'll tell him about the letter of appeal to the College and how Morris helped me. And how in the process of relating facts about Hopewell, I slipped about the molders. Let's leave it at that. He doesn't need to know the rest."

"I'll let you steer the conversation. I'm glad we got here before the Redcoats."

"Me, too. I'm so fortunate you came with me." She smiled and squeezed his hand.

Jesse searched her beautiful blue eyes as her lashes fluttered. "You are unlike any young woman I have ever known. Such ambition and determination! Even if you make mistakes, you are willing to admit them and try to make them right." *I've never felt this way before about a woman.*

Suddenly he sat up and kissed her cheek. His stubbly beard prickled. His strong arms held her for a moment after the kiss. He looked at her and sighed. "We better go down."

Lewis reclined on the settee in the living room, gazing out the window. Smoke from his pipe swirled around his head. Rachel sat beside him, and Jesse took the opposite chair.

"Father, this is my friend, Jesse. He helped me get here today. I wouldn't have made it without him."

"I know Jesse. We help him load the wagon for his trips to Philadelphia." He turned to Jesse. "I appreciate your taking care of my daughter."

There was silence between them. Trying to gauge his degree of anger, Rachel waited for her father to speak first.

Finally, after placing his burned-out pipe on the table, he said sternly, "Rachel, you caused quite a stir this afternoon. You've only been gone a fortnight, and already you have caused trouble. Tell me what happened."

She related her tale of the College, Morris's help, and her error in telling him about the molders. "He nearly pounced on my words, Father. It seemed odd at the time, but he was so kind in helping me write the letter that I trusted him. I realize now how foolish I was. Somehow, he knew I was from Hopewell. I assumed Mrs. Graydon had mentioned it, but he only aided me to glean information. When I talked with Jesse later, he said Morris was possibly a spy. Then I worried soldiers would come to Hopewell and find not just pots and stove plates, but also the cannon."

"You didn't tell Morris about the cannon, did you?" Lewis's eyes flashed.

"Oh, no, Father, I wouldn't be that stupid. But if the soldiers came looking, I knew they might find them if they weren't well-hidden. We passed Redcoats on the road but don't know whether they are coming here or not. I'm so sorry, Father. I was so gullible." She hung her head in shame.

"Perhaps the British will pass the furnace by, but if they do stop here, we hid the contraband well enough. If they come, stay out of sight, particularly if Morris is with them. We want them to think we're operating normally and that you didn't alert us. Fortunately, you arrived in time to warn us."

Lewis continued, "I felt apprehensive sending you to the city from the start, but now since you probably won't be attending school, you might as well stay home."

"Father, I understand why you think I should remain here. But there still is a chance for my education. I still have my dream, and maybe they will reconsider. Besides, my belongings are at Mrs. Graydon's, and Mr. Sterling still depends on me to help Susanna. Jesse needs to go back to Philadelphia to bring his team and wagon home, and I must pick up Missy from Levi Church's farm and take her back to Susanna."

"Well, you should conclude those details and honor your commitment to Daniel Sterling. But if they deny you entrance, you must come home. Daniel can make some other arrangement for his daughter if you're not there. We'll see what happens in the next day or so, and then you can go back. Is that all right with you, Jesse?"

"That sounds good to me," the young man said. "I can use a rest after all this excitement."

The following day, British soldiers arrived at Hopewell. Mud splattered their sodden red coats and clung to their boots, and lines of weariness and disgust at the wet weather etched their grim faces. Their general immediately went to the Big House to demand Daniel Sterling allow them to inspect the area.

Daniel and Lewis had supervised burying the cannon and cannonballs the day before. Although other molded iron goods were illegal for colonies to manufacture, they deliberately weren't hidden as thoroughly as the cannon. The ironmaster calculated that if the soldiers found that contraband, they might not look further. England probably assumed that the colonies' forges and furnaces made illicit iron products, but making weapons and shot to support the revolution was a treasonous crime.

Within short order, Redcoats swarmed over the grounds, the furnace, the charcoal shed, the blacksmith shop, the barn, the spring house, and the mansion. Combing inch-by-inch through the buildings, they were jubilant when they discovered stove parts and implements behind the bellows of the waterwheel. They lined the items up in the cast house for inspection by the commander, who after looking the pieces over, sternly rebuked Mr. Sterling. A few soldiers poked the slag pile with the bayonets of their muskets, concluded it harmless, and did not investigate further. The furnace workers had poured pig iron earlier, and the hot slag was still cooling on top.

Rachel hid in the house and didn't even briefly appear at the window for fear Morris was with them. Jesse had never met Morris, so he couldn't identify him. It was doubtful the spy would come and risk being seen with the British.

Everyone in Hopewell breathed easier when the Brits marched out late afternoon and headed toward Reading. Daniel Sterling would be fined for violating the Iron Act of 1750. General Howe would determine the exact amount when the regiment returned to the city.

After the soldiers' departure, the ladies at the Palsgrove house enjoyed their evening discussing Phebe and Nate's upcoming wedding. Jesse appeared later to set a time for their return to Philadelphia the next day. They elected to take two horses, Levi's horse and Chester, the seventeen-hand gelding.

"I'll ride Chester to Church's tomorrow, and if Missy has recovered from her stone bruise, we can exchange her for Chester. If not, we'll take him on to Philadelphia," said Rachel. "Susanna doesn't care much for riding anyway, so if Missy's not available, she won't be upset."

"I'll pick up the stable's horse from Levi's. It may take a few days for the palomino to recover. I can pick her up whenever she's fit and deliver her to town on a later trip."

Since it wouldn't take as long on horseback to get to Levi's farm as it would driving a team and wagon, they decided to depart mid-morning. "I'm glad we can take our time getting to Levi's tomorrow. I'm still sore from the ride here." Jesse groaned as he stiffly rose to his feet.

Rachel felt relieved that the soldiers had not found the cannon and shot. *The arduous trip was worth it,* she thought. *We prevented a disaster, and we've helped the Patriots' cause.*

~ CHAPTER 32 ~

The return trip to Philadelphia was uneventful. They rested for the night at Levi's farm. The next day, Missy trotted around the corral with no sign of a limp. Jesse decided that instead of leaving Chester at Levi's, they should take both Chester and Missy. They could rotate horses, so one animal would always be riderless and less tired. By riding Missy sparingly, she was less likely to become lame again. When he returned to Hopewell, Jesse could trail the extra horse behind the wagon just as he had done taking Missy to town.

On the way into the city, they stopped at Mrs. Levering's to call on Susanna. Again she said she needed no help, which suited Rachel just fine.

Rachel hated to see Jesse go on to Tun's after they arrived in Philadelphia on Sunday evening. They had talked incessantly on the trip from Hopewell. He was always the gentleman, although he occasionally stole kisses from her when she least expected it. But he didn't press her for more than kisses and subtly flirted with winks and grins and cheerful banter. When he dropped her off at Mrs. Graydon's, she felt a sense of loss and sadness. She would miss seeing his smiling face every day, but he was way behind schedule and needed to catch up. His peck on her cheek at their parting would have to satisfy her for the week.

Rachel felt both hope and apprehension when Monday morning came—her day to visit Provost Smith for the official decision. She walked several blocks to the College, which appeared as deserted as before. Miss White at the front desk smiled at Rachel and motioned her to sit.

"The Provost stepped out for a minute. Can you wait for his return?"

"Yes, I can wait," Rachel said. The room was not lavishly furnished but bespoke quality in the selection of furniture. Wood paneling covered the walls, and large multi-paned windows let in maximum light. Miss White's desk was smaller than the Provost's, and its stacks of papers threatened to topple. *Why was there so much correspondence if the school was closed?* The gray-haired woman busied herself writing in ledger books, perhaps some type of record-keeping for tuition money or grades.

Time dragged, and every minute seemed like fifteen. The clock on the wall had stopped, so Rachel couldn't gauge how long she had been sitting. She pulled some paper from her handbag and began to make a list of chores to do at the boardinghouse later. If the Trustees rejected her, she would prepare to go home as soon as Jesse arrived in town on his next delivery.

Finally, Provost Smith entered. He nodded to Rachel. "Come in, Miss Palsgrove. I'm sorry I've kept you waiting." She followed him into his office and sat in the overstuffed, green velvet chair.

He stood in front of his desk. "I'll make this brief. The Trustees considered your letter of appeal but were unable to reach a consensus about admitting you. They need more time to think about the ramifications of changing the rules. Admitting women would impact the entire climate of the school. Our standards must be upheld, so they can't make this decision lightly. If you can come back next Monday, I can perhaps give you a definitive answer."

Rachel was disappointed with the delay, but at least the response wasn't 'no'. They were still considering her request, so that was a good sign, but she didn't like the implication that women were a less desirable type of student.

"I can come back then." She rose to go. "I appreciate the consideration the Trustees are giving this matter and understand its importance to them. I hope they believe their decision is important to me also."

"Yes, Miss Palsgrove, we understand your strong desire to attend. I will encourage them to answer by next Monday."

"Thank you, Provost Smith."

"Before you go, do you have activities to occupy your time while you are here in the city?" he asked.

"No, I don't have a lot to do, but I will find a way to fill my time."

"I presume you like to read. Are you familiar with The Library Company?"

"No, what is that?"

"It is a collection of books that subscribing members may borrow. Dr. Franklin started it many years ago, and the collection is housed at Carpenter's Hall, not far from here, off Chestnut Street near Fourth."

"That sounds wonderful, but I'm obviously not a subscriber."

"They also allow non-members to borrow, but a sum of money, double the value of the book, must be deposited. When the patron returns the item, a small fee is taken from the deposit. I will vouch for you, Miss Palsgrove, so no deposit will be required, nor a fee charged. I trust I will not regret it?"

"I would be grateful for your recommendation, and I'll treat any books I borrow with great care."

"Let me write a note of introduction to the librarian, Francis Daymon, and he may lend a book or two for a short time."

"If you recommend me, I will definitely go," Rachel replied.

"Also, next to the library is a room of curiosities in which you might be interested, a so-called 'wonder room'. I'm sure Mr. Daymon will show you around."

He stepped behind his desk, grabbed a paper from a stack, and began scribbling.

"Be careful when you go. The books are on the second floor, and since occupying the city, the British use the first level as an infirmary for their wounded soldiers. I know Mr. Daymon checks the collections every Tuesday afternoon, so try to arrive then. Go to the front steps and wait for him as there will probably be a sentry posted inside the main door. Show him the note, and he can escort you into the Library."

Rachel folded the paper and put it in her purse. "Thank you so much, Provost Smith. I'm eager to visit. I'll be back next Monday."

She left, saying a quick goodbye to Miss White, who barely peered around her stacks of papers.

Outside, Rachel wondered what else she could do to occupy her time for a whole week? Since she was unsure where The Library Company was located, she decided to go for a walk to find it.

She strolled awhile and still had not found Chestnut Street. Perhaps she was going in the wrong direction. She elected to go back to Mrs. Graydon's before she got lost, and then the idea of going past Morris's office popped into her head. She knew how to get there from where she was; it was not far away. At this point, she was more angry than hurt at his imposition upon her, but even so, she did not want to see him, just spy on him as he had done with her.

After finding his building, she waited until a group of people walked past and trailed along behind them. Stealing a glance into the office, she was surprised it was empty! The overhead sign had been removed, the benches were gone from the waiting room, and no people were in sight.

She crossed the street and watched awhile, waiting for anyone to enter. She then walked to the corner and lingered, facing a store window where she could watch the office in the reflection. Shortly she moved to another window affording her a view from a different angle, but there was no activity inside. Dare she peek in and try the door? She didn't know if she was that brave, and even if she did look in, what would that accomplish? What if he came out from the back? Would she have the nerve to face him?

After debating with herself, she decided to peer in from the office's side window, so if someone *was* in there, they might not notice her. Cutting back across the street, she swallowed the lump of fear in her throat, approached the glass, and looked in. The room appeared bare and deserted. Moving stealthily in a moment of courage, she stepped to the door and gazed in the glass window. No one. Her hand tentatively turned the doorknob and discovered it unlocked. She gently pushed the door open.

Suddenly, Morris emerged from the back, looked up, and saw her. She stood frozen in her tracks, and her feet felt planted like the roots of a hundred-year oak. In three quick strides, he reached the door and jerked it open.

"Rachel, how nice of you to visit," Morris cooed. "How did your meeting with the Trustees go? Do come in and tell me all about it."

She couldn't believe he was acting as if nothing happened in her room that horrible night. Hot, intense anger welled up from her core. "How dare you ask me that after what you have done," she exploded.

"I have your best interests at heart, dear, you know that." He touched her arm, which she jerked away as if touched by a hot poker.

"You only helped me so you could impose yourself upon me." Her words spat from her mouth, and he looked surprised at the venom in her voice. She didn't dare betray the fact she suspected him of spying, or he might guess she had warned the furnace. "You have no decency, sir. You're despicable."

"Why, Rachel, I presumed that after the meeting in your room that night, you might not want to see me across the breakfast table, so I left. But now, here you are, seeking me out. Perhaps you enjoyed our time together more than you let on," he sneered.

This remark shook her. Maybe he was right. Why *was* she here? What perverted sense of injustice drove her to come here and risk seeing him? She had told Jesse she wanted to let the matter drop, so why hadn't she?

Morris stepped closer and grabbed her arm in a vise-like grip. Rachel could smell his sweaty body, and his repulsive, hot breath on her face brought back memories of that awful night. She wouldn't let that happen again, and rage filled her. She fought him like an animal, kicking his shin and then his crotch until he loosened his fingers and let her go. As his hands clutched his wounded manhood, she slapped his face hard with her open hand, leaving an angry red welt across his cheek. His hand flew to his face, and his eyes showed a twinge of fear that quickly turned to anger.

"Be gone, you whore," he roared as she turned and fled. "You'll regret doing that."

After running a block, she looked back and saw he was not following. A broad grin covered her face as she stopped to catch her breath. She felt more satisfied with herself than ever before in her life.

Morris, however, his hand covering the stinging welt rising on his face, vowed, "That won't be the last time I see you, Rachel Palsgrove. I'll make sure of that."

~ CHAPTER 33 ~

The next day, after getting better directions from Sarah about Chestnut Street's location, Rachel set off to find The Library Company. Yesterday she had been going in the opposite direction, so it was no wonder she had not found it.

Within a few blocks, she encountered Chestnut, and a short distance further was Carpenter's Hall, its name emblazoned in large letters on the front. The imposing two-story, red brick structure had huge, white double doors up a short set of steps, framed by a white pediment on top and columns on both sides. The twenty-four-paned first-floor windows sported white shutters, while the second-floor windows' crests were gracefully arched. A copper-topped cupola and weathervane crowned the peak of the building.

Rachel positioned herself beside the steps facing out, so she could survey anyone coming to the door who might be Mr. Daymon, the librarian.

Soon a little man, stooped and gray-haired, came walking briskly around the building. When he saw her, he straightened up, surprise registering on his face. She looked directly at him, holding his gaze.

"Are *vous* waiting *pour moi, Mademoiselle?*" he asked in a thick French accent.

"If you are Librarian Daymon, I am indeed waiting for you."

"That is *mon nom*, but what brings you here?"

Rachel took the Provost's note from her purse. With darting eyes, he scanned the writing. "*C'est bon, Madamoiselle* Palsgrove. So you would like to see our collection of curiosities and perhaps borrow a book. We can arrange that. Follow *moi*, and do not stare at *les hommes* in the room we enter first. The stairway is to the right as we go in, so we needn't pass anyone except the sentry. I periodically check *la bibliothèque,* but they won't be expecting you. It will be better to ask for forgiveness if they question us than ask permission and bring attention to *vous.*"

"What is '*la bibliothèque*'?" she asked.

"Ah, excuse me. I sometimes lapse into French. It means library, and there are wounded soldiers in the room if I did not make myself clear."

He unlocked the door, and they entered. Immediately, Rachel smelled the stench of antiseptic, vomit, and rotting flesh. She gasped and held her hand to her nose. Sounds of moaning and retching assailed her ears. The little Frenchman nodded to the guard, who barely looked at him, and they hurried to the winding staircase. Rachel kept her eyes glued to the librarian's back, but her peripheral vision saw cot after cot of injured and dying men swathed in bandages. Unchallenged, they quickly ascended the stairs. Mr. Daymon unlocked and swung open the door to a room filled with massive bookcases covered by wire-screened doors. He secured the door behind them.

They both sighed with relief.

"This is the library, *Mademoiselle.*" He waved his arm expansively.

Rachel gazed in wonder at the sight of so many books in one place. "I never dreamed such a place existed."

"*Oui,* there are over two thousand books here. Some of our more expensive and popular ones were removed to my house for safekeeping during the occupation, but we could not move them all. There are too many. We are quite proud of the variety of our holdings.

"But, let's go to the other side, and I will show you the curiosities in the Wonder Room before you select a book to borrow." He led her through a doorway into a large room where heavy tables and

Windsor chairs stood in the center of the room and objects in glass cases hugged the perimeter.

"Sit down, *Mademoiselle* Palsgrove, and I will show you some of our objects you might find interesting."

"Please call me Rachel, Mr. Daymon."

Rachel sat at one of the wooden tables, and the little man brought over a small case. He opened the lid, and Rachel glimpsed pieces of metal inside.

"These coins were minted in the Roman Empire 1500 or more years ago." He put one in her hand.

She hefted the palm-sized rectangular metal. "I can't believe a coin is so gigantic and heavy. It must weigh several pounds. No one would want to carry many of these around."

"It is called *aes signatum*, which means 'struck bronze.' They were the first coins of the Empire and are composed of tin bronze with a high lead content. Its unusual design on the one side reminds me of a three-candle candelabrum on a fancy iron stand. We are not sure what the picture on the other side represents."

He took another coin from the container and exchanged it with her.

She said, "This is more what I think a coin should look like." She peered at the picture of a man watching two boys nursing on a she-wolf. "What does this depict?"

"In 289 BC, a trio of men who wanted to become senators had the job of deciding what images to put on coins. They often chose an image of their ancestors. This is a coin designed by Sextus Pompeius Fostulus, showing his ancestor Fostulus watching the brothers Romulus and Remus suckling. They are the mythological twin brothers who helped found Rome."

He picked another coin from the box. "This coin is more typical of later coins when emperors depicted images of themselves. Julius Caesar's portrait was the first likeness of a living person on a coin. The emperors wished to associate themselves with divinity, so their pictures appeared god-like. An emperor named Commodus in 192 AD commissioned this one which shows him dressed in a lion skin and on the reverse proclaims himself to be the Roman incarnation of the god Hercules."

He showed her others. One coin depicted the head of Ceres, the Roman goddess of agriculture, and on the obverse were oxen pulling a plow. Proud horsemen on another affirmed Rome's military might.

"I have lots of other curiosities to show you, so we can't spend too much time discussing the coins. Perhaps if you are interested, we could view the others another time?"

"I don't know how long I will be in Philadelphia, but if I stay more than a week, I would be delighted to learn about the others."

He returned all the coins to their box, crossed the room to a tall chest with many shallow drawers, and then brought a twelve-inch round item with a handle.

"That's a mirror," she announced. "I've seen mirrors before."

"Inspect it more closely. This one is special."

As Rachel drew the mirror nearer to her face, she jerked her head away. "My face is huge."

Intrigued, she looked again into its depths, bringing it closer, then farther away. "At certain distances, my face appears gigantic, but when I bring it very close, everything becomes tiny and turns topsy-turvy. This isn't like any mirror I have ever seen before."

"This is a magnifying mirror," he said.

"How does it work? It looks like any other mirror at first."

"The surface of the mirrors with which you are familiar is flat. This one is concave, so light rays are bent toward a focal point causing the image to look larger."

"What does concave mean?"

"A concave mirror is scooped out slightly towards the middle, so it is like the interior of a bowl."

"Why does the reflection become turned around and smaller as you draw it near?"

"When you get closer than the focal point, the magnification starts to reverse itself and inverts."

"I'm not sure I understand completely, but I find it fascinating," said Rachel, as she gazed again into its depths. "But I don't know if I want to see myself that enormous."

He laughed. "We may observe things we wish were not there, like wrinkles or gray hairs, not that you need to worry about either of those."

"I hope not yet." She handed it back.

Then the librarian gently placed a scroll-like object about fifteen inches wide at the end of the table. "Would you care to unroll this, Rachel?"

She stood and cautiously unrolled the scroll, which extended the entire length of the twelve-foot table.

"What beautiful colors. It is so finely made with beautiful small designs."

"Would you believe you are looking at the skin of a snake?"

Rachel's eyes widened. "I would never believe a reptile could grow to such a size. What kind is it?"

"An anaconda from South America. They can swallow deer and cattle and even a man. They are not venomous but are constrictors and squeeze their prey to death. The biggest of them are twice this large."

"I'm glad snakes aren't that big in Pennsylvania," she exclaimed.

"These snakes live in the jungle, where there are few inhabitants. Of course, when people find one, they kill and eat it. Snake meat, I hear, is delicious."

"I hope never to eat a snake, even if they taste good. That snake could feed an entire village."

"Many other countries' cultures are different than ours, and the people consume a variety of plants and animals foreign to us."

He re-rolled the skin and replaced it in the drawer.

Next, Mr. Daymon pulled a large fuzzy garment from a cloth bag and laid it in front of Rachel.

"That's a coat," she said, relieved that she could finally identify an item and not seem so ignorant. She ran her hands over the surface. "I don't recognize this fur."

"The coat is called a parka. Caribou hide comprises the body of the parka, and wolverine fur edges the hood. The Eskimos, also called Inuits, of the far North, wear parkas to keep warm in the sub-freezing temperatures of the Arctic."

"I'm familiar with wolverines but have never seen one. What kind of animal is a caribou? The nap is luxurious and thick."

"Caribou is a type of deer common in that region. The wolverine fur repels the ice crystals formed from the water vapor the wearer exhales."

"Where did the library get such a coat?" she asked.

"The North West Company explored that Arctic area seeking a water passage across the continent of North America to the Orient. They encountered these people and were fascinated by how they live in such a frigid climate. Although their trip was unsuccessful, they brought back information about this culture. We also have some unique utensils and instruments from them in our collection." He stowed the coat in its bag.

He then placed a wooden box measuring eighteen inches long, six inches wide, and six inches high in front of her. "Here is one last item to show you today. Are you squeamish?"

"What do you mean, sir?"

"Some visitors to the Wonder Room, particularly women, find this item disturbing. I don't want to repulse you if you get upset easily. In the box is a preserved ancient human body part. Would you like to see it?"

Rachel tried to imagine what part might be in there and whether she would want a peek. "I'm a country girl, Mr. Daymon, and I help my mother butcher chickens and other animals for the family table. So I think I would not be overly upset over a part, no matter how gruesome."

"In that case, I'll let you open it gradually, and you can decide if you wish to see its entirety. The top lid slides off, so view it as slowly as you are comfortable." He pushed the box close.

With a combination of keen anticipation and nervous trepidation, she slid open the lid. Inside, on a yellowed bed of cotton, were a human's blackened fingers, hand, and wrist. Rachel felt the bile rise in her throat, but she swallowed it down as her curiosity about the hand took over her thinking and pushed down her gut reaction. "Why would anyone want to keep the hand of a dead person?"

"This hand belongs to an Egyptian princess whose body was mummified after her death. The Egyptians built elaborate tombs for their royal dead and preserved their bodies for the afterlife. Once the internal organs were removed and put into canopic jars, the corpse was dehydrated using salts then wrapped with cloth to prevent decay when placed in the tomb."

"May I touch it?" Rachel asked.

"Handle it carefully. It is delicate and over two thousand years old."

She gingerly raised the hand from its bed and turned it over. She could see fine details of the skin and bones, and traces of cloth were still clinging in places.

"This may be the oldest remains of a human on Earth. But why was it removed from her body?"

"Unfortunately, fortune hunters in Egypt robbed the royal tombs to steal the valuables inside. The hand was taken as a souvenir and later sold to a collector. We are grateful for this example of a mummy, but it is disrespectful to the Egyptian dead to possess it. The original buriers never intended to have the princess moved from her tomb or her body parts to be severed and separated. We try to be respectful and honor her and her culture."

"Do you know who she was?"

"No, we do not know from which tomb she came."

Rachel reverently replaced the hand into the box. "I'll say a prayer for her and ask for forgiveness of the greedy persons who dishonored her. I'll also thank her for allowing me to learn from her misfortune."

"Some people believe curses follow tomb robbers, so ask a blessing for us all."

Rachel slid the lid back and handed the container to the librarian.

"There are many other curiosities here," he said, "but we need to save some time for you to choose a book or two to borrow. Do you plan to be in the city long?"

"I'm not sure how much longer I will be here," she said. "I'm waiting for the Trustees at the College to decide whether they will admit me as a student. If they do, I will be here quite a while. If not, I may be gone in a week or so."

"That would be unfortunate to return home so soon. There are many more wonders to see and books to read. When will they make their decision?"

"They told me to come back next Monday, but they have put me off before."

"If you find you will not be staying long, I can show you a few more things when you return the books before you go home. I'll be here next Tuesday, and you can meet me like you did today."

"What other sorts of curiosities are there?"

"We have fossils and minerals, a microscope and telescope, an air pump and an electrostatic machine, marble from the ruins of Herculaneum, some beautiful conch shells, scrolls in the Russian language, some other medals, and curious snakes and scorpions preserved in bottles of spirits. It would take numerous hours to see everything."

"I'm grateful you showed me these things today. I am afraid I took you from your important work."

"I enjoy sharing our collection, and as for my time, the library gets few visitors since the British invaded Philadelphia. Your enthusiasm is a delightful diversion."

She blushed at this praise. "I'm eager to learn everything I can."

"Let us go to the book room and find a suitable book for you. Do you have any idea of what you would like?"

"I'd like to learn more about any of the things you showed me today," Rachel replied.

"I know some books that would be perfect," he said. He led her to the other room and pulled a tome from the shelf. "This book is titled *Antiquities of Rome* and describes other Roman artifacts, not just coins."

She perused the drawings inside. "This looks interesting. May I borrow it?"

"Yes, of course."

He pulled another volume from the shelf. "This book, by Sir Isaac Newton, is called *Opticks* and tells about reflections, refractions, and colors of light. It might clarify some of the properties of the magnifying mirror, as well as help you understand our microscope and telescope that you will learn about on your next visit."

The book was weighty, and the reading looked very scientific. Rachel decided that if she were to be a college scholar, she would need to read and understand many scientific principles of which she had never heard.

Mr. Daymon noted her dismay. "We do not expect you to become an expert by reading one book. You will get a feel of what college is like, as well as perhaps a better explanation than I have given today.

"However, on second thought, there is a more suitable book on that subject for you." He replaced the Newton book and pulled an adjacent one. "This volume is also called *Optics*, in three parts. The first part discusses vision by rays reflected from mirrors and polished surfaces. The second talks about light refracted through lenses. The third part shows examples of useful optical instruments and machines.

The author is Benjamin Martin. I think you will find it less theoretical and more practical than the Newton book."

"Yes, that seems like a book I can better manage," she said, as she took it in her arms.

"Let me record these books in my log, and I'll escort you out. You can put them on this table while I get my record book."

She put the books down, and soon Mr. Daymon appeared with quill and ink. "Where are you staying?"

She recited the street and number, and he completed his entries. He rose to go. "I just had another thought. Since you are here this week, you may want to attend a concert Miss Marianne Davies is giving tomorrow afternoon. She will be playing the glass armonica. Are you familiar with this musical instrument?"

"No, what is it? It sounds intriguing."

"It makes the most beautiful, ethereal sounds you will ever hear. Dr. Franklin invented it and is an ardent fan. Miss Davies is one of the few people who have mastered it, and she will be touring soon in London. I'll write down the address for you with a note of introduction. The concert is by invitation only since it is so popular, but I know her personally, so I am sure you will be welcomed."

He handed her the note and rose. "We'll try to leave as unobtrusively as when we came, *Mademoiselle* Palsgrove." He winked at her as she picked up her books. They left the library, and he locked the door behind them.

~ CHAPTER 34 ~

Rachel's thoughts spun as she walked home from the library. There were so many things to learn in the world. Simple life at Hopewell revolved around the rhythm of the furnace and its voracious appetite for fuel. Workers' lives consisted of crafting the molds, gathering iron in the mines, cutting wood and making charcoal, or tending the pours—a constant repetition of chores, day and night, week after week. The furnace ran continuously for years, and the jobs required a precise set of skills. Women in the village played supporting roles by running a household and raising the children who were the future workforce. There was little time for intellectual pursuits as twelve-hour workdays drained the workers' energy. Everyone spent their time at home eating and resting to refuel their bodies.

But Rachel knew there was so much more to life—exploration and science and history. She realized how sheltered her existence had been so far. A whole new intimidating but exciting universe was opening up for her. What would be her place? What role was she willing to accept?

The following evening, Rachel arrived at the mansion for the concert. The house reminded her of Susanna's boarding school, with a pillared veranda and stately doors. A servant who answered her knock looked at her note from Mr. Daymon and instructed her to join the other guests in the drawing room. Selecting a seat near the front, she hoped to get an optimal view of the large cherrywood box on a stand, which she presumed was the glass armonica. She hoped no one would notice that her attire was woefully inadequate for the occasion compared to the other guests' fancy dresses and hats.

Soon the room filled with tittering ladies, their high-pitched voices chirping like noisy birds around her. Rachel smiled at them, but no one made a move to include her in their conversation.

The attendant left his position at the door and proceeded to the front of the room, where he patiently stood, waiting for silence. "Good afternoon, ladies. We appreciate your attendance to hear Miss Marianne Davies, who will explain the glass armonica and favor you with a performance on this wonderful instrument."

A lithe young woman stepped up and nodded toward the servant, who said, "I present to you, Miss Davies."

As the audience politely clapped, Miss Davies smiled and sat down behind the armonica, placing her feet on the treadle on the floor.

"Thank you for coming. I doubt many of you have ever heard the glass armonica, so I will briefly explain how it operates. Our dear Dr. Franklin of this city is its inventor. It consists of many finely-tuned glasses mounted on a spindle powered by the foot treadle. I place my wet fingers on their rims, and they vibrate, producing a sound. Since I have ten digits, I could simultaneously play up to ten notes, but mostly, I will be playing single tones and harmonizing chords. I think you will find the sound pleasing and unique. After the concert, if you like, you may approach the armonica for closer inspection and a demonstration."

Miss Davies checked her foot position, straightened her back, and dipped her fingers into a bowl of water. Her feet began rocking with a slow rhythm. Suddenly, ethereal, ghostly sounds filled the room. The song had a halting, haunting rhythm that entranced the audience. Her next melody featured a lilting tune familiar to all, which brought smiles to the ladies' faces. She played several classical songs, a church hymn, and finally, a well-known romping ditty that had the ladies tapping their feet.

As she concluded, Miss Davies let the final tones fade into the air, held her head down coyly as the music faded, then stood and curtsied. The audience applauded enthusiastically, their gloved hands making muted puffs of sound.

Rachel was completely enthralled, and as soon as possible, rose from her seat and positioned herself beside the instrument to congratulate the musician on her performance and watch her demonstration.

Miss Davies shyly accepted compliments and seemed more nervous talking to them than she was while playing the instrument. After a few minutes of polite conversation, she said, "Let me show you how it is played."

She sat down again and wet her fingers. "As you can see, the spindle turns, spinning the glasses which are arranged from low to high notes. The edges are painted different colors according to the pitch." She played a scale, then played harmony with two or three notes played together.

"How do you know which glasses to play?" a lady inquired.

"It takes many hours of practice, and I memorize all the songs. This instrument is my career in life, and soon I will be going to Europe to demonstrate it. Thank you for coming today. Your attendance has allowed me to polish my skills."

The ladies began to file out of the room. Rachel made sure she had not forgotten her purse or shawl and proceeded to the exit at the rear. She glanced up and was startled to see Susanna chatting with some women.

"Susanna," called Rachel across the room.

Susanna looked up, saw Rachel's smiling fresh-scrubbed face, then scowled and continued to converse with her friends as she exited. As Rachel drew closer, she heard one of Susanna's friends ask, "Who was that?"

"Just a worker from my village. I don't know what she's doing here. Probably just visiting Philadelphia."

Rachel was stung by the rebuke and hung back in the crowd. After a minute of reflection, she thought, *at least I tried to contact her, and I can report she has made friends and is attending social events. I'm not going to let her snub bother me; I've got better things to do.*

~ CHAPTER 35 ~

As Jesse pulled the team and wagon into the outskirts of Philadelphia from his trip from Hopewell, he contemplated the past week. He was two days behind schedule due to the quick trip back to Hopewell and hoped Theuben Bailey wouldn't be too upset at the late arrival of the pig iron. Since ships bound for England regularly arrived, if he missed one boat, another would come soon. His tardy arrival to the warehouse to deliver iron pots and stove parts also should not be a problem. They could process a shipment any day except Sunday.

However, Jesse was deeply concerned about his lack of delivery of the cannon to 'Frederick,' who expected his arrival precisely on Wednesday. He had no way to inform him he would be late and hoped Frederick would come on subsequent days looking for him. What could he do with the cannon and balls if Frederick wasn't there? It would be a considerable risk having them in the city overnight and then hauling them back to Hopewell. The British soldiers were everywhere, poking their noses in any suspicious-looking wagon or carriage. He had hesitated to bring them since he was off schedule, but he knew how desperately the colonial navy needed them. Daniel Sterling and the Patriots were depending on him.

While these worries were troublesome, they were out of his control, so he stopped fretting. Thoughts of Rachel loomed larger on his mind, and those ideas were less easily put aside. He felt a strong connection with her after their brush with the British at Hopewell. Visions of her invaded not only his waking hours but also his dreams. *If I could only get her out of my head!* He felt a strange and uncomfortable giddiness when his brain whirled with images of her smiling face and blue eyes. He could hear her voice even though no one was around. He ached to see her, longed for her touch, and wanted to be with her. He had never been fascinated with any female before, and the feeling was both frightening and exciting. The only woman he had known for more than just casual conversation was Hetty at Tun's, and he didn't feel the same way about her as he did about Rachel.

When he pulled into the location where he'd met Frederick the last time, everything looked deserted as it had before. He tied the team and waited. But Frederick didn't come. Jesse poked around the abandoned shack on the pier to kill some time. What now? He wished someone would show up.

After another hour, he decided to unload the pig iron at Theuben's. Fortunately, the pigs had been loaded last in the wagon with the cannon and balls stowed in the middle, separated by a sliding divider and thoroughly covered by straw and a tarp. Theuben would be curious, and Jesse would stay with the rig during the unloading to protect it from his prying eyes. After delivering the pigs, he could come back, and perhaps Frederick would appear.

As he pulled into the dock at Theuben's, the big man waved to him. "Expected to see you two days ago," he admonished. "The ship sailed yesterday morning."

"Do you have a place to store the iron until the next boat comes? I'm sorry I'm late. I had an unavoidable delay."

"You're in luck. Another ship is due later today." His whistle beckoned his helpers, who poured out of the shack and quickly unloaded the pig iron. The men finished the paperwork, and Jesse was on his way.

At the store's warehouse, he unpacked the crated pots, skillets, and stove parts from the front of the wagon, while carefully hiding the cannon. He left the order for store supplies needed by Hopewell. "I'll be back tomorrow morning," he called.

Arriving again at the dock to meet Frederick, he noted everything still looked deserted. The sun was sinking in the sky. No one would come after sundown. Reluctantly, he headed for the stable.

At the livery, he asked, "Can I pull the wagon into your shed out back, Caleb? I have some merchandise to go back to Hopewell that I don't want ruined by rain."

"The shed's full, but you can park it under the overhang at the end of the barn. That should keep it dry. I don't think it will rain anyway."

Jesse preferred a spot inside a building away from curious eyes, but he couldn't make a fuss and arouse suspicion. "All right, I'll pull in over there, but are you sure everything will be safe?"

"Yes, we close the gates at night, and the dog roams around. He'll tell us if anyone trespasses. We've never had a problem before."

"That's good," said Jesse, feeling somewhat reassured. "I'll be in trouble if this load doesn't return."

Jesse parked the wagon as directed and anchored the tarp over the top. He unhitched the horses, bedded them down in the barn, and hung up the harnesses. He prayed everything would be safe.

Walking the blocks to Mrs. Graydon's house felt refreshing after sitting for hours on the wagon's hard seat. Andrew answered the bell and escorted him inside. Rachel didn't expect him today; how would she react?

Jesse sat in the parlor, and in no time, Rachel was flying down the stairs into his arms. He caught her and instinctively squeezed her tight. She floated light as a bird, her slender body all curves and muscle. He noticed her hair piled atop her head, her long, pale neck gracefully rising above her calico, lace-trimmed collar. As the scent of soap rose to his nostrils, he realized other people in the house were staring at them, and he put her lightly down. She gave him a quick peck on the cheek before he could pull entirely away in embarrassment.

"I'm so glad you're here. So much has happened. I can't wait to tell you everything!" she exclaimed.

Acutely aware of the other boarders' eyes on them, he said, "Let's go to Tun's for supper, and you can tell me everything. There's a lot to tell you too. Do you need to change before we go?"

"No, I think this dress will be fine. But let me tell Mrs. Graydon I'll not be here for dinner, so she doesn't set me a plate."

"Take a shawl. It's getting much cooler outside."

"I'll be back in a minute." Rachel ran up the stairs.

She returned with the wrap, a muted blue shade of wool, and dashed to the kitchen. Breathless, she rejoined Jesse.

He helped turn her shawl around her, the caress of the soft fabric on his fingers making him want to fondle more than the cloth. As they strolled to the tavern, he clenched her hand, grasping her slender, strong digits with his stout, calloused ones. She squeezed his hand playfully, and his heart thumped in his chest. They matched their strides step for step as dry brown leaves skittered down the street beside them in the slight breeze. The sun dropped below the horizon behind them, spraying brilliant pinks and yellows into the sky. The chilly air foretold the winter to come.

In youthful exuberance, Rachel began to skip, urging him to follow her lead, dragging him along. Her excitement lifted his spirits, and he put his concerns about the wagon aside for the moment. He hadn't skipped in years, but somehow with her coaxing him on, he relived carefree boyhood times and skipped too. Soon, they stomped up the steps of the porch at Tun's, where a cacophony of sounds erupted from the open door—clinking glasses, twinkling notes from the piano, and raucous laughter. It was Friday night, payday for many, and people were celebrating another week's work done.

Jesse found a table for them and held her chair. The waitress promptly appeared and took their order.

"Now, tell me all about your week," he said. "You must be accepted at the college to be this happy."

She scowled, but her eyes were still lively. "No, they've put me off again. But meanwhile, I've had the best time. I discovered the library, and the librarian showed me some of the oddities in their collection." Rachel detailed the unusual things she had seen.

"I didn't know such things existed," he marveled.

"Neither did I. I'm so happy Provost Smith suggested I go. I also borrowed two books." She began to tell him about the tomes she had selected.

Jesse put his hand on her arm and stopped her mid-sentence when his eyes spotted his contact, making his way across the room. "I need to talk to the man who just came in."

Rachel smiled. "I'm warning you. If you're not back before the food comes, I may eat your meal too. I'm famished."

"Don't worry; I won't be gone long. I'm starving, so you better leave my plate alone." He grinned as he rose from his seat.

Jesse slipped onto the bench across from his contact. There was no danger of anyone overhearing their conversation above the din of Tun's patrons.

The man stared at him. "What happened?" he demanded. "You were expected several days ago."

"We made an emergency trip back to the village after you told me your suspicions about Morris. It's fortunate we did because soon after we arrived, the British showed up for an inspection."

"Was anything found?"

"They unearthed some household goods we planted, but that was all. Sterling will get cited for those, but the soldiers didn't find anything else. However, the extra trip threw off my schedule, so I didn't make it back until today with more products."

"That explains why Frederick didn't meet you."

"I went today, but no one was there."

"Frederick and his men had other things to do today, and they were tired of waiting around. They figured you probably weren't coming until next week."

"I shouldn't have come, but I remembered how much you needed the goods."

The man's brow furrowed. "Where are they now?"

"They're still on the wagon stowed at the stable."

"Is the wagon concealed?"

"No, just under an overhang at the end of a barn. The liveryman didn't have room for the rig anywhere inside. When can I deliver the cargo?"

"I'll get in touch with Frederick this evening, and you can come to the dock at sunrise tomorrow morning."

"I'll be greatly relieved when I can unload them."

"Yes, you've taken quite a risk bringing them off schedule."

Jesse shook the man's hand and met his eyes with a nod, then rose and zig-zagged through the crowd back to his table.

"That didn't take long," he said to Rachel. "I see our food has come, and I've gotten back before you ate everything on both plates."

Rachel put her fork down and leaned in close. Glancing to either side, she whispered, "Are there problems?"

"Yes, but nothing we can't handle." He told her his dilemma. "I realize now I shouldn't have brought them, but it's too late for regrets. I think they'll be safe for the night where they are."

"I feel bad. All the chaos in your schedule was my fault. If I hadn't been so stupid and gotten involved with that person, none of this would have happened."

"I hope you never see him again," Jesse said.

"Well, I don't know if I should tell you, but–"

"Did something happen?"

"Yes, I encountered Morris at his shop."

"At his shop! Why would you go there?"

"I can't explain why. Some force compelled me to want to spy on him."

"That seems very foolish. What happened? Are you all right?"

"I was peeking in the door when he suddenly appeared and tried to grab me. I made him regret doing that. I slapped his face and kicked him."

"I would have liked to see the shock on his face," replied Jesse. "I'd like to do some slapping and kicking myself. But you must avoid him. Promise me you won't go back."

"I promise. I think he is moving out. His office was bare."

"He must be moving elsewhere." Jesse paused. "Now, let's eat before our meals get cold. And tell me what other exciting things you did this week."

She smiled and began to talk about the concert. As they were eating, Hetty approached the table. She sat down beside Jesse and touched his arm. "Who's your friend, Jesse?" she asked.

He brushed her arm aside. "This is a friend from Hopewell, Rachel. She's here in the city to get an education to become a teacher. Rachel, this is Hetty. She works here."

Hetty softly whistled. "You must be brilliant, Rachel. I can't imagine teaching children."

"I may not be here long if I can't get into the university," said Rachel.

Hetty saw a patron at the bar beckon her. As she stood up, she asked, "Jesse, will I be seeing you later?"

"No, I have other plans this evening."

"That's too bad. Nice meeting you, Rachel."

Rachel began to ask Jesse about Hetty when four British soldiers entered Tun's. A hush fell over the tavern, and conversation didn't resume until the soldiers were seated. Rachel and Jesse looked at each other, then down at their plates. Would the soldiers find the wagon?

~ CHAPTER 36 ~

Jesse and Rachel returned to the boardinghouse, both feeling reluctant to part again for another week. On the steps, he gave her a shy kiss on her cheek. She went inside to read the letter he had brought from her parents and Phebe, detailing more wedding plans. She was happy her sister had found a husband. In her room, she fell into bed to dream warm, delicious thoughts of Jesse.

At dawn, a sharp rapping at her door snapped her awake. "Miss Palsgrove!" yelled Andrew. "Your young man is here, and it's urgent he see you."

Alarmed, she said, "Tell him I'll be down in a minute. I need to dress." Andrew's feet pounded down the stairs.

Rachel dressed, pulled on her socks and shoes, and ran the brush through her hair. They had said their goodbyes last night, so she couldn't imagine why Jesse was here. Perhaps something had gone wrong.

She hurried down the steps. One glance at Jesse's ashen face told her the news was not good. He was biting his lower lip to the point of drawing blood.

"Jesse, what's happened?"

"Can we go to the barn to talk?" he whispered.

"Yes, we can go out the back door." She led him through the house and down the back steps to the barn. Missy nickered from her stall expectantly. "Let me give Missy her oats and hay so she won't bother us."

While Rachel measured the feed from the barrel and spread it in Missy's trough, Jesse pitched down hay from overhead. Rachel retrieved the water bucket from inside the stall, threw the stale water on the garden by the building's side, and refilled it with fresh water from the pump.

Jesse paced and wrung his hands while she finished hanging the bucket. She had never seen him this upset.

She laid her hand on his arm to comfort him. "Now, tell me what has happened."

"I was to deliver the cannon first thing this morning, but when I arrived at the stable, British soldiers were guarding the property. I peeked through the back gate, and the wagon isn't there."

"Are you sure it's gone?"

"Yes."

"What about your horses?"

"I couldn't see inside the barn, and Caleb wasn't there. What happened to my wagon? My only thought was to come here. If the soldiers found the cannon in the wagon, Caleb might be in big trouble. Maybe you can ask at his house to borrow a horse and buggy for the day and can find out something."

"Yes, it is a reasonable request for a Saturday."

They hurried to the livery, sticking to the alleyways rather than the main streets to avoid any soldiers who might be patrolling. When they arrived, Jesse found a hiding place across the street to observe the scene. Guards were posted in the front and back of the barn and shed but not at Caleb's house next door.

Rachel rapped lightly on the house door. No one answered, so she tapped a little louder. A small, thin woman with bags under her eyes and wild hair around her face cracked the door.

"Oh," she said. "I thought you might be more Redcoats. What do you want?"

"I was hoping to rent a carriage and horse today, but I was afraid to go past the soldiers. Might one be available?"

"No," the woman spat. "My husband was arrested in the middle of the night. They confiscated all the animals, carriages, and wagons."

"Arrested? Why?"

"They said they found contraband, so they declared him a traitor. He'll be lucky if he's not hanged. I don't know what I'm going to do with five children to feed and no husband nor business." She wailed and wrung her hands.

"Oh, dear, I'm sorry to hear that. Perhaps the authorities will find they have made a mistake."

"Even if they find the person responsible, I doubt they'll let Caleb go. It looks like he was involved since the goods were in his barn." Rachel heard an infant squalling inside.

"My apologies for bothering you."

The woman slammed the door.

She walked back to where Jesse was hiding.

"Yes, they discovered the contraband, and Caleb is in jail. The soldiers have taken everything. What are you going to do?"

"I need to tell my contact at the dock what happened. Then I'll go to the store and cancel Hopewell's order since I have no way to haul it back. Then, may I borrow Missy to ride to Hopewell to get another wagon and team?"

"Of course, you can take her. To save time, I can go to the warehouse while you go to the dock. We can meet back at Mrs. Graydon's."

"Yes, that will be quicker. I'll see you back there." He gave her a quick hug and ducked down the alley toward the waterfront.

He walked briskly but not so fast as to draw attention to himself. When he arrived opposite the pier, he saw Frederick and his men waiting for him at the shack. He darted across the road, narrowly missing several passing wagons. When Jesse reached the shack, eight

British Redcoats on horseback stormed the dock. With the ocean at their back, Frederick, his men, and Jesse had nowhere to run.

"You traitors must come with us!" the captain shouted as the soldiers took them prisoner. Outnumbered, Jesse, Frederick, and his crew were led away without a fight. As they marched away, the captain nodded to some men watching the action from a storefront across the street, where Edmund Morris stood.

Morris chuckled to himself. *I told you I'd get even, Rachel Palsgrove.*

~ CHAPTER 37 ~

Rachel sat in the parlor of the boardinghouse, waiting for Jesse's return. She thought about the discovery of the cannon and the possible implications. Would Caleb, the liveryman, tell the British he was not responsible and that Jesse was? Rachel didn't know whether Caleb's loyalty lay with the revolutionists or with the British. She couldn't fault him if he gave up Jesse; the wagon had been parked in his yard without his knowledge of its contents. But as far as the British knew, Caleb played a part in hiding and delivering the munitions. If Caleb chose to tell, the British could be seeking Jesse, too.

The hours dragged on, and Rachel alternately paced, peeked out the window, or looked down the street. She went to the barn several times to see if Jesse had arrived surreptitiously and might be hiding there. On one visit to the barn, Arthur Brown arrived by horseback from his weekly sales trip. He observed her checking up and down the alley.

"Hello, Rachel," he called. "You look worried. Is anything wrong?"

"I'm waiting for my friend to arrive, and he's late."

"Would this be your gentleman friend that my wife, Sarah, has been telling me about?"

"Yes, he's the one."

"I'm sure he'll be along soon. He probably is delayed somewhere. There was a bit of commotion on Water Street when I came through earlier. Perhaps he had to detour his wagon around that."

Rachel was startled by this news. "Yes, it seems several areas of the city have problems today."

Arthur unsaddled his horse, wiped down his tack, and curried the animal before leading it into its stall. After filling the water bucket, he climbed the ladder and threw down some hay from the loft. He jumped off the last two rungs to the ground as she again scanned the alley, and said, "Be patient. He wouldn't miss visiting a pretty girl like you."

"You're right, Mr. Brown. I'm no doubt worrying about nothing."

By suppertime, Rachel feared something terrible had happened to Jesse. Arthur Brown was correct. Jesse wouldn't miss being with her if he could help it.

She also worried about Jesse's team of horses. It would be a blow for him to lose them. They were like children to him—his family when he traveled.

Darkness fell, and Saturday ended with no word from Jesse. The weather was stormy with heavy rain and gusty winds on Sunday, but she wandered the streets looking for him despite the downpour. She came home wet and shivering, and quickly went to her room to change clothes.

Although she had no appetite, she needed to eat something; she couldn't search if she got sick. In the kitchen, she found a plate of cold chicken and a biscuit Mrs. Graydon had saved her from supper.

Rachel passed the parlor on her way back to her room. Sitting on the divan beside Arthur, Sarah asked, "You didn't have any luck finding him?"

"No, but I'll go again tomorrow. I'm tired, so I'm going to bed."

"He'll turn up. Don't worry."

Rachel trudged up the stairs. She felt a little better having eaten something, but her face in the mirror appeared haggard. She crawled into bed and tried to get warm, not even glancing at the enticing books on her bedside table.

Sunday's weather was dry but chilly. Rachel looked for Jesse most of the day but didn't find any sign of him. She despaired whether she would ever see him again. Her chest and head hurt from worry. Her raw eyes were puffy and red from crying.

Monday morning, she tidied herself the best she could and walked to the College. Her heart wasn't in it, but nothing further could be done at home. Perhaps if she got some good news about school, she would feel better.

When she arrived at the College office, Miss White ushered her into Provost Smith's office. Rachel tried to put on her best face so as not to betray her troubles.

Upon seeing her, the Provost pointed to a chair and finished writing on the papers at his desk. He placed his fountain pen in its stand, capped the ink bottle, and glanced up. "Miss Palsgrove, I see you're here early this morning. You'll be happy there's a decision about your admission. But before I tell you about that, I wonder if you had an opportunity to visit the Library this week?"

She brightened a bit at the thought of good news. "Yes, I visited The Library Company and found the place fascinating. Mr. Daymon was most accommodating. He showed me some of the curiosities and let me borrow two books. I appreciate your introduction to him."

"I'm glad you enjoyed your excursion. It's a wonderful place."

"So, what is the trustees' decision?"

Provost Smith sat tapping his fingertips together, contemplating his next comments. He looked directly at her. "They gave your application and letter of appeal much thought. Unfortunately, they decided they will not be able to grant you admission to the College."

Rachel's face fell, and tears flooded her eyes. This news was too much to bear! They had ruined her dreams, and she would have to return home. She pulled herself together enough to ask in a wavering voice, "Did they give any reasons why they are denying me?"

"Yes, they believe they are doing what is in *your* best interest. If they admit you, you would be the only woman in the College, and I'm sorry to say the male students would make you very uncomfortable.

They can be a rowdy group at times, and their manners and language don't always reflect the high ideals we are trying to foster here.

"And even though you have a solid foundation of academic studies, most of our pupils have attended the Academy first, many of them coming to us at nine years of age. They have been studying intently for three or four years with the sole goal of admittance to the College. An extensive examination process for applying to the College eliminates many students.

"Since our rigorous curriculum spans many years of advanced study, you couldn't keep pace. Unlike other institutions whose main aim is to train men for the clergy, we train young men for careers as future leaders of our communities and country. They will become mayors, judges, governors, surveyors, scientists. Only our less talented students will become schoolmasters to teach children reading, writing, arithmetic, and grammar. Our primary focus is not to instruct teachers, and therefore, your goals are not compatible with the objectives of the College."

Rachel felt her face turning red as her temperature rose in anger. She heard the Provost telling her she was not smart enough or the correct gender to be a student here. While some of what he said made sense, her fists tightened at his words, her tears dried up, and her jaw clenched. The trustees were not going to give her a chance.

She weighed her thoughts carefully. "So, if I understand you correctly, the College is not going to allow me to attend because I might be a distraction to the other students and because they think I am not intelligent enough to master the work," she said bitterly. "Will they not give me the entrance examination to test my qualifications?"

"No, I am sorry, Miss Palsgrove, they will not do that for the reasons just stated. The trustees *do* admire your desire to become a teacher, so they are offering you an alternative they think is more suitable to your situation."

"What would that be?"

"We have a school called the Charity School for Girls. Elizabeth Gardiner is the headmistress. The students are children of working people of our city who would not otherwise receive any education. The Charity School for Boys is located on the campus here, but the girls' school is in a house nearby. Miss Gardiner is an excellent teacher, and she can always use bright volunteers to help students having difficulty with their studies. You could learn a lot from her and gain valuable experience. Would you like to go to the School and investigate whether or not that placement would suit you?"

"I appreciate the offer, Provost Smith, but that position sounds greatly different from what I desired."

"You could also continue your studies at The Library Company while you are still in the city."

"Since the Trustees will not admit me to the College, I don't have any other options, and I would like to continue visiting the Library. But first, I want to observe the School and talk with Miss Gardiner."

"Excellent. Here is a letter of introduction." He handed her an envelope. "I've already talked with her about the possibility of your working there, and the idea has her approval if you decide you would like it. The school starts at eight in the morning. You are free to stay the entire day any day you choose."

She rose. "Thank you. I will."

By Thursday, Rachel was a wreck. She had not yet gone to the Charity School and was still smarting from the College rejection. She wouldn't be able to concentrate on school anyway until she found Jesse.

Her gut told her something terrible had befallen him. He would not leave the city without contacting her. She feared the worst; perhaps he'd been killed or was lying wounded somewhere, unable to reach out for help, bleeding slowly to death or sick with infection and fever. Maybe he was in hiding from the British, trying to elude capture, holed up in some barn or shack without water or food, waiting for an opportunity to escape. Perhaps, she would never learn his fate.

At mealtime, she pushed the morsels of food around on her plate. Dark circles ringed her eyes, her hair was uncombed, and her clothing soiled. By day, she roamed the city, searching alleyways and abandoned buildings, hoping to find someone who knew his whereabouts. But she dared not ask too many questions for fear the wrong people would become suspicious. By night, her dreams sought answers to where he might be, and she turned restlessly in her bed. How could she find him? Where hadn't she looked?

After another fruitless search around the city in the morning, Rachel returned to see Ben sitting on a wagon with a team of horses in front of Mrs. Graydon's house. He saw her coming and jumped down. She flew into his arms.

"Oh, Ben, I'm so relieved you're here." The tears made dirty rivulets down her face. "I don't know what happened to Jesse. I can't find him anywhere."

"That's why I came. When he didn't show up at Hopewell, we became alarmed and feared something had gone wrong. We had pig iron to bring to town, so I came to deliver it and ascertain the situation. When did you last see him?"

Rachel told him of the delivery's failure and the cannon, wagon, and horses' confiscation. "He went to tell Frederick at the dock what happened, and that was the last I saw him. I've looked everywhere."

Ben said, "I have some places I can ask, but I can't take you with me as they don't allow women. I already delivered the iron to Theuben, so the rest of the day is free. Wait here and get cleaned up. Have faith that we'll find him. I'll be back as soon as I can."

"Oh, Ben, I hope you locate him." Her face lit up.

He gave her another hug. "Now, go wash up, and don't worry."

Ben found Jesse at the Walnut Street Jail. An imposing limestone structure two stories high, it was topped by a red roof and cupola with a weather vane. An eight-foot wall surrounded the building. Steps led to the entrance, which was barred and guarded. The jail, located near the statehouse, was built in 1773, so it appeared new and clean from the outside. Inside was another story.

Ben went to the door where a guard asked what prisoner he wished to visit. He asked for Jesse, and a guard escorted him inside. Even before Ben stepped through the heavy wooden door, he smelled the stench of urine, feces, and unwashed bodies. His eyes began to water, and he started to cough. He pulled the handkerchief from his back pocket and held it over his nose.

They marched halfway down the hall, passing large cells of men on either side until the guard stopped outside a crowded cell housing twenty men. The jailer barked, "Jesse Quinter!" through the bars. Some of the prisoners lay on the floor, some leaned against the wall, and others paced back and forth. Most had matted hair, many were scratching themselves, some had open running sores on their face or hands, and all had a hollow, gaunt, desperate look about them. Their garments hung in rags, and some men were almost naked.

Ben caught sight of Jesse, shuffling across the cell, trying not to jostle his cellmates. Although Jesse had been in jail for less than a week, Ben could tell by looking at him that he had been through a lot. One sleeve gaped open where it joined his shirt at the shoulder, his pants showed stains at the knees and seat, and he had purple bruises on one side of his face. Despite his condition, Jesse smiled broadly.

"Ben! Am I glad to see you." He shook Ben's hand through the bars. "I didn't know if anyone would ever find me here."

"We became worried when you didn't return to Hopewell. What happened to you? You look terrible."

"When I went to the dock to tell them the packages had been confiscated, soldiers were waiting for me. I don't know how they knew where I would go. My contact and his men are in another cell down the hall. Caleb from the livery is somewhere here too. The Redcoats must have found the goods in the wagon parked at his stable. When I was brought here, several men who wanted my clothing tried to strip

DREAMS OF REVOLUTION 197

me. I fought them off, but not before they got in a few good punches and tore my shirt."

"Are you getting enough to eat? From the looks of most of these men, they are starving."

"Food rations come only Tuesday and Saturday, so I've had one meal so far. We're only allowed a cooking fire once a week, but usually, the victuals are gone before we get the fire going to cook them. The bread is moldy, and the vegetables are rotten. We're lucky for a small chunk of meat, and it's often rancid."

Ben noted, "But some of the men appear fairly well-fed. Is that because they're new here, like you, or do they have a means of procuring more food?"

"Some men's families deliver food to them or give them money to buy extra rations from the guards. The jailers also run a bar where prisoners can purchase spirits."

Ben emptied his pockets and came up with a few coins. "That's all the money on me, but I can bring more later." Ben looked around the cell. "Do you have water to drink?"

"Every morning, they take away all but one of the pots we eliminate in and return them full of water. That's all to drink unless you buy liquor."

"Have they charged you with anything? Do you have any idea when you might be released?"

"They told me I'm charged with treason and will be hanged."

Ben said, "Jesse, the British aren't hanging prisoners, even for serious crimes, because they don't want their captured officers to suffer the same fate. Your best chance of release is an exchange. When I return to Hopewell, Mr. Sterling can contact someone to set that up."

"I hope Sterling isn't in jeopardy for this," Jesse said. "He's probably the only one who can help me."

"I'm sure there are other people in the city we can turn to also," said Ben. "We weren't making our products just for ourselves."

"I suppose we won't be casting any more for a while?"

"No, not until this situation gets resolved. We'll stop those operations in the meantime."

"I'm sorry I brought them into the city when we were off schedule. It's all my fault."

"I don't blame you. After soldiers came to Hopewell, they were still undoubtedly watching us. We're so grateful to you and Rachel that the furnace wasn't caught making them."

"Speaking of Rachel, how is she? I'm sure she was worried sick when I didn't show up."

"Yes, she's been distraught, thinking the worst. She'll be relieved to learn you're alive even though you're here."

"They allow prisoners to receive letters, so I hope she can write to me. I can't write back, but you can tell her how I am. I don't want her coming here under any circumstances. She would worry too much if she saw me in these miserable conditions. She's got enough on her mind."

"I'll let her know where you are. She'll be relieved that you've been found alive."

~ CHAPTER 38 ~

George Coggins's behind ached from bouncing on the wagon seat over the icy, rutted road to Philadelphia. He had taken over Jesse's job making deliveries. Ben sat beside him to show him the route since George was unfamiliar with the city. He had a good idea why Jesse was in jail, and he hoped the job wouldn't land him in the same predicament.

After the long ride, they were finally entering Philadelphia. They had already stopped at Susanna's boarding school to deliver a letter from her parents and pick up one from her. George was amazed by the stately mansions and cobblestone streets. As they drew further into town, block after block of row houses lined both sides of the avenue. Ben instructed him to pull to the side of the road.

"This is where Rachel is staying," he said. "Get down, and I'll introduce you."

Coggins got down gingerly and rubbed his backside.

They knocked on the door, and Andrew let them in. He skipped upstairs to fetch Rachel.

"Rachel, this is George Coggins. He's taking over the deliveries."

"Hello, George. I didn't ever expect you here."

"You know each other?" asked Ben.

"We've met a time or two at the furnace," Rachel replied.

George appraised Rachel's looks approvingly. Since he had seen her last, she had matured into a young lady. She was wearing a perky print dress, and her brown hair was pulled up on her head in curls. It was quite a difference from the tomboy he knew back at the village.

"George, this is one of your regular stops in the city," Ben said. "You'll pick up any mail for home or the jail, your next stop."

Rachel fished two envelopes out of her dress pocket. "Here are two letters, one for my family and one for Jesse. Don't mix them up." She blushed.

"Let's go, George," said Ben. "There are several more stops to make today."

"Ben," said Rachel, "I'm planning on coming home at Christmas for the festivities."

"Your sister would be distraught if you didn't."

"My school closes for the holidays, so I won't miss anything here. George, don't forget to pick me up the week before Christmas. I wish Jesse could join us too. Maybe by then he'll be free."

"I'll be sure to take you," George said. "Good day."

Ben and George walked down the front steps and waved to Rachel as they pulled away.

A few blocks from the boardinghouse, the men stopped the wagon beside the jail. "Bring Rachel's letter and that package under the seat," said Ben.

Ben showed George the entrance gate and introduced him to the guard posted at the door. The jailer inspected their package and ran his hands over their bodies, searching for concealed weapons. As they entered the hall, George wrinkled his nose at the pungent stench. The bellowing of angry, upset voices assaulted his ears. When they reached Jesse's cell, he noticed the filthy, ragged condition of the prisoners' clothes and the skeletal look on their dirty faces.

The guard escorting them called Jesse's name, and Jesse shuffled over to the cell bars. Ben noted he looked even thinner and dirtier than before. The bruise on his face had turned yellow and green instead of the ugly dark purple it had been.

"Jesse, this is George Coggins. He's taking over the deliveries from Hopewell and will be visiting you every week. How are you doing?"

"I'm not too bad, considering, but I can't wait to get out of here. I caught a bad case of lice." He scratched his head. "But so does everyone here. Don't stand too close, or you'll regret it," he warned.

George handed him the package. Ben said, "Here's food from home." He dug into his pockets. "And here's some money. George, don't forget to give Jesse the letter."

"This is from Rachel." He handed over the envelope.

Jesse took it and smiled. "How is she doing, Ben?"

"She's sorry you're here, of course, but relieved you're alive. She was anxious about you."

Jesse looked at Ben. "Next time you see her, tell her I miss her a lot."

"We hope you soon can tell her that yourself."

"Is there any word regarding an exchange for me?"

"No, but Mr. Sterling is asking his contacts. Unfortunately, these things are difficult to arrange. It takes more time than we would like."

"They released Caleb yesterday. He was in the cell next to mine, and I saw them take him down the hall. They needed room for other prisoners and couldn't connect him with our delivery other than the goods were in his stable yard. He must have told them it was my wagon."

"Caleb's wife will be relieved. I hear he has five children to support," Ben said.

"Have you seen my team of horses?"

"No, there's no sign of them. No doubt, the Redcoats confiscated both the team and the wagon."

"The horses are probably hauling goods for the British," he lamented. "I hope I can get them back."

"First, we have to get you out of here. Then we can worry about them. Is there anything we can bring you next time? More food?"

"Yes, I'd rather you bring food from home, instead of money. Everything costs so much here that the shillings don't go far. A bit of pocket change is all I need. Anyone with much more than that is a target for thieves."

"Since the British occupied Philadelphia, the price of everything has increased tenfold. Mr. Sterling is trying to procure his staples from other cities such as Reading and Lancaster."

Jesse stepped closer and whispered, "Are you hauling those special items anymore?"

"No, we can't risk getting caught again. We're laying low."

George knew the 'special items' they were talking about and that the furnace had temporarily suspended their production. There was too great a risk currently with the British army being so close in Philadelphia. "I'm glad to hear I won't be hauling those," he said. "I certainly don't want to end up here."

"No, you don't," said Jesse. "Be careful."

~ CHAPTER 39 ~

After eating some of the food Ben brought, Jesse stowed the rest under his shirt, safe from prying eyes and thieving hands. It felt good to have a full stomach for a change. He would defend those scraps if he had to, but he had already earned a reputation as no pushover, so most men left him alone. Every day he saw prisoners who didn't have resources outside the jail succumb to the harsh conditions.

He slid down the wall to read Rachel's letter and raised the envelope to his nose, inhaling its gentle scent of lavender perfume. Closing his eyes, he conjured up an image of her smiling, beautiful face. How he missed her! Not seeing her hurt him more than being in jail. His whole being ached. He opened the envelope and pulled out the paper covered with her flowing handwriting. A small object fell into his lap. He read:

My dearest Jesse,

I was so thankful Ben discovered you! After searching everywhere you might be, dead or alive, fearing the worst, I thought my heart would break. While I am glad you were found, I am distressed about your imprisonment. Ben won't tell me about the conditions there, so I can only imagine how terrible they are. I know he wants to protect me, so I don't push him to tell me more. Keep safe. I'll send whatever food I can when I write each week.

You've probably found the small, smooth stone in the envelope. Save it in your pocket as a remembrance of me. I didn't want to send anything valuable for fear someone would rob you for it, but whenever you feel the stone, know that I am praying for your safe return.

Let me tell you about the weeks since I've seen you. I met with the Trustees at the college, and they denied me entrance. Their reasons do not seem valid to me, but I can understand them and have no other way of fighting them. Instead, they offered me a position at the Charity School for Girls. The headmistress, Miss Gardiner, is a knowledgeable, dedicated person, and she can certainly use my assistance. About twenty-five pupils attend, and many of them need extra help with their lessons. She guides me on methods to instruct these students, and I hope if I do an excellent job, she will give me a favorable reference. Meanwhile, I can borrow books from The Library Company and continue my education that way too.

So I am staying in Philadelphia, not only for the experience at the School but because you are here. I will not abandon you, and even though I can't visit, perhaps my letters can provide a little distraction from your dreary circumstances.

Ben tells me Mr. Sterling is working on an exchange for you. Be patient! I am confident he will find a way to secure your release.

Until then, be sure I am thinking about you always,

Love forever,

Rachel

Jesse reread the letter, then folded it into its envelope and put it in his pocket along with the pebble. Although he longed for her, his mood brightened. *I'll keep strong for you, Rachel, and see you soon.*

~ CHAPTER 40 ~

The din of high-pitched, shrieking, girls' voices reached Rachel's ears before she opened the door of the Charity School. As she stepped into the large room, some girls huddled in one corner crying, while others pranced around the room in glee. Rachel grabbed the ringleader's arm as she passed. Harriet was a big-boned, awkward girl with matted hair and tattered clothes. She let out a squeal when she realized she was caught. Rachel steered her to a chair at the side of the room and commanded her to sit. The bully meekly complied, hoping to avoid harsher punishment by pretending innocence now. Harriet's accomplices scattered in their attempt to disassociate themselves from the situation. Sally, Harriet's second-in-command, approached the crying girls and attempted to soothe their tears, but they only wailed louder when she came near. Rachel ordered Sally to another chair across the room from Harriet and then went to the whimpering girls.

Kneeling beside one of her favorite students, Rachel dabbed Caty's tears with her handkerchief and anchored a stray dark curl behind the small child's ear. Great sobs wracked her tiny body, but with Rachel's gentle, soothing circles on her back, and the threat of imminent danger thwarted, her weeping lessened.

"Tell me what happened, Caty," prodded Rachel.

Caty glanced at the other tearful girls, then scrutinized the faces of the bullies across the room, assessing whether snitching on them would have repercussions later.

Miss Gardiner burst into the room. "Rachel, what's going on here? I heard the commotion all the way in the kitchen. Violet fell and skinned her knee, and while I was cleaning her wound, chaos broke loose in here." She looked sternly around the room. "I'm ashamed of you girls." Her gaze fell on the two seated girls.

"When I arrived, Miss Gardiner, a group led by those two were terrorizing the others. I caught them red-handed," Rachel said.

"Harriet and Sally, I'll be telling your mothers. And Harriet, since this is the second time this week you've been disobedient, you'll receive two whacks immediately."

A gasp escaped from the girls' mouths. Everyone feared the paddle more than anything, especially when wielded by the headmistress. Miss Gardiner was as round as she was tall, and her massive weight could deliver a wallop. The crying girls dried their tears and felt vindicated for the hair-pulling and pinching they had endured. After receiving a paddling, most students never made such a severe transgression again.

"Now, let's put these chairs back in order and start the morning lesson. Rachel, take over today's grammar assignment while I deal with Harriet."

With much screeching of wooden chair legs on the hardwood floor, everyone pushed their seats back into neat rows while Miss Gardiner towed Harriet to her office. Soon two loud whacks reverberated through the room, and the girls raised their heads from their slates to listen for an ensuing wail, but there was none. They quickly stared at the floor as Harriet entered the room, rubbed her bruised backside, and sat down in her place. Rachel noticed a single tear streaking down her face. *She's a tough one,* she thought. *I'll try to make friends with her. What can her home life be like if she acts this way in school?*

After lunch, the students went outside to play in the schoolyard. "Harriet, can you stay behind a minute, please?" Rachel asked.

Harriet sighed and pursed her lips in defiance while the others left.

"I want to talk to you about this morning."

"Me already got me whacks and 'twill be more from Mum when Miss Gardiner tells tales. What more do ye want?"

"First, you need to speak respectfully to me. I'm not trying to get you in more trouble. I'm trying to understand why you always have these problems. I want to find a way to help."

"I hate this school," Harriet proclaimed. "The other girls don't like me and won't let me play with them. They call me names, so I pinch 'em and pull their hair."

"Why do you think they don't like you?"

"My clothes aren't nice, and I don't have dolls and things like they do. They don't want to share, and I don't know how to play the silly games they like."

"Perhaps we can find some ways for you to fit in better."

"They still wouldn't like me. There's nothing ye can do. Ye can't make 'em like me."

"No, but maybe we can change a few things that will make them want to be your friend."

"Like what?"

"When you pinch them and pull their hair, they become afraid of being near you. You wouldn't want a friend who hurts you, would you?"

"No, but I only do that when they're mean to me."

"Do they hit you?"

"No, but they call me mean names."

"What kind of names?"

"They say 'hairy hatchet face,' and I don't like that."

"Yes, no one would like to be called that. But I'll tell you a secret." Rachel pulled Harriet closer. "Girls called me names when I was younger too."

Harriet's mouth fell open. "I don't believe ye–ye're just telling me that. What did they call ye?"

"They called me 'horse face' because my face is long and narrow and not too attractive. Also, I look homely next to my beautiful sister. I know names can hurt."

"Ye look pretty to me, Miss Palsgrove," Harriet exclaimed.

Rachel smiled. "The point is, children often make up names from the sound of your name or about your looks. When you do something back to them, you get in trouble. Do you think that sometimes happens?"

"Well, I'm the one in trouble all the time. They're never punished."

"I'll talk to them about name calling, but if they do call you a name, can you ignore them?"

"Why would I do that?" Harriet asked.

"So you won't get in trouble."

"Oh, I see," Harriet said. "Then they might get the paddle for calling me names."

"That's right. Can you try?"

"'Twill be hard, but I'll try," Harriet replied.

"Good girl, Harriet. You can do it. You're very smart, you know."

Harriet beamed.

"Now, another question. Do you have another dress at home?"

"I have me Sunday one, but Mum doesn't let me wear it to school."

"I'll talk to your mother, and if you can wear something else to school for a day or two, I can mend your school dress. I bet your mother doesn't have much time to sew after tending all your brothers and sisters."

"T'would be kind of ye, Miss, but me mum would be insulted if you asked to mend my dress."

"Perhaps I can think of some words to convince her differently. Maybe if she thought it would help you make friends at school, I'll bet she would be willing. I'm sure she doesn't like hearing from Miss Gardiner so often."

"Fer sure, miss."

"Also, I'd like to fix your hair a little. Would you and your mother mind if I cut it a bit to remove some of the knots? It would be easier to comb. I could show you how."

"Miss Palsgrove, we nay have a comb, nor a pair of scissors."

"I could trim it one day after school, and I'll bring a brush we can keep here. If you come in a bit early every day, we would comb it before school."

"That'd be grand, Miss. Can I go out to play now?"

"Yes, Harriet. I'll talk to your mother and tell her our plan. You can go out now."

Harriet smiled shyly and scampered out the door. Rachel smiled to herself. *Perhaps I've made a new friend.*

~ CHAPTER 41 ~

A few weeks later, as the wagon topped the rise overlooking Hopewell, Rachel gasped as she scanned the beautiful sight below. "Pull up here," she asked, touching George's hand on the reins.

A serene mantle of sparkling white snow bathed the village, and bare tree branches covered with shimmering, crystal cloaks reached high into the clear, cloudless, blue sky. Tiny columns of white smoke twisted skyward from house chimneys and the furnace. The only sound was the stamping and puffing of the woolly horses anxious to go home.

"Isn't it gorgeous?" Rachel sighed.

"I guess it would appear beautiful to someone who hasn't been home in a while," George responded. He sat a minute, as restless as the animals, then clucked to the team, and the wagon lurched down the road.

As they neared the barn, the horses whinnied to their friends in the field. "They're glad to be home too," she said.

When they pulled up to the Palsgroves' house, a broad smile crossed Rachel's face as Nick came tumbling out to welcome her. She jumped from the wagon seat, grabbed and hugged him, then danced around in the snow as her mother and Phebe laughed from the doorway. George turned the wagon to take the team to the barn.

"Come in, come in, Rachel. It's cold out there," her mother called, pulling her shawl closer around her. "Nick, you don't have your coat. Come in and get warm."

Inside the cottage, the smell of freshly baked bread and beef stew made Rachel realize how much she missed home and her mother's cooking. She embraced Phebe and her mother, and thought her mother was never going to let her go.

"We've yearned for you so much. I hope you're home to stay."

"I can't, Mother, but I'll be here for a week or so. I wouldn't miss Phebe's wedding for anything."

Nick approached, balancing a plate of gingersnaps. "Want a cookie? I helped bake them this morning."

Rachel tousled his hair, picked the largest one, and took a bite. "These are the best gingersnaps ever."

"Yes, they are, aren't they?" her little brother boasted. "I've eaten three so far."

"And if you gorge on any more," their mother admonished, "you won't eat any supper. Speaking of which, I better stir the stew and set the table."

"I'll help you, Mother," Rachel said.

"No, no, you go in and visit with Phebe. Nick and I can manage everything here."

Rachel savored her cookie as she walked into the living room. She plopped into the chair opposite her sister, who had taken up her sewing.

"Was it a tiring trip from the city? It seems like such a long way."

"Yes, the winter cold freezes you to your bones. The summer is not so bad. Is Father at the furnace?"

"Yes, he'll be home after the evening pour. We'll dine then. Are you hungry?"

"This cookie will hold me. How are your wedding plans coming? There's not much time left before the big day."

Phebe lowered her work into her lap. "Almost everything is in place for the ceremony. My dress is nearly finished, and Mother made a new frock for you, but don't tell her I told you—I think she wants it to be a surprise. I'm so joyful! I wish you could find someone here to make you happy so you don't go back to Philadelphia. We all miss you so."

"Will the wedding be here at the house?"

"No, Mr. and Mrs. Sterling insisted we have the ceremony at the Big House with the festivities in the basement dining hall. Nate and I declared our intentions the last three Sunday church services and no one objected, so we obtained our certificate to marry. Reverend Clements will pronounce our vows."

"Where will you live afterward?"

"We're renting old widow Anderson's house down the lane. You know she died last month of pneumonia?"

"No, I'm sorry about her. She was always so sweet to us, particularly Nick. I think he reminded her of her son, who passed young."

"Mother and I are cleaning the house out, and it's looking quaint. We were fortunate to buy most of the widow's furniture, bed and settee, and kitchen items. It has everything we'll need."

Rachel grew pensive. She gazed at her sister's pretty, radiant face, her lustrous, red hair with its tightly wound curls, and heard the lilt in her voice. Phebe looked healthier than she had in a long time. "It sounds like everything is well-arranged. You'll make a beautiful bride."

Phebe took up her sewing again. "Are you seeing anyone special in Philadelphia?"

"I have a friend I'm fond of, but I'm busy helping at the Charity School and working on my studies at night. Miss Gardiner, the headmistress, gives me readings about children's education and then quizzes me on them. I also borrow books from The Library Company on various subjects. They're fascinating."

Phebe was not about to be sidetracked into talking about school. "So who is this person you're 'fond of'?" she laughed. "Do I know him?"

Rachel's cheeks got hot, and her face turned red. "You know him. Jesse Quinter, who drove the team into Philadelphia from the furnace before George Coggins got the job."

"The man who's in jail? He's the one who came home with you when the soldiers came, right?"

"In his wagon, the British discovered those things the furnace has been making. Mr. Sterling is trying to arrange an exchange for him. We hope he's out soon."

"It seems you're more serious about him than you like to admit," Phebe teased. "I suppose you can't go see him."

"No, but I write letters that George delivers each week. I'm glad I can't see Jesse. If I saw firsthand the conditions, I would feel worse for him than I already do. I can hardly imagine how bad it is."

"We all will be a lot happier when Jesse's free." She studied Rachel's face.

"You seem tired, Rachel. Why don't you go upstairs and lie down? Your old bed is freshly made. We'll call you when Father gets home."

"That's a good idea," said Rachel, stifling a yawn. "I'm more exhausted than I thought."

~ CHAPTER 42 ~

On Christmas morning, the sky was gray and cold. Snow appeared imminent. At the Palsgrove house, Phebe sewed the last tiny stitches in the hem of her wedding dress. It was good luck for the bride to sew the final stitches on the day of the wedding. She would get dressed at the Big House so she could make a grand entrance.

Upstairs in her room, Rachel smoothed her new dress of light blue silk over her petticoat. It was not fussy with lace and embroidery. Although she preferred breeches to dresses, at least she felt comfortable in this one. She had seen her sister's fancy gown and was grateful for her frock's simplicity. She wished Jesse could see her in it. He would have liked the way the blue matched her eyes and contrasted with her dark hair.

Mother, Father, and Nick, dressed in their Sunday best, waited in the kitchen for Rachel and Phebe to finish their final preparations. They were relieved to have the ceremony and festivities at the Big House since their home would not have accommodated the entire village, and the church was a long way down the road.

"Let's go, girls," Martha crowed. "We don't want the guests to arrive before us."

Rachel bounded down the steps and watched Phebe roll her creation in a clean, white sheet.

"I'm ready, Mother," Phebe announced.

As the family pulled the cottage door shut behind them, puffy fat flakes of snow began to fall, blanketing the lane to the Big House.

Martha said, "Phebe, let me take the dress while you and Rachel hold your father's arms, so you don't slip." Nick carried a small burlap bag containing the girls' dainty shoes and last-minute accessories such as jewelry and hair bows. The snow fog enveloped them in a peaceful white cocoon. Silently the little procession made its way up the slope to the Big House's wide porch. Inside, the ladies climbed the stairs to a bedroom where Phebe would dress.

The bride stepped into the mound of fabric then pulled it up over her shoulders. Her sister laced up the back while Martha placed a gold bracelet on Phebe's wrist, piled her hair high, and positioned her veil.

Phebe's gown was magnificent, crafted of beautiful dove-white silk, embellished down the front with dainty flowers and flowing vines embroidered in gold thread. Rows of gathered material stood at the edge of the V-shaped bodice around the low but modest neckline, and the skirt below her waist flared out in graceful cascades of white. The sleeves ended at mid-arm, then puffed out in drapes of delicate lace. Rachel marveled at the time she spent creating such a masterpiece.

"You are the most beautiful bride ever," Rachel said, surveying the complete package. "You'll take Nate's breath away."

Martha agreed, her eyes misting as she surveyed her gorgeous daughter. "Rachel," she sighed, "we're finished here. Please go downstairs, and when they're ready, come get us."

In the Big House's living room, the younger guests lined the walls while old folks teetered on chairs and benches in the center of the room. Stragglers spilled over into the adjacent parlor. Everyone wore their Sunday clothes, and the maids heaped their heavy winter coats on an upstairs bed. Even Isaac, the charcoal wagon driver, looked freshly scrubbed and hardly recognizable from his usual dirty appearance. Fires blazed in the grates, and candles in wall sconces twinkled.

Phebe descended the staircase, and the ladies oohed and aahed at the sight of her. Nate wore a navy blue velvet frock coat boasting brass buttons down the front with a flapped pocket on each hip and matching navy blue breeches. His vest buttoned over a white shirt whose top tail encircled his neck while white cuffs peeked out below the sleeves of his coat. His eyes, smiling and confident, drank in the beauty of his lovely bride.

With bridesmaid Rachel and Nate's groomsman at their sides, the handsome couple faced Reverend Clements so both rooms could observe the ceremony. The minister raised his arm for silence, then joined the bride and groom's hands. After a brief exchange of vows, the wedding was official. A cheer went up from the guests, and Martha and Margaret Zerbey, the groom's adoptive mother, dabbed their tears of joy with their handkerchiefs. After a round of congratulations, Mrs. Sterling rang a tiny, tinkling bell. "Everyone, please go downstairs to the dining hall, and help yourselves to the refreshments."

The hungry crowd surged toward the stairs, the children skipping ahead to be first in line. The villagers were always grateful for free food and liquor and a chance to socialize, especially on a snowy holiday when many workers had the day off. The furnace still operated with a skeleton crew, but those men working now would join the festivities when the shift changed later.

Platters of steaming venison, beef, and ham were the main courses, with various vegetables as side dishes. The children drank milk or sweet cider, and the adults chose beer, hard cider, or rum, with many women preferring a toddy of sweetened rum and water. For dessert, everyone enjoyed peach or apple pie with a spoonful of whipped cream on top, but the unmarried girls and women received a slice of the special bride's pie. Soon Rachel squealed when she discovered the hidden lump of nutmeg, which predicted she would be the next to marry. *Does this portend my future,* she wondered.

After the meal, the men pushed the tables and benches against the walls. The musicians began tuning their instruments.

The first number was the dance of the bridal crown. Phebe stood in the center of a circle of married women, and a wreath of evergreens and berries woven together with ribbon adorned her head. While the ladies danced around the bride, Nate skirted the outside, and the women locked their arms tightly together. He attempted to sneak under, but they ducked low; he tried pulling their arms apart, but they were as entwined as a vine that clings to a tree. As the music's pace quickened and the toddies began to take effect, the ladies' grip loosened. Nate broke through and snatched the crown from Phebe's head. It tore into pieces, scattering on the floor, and maidens scrambled to take home a portion that also predicted a marriage within the year.

Then adult dancers formed two facing lines to dance the ever-popular reel, but the youngsters began to run around, pushing and teasing each other. Mrs. Sterling suggested the children go outside to play in the snow, an idea that met with the adults' approval. The youngsters were eager to play in this first deep snowfall of the year. Nick begged to go too, and Martha let him. The newly fallen snow would be perfect for sledding down the hill behind the Big House. A maid took the children upstairs to find their coats.

The band played for hours, taking short breaks for food and libations, and the tunes got more raucous as time went on. Phebe only danced slow ones due to her heart condition, but the mothers and Rachel danced with Nate several times. The bride and groom received a steady stream of well-wishers at their table, which kept them busy.

The afternoon drew late, and darkness began to fall on the short December day. The children were rounded up and brought in to warm up before their trek home with their parents. They were hungry and thirsty from their day outside and tired from their play in the brisk air.

While the children settled, Martha approached her husband. "Lewis, where's Nick? Do you see him?"

"No, I don't see him. I also haven't seen Nick's friend, Timothy. Rachel, ask the maid if she saw them when she was bringing in the others."

Rachel returned with the maid, looking worried. "Mrs. Palsgrove," she said, "I saw Nick and Timothy sliding down the hill by the furnace earlier in the day. But they didn't come in with the others."

Lewis and Timothy's father gathered some men together. "We'll go out and look for them, Martha. Don't worry. They probably went exploring and didn't hear the maid call. We'll be back soon."

The men retrieved their coats from upstairs and hurried out to search for the boys. Rachel tried to comfort her mother, whose hands were trembling. "I'm sure they'll find them. You know how curious Nick is. They just wandered out of earshot."

The party continued. Men who had been working at the furnace came in and ate while the night shift workers left. But Lewis and the searchers did not return.

As time passed, everyone quieted with worry. Martha mindlessly twisted her handkerchief in her lap. The sun had set, and darkness closed in.

"Here they come!" someone shouted. The men entered the hall with snow heaped on their hats and covering their shoulders.

Martha rushed to her husband's side. Lewis said, "After searching everywhere close to the house, barns, and furnace, we could find no sign of them. We need more men and torches."

"Aren't there any footprints in the snow?" someone asked.

"No. It's still snowing, so any tracks that might have been are covered."

Small groups of men took off in different directions with lit torches, soon gone from sight into the darkness. While the ladies and children waited, the band played comforting old favorites. Everyone tried to keep their spirits up, but the group became more discouraged as time dragged on. Finally, some of the mothers approached the Palsgroves and Timothy's mother.

"We're sorry they're not back, but we're sure they'll find the boys. Since it's late, we're going to take our children home, but we'll be praying for you." They hugged the families, gathered their coats from upstairs, and left. As the crowd dwindled, the band stopped playing and began packing their instruments. The maids removed the leftovers. Sick with worry, the two families huddled together. Reverend Clements sat with them, and they prayed for the boys' safe return.

After several hours, the men returned empty-handed. Martha approached Lewis, her eyes pleading. "I'm sorry, Mother. We couldn't find them. Our torches burned out, and we looked everywhere. There's nothing more we can do tonight. We'll go back out in the morning."

Martha wailed, and her knees buckled, but Lewis caught her before she slumped to the floor. "We must hope for the best, Mother. Be strong. It's in God's hands for now."

~ CHAPTER 43 ~

Dearest Jesse,

I am so sorry I could not write or send food last week. I hope you didn't worry or suffer too much. You are in my thoughts every second of every hour.

A tragedy befell my family. On the beautiful day of my sister's wedding, my younger brother, Nick, and his friend, Timothy, went out to play with the other children in the snow and were lost. The village men didn't find their frozen bodies until the next morning. The boys had wandered to the pond way behind the barn and had fallen through the thin ice. Since the water is shallow, no more than three feet in most places, they climbed out and began to make their way home. But the cold water and winter weather took a toll on them, and they lay down to rest. The falling snow covered them, and they were already gone by the time they were missed. I hope God took them quickly and they didn't suffer.

Nick's funeral was at our house. Mother, Phebe, and I washed his pale body, and Mother made a long white shroud of linen for him. Timothy's father and Father made the two pine coffins, and my brother's body rested in our drawing room on the dining table moved from the kitchen. We draped the pictures and mirror on the walls with white cloths. Everyone in Hopewell came to pay their respects and joined the procession to the graveyard beside the church. Reverend Clements said kind words over the boys, and a few friends offered poignant memories of the boys' antics.

After the men lowered their caskets into the ground, a mound of straw on top deadened the horrible sound of the hard, cold clods of dirt shoveled over them.

Leftover food and drink from the wedding feast fed the mourners at our house. Poor Jack, the cat, hid under the bed upstairs most of the time, and when he did come down, he mewed piteously looking for his buddy Nick.

Mother, in particular, takes Nick's death to heart, and it saddens me to think I'll never see his innocent, freckled face again or hear his sweet laughter. We will forever remember Phebe's joyous wedding day with sorrow.

I am grateful to return to my students at school to provide a diversion and remind me that life continues no matter how heavy our hearts.

My studies beckon now, as my absence has put me far behind. At least I can now sleep from exhaustion, although my appearance would shock you. My eyes are puffy and red with dark circles under them, and my usual joyous manner is weary and slow.

I pray for your release daily and trust the Lord keeps you well during your confinement. Pray for me too, that God will lift my crushing heartache.

With my love,

Rachel

Jesse reread the letter and swiped his eyes with his dirty sleeve. He didn't know Nick well, but could picture the impish boy around the dinner table. When he didn't hear from Rachel, he had been feeling sorry for himself, thinking she had abandoned him. His hunger had subsided into a dull constant ache. His ribs and hip bones felt sharp under his shabby, disgustingly filthy clothes. He stank and itched all over. Her letters and food were the highlight of his week and kept him going. He realized that Rachel would never abandon him. She was a loyal and faithful friend, and only her own tragedies would keep her away. Thinking of her, he fingered the stone in his pocket she had sent him. He folded the paper and tucked it into his shirt, along with her other letters.

He'd had no further word of his exchange and felt discouraged about ever getting out of jail. Rumors swirled around the prison that release would come soon. It was hard to stay hopeful, but hope was all they had.

~ CHAPTER 44 ~

Rachel bent over her writing table in her room at Mrs. Graydon's, creating math problems to be presented to her students the next day on the blackboard. Her quill scribbled over the paper with frequent dips into the inkpot. She rolled the blotter over the numbers as she wrote so they wouldn't smear.

She created problems for each level of pupils which they would copy onto their slates. Her direct work with the girls would center on the middle-level group. The more advanced students would help the younger ones.

With math finished, she decided which concepts to present for the grammar lesson. As she pondered and made notes, her pen dragged slower and slower, her eyes gradually closed, and her head drooped. Soon she slipped down in her chair with her head slumped on her arm. The quill clattered to the floor, but she was oblivious in her slumber.

A sharp rap at the door roused her, and she glanced around, startled. The knock came again, and she rose to answer. "Who is it?" she asked.

"Sarah."

Rachel opened the door, and Sarah entered with two steaming mugs of tea. "I thought you could use a cup. You looked so tired at dinner."

"Thank you, Sarah." Rachel gratefully took the tea from her and placed it on the table. She rubbed her fists in her eyes. "I must have dozed off," she said, picking up the pen from the floor and capping the bottle of ink. "Come talk a little while we drink the tea."

Sarah seated herself and gazed at the plethora of paperwork and books on the table. "Oh, you're working. I won't stay long." Rachel pushed aside some papers for more room.

"Since I've returned from Hopewell, I'm always behind. I can't seem to catch up. I'm so exhausted."

"Your brother's death was a terrible shock. Are you sleeping at night?"

"I'm sleeping better, but it's not a peaceful, relaxing sleep. It's more a restless tossing."

"I noticed you didn't eat much tonight. Perhaps I should have brought two muffins along with the tea."

"I haven't much appetite lately. Even the thought of most food makes me nauseous." She sipped the tea. "This tastes delightful though."

"Has your mother written since you've been back?"

"I had a letter yesterday. She tries to sound cheerful as she tells me the news at Hopewell, but she's very melancholy. She not only lost Nick, but Phebe is gone from the house as well as me. I'm sure she was secretly hoping I would stay home and not return to Philadelphia, but I can't do that. I committed to the School, and I need to be near Jesse, even if I can't see him."

"Any word on an exchange for him?" Sarah enquired.

"Not yet, but Mr. Sterling, Hopewell's ironmaster, told me when I was home that he has appealed to General Washington to find a British officer to trade for him."

"I'm puzzled why they are still holding him," Sarah pried. "I heard they released Caleb, the stable owner, weeks ago, so why aren't they letting Jesse go? Why is he more valuable than Caleb, and why is he worth the exchange of an officer? No insult intended," her friend quickly added.

Rachel dodged Sarah's questions and wondered how she knew or cared about Caleb. "I don't know." She shook her head. "I don't understand all the politics. But I hope his release happens soon. I miss him so much."

"May I ask you a personal question? You don't need to answer if you choose not to."

"I'll reply if I can. We are such good friends."

"Do you think there's another reason you're tired and feel sick besides Nick's death?"

"What do you mean?" Rachel asked.

"Well, I will try to put this delicately, have your courses changed?"

"My courses? I'm a little irregular, that's all. There are many stresses in my life lately. School, Phebe's wedding, Jesse's imprisonment, Nick's accident. I'm sure they'll straighten out soon."

"Lots of young women get interested in a beau, and before long, there's a wedding."

Rachel blushed. "Jesse and I are close friends, but nothing like that."

"I thought by the way you talk about him that there might be more than friendship. I'm sorry if I embarrassed you."

"You didn't. I'm just sad and overly sensitive."

"Arthur and I have wanted a child since we married, but so far, nothing has happened. Every month I pray to be blessed."

"Perhaps his frequent traveling causes the problem," Rachel suggested.

"That might be the reason." Sarah slurped the last of her tea from the saucer, then rose and held out her hand for Rachel's cup. "I'll take these to the kitchen so you can resume your studies."

Rachel escorted Sarah to the door. "Thanks again for the tea. I might have slept all night on my desk if you hadn't come."

"If you need anything else or want to talk, you know where to find me. Goodnight, Rachel, take care."

Rachel shut the door and sat down to think. A feeling of dread came over her. What if Sarah was right and she *was* expecting a baby? That would be a disaster. If she was, there could only be one father— Edmund Morris. Bile rose in her throat at the thought of bearing his child. She ran to the bowl beside the pitcher on the dresser and vomited her tea. Breathless, she sat back down, a sour taste in her mouth. After a few minutes, when she felt better, she rinsed her mouth with water from the pitcher, then pulled on her robe and slipped her feet into her shoes for her trip to the privy to dispose of the mess.

On the way outside, dark thoughts tumbled through her mind. If she were with child, what would happen to her school position? As an unmarried woman in a family way, she knew Miss Gardiner wouldn't allow her to continue to teach, and going home would bring shame to her family. She could try to get rid of it, but how? And if she had a baby, how would she raise a child by herself?

Back in her room, she was too disturbed to continue working. She snuffed out the candle, lay on her bed, and cried herself to sleep.

~ CHAPTER 45 ~

Sarah hurried out of the house soon after Rachel left for School. She walked several blocks, turned into a narrow street beside an empty-looking storefront, and then ducked down the alley running behind. Opening the store's unlocked rear door, she banged on the sturdy inner door. It opened a crack.

"Who's there?" barked a deep, gruff voice.

"Sarah Brown. I have information for you."

"Come in."

Edmund Morris opened the door wider, and Sarah entered. The large room was empty except for a table in the center covered with writing materials.

"I wondered when you might come to tell me about Miss Palsgrove's activities. Ever since I left the boardinghouse, I expected to see you regularly. Surely you or your husband have something to report about her or the colonists' movements. I thought you were eager for the money we're offering for information."

"The boardinghouse has been quiet until lately, and Arthur hasn't learned anything new on his travels."

"Be brief; I have much work to do," he hissed.

"Rachel told me Hopewell's ironmaster, Mr. Sterling, contacted General Washington to attempt the trade of a British officer for Jesse Quinter."

Morris's eyes narrowed. "I would be quite displeased if Mr. Quinter were released. I had hoped he would stay in jail forever since it took us so long to catch him transporting the cannons."

"Arthur and I like him where he is now too. We don't want him nosing around and discovering that Roy, who robbed him at Berry's, is my husband, Arthur Brown. As long as he's in jail, he won't see Arthur's horse in the barn or accidentally run into him in town. We also love having that handsome team of cream horses you gave us after his capture."

"Those horses were a well-deserved reward for the information you gave me about the wagon being stuck overnight in the city. His arrest restored my credibility with my superiors after the farce at the furnace. I trust the animals are well-hidden? They are extremely recognizable. You need to be careful."

"Yes, Roy stabled them far outside town where a farmer is putting them to good use in barter for their upkeep. They will be invaluable when we move West. Roy fawns over them every time he visits."

"Was that all you wished to tell me?" He fumbled in his purse for some coins.

"No, there's more. Rachel, I believe, is with child. She denies having had relations with Quinter, but the signs of a child are there. Extreme fatigue, nausea, sleeplessness. She's dragging around like she's carrying a fifty-pound sack of grain on her back. Those symptoms can't be entirely due to grief about the death of her brother, which happened several weeks ago."

"That news also interests me," Morris replied. "She thwarted our plans to surprise Hopewell making contraband, so I welcome any complications to her situation. You earned a little extra today, Mrs. Dickenson, or should I say, Mrs. Brown?" He counted more money into her hand.

As she turned to leave, Morris instructed, "Let me know when you confirm any of this information."

On her way home, Sarah bought several custard tarts from the bakery with her informant's money. Chuckling to herself, she thought, *I'll share these with my benefactor, Rachel, when I get home.*

Morris sat at the table, his thoughts churning. An exchange for Quinter would ruin all the hard work that went into his capture. Captain André, of the British army, now had confirmation that Hopewell was helping the colonists, and that Morris's information was correct. As for Rachel, most young ladies he bedded didn't make a fuss, let alone track him down and assault him. Now she might be bearing the fruit of his seed. She wouldn't be the first in this town. Maybe a child will send her packing back to Hopewell with her reputation in shambles. Yes, Jesse Quinter must stay in prison, so he can't come to her rescue.

~ CHAPTER 46 ~

Jesse, Charles, and a handful of other prisoners plotted among themselves. "When the guards come to bring firewood for the stove today, their hands will be full. That would be a good time to overpower them. We can use the logs as weapons."

Charles said, "Two men each can take down the guards with the wood, but the other guard watching them has a gun. Who volunteers to rush him? They are liable to be shot."

The men were silent. After a few moments, Jesse said, "I'll rush him. I'm probably stronger than most of you here. If I can get the gun away from him, we can get past the guard at the gate. But he might also have a knife on him."

"Jesse, I can help you," said Charles. The other men paired up to tackle the other guards. Men in the cell who were too weak to take an active part in the plan would help however they could.

When they heard movement in the hall, the prisoners positioned themselves between the stove in the center of the room and the cell door. "Here they come," whispered Charles. "Get ready."

The guard with the musket unlocked the cell, and the other guards lugging the firewood entered, followed by the armed guard. When they were all inside, he relocked the door and stood near it. As the men neared the stove, a prisoner in the corner shouted, "Hey, you!" The soldiers looked in his direction, and the prisoners jumped them from behind. The logs crashed to the ground, and the prisoners scrambled to pick them up to use as clubs.

Meanwhile, Jesse and Charles rushed the armed guard. Jesse grabbed the gun and wrestled for its control. After a brief struggle, the gun went off with a roar, but the bullet slammed harmlessly into the ceiling of the cell. The now useless musket clattered to the ground. Before Jesse could search for a knife and get the door key out of the guard's pocket, other Redcoats came running down the hall with their guns drawn.

"Stop, or we'll shoot," they commanded, and the men ceased struggling. One guard dragged an injured comrade, who had been hit on the head with a log, to the front of the cell. All the guards backed out. The commander of the guards appeared at the door.

"Who's responsible for this?" The prisoners were stone-faced. The armed guard said, "Quinter tried to take my gun."

The commander roared, "Quinter, come to the front."

Jesse squared his shoulders and strode to the cell door, where the guards pulled him out.

"I'll show you men what happens to prisoners who assault my guards." He nodded to the soldiers holding Jesse. "Take him away."

Hours later, the cell door opened, and the guards tossed Jesse's battered body into the cell. He was unconscious, and his face was bloody. Both eyes were black, and his lower lip was split. "Here's what happens when prisoners don't behave," the guard said as he relocked the cell.

~ CHAPTER 47 ~

Phebe trudged through the newly fallen snow to her parents' house. She flipped up the collar of her coat to cover her numb ears. The temperatures this winter had been brutal. The cold never seemed to end. She wiggled her fingers in her gloves, trying to start the circulation. She would like to be sitting by a warm fire in her cabin but inside felt barely warmer than outside. Nate never seemed to chop enough firewood for her to make it through the week while he was gone, and she always tried to save enough back, so when he came home, the cabin would be warm. Feeling chilled to the bone most of the time, she put on woolen sweaters, a hat, heavy hose, sometimes even mittens, but she still couldn't get warm. Even sitting in the wing chair close to the fire, with a blanket covering her, provided no relief. Nighttime was the only time she felt halfway comfortable after the bed warmer filled with the remaining hot embers from the fire had warmed the sheets, and she could lay under the down comforter. But she couldn't stay in bed all day.

With the firewood almost gone, the cabin became unbearable, and she braved the weather to go to her parents' house to warm up. If she asked for some wood, she knew they'd provide, but her pride wouldn't let her. She was now a married woman, and a new couple should be self-reliant. To ask for help would make Nate feel like he wasn't a good provider, and he would be upset. It was ironic that Nate was cutting wood all day, but the cabin never seemed to have enough.

Arriving at her destination, she rapped lightly at the door and let herself in. The warmth of the room flooded over her like a mid-summer day. Her mother came from the parlor and welcomed her with a hug.

"Let's take your coat off," her mother said, helping her hang it on the peg by the door. "Why, you're shivering. Come by the fire and warm up."

Phebe sat close to the roaring blaze, vigorously rubbing her hands together, holding her fingers out to the delicious warmth, savoring the feeling. Suddenly, a gurgling cough erupted from her lips, and she drew a soiled handkerchief from her sleeve to cover her mouth.

"Are you all right, dear? You've got dark circles under your eyes, and it looks like you're losing weight. Your dress is hanging on you. Now that you're in a family way, you need to eat more."

"I'm better now that I'm warming up. The weather is so cold outside. Will winter ever be over?" Phebe smiled weakly at her mother.

"Let me make you some peppermint tea. It will soothe your throat."

When her mother returned from the kitchen, Jack, the cat, lay curled in Phebe's lap, purring and kneading her arm.

"I've missed you so much, Phebe," her mother exclaimed, stopping to squeeze her daughter's bony shoulder and to stroke Jack's head before handing the cup to her daughter.

"Me, too," Phebe sighed.

"It must be lonely at the cabin when Nate is gone. How are you occupying your time?"

"I'm sewing some and cooking, of course. I started reading some of Rachel's books too."

"Keep yourself busy if you can."

"I do, Mother, but I spend a lot of time staring into space thinking about Nick. Whenever I come here, I expect to see him around every corner and to hear his laugh. How do you stand it?" Tears ran down her face.

Martha pulled her chair next to Phebe's and took her cold hands in hers. "I have my days of melancholy when I think of Nick, but I remind myself that his passing is God's will and that my son is in Heaven. We must accept what we can't change and live our lives until we meet him again when our time on earth is over."

Phebe stroked the cat, who raised his chin to be scratched. "I wish I could be more like this cat. He accepts each day as it comes and is happy."

"Jack misses Nick too. Sometimes he searches the house howling for him. He feels the loss at that moment but doesn't dwell on it. Perhaps you need a cat at your house to give you comfort."

"Oh, Nate hates cats. He would never let me have one. They don't seem to like him much either. At least Jack doesn't."

"Animals can sense when they're not wanted. They don't understand people's words, but they know what's in their hearts. Now, show me your sewing project."

Phebe drew a blue calico dress from her kit.

"It's pretty," Martha said, examining it.

"My heart's not in this sewing. I don't desire a new dress, and it keeps me occupied, but I don't seem to be able to sew with my usual precise, tiny stitches."

"Perhaps you need better light at your cabin."

"Yes, that might be the cause. I'll try to sew near the window during the day rather than at night."

"Would you be interested in making some men's shirts for pay instead of your dress? I received an order for three that I don't know how I'll ever finish, and the men would like them right away."

Phebe brightened. She could earn some money to buy more firewood and also feel more useful. "Yes, that would be wonderful."

Opening her sewing basket, Martha said, "Let me show you the pattern and materials, and you can choose which you would prefer."

~ CHAPTER 48 ~

Rachel struggled to saddle Missy for her ride to visit Susanna at Mrs. Levering's School.

"Stand still, Missy," she admonished the palomino, who danced around at the end of her tether. "Oh, it's not your fault you're so full of energy. You're bored being cooped up so much this winter, just like I am." Rachel fought to position the saddle and tighten the girth.

"Can I hold her head while you mount?" offered Arthur Brown, Sarah's husband, who had arrived last night from his weekly travels, and was now mucking out his horse's stall.

"I would appreciate your help," replied Rachel. "She'll probably take off running as soon as I place my foot in the stirrup."

Rachel led the mare from the barn to the mounting stump, and Arthur held the horse's head as Rachel hopped on. She spun the horse in tight circles until Missy settled down and would respond to the pressure on the reins.

"Thanks for your help," she called to Arthur.

"Enjoy your ride." Arthur hefted the muck basket and spilled its contents on the manure pile behind the barn.

Rachel slow-trotted Missy until the animal warmed up, then allowed her to break into a controlled canter. Soon they were several miles from town on a beautiful tree-lined stretch of road. The day was sunny but cold. A light dusting of snow lay on the ground and sparkled on the tree limbs above. From what Jesse had told her, the city didn't usually get as much snow as Hopewell. The fresh air felt exhilarating, clearing her head of worries and reminding her of the glories of nature. Friendly people waved as she passed them. Everyone hoped spring would come soon and relieve the frigid weather.

After a while, Rachel reluctantly turned Missy back toward town and Mrs. Levering's School. She hadn't visited Susanna in several weeks per her request but needed to put in an appearance so she could honestly report something back to her parents. Her last letter detailed her brief meeting with Susanna at the glass armonica concert and that she was enjoying socializing with her friends.

She walked the horse the last half mile to let her cool down so the sweat wouldn't freeze on her while she popped in to see her former classmate. Rachel tied Missy at the iron horse-head hitching post and strode up the walk, which had been sprinkled with cinders to cover any slippery spots. The maid who answered her knock recognized Rachel from previous visits and asked her to wait in the vestibule while she fetched Susanna.

After a few minutes, Susanna primly descended the wide staircase. Her tight-waisted dress accentuated her hips, and lacy petticoats peeked out from the bottom hem. She wore carefully applied makeup that reddened her cheeks and lips. A beauty spot dotted the left corner of her mouth.

"Hello, Rachel," she cooed in a soft, pearly voice. "I didn't expect you again, but I'm glad you've come. I have some news."

Susanna's friendly reception and appearance surprised Rachel.

"First," continued Susanna, "I hear your sister's wedding was a success, but the untimely death of your brother greatly saddened me. My condolences."

Rachel lowered her head. "Thank you for your kind thoughts. His death was a shock to us all on what had been a joyful day." After a moment, she said, "Everyone asked for you at Christmas and expressed surprise you weren't there."

"There were so many exciting events in the city during the holidays that I decided to stay here."

"The weather has been dreadful for traveling too. What is your news?"

"I have not made a formal announcement yet, but I'm planning to be married this summer. You don't know him. He's a barrister from England. We've been courting awhile now, and he has asked for my hand."

"I've met a few people here. Perhaps I do know him. What's his name?"

"His name is Edmund Morris. He's very handsome and sophisticated and quite a catch. All the young ladies here flirt shamelessly with him, but I'm the lucky one he chose. Have you made his acquaintance?"

Rachel's breath caught in her throat as she tried to control her surprise. "No, no, I don't think I've had that pleasure." Her voice quavered. "Congratulations."

"I'm telling you now because after our marriage, your services won't be necessary. I hope the news gives you enough time to finish your educational endeavors."

"That should be sufficient time for me to decide what course I'll take. I appreciate the notice. Are your parents delighted at the happy surprise?"

"My fiancé hasn't yet made the trip to see Papa. Edmund's so busy here. I'm not sure when he'll go. Perhaps he'll write a letter instead. So, please keep the engagement a secret."

"I'll be sure not to tell anyone." Rachel moved toward the door. "I best be going before the sun goes down. Again, you have my congratulations."

"Thank you, Rachel, and good day." Susanna closed the heavy door behind her. With her thoughts spinning, Rachel mounted Missy to return home.

~ CHAPTER 49 ~

"My God, Jesse, what happened to you?" exclaimed George when he visited the jail.

Charles helped Jesse stand and limp his way to the front of the cell. Jesse's lips and eyes were swollen, and his face was shades of yellows and greens. He peered at George through half-closed lids. "I ran into some bad luck," he said.

Charles said, "Our revolt was unsuccessful, and Jesse got the worst of the punishment. Everyone in the cell is on half rations."

"Don't tell Rachel," Jesse said. "She worries too much as it is."

George handed the parcel of food he had brought through the cell bars. "Charles," said Jesse, "take some of this for yourself and give a bite to each of the other men."

"What about you?" asked Charles.

"My jaw hurts so much, I can't eat. Give it to them."

George said, "I also brought your winter coat." He stuffed it through the bars.

Jesse slowly put the coat on. His stiff arms had trouble sliding into the sleeves. He tried to smile through his cracked lips as he savored the feel of the cloth. "That feels better than you can imagine. My clothes are threadbare with holes on the elbows and knees. I'm grateful you brought it."

"Here's a letter from Rachel too. Do you want me to read it to you?"

"No, I'll manage. There might be some personal lines in there. I'll be better next week when you come."

George turned and left. Charles steered Jesse over to the wall, where the battered man slunk down to a sitting position on the floor. Holding the letter to his nose, he inhaled the scent of her perfume. With shaky hands, he opened the envelope.

Dearest Jesse,

Here's hoping this writing finds you reasonably well. I'm sending you as much food as possible, but unfortunately, it is less than usual because the Patriots' blockade causes great shortages and very dear prices. As long as they control Fort Mifflin on Mud Island and Fort Mercer on the New Jersey side of the Delaware River, supplies will be scarce. I hope George brought some food from home to help make up the difference.

At my sister's wedding, Mr. Sterling told me how guilty he feels about putting you at such risk even though you willingly volunteered for the job. I hope General Washington, encamped at Valley Forge, has not forgotten you. He and his men endure horrific conditions this winter too. Major General Baron Von Steuben has arrived to train the soldiers for when the fighting resumes after the weather abates. Perhaps I should not have written that if this message falls into the wrong hands, but I wish to give you hope the war will be over soon.

Other, more disturbing news transpired. Susanna tells me she is engaged to be married, but her fiancé is the person with whom I had difficulty earlier. He is incredibly devious and probably thinks he can get information from her, but I doubt her father confides much about his activities. I couldn't warn her as I am sure she would not believe me, and she might ask questions I did not want to answer.

Unfortunately, my situation might jeopardize my place at the Charity School. I pray it is not true, and I won't burden you with conjecture until I know it is a fact. But if you think back to the previous difficulty I referenced, you may guess at my dilemma.

Some happy news from home is that my sister, Phebe, is expecting. My parents are delighted at the prospect of a grandchild and are distracted from dwelling on poor Nick's fate. But they are worried about Phebe's heart. They will leave that in God's hands.

I continue to go weekly to The Library Company and explore more treasures there, such as fossils and specimens of exotic creatures, and to borrow additional books you would find dry as dust. But I would gladly trade all the books in the world to be with you again.

My heart aches to see your handsome face, to hear your kind voice, and to feel your strong arms around me. I'm counting the days until we can be together again. I send you,

All my love,

Rachel

Upon reading the last paragraph, Jesse felt the sting of tears in his eyes and longing in his soul. *I'm so glad she can't see my sorry state.*

Yes, the blockade has also affected the prison's food supply. Our meager rations come just twice a week, usually consisting of a half-pound of biscuit with a smattering of pork, one cup of peas, one-half gill of rice, and half an ounce of butter, and now, because of our actions, we only get half of that.

Rereading the letter, Jesse balled his fists in anger on learning of Rachel's possible predicament. He thought, *she's worked so hard to get her placement at the Charity School.* Susanna's engagement with Morris was a problem too. How much did she know? She might be falling into the same trap Rachel did and reveal information that could jeopardize the furnace. Her father's life might be in danger if he was labeled a traitor to the crown. Rachel could try to warn her, but he knew Susanna wouldn't listen. He hoped Rachel would write Mr. Sterling with the information since she had previously saved the furnace from being discovered, but would it be in time? Jesse felt so helpless. He couldn't do anything in jail except try to survive. It was hard to keep one's sanity and hope, yet he vowed to stay strong. But could he hold on?

CHAPTER 50

Rachel toiled by candlelight at the table in her room, making notes from a book she had borrowed from the Library. She ate little at dinner, and now her stomach was rumbling. A tear dropped on her writing, smearing the ink into illegibility. In a fury of despair, she crumpled the paper into a ball and threw it at the door.

A soft knock startled her, and she dabbed her eyes with her handkerchief. "Who's there?"

"Sarah. May I come in?"

"Yes, the door is unlocked."

Sarah entered carrying a salver of two steaming cups of tea and some biscuits smeared with butter and strawberry preserves.

"You hardly ate anything tonight. Can you use some refreshment?"

Rachel gratefully accepted the tray. "What would I do without you, Sarah? You're always looking after me."

"That's what friends do," she replied, as she sat on the bed. Rachel cradled the cup in her hands, feeling its warmth loosening her cramped fingers. They took a bite of biscuit and sipped the tea. "You seemed distracted at supper. Is something bothering you?"

"Oh, Sarah, I got dismissed from school today."

Sarah gasped. "Why would they do that?"

"Before class started, Miss Gardiner, the headmistress, noticed my dresses are tight and asked if I was expecting. I couldn't lie to her. She said my condition was disgraceful, and I was a poor example for the students and would have to go." Tears streamed down Rachel's face. "I wasn't even allowed to say goodbye to them."

"So, you know for sure you're in a family way?"

"I can't deny it further. My courses haven't come, and even though I'm no longer sick in the morning, my stomach flutters. It wakes me up at night sometimes."

"That's the baby moving," squealed Sarah. She clasped Rachel's hands in delight. "How exciting!"

"I don't feel excited. I can't be having a child. It's ruined all my plans," Rachel said in despair.

"But a baby is a gift from God." Her gentle hug showed her pleasure.

"This 'gift' has gotten me ousted from teaching, and I can't wear most of my clothes or ride my horse. Mrs. Graydon will probably soon ask me to leave once she learns of my condition. If I have to go home, I'll disgrace my family."

"All those things are temporary inconveniences and indignities. You're not the first young lady in this predicament, and you won't be the last. Your family will love you, no matter what. Mrs. Graydon won't ask you to leave. She needs the money, and there aren't any prospective boarders in town. Everyone who could leave has already fled."

"I'm so alone. I don't know what to do."

"First, you are not alone. I'm here. Let's think about your choices logically rather than emotionally. Can you go home to deliver the baby?"

"I don't want to go back to Hopewell. I've worked so hard to get here, and I want to finish my education at the Charity School. I can't leave Jesse either."

"Think of the situation as a brief setback. Perhaps you can continue school just a few months later."

"I can't take an infant to school with me."

244 LINDA J. COLLINS

"Again, you forget, you have my help. I could watch the baby while you are there."

"Oh, I couldn't impose on you like that," protested Rachel.

"You wouldn't be imposing. There's little to do all day with Arthur gone all week, and I love children. I would be delighted to assist you. Remember, too, Jesse will be out of prison soon to support you."

"Sarah, you are so optimistic. Maybe I *can* get through this with your help."

"What will you do while you're waiting for the baby's arrival?"

"I can still borrow books from The Library Company. I would like that."

"See, you'll still be continuing your studies."

"How will I explain a baby to my parents? They'll be so ashamed of me. I'll be an outcast in Hopewell."

"Tell them the truth. They've been in love and will understand. I think you underestimate the power grandchildren have over grandparents. As for everyone else, do you care what they think? Their opinions never stopped you before," she joked.

Rachel finished her tea. "You might be right. You are such a good friend to me." She hugged her. "I am encouraged by your kind words."

"Why don't you write a letter to Jesse and then plan your day for tomorrow? Do you have any money to shop for more suitable clothes?"

"I have some saved from my allowance from Mr. Sterling."

"Good! We'll go shopping tomorrow. If you keep busy, the time will pass much faster. Look forward to bringing a new life into the world. Families are our most precious possession."

Sarah gathered the dirty dishes, and Rachel pulled open the door.

"I'll see you in the morning," Sarah chirped, smiling.

~ CHAPTER 51 ~

The following Tuesday, Rachel met Francis Daymon, the librarian, in front of Carpenter's Hall at the usual time. After ascending the stairs and entering the library, they settled themselves at a table. Mr. Damon opened his ledger to record the return of her books.

"Before I choose books today, sir, I need to ask a favor," said Rachel.

"How can I help you, Miss Palsgrove?"

"Could I possibly borrow some additional books in the weeks to come instead of my normal two?"

"I would not mind for you to take additional books each week, Mademoiselle. You have been very careful with those you have borrowed so far and have returned them faithfully. But," he paused, "how will you have time to read more with your school obligations?"

"Unfortunately, for now, I am no longer attending school." She bowed her head and raised her clasped hands to her chin, wrestling with how much information she could share with him. She looked up. Her eyes met his soft, gentle gaze, which made her decision. "You see," she hesitated, then plunged on despite her embarrassment, "I am expecting a child and cannot be at school during this time. I hope to resume my studies after the baby is born. Meanwhile, I need something to occupy my extra time."

"I see," he replied, shifting uneasily in his chair. "And what has happened with your friend in jail? Will he be released soon?"

246 LINDA J. COLLINS

"We are not sure when Jesse will come home. An exchange for him seems to be taking forever."

"I presume Jesse is sympathetic to the revolution?"

"Yes, as am I. I regret not being able to help more."

The librarian sat quietly, deep in thought, his fingertips bouncing gently against each other. Finally, he spoke. "What risks are you willing to take to help him and the Patriots' cause?"

"I'm not sure what you mean, but I would do anything to help. I love him. Hopewell's future depends on the revolution's success. Mr. Sterling, Hopewell's ironmaster, would be ruined if his activities were discovered, and my entire community would perish without the furnace."

"I am good friends with Dr. Franklin, who is aware of Mr. Sterling's activities."

"So, you know why Jesse is in jail?" she asked, shocked.

"Yes, I do. Dr. Franklin is involved with many aspects of the revolution."

Rachel sat back in her chair, surprised. She didn't know Dr. Franklin was associated with the Patriots' cause. "Oh, I'm speechless. I knew he was associated with many institutions in the city."

"Yes, Dr. Franklin wants the revolution to succeed."

"Have you heard of the Committee?" he asked.

"Committee?"

"The Committee of Secret Correspondence."

"No, what is that?"

"General Washington needs information to plan his next moves when the war resumes after winter. He wants to know about British troop movement in the city, the number of ships in the harbor, and British soldiers' health and morale. The Committee has contacts who gather such information. Would you like to be a part of the Committee?"

"You mean, spy on the British?"

"Yes. The Tories have people all over the city and countryside sharing crucial information with the enemy, and we must do the same if we are to win the war."

"Yes, I have already had an unpleasant encounter with one of their spies, Edmund Morris."

"Yes, Monsieur Morris is a problem for us."

"Susanna Sterling is engaged to marry him."

"*Mon Dieu!* I hope she does not give away any information."

"I can't warn her as she won't believe me."

"Perhaps, I can get a message to Monsieur Sterling."

"I hope you can. I don't want to put such information in a letter for fear it might be intercepted."

"You see the importance of transmitting information that will help our cause. As a woman, particularly one expecting a child, you may be able to go places and see things our male contacts cannot witness. However, this endeavor is not without risks. Patriots caught spying may be hung."

She gasped. "Can you tell me how the process works before I make a decision? How is the information transmitted?"

"Dr. Franklin directs the Committee work. We give messages to an intermediary, Major John Clark. The notes are written in code in invisible ink and contained in an ordinary-looking letter. If intercepted by the enemy, they appear innocent. So far, none of our contacts has been found out. Do you think you are willing to take the risk?"

"Yes, certainly. How do I get started?" Her eyes shone with eagerness.

"What kind of information do you think you could obtain?"

"Hopewell ships their pig iron to England through a man at the docks named Theuben Bailey. Jesse knows him well, but I have never met him. I believe he is sympathetic to our cause. He could apprise me of British activity in the harbor and relay conversations he hears from sailors. While visiting him, I could count ships and note any activity. And if I visit Jesse in prison, he could tell me what he hears from newly captured men and the guards. I could also frequent Tun Tavern in hopes of overhearing British soldiers' conversations."

"All that information would be beneficial. See what you can gather this week, and when we meet next, I'll show you the code."

"I can't wait to start helping."

"But miss, do not reveal any of this to anyone, except Mr. Bailey and Mr. Quinter. You don't know whom you can trust in this city."

~ CHAPTER 52 ~

George Coggins arrived at Mrs. Graydon's on Thursday with Hopewell's letters and to pick up messages and food for Jesse in the jail.

"George, I am so glad you're here," exclaimed Rachel, as she opened the door.

"Here's your letter from home." He handed her the envelope, then spied her empty hands. "Where's your parcel for Jesse? Hurry up. I'm behind schedule."

"There's been a change in plans. I'm going with you to the jail today."

"That's a bad idea, Rachel. I know you miss him, but the jail is a disgusting place. Jesse wouldn't want you to see him in his current condition. You should stay here."

"No, George. I'm going," she insisted. "I have important things to discuss with him. I'm going to the docks too. Don't try to stop me."

George shook his head. "Neither place is appropriate for a female," he argued. "I won't be responsible if something happens to you. Your parents and Jesse would never forgive me. Now, give me your package. I have to go."

"Do you never see women in the jail or at the docks?" Her stern voice rose in volume.

He pursed his lips. "I don't know why you're so stubborn. I said you can't go, and that's that."

"Answer my question, George Coggins! You know you see ladies in those places. You will not tell me what I can and cannot do."

"Yes, I see women there occasionally. But they are females of questionable character, not ladies, if you know what I mean. Not someone like you."

"That settles it. I'm going. I'll get my shawl and basket. Wait here."

George huffed in anger and muttered to himself while Rachel darted up the stairs. When she reappeared, she was wearing a plain dark dress she usually wore around the house and had twisted her hair into a bun on the back of her head covered by a matching bonnet.

When they arrived at the jail, the guards laughed and eyed Rachel. "I see you brought some help today, George. We're glad to see a pretty face instead of your ugly one. You can leave her here while you go see the prisoner." The guards winked at each other.

Rachel snapped, "Get used to seeing me here, gentlemen, as I will be a regular. I will not be staying with you men here, either, as I intend to visit the prisoner too."

"Oh, she's a feisty one, George. You better watch out," they jeered.

"Give me your basket, miss," the guard ordered.

Rachel handed him the basket. He rooted through it and removed some of the oatmeal cookies she had baked for Jesse.

"Hey," she said, "what are you doing?"

The guard began munching a cookie and passed one to his cohort. He handed the basket back.

"You won't need all of these, ma'am. Consider them the price of admission. Go on down and see the prisoner. George knows the way."

The visitors went down the hall past several cells of men. Rachel held her perfumed hanky to her nose, partially to hide her face but mainly to mask the horrible odor of unwashed bodies, urine, feces, and rotting flesh. It was the same smell she experienced every week at the Library when she passed through the lobby of wounded British soldiers, but it was ten times worse here. Men hung onto the bars of the cells begging visitors for any scrap of food they may have. When she ignored them, they made rude remarks and catcalls. George stopped at the next cell, but there was no sign of Jesse.

She looked over a sea of heads packed together. Some men stood while others sat on the floor. Forty or fifty men crowded together. Straw littered the floor in a crude attempt to insulate the men from the biting cold. "Is this his cell?" she asked.

"Yes, but I don't see him. Usually, he stands near the front because he knows it's my day to visit."

Fearing the worst, they scanned the filthy faces.

George shouted, "Jesse Quinter!"

A ragged, emaciated skeleton in tattered clothes rose and worked its way to the front. Rachel gasped at his smudged face and scraggly beard. His hair was oily and matted. Only his eyes looked like the Jesse of old she knew and loved. She stifled a moan rising in her throat.

"Rachel, why are you here?"

"I made George bring me. I couldn't stay away any longer."

"I hate for you to see me looking so poorly, but I'm glad you've come." He searched his pocket and held up the stone. "I never thought such a simple thing could give me courage and hope. I'm so grateful you sent it with your wonderful letters."

She touched his hand. "Don't ever forget I'm always thinking of you."

Jesse eyed her basket. "I hope there's food in there. I'm famished."

"Yes, yes." She pulled out a sandwich wrapped in newspaper.

He took it with trembling fingers and began to eat.

She was aware other prisoners and George were listening to their conversation. "Jesse, can we work our way over to the corner? I have something personal to tell you."

He offered scraps of his sandwich to prisoners in the way, enticing them to move. George didn't follow.

In the corner, she leaned in close and whispered, "I'm working with Mr. Daymon at The Library Company to provide information to General Washington. If you can get details from any prisoners, particularly newly captured ones, I can relay the information. Our efforts may help the war end sooner."

Jesse looked into her eyes and furrowed his brow. "That's very noble of you, but aren't you taking a big risk? The British don't look kindly upon spies. I think it's too dangerous."

"Mr. Daymon says they seldom suspect women of passing information. Everything will be in code, so even if the message is intercepted, no one will be able to read it. The Charity School has dismissed me due to my condition, so I have extra time on my hands. I want to help the cause."

"I'm helpless to forbid you from doing it, and I know how much you want to help. Just be very careful. I'll try to get information, but it'll be a joy to see you every week even if I don't. That alone will help me survive."

A guard appeared at the end of the hall and shouted, "Visitors must go now."

Rachel gave Jesse the remaining food in her basket, which he stuffed in his shirt, and pressed a letter into his hand. "I love you," she whispered, leaning in close to kiss his cheek as George pulled her away.

"I'll be anxiously awaiting your arrival."

George and Rachel hurried out. "Next stop is the docks," she announced, as George shook his head.

A few blocks later, their wagon arrived at the waterfront. "Have you met Theuben Bailey?" George asked.

"No, I haven't."

They strode down the dock and entered the shanty where Theuben sat poring over a ledger book. He looked up as they approached. "Hello, George. I'm glad you're here to save me from reconciling these accounts. I never was particularly adept at math, so these figures have me baffled. Who have you brought with you?"

"This is Rachel Palsgrove. She's from Hopewell and is Jesse Quinter's friend."

"How do you do, Rachel?" Theuben stood and tipped his sailor's cap.

"I'm fine, Mr. Bailey. Please sit down."

"Is Jesse being released soon? I sure miss his face around here. No offense, George."

"Perhaps Rachel could help with your accounts, Theuben. She's a school teacher."

Rachel said, "I'm not a teacher yet. I'm still learning, but I'm good at math. I could help you if you like."

"That's a very generous offer, but I need lots of help almost every day. I'm sure you wouldn't want to come here that often."

"On the contrary, Mr. Bailey, I would like to be here every day," she replied.

"Surely you have better things to do."

"I am temporarily on leave from my teaching assignment, so I'm available. Could I speak to you privately?"

George said, "I'll start unloading the wagon."

"I'll send the boys to help." The men strode out the door. Theuben's shrill whistle brought his deckhands running. "Help George unload his iron, boys," he commanded.

"Yes, sir." They headed down the dock toward the wagon.

Back inside, Theuben offered a chair to Rachel. "Now, what did you want to speak to me about?"

She hesitated, not quite sure where to begin. "I don't know how to ask this, Mr. Bailey..."

"Call me Theuben."

"Theuben, I know you ship Hopewell's pig iron to England."

"Yes, that's correct. For several years."

"Are you aware Hopewell makes iron items for sale here in the colonies?"

"I suspected as much since the wagon from Hopewell usually isn't empty when it leaves here."

"You know that's against the Iron Act, don't you? I know you haven't turned Hopewell in to the authorities."

"I think the Iron Act is an insane way to keep the colonies dependent on England. Why mandate shipping iron across the ocean only to employ British ironworkers to make products to be shipped back here? It's a waste of time, and the finished goods can be made here just as well and cost less."

"So, if the colonies win their freedom from Britain, and Hopewell no longer ships pigs, won't your business be ruined?"

"There will always be trade of some kind. Britain will still need iron to make goods for its people. Is Jesse in prison because Hopewell is selling iron products? George never told me why he was arrested."

"Hopewell was making cannon and balls for the colonies' navy, and Jesse was caught delivering them. That's why he's in jail."

Theuben whistled. "That's a serious crime. I'm surprised he hasn't been hanged."

"They are trying to arrange his exchange for a captured British officer. I've just seen him in the jail, and conditions there are horrendous."

"I've heard it's a nasty place. But why are you telling me this?"

"You seem to be sympathetic to the Patriots' cause, and I need your help. General Washington wants information to help him win the war."

"What kind of information?"

"He needs to know what British ships are coming into Philadelphia, how many soldiers are on them, and where they are going. Surely you see and hear things."

"What's your role in this?"

"I'm a contact to gather information."

"But how does the information get to Washington?"

"My messages will be written in code and given to another person who will pass them to the General. The sooner the war is won, the sooner we can reclaim Philadelphia. Can I count on your help?"

Theuben scratched his head. "That's a risky undertaking, but yes, I'll help. I have some observations now if you want them."

"What are they?"

"Just today, I noticed two British ships come into port. Each one carried about two hundred men who headed to the British camp outside town. The soldiers all wore uniforms and had muskets. They were well-organized."

"Yes, that's the sort of thing the General would want to know. I'll send the message to him."

"You won't use my name in any way, will you?"

"It'll be our secret. Now, show me your ledgers."

~ CHAPTER 53 ~

The following week Rachel and Francis Daymon met again at the Library.

"Were you able to learn anything about our enemy this week, Miss Palsgrove?"

"Theuben Bailey at the docks told me some British ships arrived carrying soldiers. I'll see Jesse later this week, and I may have news from him too."

"Very good." He placed a book, several sheets of writing paper, a quill pen and ink, a bottle containing a cloudy white liquid, and a small paintbrush on the table before her. "You begin by writing a letter to an imaginary romantic friend. Pick a common male name."

"How about Henry?"

"Now, write a few lines to your imaginary friend, Henry, but when you write, space each line far apart so you can later add an invisible line in between."

"The invisible lines will contain my secret message?"

"Yes. Now write a few lines with your pen and ink. Your friend will be a person with whom you are secretly involved because you will be hiding the letters in a hollow tree for the messenger to retrieve."

She began writing, and after six lines, the librarian stopped her. "That is enough writing for our demonstration today." He pushed the book toward her.

Opening the cover, she said, "*Gulliver's Travels* by Jonathan Swift. I've read this book already."

"Yes, it is entertaining reading, but it serves another purpose. It's the codebook for your secret messages."

"How is this a codebook?"

"I'll show you. First, write your message to the General on another paper, keeping it as brief as possible. Let's choose a simple one for practice. For example, 'Two ships arrived in harbor.' Look anywhere in the book for the number two. Can you find it?"

She leafed through the book slowly. "Here's one." She pointed to it.

"Notice the page number it is on."

"Page 26."

"So the code line will start with the number 26. Next, count the words from the beginning of the page down to and including the word two. By the way, you don't have to find a grammatically correct word 'two' or the number 2. It could be the word 'to'."

"The number four could be spelled 'for'?"

"Yes, that's right."

She counted carefully with her finger. "It's the eleventh word on the page."

"So, your next number will be eleven. Now you have 2611. Next, look for the word ships or ship or boat. That will be more difficult to find. As you become more familiar with the book, you will learn where certain words are located but don't repeatedly use the same ones. Try to vary the pages you choose. In the beginning, it will be very time-consuming to find the words."

"I have lots of spare time," she replied, as she thumbed through the book. After a few minutes, she exclaimed, "Here is the word 'ship'." She counted. "Page 47, word 56."

"So now you have 26114756. You continue with your message, stringing the numbers together."

"But how will the receiver decipher the numbers?"

258 LINDA J. COLLINS

"They have a copy of the same book and will apply the procedure in reverse. It is sometimes challenging to get the right page and word, but they are very skilled at figuring it out. For example, the start of your message could be page two, word 61, which would be incorrect."

"How do I write the numbers so they appear invisible, but the receiver can read them?"

He handed her a bottle and a brush. "The bottle contains a solution of half baking soda and half water. Dip your brush and write your numbers between the lines of your letter."

She did as instructed. "But I can see the number I wrote. They are not invisible at all."

"Wave the paper around until the liquid dries."

After a few minutes of waving, she looked again at the paper. "The writing is gone, but how does the receiver make it reappear?"

He pushed the burning oil lamp close to her. "Bring the paper close to the hot part of a lamp or a candle flame. Be careful not to set it on fire, but let it get hot."

Upon heating the paper, the baking soda scorched, and the numbers reappeared. "It's like magic," she marveled.

"Your contact gets the paper, heats it, and deciphers the code. The message is then passed on to General Washington. Even if the letter falls into the wrong hands and the numbers appear, they will be meaningless without the book. Make sure you destroy your message with the numbers when you are finished."

She sat back in her chair and looked at him. "It's an ingenious system."

"We try to make sure the enemy does not discover our contacts and their messages. Now, pack up these items, and we'll find a hollow tree in the park where you can hide the letters."

"How will the receiver know when there will be a note in the tree? He won't want to be constantly checking it."

"Do you hang your laundry on the line in the back of your boardinghouse?"

"Yes," she answered, puzzled.

"What day is wash day?"

"Monday, usually."

"Do you have any colored handkerchiefs?"

"I have some lavender ones."

"If you have any messages, put them in the tree on Sunday. On Monday, hang a lavender handkerchief first on your line, closest to the house. That will signal the receiver to look in the tree for your note."

She finished packing the items in her bag.

"Let's go find that tree," he said.

~ CHAPTER 54 ~

All day Saturday, Rachel labored at her desk writing code. She had revisited Jesse in jail, and he told her one of the newly captured prisoners had witnessed British troops raiding hay and livestock from citizens on the outskirts of the city. He reported that when the soldiers are on these foraging raids, the city is low on defenses.

She had composed her romantic letter to 'Henry' when a knock startled her, and Sarah burst in through the unlocked door. Rachel scrambled to hide the papers under the blotter on her desk while chastising herself for not securing the lock.

Sarah plopped onto the chair beside Rachel's desk and handed her a biscuit wrapped in a napkin. "You've been hiding all day in this stuffy room. I thought you might need some nourishment."

"Thanks," Rachel said, as she nibbled on the biscuit. "I've been busy writing letters all day." Papers littered the desk. The inkpot and jar of watery baking soda stood open.

"What have you hidden under the blotter?" Sarah asked, as she moved to retrieve the paper.

"Nothing," Rachel replied, defensively placing her arm on top. "It's private."

"We don't have any secrets from each other," Sarah chided. "Show it to me." She leaned into Rachel, raised her arm, and lifted the blotter. The letter to Henry lay exposed to view.

Sarah snatched it. "What's this? A letter to Henry? Who's he?"

"Just someone I met recently."

"Dearest Henry," Sarah read. "My heart yearns to be near you…"

Rachel grabbed at the paper, but Sarah spun away from her, still reading aloud. "I cannot wait to see your face and feel your strong arms around me…" She paused reading. "You sound serious about this Henry. I'm surprised you haven't abandoned Jesse before this since he'll never get out of jail. Now, tell me all about Henry. I want all the details."

"I… I… I'm not telling you about him," Rachel stammered, as she snatched the letter, folded it, and tucked it into her dress pocket.

"At least tell me how he looks. He must be handsome to turn your head from Jesse."

Rachel's brain scrambled to conjure an image of Henry she could tell Sarah. David Sterling, Susanna's brother, popped into her head. "Well, he's tall and lanky, and wears his brown hair in a short braid down his back. He's got a rather high forehead and beautiful hazel eyes. He dresses well, usually in knee-high black boots and a waistcoat and vest."

"Where did you meet him? Not around this boardinghouse, that's for sure."

"I met him at the college a while back. He's one of the Trustees."

"So he's one of those who denied your entrance into college?"

"Yes, I suppose so."

"But why is he interested in you now, in your condition?"

"I'm not sure," Rachel faltered, no plausible reason coming to mind.

"I'll bet he felt guilty about voting against you but admires your ambition and tenacity."

"That's probably it," she agreed, grateful that Sarah had provided a reason for his interest. "We don't talk about it since it's all in the past."

"He must be older than you to be a trustee."

"Yes, about ten years older."

"He probably pities your dismissal from the Charity School too."

"Perhaps. We simply have a mutual attraction."

"He seems quite a contrast to Jesse. I can see why you would be attracted."

"I still like Jesse, but you're right. The British will probably never release him from jail, and I have to provide for my baby." She wiped her mouth with her napkin and tossed it to Sarah. "But enough about Henry. I have to finish my letter, so you'll have to go." She walked toward the door.

"What's in this bottle?" asked Sarah, holding up the watery jar of baking soda, shaking and sniffing it.

"Give me that," Rachel shouted, grabbing for the bottle.

Sarah lost her grip, and the jar dropped on the desk, spilling liquid over the papers.

"Look what you've done," cried Rachel. Sarah tried to blot the papers with the napkin, but the ink had run, ruining them.

"I'm so sorry," Sarah said, still blotting. "What was in there?"

"Just a mixture for when my stomach is upset. Now I'll have to start the letter all over." Her anger rose as she thought about the extra work ahead of her. "Get out of here," she shouted, pushing her toward the door.

"All right, all right, I'll leave." Sarah kissed the back of her hand and winked as she left. "Send a kiss to Henry for me."

Rachel slammed the door behind her.

~ CHAPTER 55 ~

The next evening in the boardinghouse parlor, Sarah and Mrs. Graydon sat mending while Rachel attempted to knit wool socks for Jesse.

"Your knitting is progressing well, Rachel," noted Mrs. Graydon.

"Thanks for the encouragement, but I'm dismayed at how long it is taking to finish. By the time one sock is done, winter will be over, and there will be no need for heavy socks." She held the half-completed work up to the light of the fireplace. "It looks like it may be too small, too. More the size for a rabbit's foot than a man's."

"It will stretch, dear. It looks fine to me. Perhaps you should be knitting a blanket for your impending arrival instead."

"I'm so grateful, Mrs. Graydon, you are letting me stay here in my condition. I have nowhere else to go."

"I've grown quite fond of you, Rachel, and I know how much you want to be near Jesse. If times weren't so hard, I might send you packing, but I need the money as well as wishing to help you in your predicament. Besides, I love babies. It's been a long time since Andrew was small."

"Mrs. Graydon," asked Sarah, "you've never told us what happened to your husband. If it's too painful to talk about, please pardon my inquiry."

The older lady put down her mending. "No, it's not so distressing anymore. As they say, time heals all wounds. My husband, Joseph, passed in the winter of 1773 from smallpox. The worst part was that he contracted it from our son, Andrew. We all suffered so."

"How did Andrew get smallpox?" asked Rachel.

"Philadelphia has had several smallpox epidemics. The ones in 1756 and 1759 killed over fifteen hundred people. Doctors in the city recommended inoculation against it."

"What's that?" asked Sarah.

"An inoculation gives the person a mild case of the pox, so if one is exposed to the disease later, the body won't get it. Joseph and I were concerned about Andrew, so Dr. Redman gave him the inoculation."

"How did Joseph become ill?"

"Andrew took a long time to recover. The doctor gave him the pox in a small incision in each arm. After four days, the rash and fever started, and he was so ill we thought he would die. Joseph and I became sick as we cared for him, but Joseph's case was much worse than mine. We had nausea and vomiting at first, and after two days, our skin erupted in pustules. You can still see the scars on my face. The fever and aches were unbearable. My sister came to help us, and thank goodness she didn't fall ill. Joseph was poorly for days, the fever raging inside him. Then he developed pneumonia. His raspy breathing and gasps for air were horrible to hear. He fell into a coma and died. Andrew and I recovered, but we were sick for months."

"What an ordeal," exclaimed Sarah. Rachel sat with her hands in her lap as a tear ran down her cheek.

"Yes, it was a horrible time. Fortunately, Joseph had purchased the boardinghouse a year before he died, so I could support Andrew and myself after he passed. It's enough income for us to live fairly well, but all the chores are difficult to manage. Now that Andrew is older, he can help more."

"I imagine you wish your empty room was rented," said Rachel.

"Yes, I wish it was, but finding a new tenant these days is impossible. When the British came to town at the end of September, the active Whigs fled the city. The Tories welcomed the soldiers, and the Quakers have remained neutral. British officers occupied any empty Whig houses they could find and demanded to room in other houses. When they first arrived, all my rooms were rented. But since Mr. Morris left, I've lived in fear that they would want to move in."

"What would be so terrible if an officer came to live here?" Sarah asked. "It would fill your empty room."

"The room would be filled, but the officers don't pay for their lodging or meals. I'd have more cooking and cleaning, and then if I could find a paying boarder, I wouldn't have an empty room. It would run me into the poorhouse."

As if on cue, a loud knock at the door startled them. "Andrew, see who's at the door," Mrs. Graydon called.

The open door revealed a British officer standing on the stoop.

"Hello, rebel," he said to Andrew.

"Bloody-back!" exclaimed the boy, as if they were old friends.

"Is your mother home?"

"Here she is." Mrs. Graydon hurried to the door.

"I'm sorry to interrupt your evening, ma'am, but I hear you have a vacant room, and I require lodging."

Andrew piped up. "Mother, this is Captain Crammond. We talk on the corner when he's in town. I told him Mr. Morris had moved out, and you needed a boarder."

Andrew's mother glared at him. "I have a room, but I fear it would be much too small for your needs."

Captain Crammond pushed open the door and entered despite the landlady's feeble protests. "I'm sure it will be fine. Show it to me, and also the rest of the house and barn. I desire to move in this evening."

"We will be happy to have you," she lied, as she fished the key to Morris's old room out of her pocket.

"I'll show him around," offered Andrew. Captain Crammond smiled and tipped his hat to the dumbfounded ladies as he ascended the stairs behind Andrew.

Rachel thought, *how will I code my messages with an enemy soldier in the house? On second thought*, she mused, *perhaps he will be my best source of information. Maybe I'm lucky he came.*

~ CHAPTER 56 ~

Rachel was startled to see three new faces around the breakfast table. Captain Crammond rose as she entered the room.

"Good morning, miss. Due to the lateness of my arrival last evening, I did not make your acquaintance. I'm Captain Crammond. May I ask your name?"

Rachel gave a slight curtsy. "I'm Rachel Palsgrove. I'm pleased to meet you."

"Let me also introduce my two servants, James and Thomas." The men nodded in her direction, their mouths full of food.

"Here's some breakfast, Rachel," said Mrs. Graydon, coming from the kitchen and handing her a platter of scrapple, eggs, and biscuits. Rachel took a helping of each and passed the dish to Sarah, who continued it around the table. In a flash, the plate was empty, smeared with only a greasy residue. The landlady brought out a steaming pot of tea and frowned as she removed the empty dish to the kitchen.

The back door slammed, and Andrew appeared carrying five eggs. "Here are more eggs, Mother," he called.

Sarah piped up. "I didn't know we had chickens, Andrew."

Captain Crammond said, "I took the liberty of putting my chickens in the old coop out back. There is fresh milk too, from my cow that also came with me. Thomas milked her this morning."

"Fresh milk and eggs every day will be a treat for us, Captain Crammond," Sarah said.

"It is the least I can do since we have imposed greatly on Mrs. Graydon's hospitality."

Rachel studied the Captain's face as she ate. He looked to be in his mid-thirties and wore his brown hair tied with a bow at the nape of his neck. His green eyes, clean-shaven face, and strong chin made a handsome combination. He was wearing his red uniform and had tucked a white cloth napkin neatly under his chin. His servants were younger than him and wore rough woolen shirts and breeches.

"What are your duties with the army, Captain Crammond?" asked Rachel.

"I command a platoon of men camped near Germantown. We drill each afternoon and march around the city. Our main task is to procure firewood for the camp, which is no small matter."

One of the students asked, "Were your men the ones taking down the wooden building a block over?"

"Yes, that's where I met Andrew, who watched us work. The building was in poor condition, so General Howe authorized us to dismantle it for firewood."

Rachel finished her meal but lingered over her cup of tea. Captain Crammond motioned to the servants, who rose to perform their chores in the barn.

As Sarah began to leave, the Captain said, "Sarah and Rachel, would you like to see a play tonight?"

"That sounds interesting, Captain, but how could we do that?" Sarah asked.

"The other officers and I find that our duties in Philadelphia only occupy a small part of our time, so we have formed a theater troupe and perform two plays every Monday at the Southwark Theater. Tonight's performances are *Henry IV, Part I*, and *A Trip to Scotland*. I have a small part in the latter. They are strictly amateur productions, but I think you would find them enjoyable. Would you please join me? I promise not to keep you out too late."

Rachel didn't hesitate. "I've read *Henry IV* and would love to see a performance if Sarah will come too. *A Trip to Scotland* sounds interesting as well."

"Sarah, will you come?" he asked.

"Yes, an evening out would be delightful."

"Good, it is all set. I will meet you in the parlor at six."

Promptly at six, the threesome, Captain Crammond, Sarah, and Rachel, departed from the boardinghouse. The Captain's guard trailed them and carried an unlit lantern in addition to his musket. Captain Crammond explained, "General Howe decreed that no person should be out after eight without a lantern, and a guard always accompanies me. You may have seen him in front of the house all day. Several guards rotate their duties throughout the day."

As they neared the theater, the sidewalk became more crowded with people headed the same way. The Southwark Theater at South Street above Fourth Street was a towering, red brick and wood structure. In front of the theater, bejeweled ladies in elaborate feathered hats descended from fancy carriages. Dapper gentlemen in waistcoats and breeches with knee-high gleaming black boots accompanied them.

"Half the town must be here," exclaimed Sarah, as they jostled their way inside.

"My box seats are down the left aisle, ladies." The entourage drifted down the aisle toward the stage and saw the servant, James, waving to them from seats ten rows from the front. "James has been here since the doors opened at four, so no one else claims our seats."

James exited the box to allow them to enter, and as he did so, an intoxicated patron backing down the aisle bumped into Rachel, nearly knocking her down. The Captain caught her, then shouted, "Watch your step, man, there are ladies behind you."

The drunk turned around, ready to assault his confronter, but saw the uniform and hesitated. His friend behind him pulled him away, grumbling. "He's sorry, officer; he meant no offense."

Captain Crammond huffed. "They should not have let a person in that state into the theater. Are you all right, Rachel?"

She nodded and straightened her gown.

"Let's sit down, ladies." He grasped Rachel's elbow and guided her into the box. "I'll sit on the end so I can leave before the second play starts to get into costume. James, you may go home."

With open mouths, Sarah and Rachel gawked at the sights around them. The lights in front of the stage were oil lamps without glasses, and in the rear of the theater, sturdy pillars supported the balcony. Playgoers occupied almost every seat, and the chattering crowd created quite a din.

"Look at the beautiful scenery on the stage," commented Rachel, sitting next to the Captain.

"We are fortunate to have several very talented artists in our ranks, Captains John André and Oliver Delancy. Everyone marvels at the scenery's realism. We also boast some wonderful actors in our troupe. Dr. Hammond Beaumont, our surgeon general, often has a starring role. Some performances also feature Miss Hyde, a professional actress. The men are awkward playing the women's parts, but it often adds great hilarity to the production."

Sarah pointed. "Who's over in that box with all the guards around? He looks important."

"That's our commander, General Howe, and his mistress. They attend all the plays."

"Does no one object to her presence?" asked Rachel.

"He's in charge, so no one questions whether his behavior is proper or not."

Stagehands appeared and snuffed out the wall sconces. As the theater darkened, the audience hushed. In the darkness, Captain Crammond snaked his hand into Rachel's and gently squeezed. Startled, she looked at him, and he smiled mischievously. She didn't squeeze back but also didn't withdraw her hand. As the play started, she turned her attention to the stage. The Captain leaned over, and she felt his hot breath in her ear. "You look very lovely tonight, my dear."

She smiled politely and whispered, "Thank you," then held her finger to her lips for silence. Rachel felt enveloped in a real dilemma. She didn't want to encourage him, but he was an officer and a potential source of valuable information for General Washington. He could discern her condition from her shape, so what did he want? She turned her attention to the play.

The actors often bumbled their Shakespearian lines to the amusement of patrons familiar with the play, and the crowd roared with laughter when Falstaff's stomach pillow stuffing slipped to his knees. Soon the Captain gave her hand a final squeeze. "I'll see you after the next play," he said, as he exited the box.

A *Trip to Scotland* featured actors attempting Scottish accents while describing the sights of Scotland. The changing backdrops offered such breathtaking views of the Scottish countryside that the audience felt they were there. The Captain had a major part as a tour guide describing the points of interest.

After the final curtain, Rachel and Sarah waited for the Captain and his guard to return. Most of the crowd had dissipated when they finally appeared. "Sorry I took so long, but I had to change out of my costume. How did you ladies like the productions?" he asked.

"*Henry IV* was delightful. I haven't laughed so much in a long time," said Sarah.

"I feel as if I have traveled to Scotland and back," said Rachel. "You played your part expertly."

The Captain beamed. "I'm glad you enjoyed it. Perhaps you will join me again next week for a new set of plays. Let's start for home." He motioned for the guard to lead them out. Once outside, the guard lit the lantern to light their way home. The Captain kept his hands to himself, but Rachel caught him several times, gazing at her in the moonlight. *What is he up to?*

~ CHAPTER 57 ~

Sarah tried to turn the knob on Rachel's door while balancing the tray of teacups but found it locked. She kicked the door with her foot. "It's Sarah. May I come in?"

After the sounds of papers rustling and footsteps, the key rattled in the lock. As the door opened, Rachel smiled at Sarah and took the tray from her. "Come in."

Sarah sat on the bed to sip her tea. "Why is the door always locked now?" she asked.

"I lock it because of all the strange men in the house," Rachel replied.

"You and the Captain aren't strangers. You were mighty close at the play. Don't think I didn't notice."

Rachel blushed. "That was his idea, not mine. I couldn't be rude to him."

"You needn't encourage him though. I felt awkward being with you two lovebirds."

"Lovebirds! You exaggerate, Sarah. I believe you're jealous."

"You seem to have it all, Rachel. First, Jesse, then Henry, now Captain Crammond."

"You surely aren't envious of me," Rachel said. "I'm alone in a strange city, my schooling has collapsed, I'm expecting a child, and Jesse's in jail and may be hanged. Sarah, you have a husband."

"I may have a husband, but he's seldom home. I'm lonely. And you've got what I want most—a child. Yes, I'm jealous!" Tears ran down her face.

Rachel sat beside Sarah on the bed, offered her handkerchief, and put her arm around her. "You'll have a child soon, don't worry. I'm sure of it. God knows you'd be a wonderful mother."

"I hope you're right," Sarah sniffed.

Later that day after lunch with Rachel and the servants, Sarah announced, "I'm going for a short walk. I'll be back soon." She gathered her shawl and set out to meet Morris to share her information about the Captain's arrival and his interest in Rachel. Her mouth watered at the thought of more bakery treats as her reward.

She hurried through the alley behind Morris's storefront and knocked on the door.

The door cocked open, and Morris's face appeared. "Sarah, come in. We were just talking about you."

Puzzled, she entered to see Captain Crammond lounging in a chair smoking his pipe.

"Good to see you again, Sarah," he said.

"What are you doing here, Captain?" she asked.

"Surely you don't think it was by accident that I chose Mrs. Graydon's boardinghouse to stay. Mr. Morris highly recommended it. How better to monitor the activities of our mutual friend, Miss Palsgrove?"

"I thought that was *my* job, Captain," she replied.

"It *was* your job, but now it's mine, and I am thoroughly enjoying it. Young ladies in this dreary town are hard to find."

Morris said, "You may go, Sarah. You're not needed anymore."

Sarah clenched her jaw and marched out the door.

"I hope you can discover whether or not Hopewell is still sending cannon and shot to the rebels, Crammond," said Morris. "Sarah hasn't been very helpful on that score."

274 LINDA J. COLLINS

"I'll ply Rachel with my charms," Crammond grinned, "and if that doesn't work, I'll monitor her activities. If Hopewell is still in operation, I'll find out, and I'll have some fun doing it. Our informer there hasn't had any news for quite a while."

"Watch out," Morris warned. "So far, she's not suspicious of your spying, and we want to keep it that way. She seems demure and naïve, but she can also be a spitfire. Trust me, I know."

~ CHAPTER 58 ~

The following day, the Captain found Rachel in the barn, mucking out Missy's stall. The palomino stood at the hitching rail, occasionally stamping her hoof.

"This is a handsome horse, Miss Palsgrove," he remarked, running his hand along Missy's neck.

"Oh, Captain, you startled me." She wiped her dirty hands on her shift. "She's a fine animal but can be very ornery."

"What's her name?" He took up the bristle brush and began grooming the mare with vigorous sweeping strokes.

"Her name is Missy—short for Miss Behaving—which you can take either way."

He chuckled. "A double entendre. Very clever." Missy nickered as he moved to her other side. "She seems well-behaved at the moment."

"That's because Andrew rides her early each morning and tires her out. Otherwise, she would be antsy, although she seems to love your touch."

"I've been told that before," he said. She blushed. "Andrew is a big help around here. He faithfully gathers the chicken eggs every morning too."

"I don't know what I would do without him. I certainly can't ride in my condition."

He stopped brushing and looked at her over the mare's back. "Are you busy tonight?"

"What did you have in mind?"

"I wondered if you would accompany me to the ball at Smith's Tavern this evening."

"A ball? I'm not much of a dancer, especially now. At the last dance I attended, I was so clumsy that I fell and tore my dress. Surely there is someone better suited than me to ask to the ball."

"Well, there is a shortage of female company around Philadelphia these days, but even if there were lots of ladies from which to choose, I would still ask you. I'd like to know you better."

"I'm flattered, Captain, but why me?"

"I thought you would enjoy the music, and we could dance the slow dances if you like. I think you would find me a more than adequate partner. You intrigue me, Miss Palsgrove."

"All right, it does sound entertaining. The last music I heard was a concert given by Miss Davies on the glass armonica."

"I assure you, the music at the ball will be more exciting than that. Can you be dressed at six?"

"I'll be ready. But now, I must get back to my stall cleaning. I've lots of chores to complete if I'm going out this evening."

"Let me help you," he replied, tossing the brush into the tack box and taking the pitchfork from her. "I have a few minutes before I leave for practice with my men."

At a little past six o'clock, Captain Crammond waited for Rachel in Mrs. Graydon's parlor. Soon she descended the stairs, dressed in her Sunday best. "I'm sorry to keep you waiting," she said.

"I anticipated your arrival with bated breath." He rose and held out a slim white box. "This is for you."

"What's this?" she asked as she opened the lid. Nestled in tissue paper was a pair of white kid gloves. She gently caressed them. "They're lovely, but I can't accept them. They're too extravagant."

"All the ladies at the ball wear gloves. Do take them. I hope they fit."

She smoothed them onto her hands, wiggling her fingers. "I've never felt anything so soft. They feel like silk and fit perfectly. Thank you." He smiled his approval.

They went out the door, and the Captain held her gloved hand as she navigated the steps. After a short walk in silence, he said, "Tell me about yourself, Rachel."

"There's not much to tell. I'm from a village called Hopewell, about forty miles from here. It's an iron-making community. I have parents and a sister there."

"And what brings you to Philadelphia, so far away from your family?"

"I came to the city to learn to be a teacher. However, I lost my position at the Charity School due to my condition."

"So, you chose not to return home because your beau is here in the city?"

"No, my beau has deserted me," she lied, unwilling to tell him about Jesse in jail. "I am alone here except for my good friend, Sarah. I stay because I hope to return to school after the baby comes."

"You have ambitious plans, young lady."

"What about you, Captain? Do you have a wife and children back in England?"

"No, I'm not married. It is difficult to have both a military career and a family."

"You aspire to move up the ranks?"

"Yes, I hope someday to be a general. I attended the Royal Military Academy at Woolwich and have the credentials, but I need more experience, although I'm not learning much about battle strategy parked here in Philadelphia. I hope when winter is over, the troops will resume their fighting to preserve this colony for England. Where do your loyalties lie?"

"I have no interest in politics, sir. I only desire to finish my education, return to Hopewell, raise my child, and teach."

278 LINDA J. COLLINS

They arrived at Smith's Tavern. Rachel was relieved to see women of all ages and in all manner of dress. Most, indeed, wore gloves, so she was glad the Captain had given her a pair, although she was wary of accepting a gift from a man. The last gift from Morris had not turned out well.

The tavern overflowed with dancers. After a few slow dances, Captain Crammond found a chair for Rachel to sit out the faster ones. Her foot tapped to the rhythm, and her head nodded in time to the music. He stood beside her, his hand gently keeping time on the back of her seat.

"Captain, why don't you ask some of the other ladies to dance? I won't mind. I feel I am dampening your enjoyment of the evening."

"I am perfectly content to stay by your side. No one else here interests me but you."

She resumed watching the crowd, but suddenly a figure sailing by in the distance caught her eye. *Could it be? Surely not*, she thought. The man came closer, and indeed it was Morris, dancing with a pretty brunette, not Susannah. As she stared, he turned, and they briefly locked eyes. His eyebrows raised in surprise, and his mouth silently blew her a kiss. Shocked, Rachel jerked her head away. Her heart pounded, her mouth felt dry, and she began to sway in her seat, feeling close to fainting.

The Captain asked, "Rachel, are you all right?"

"Captain, I need some refreshment if you please. I'm feeling a bit faint from all the excitement."

"I'll be back shortly." She watched him weave his way through the dancers to the refreshment table, then looked down at the floor, hoping the room would stop spinning.

Suddenly a pair of black boots invaded her field of vision. Edmund Morris stood in front of her, and his hand snaked under her chin and lifted her head. She gasped and shrank away from his touch, but the arms of her chair held her prisoner.

"Miss Palsgrove," he cooed, "I'm pleasantly surprised to see you here. May I have the next dance?"

"No, Mr. Morris, I have no desire to associate with you. Please, leave me alone."

"Oh, that is a poor attitude to take with an old friend. I have no animosity toward you despite your rudeness at our last encounter."

"Your previous attentions toward me have caused me much anguish, so I have no wish to be near you. Again, please, leave," she commanded.

"I regret any misunderstanding in our past. My apologies. I'll go, but I'm sure our paths will cross again sometime."

"Not if I can help it," she hissed.

He retreated, skirting around the dancers, walking on the same path on which Captain Crammond was returning with the refreshments. As Morris passed him, he winked at the Captain, who smirked in return.

"Here's some lemonade, Rachel." She took the cup with shaking hands and carefully raised it to her lips. "It tastes wonderful. Thank you so much."

She sat a few minutes more, regaining her composure. "I'm sorry, Captain, but I'm feeling exhausted. The music has been enjoyable, but would you mind if we went home now?"

"I don't mind at all. I'll summon a carriage to take us to Mrs. Graydon's."

Shaken to her core, she rose on wobbly legs and took his arm as they left the ball.

~ CHAPTER 59 ~

Several weeks passed, and Rachel faithfully coded her messages. She visited Theuben almost daily to help with his bookkeeping, and he informed her about ships in and out of the harbor and sailors' and soldiers' conversations he overheard. The weekly visits with Jesse continued, but her love had little news of value to report. His condition steadily worsened, and she was more disheartened about his survival every week. Each time she visited, she railed at the guards, insisting that the 'father' of her child must be released to support her, but her pleas fell on deaf ears.

At The Library Company, she asked Mr. Daymon if her messages were helpful. "Yes," he said, "your information has been beneficial. Has the coding become easier?"

"It's easier but still a tedious process. I memorized the locations in the book for many of the words I need, but I'm careful to use new places too."

"Do you learn much from the officer quartered in your house?"

"I overhear bits and pieces when he talks with his servants, and last week he entertained twelve other officers at a dinner party at Mrs. Graydon's. She complained about preparing food and drink for so many, but the wine flowed freely, and by the end of the evening, they were all fairly drunk. They chattered about some grand party coming soon. It's a coveted invitation in the city, and only Philadelphia's wealthiest ladies, loyalists, and officers are invited. The city's seamstresses are frantically working on elaborate gowns designed by one of the officers, Captain John André, who was present at the dinner. Of course, I didn't receive an invitation."

"Have you attended any more plays or balls with the Captain?"

"He continually asks me to go, but I decline, using my condition as an excuse. I certainly don't want to reencounter Edmund Morris."

"You must be very careful, Rachel. These are powerful men with whom you are dealing."

"I don't discuss anything with the Captain of any importance, although he asks me about Hopewell and my activities frequently. I'll watch my step, Mr. Daymon, don't worry."

At the docks, Theuben met her at the door.

"There's a stack of paperwork today, Rachel," he said, as she entered the shack. "Several ships came in overnight."

She glanced at the piles of papers littering the desk. "These may take me several hours today."

"I'm thankful you're doing this work instead of me. My books have never looked so orderly and balanced. I wish you would accept some payment."

"I'm happy to help. Your information is payment enough."

He poured a cup of tea from the kettle on the stove and placed it before her. "I have some news for you too." He pulled a chair near and whispered, "Numerous British ships have come into the harbor lately. But their loads are puzzling—unusual goods and crates of wine and liquor."

"I hear they're planning a big party, although I don't know what there is to celebrate."

"The soldiers have been grumbling that they aren't getting any of these fancy rations. They are very disgruntled." He rose from his chair. "I'll let you get to your books."

As Rachel returned to the boardinghouse, she passed Tun Tavern. The day was warm, and she decided cold lemonade would taste good. These days her belly felt huge, the baby was kicking a lot, and her gait was more a waddle than a walk. She headed to the privy in the back before she went in. She needed to make an increasing number of trips to the facilities as each day passed, much to her dismay. But despite all the inconveniences of expecting a child, she accepted that soon she would have another life to care about, although she felt overwhelmed with the impending responsibility.

Soon she was seated inside, sipping her drink, when Captain Crammond entered the tavern. He spied her, looked surprised, and sat down at her table.

"Miss Palsgrove," he said, "I am amazed to see you here. I thought I saw you at the docks earlier too."

"Are you following me, Captain? Aren't you drilling your men this afternoon or scavenging wood?"

"We are well-stocked with wood since the weather has warmed, so I have free time. I've just come from play practice." He nodded toward her drink. "How does the lemonade taste today?"

"It's fine, but you didn't answer my question. Are you following me?"

"I'll admit that I'm curious about how you spend your afternoons. Your travels are mysterious to me. I mean no offense, but I am concerned for your safety. This area is a rough part of town for a lady in your condition."

"You needn't be concerned about me. I can take care of myself."

"I can see that. I'll be going and let you be. I'm sorry if I intruded."

"Thank you, Captain. I'll see you later at dinner. *I need to be more careful where I go. I don't know who might be watching.*

~ CHAPTER 60 ~

"Jesse, do you want the water left in this pot? Charles needs to use it." Jesse's prison mate held out one of the chamber pots that were emptied daily of excrement and refilled with fresh water each morning for drinking.

"Sure, I'll drink it," he said. He raised the vessel to his lips, carefully avoiding the crusted feces on the chipped rim.

As he was drinking, the dead prisoner patrol arrived. The prisoners moved any inmates who had died during the night to the front of the cell for burial. One skeletal body in Jesse's cell was rigid with cold and rigor, and nearly naked, having been stripped of his clothes by cellmates trying to keep warm on the frigid days and nights. One soldier held the door while two other guards added the corpse to others in a cart in the hall. George had told him a large pit was not far from the jail where the dead were thrown.

Shortly after the carcass detail, the prisoners' meager food rations and firewood arrived, three days since the last delivery. The prisoners scrambled to form a line. Jesse took his turn warming his tin of rations over the wood stove, and his battered body drank in the delicious rays of heat. The men gathered around as close as they could, but the weaker ones stayed on the outskirts, lethargic and unable to expend any energy to fight for a spot in front. Some of the sickest men had already lost their food to stronger prisoners. There was little humanity among people in this life and death situation.

Cooking completed, Jesse retreated to the perimeter with his plate. He greedily devoured the mixture of peas, gravy, and a tiny sliver of pork over a handful of rice, using his two biscuits to sop up every drop of the gruel. He licked the tin clean and placed it under his shirt for safe keeping. Jesse felt himself growing weaker every day from lack of food. His clothes hung on him, and when he walked, he held his pants up to keep them from falling to his ankles. The dead patrol removed more and more bodies every day from the cage. *Would he be next?* Depression and desperation wielded an ever-tightening, vise-like grip on him as each day crawled by.

When George and Rachel's faces appeared outside the cell bars, Jesse cried with relief. He wiped tears from his eyes with his dirty sleeve. The rations they brought were a wonderful treat, but their presence buoyed Jesse's spirits even more than the food. He had no news to report to Rachel, and the guards demanded their visits be brief. He longed to kiss and hold her but seeing her face and hearing her voice was better than no contact at all.

"Thank you for the food and letters." He sadly watched them depart down the hall. Jesse found a quiet corner where he could sit on the floor by himself to savor Rachel's words. He took out the smooth stone from his pocket and held it while reading.

The first letter was her usual recounting of daily activities. But the second caused him great concern. His brow furrowed as he read it.

Dearest Jesse,

I hate to burden you with bad news. His heart clenched in anticipation. *I discovered Susanna's fiancé is indeed who I suspected he might be. I'm not surprised at his deviousness and that she has fallen in love with him, as he can be so charming and manipulative. Does he suspect my connection with her? He knows we're both from Hopewell but probably nothing more because I'm sure she wouldn't talk to him about me. I don't want to visit her in my condition to warn her, and I don't think she'd believe me anyway. She might be in danger if she confronts him with my allegations.*

As my time of confinement grows near, my good friend at the boardinghouse, Sarah Brown, is very comforting and willing to help me. Mrs. Graydon also has accepted my situation and will be an experienced support. Even though I miss the Charity School children tremendously, I am using my extra time on my studies at The Library Company, helping Theuben with his bookkeeping, and pursuing my other endeavors.

Please don't fret about me, Jesse. I can persevere, and so must you.

Love,

Rachel

If only I were out of here! He pounded his fist on his thigh. *I have a score to settle with Edmund Morris in more ways than one. I'd marry Rachel and make things right. Even though the child isn't mine, I would treat it like my own. I hope her "other endeavors" don't get her in trouble.* He reread her letter and resolved to stay strong until the day their reunion would come. He was helpless to do otherwise.

~ CHAPTER 61 ~

Rachel strolled down Chestnut Street in the chilly spring air toward The Library Company. She pulled her thin coat tighter around her, but her burgeoning belly prevented its closing. Her swaying gait made her feel embarrassed and conspicuous, but the walk invigorated her. Now she was anxious to return the books she had borrowed last week and gather new selections. Since she no longer had school work to complete, she spent lots of time in her room poring over each book, trying to fill the long hours either reading or producing her coded messages.

Arriving at Carpenter's Hall, she spied Mr. Daymon, who always greeted her faithfully at the door every Tuesday, no matter what the weather.

"Hello, Mr. Daymon," she called. "It's a beautiful day today, isn't it?"

"*Oui, Madamoiselle* Palsgrove, this splendid temperature is most delightful after the dreadfully cold winter we've had." He reached out his hands. "Let me take those books. They must be heavy."

"Thank you," Rachel said, as she piled the volumes in his arms. "I thought my back would break by the time I got here. I'll have to remember to choose smaller ones to borrow today."

Mr. Daymon opened the hall door. The sentry briefly looked up and nodded to them, used to their presence each week. Passing through the foyer to the staircase, they averted their gaze from the wounded British soldiers on the first floor. The little Frenchman bounded up the stairs, but Rachel trudged rather than bounded and was panting by the time she reached the top landing.

He unlocked the door, and they entered the library—she now associated its musty smell with this wonderful place.

While the librarian updated his logbook with her returns, Rachel perused the shelves. "My baby is due soon," she said, noticing his quick look at her belly, "and I may not come back for a week or two after he or she is born."

"I know you'll return the books when you can. Next Tuesday, I'll wait awhile outside as usual, and if you don't arrive in a few minutes, I'll understand to come ahead inside."

Keeping her walk home in mind, she chose four slim texts and took them to the table where he was sitting.

He recorded them in his ledger. "Are you ready to leave?"

"Yes, I think your collection of wondrous items no longer holds many mysteries for me, so I think I'll go and enjoy the weather while I can."

"You are always a welcome guest. I'll see you whenever you can come." He picked up her books and escorted her out of the Library and down the steps.

Outside he handed her the load, and said, "*Bonne chance* to you. I'll see you soon."

On her way home, she took a short detour to a small park and sat on a bench. The trees were sprouting new leaves, and crocuses were peeking their heads through the soil. Warm rays of sunshine caressed her back. Swarms of people were out enjoying the day, too, and she watched them flit around like bees up and down the sidewalks and tried to imagine their destinations and lives.

Suddenly a hand grasped her shoulder from behind, startling her, and a familiar voice boomed. "Why, fancy seeing Miss Palsgrove out and about on this fine spring day," Edmund Morris's voice jeered. Rachel turned as best she could to confront him, pulling her body away. "May I sit with you a moment?" he queried as he rounded the bench.

Before she could protest, he settled on the seat beside her, much too close for comfort. "I wish you wouldn't," she stammered.

"You're not very friendly," he admonished. "When is your baby due?" He stroked her belly, and she recoiled as if burned by a hot flame.

"That's a rude question to ask. Get away from me," she replied indignantly. Quickly gathering her books, she struggled to her feet and turned to go.

"You don't have to leave because of me." He laughed at her receding form as she wobbled down the street without a backward glance.

Shaken by another encounter with Morris, she hurried home as fast as she could. Exhausted and still trembling with fear and rage at his audacity, she sat in the parlor, trying to calm herself. Halfway home, her back had started hurting, with a sharp pain intensifying every minute. After a short while, she decided to go to her room to lie down, but a sudden gush of water splashed to the floor when she rose from her seat. "Oh, no!" she cried, which brought Mrs. Graydon rushing from the kitchen.

"I don't know what happened," exclaimed Rachel. "I'm sorry I've ruined your chair and carpet."

"Don't worry, dear," soothed the landlady, assessing the situation. "Let's take you to your room and call for Sarah and the midwife. I believe you're having a baby."

~ CHAPTER 62 ~

Rachel lay in bed with her new baby boy in her arms. Mrs. Graydon, Sarah, and Rebecca, the middle-aged, plump midwife, surrounded her. The bun at the back of Rebecca's head was still tightly wound despite her efforts to help Rachel. Her authoritative but gentle manner exuded confidence and experience, and soothed the other ladies in the room. She had just finished washing the newborn after cutting his umbilical cord, and he was squalling mightily.

"He's got a fine set of lungs, miss," remarked Rebecca. "We'll wait for the afterbirth, clean you up, and change the bed. After that, you can try nursing him. I'll show you how if you like."

As they gazed at the new arrival, the baby stuck his thumb in his mouth, and his squalling quieted into noisy sucking.

"He'll be a good nurser. When they find their thumb that quickly, you know he's been at it afore he was born."

"He sure came fast for a first baby," said Sarah. "He looks perfect, Rachel."

Rebecca observed, "Usually first babies take longer than that, but the miss is young and healthy, and that helps a lot."

Mrs. Graydon said, "Supper needs tending, but can I hold him a minute before I go, Rachel?"

"Of course you can, Mrs. Graydon." She clumsily handed the baby to her.

"Remember always to support his head until his neck gets stronger," Rebecca told her.

"There's so much to learn. I can't believe he's here."

Mrs. Graydon cooed to the infant, who closed his eyes. "How wonderful it feels to hold a new life in one's arms. My boy hasn't been this small for a long time."

Sarah asked, "Mrs. Graydon, could Rachel borrow the rocker from the parlor for a while? I've heard rocking is soothing to small babies."

"That's a wonderful idea. After supper, I'll ask Andrew to carry it up. And when the food is ready, I'll ring, and perhaps you can bring Rachel a plateful of food." She looked at Rachel's flushed face. "You must be famished."

"Both the rocker and the meal will be delightful," Rachel replied. She squirmed a little in the bed. "Oh, Rebecca, I think something is happening down below."

The midwife peeked under the covers. "Yes, the afterbirth has come. Let's get you cleaned up."

"May I hold the child now so Mrs. Graydon can leave?" requested Sarah.

"Yes, please do. I know you're as excited about the baby's arrival as I am. I couldn't have survived this without your help, Sarah. I'm so grateful to you."

Mrs. Graydon passed the baby to Sarah. "Don't forget, I'll ring the bell. Congratulations again, Rachel." She stooped and kissed the top of the baby's head.

Cradling the baby in her arms, Sarah sat down and began swinging him gently, gazing lovingly at his face. "He's got such long eyelashes and blue eyes, Rachel, just like you. When he grows up, all the girls will swoon over him."

"It will be a while before he needs to worry about girls swooning, I hope," joked Rachel.

"They grow up too fast, miss," said the midwife. "Enjoy this time with him while you can, for soon he will be a strapping young lad like Andrew."

Rachel accepted the warm washcloth for cleaning, and Sarah relinquished the chair for her while Rebecca changed the linens. "I'll have this bed changed in a moment, and then we can see if he'll nurse."

Within minutes, Rachel was back in bed with her head and back propped with pillows against the headboard. Sarah handed over the baby carefully. "Here's the wee one."

Rebecca showed Rachel how to nurse the child. "Look how he latched on right away. I don't think you'll have any trouble with him feeding. Your milk won't start for a while, but keep nursing him every two hours for about fifteen minutes on each breast. Your foremilk helps his digestion and will aid your milk coming in." She rooted around in her medical satchel. "Here's some lanolin cream for your nipples. Rub some on after he nurses. It will help keep them from getting sore and cracking."

"Is there anything else I need to know to take care of him? Mrs. Graydon gave me some advice, but it's been a while since Andrew was a baby."

"If he has a black stool in his diaper, don't be alarmed, as the first couple ones are cleaning out his insides. After a few days, they'll look more normal. Do you know how to swaddle him?"

"I can show her that," said Sarah. "I learned when I helped my sister with her baby. It's a special way to wrap him in his blanket."

"The wrapping soothes them by making them feel more secure. How about a cradle in which to sleep? If you don't have one, pull out a drawer in your bureau and lay him there. Try not to fall asleep with him in your bed. Many an infant has been accidentally smothered by its mother in bed."

"How awful." Rachel winced at the thought.

A bell rang downstairs. "I'll go fetch a plate of food," said Sarah.

Rebecca packed away her equipment. "Any other questions?"

"I can't think of any now, but no doubt some will come to me later."

"I'll return tomorrow afternoon to check you both. I'll show you how to bathe him too."

"Thank you so much for your assistance. Some money is on the bureau for you."

"You are welcome, miss."

As Rebecca left, she held the door open for Sarah, who was coming up the stairs with a plate full of food and a big glass of milk, which she put on the table.

"If you've finished nursing, I'll hold him while you eat." Sarah eagerly reached for the infant.

Rachel began to devour the food while Sarah rocked the baby and cooed to him. Soon the plate and glass were empty. "I can't believe I ate all that!" she exclaimed.

"You've worked hard today, so don't be bashful about cleaning your plate. Now, let's change his diaper, settle him in, and you can sleep. He's going to want to eat again soon."

Sarah showed her how to change him and cleared a drawer in the bureau, placing a layer of soft blankets in the bottom.

Rachel inspected every inch of the baby before swaddling him with Sarah's help. "His body seems perfect. Every finger, every toe, every part of him is so tiny and beautiful, even if his head is an odd shape."

"His head will round out. A baby's head is pliable to fit coming out. Have you chosen a name yet?"

"I decided to name him Nick, in remembrance of my poor dead brother. My parents and sister will like that name too. We miss him so. But I'll call the baby 'Little Nicky' for now."

"You're so sweet to honor your brother. Let's put you both to bed. When he wakes up tonight, I'll hear him cry and come help you with him."

"You are so kind and thoughtful, Sarah." Rachel climbed into bed, and as she sank into it, she fell immediately asleep.

Sarah peered longingly at Nicky's peaceful, innocent face. She settled him in his drawer, then snuffed out the candle and tiptoed out the door.

~ CHAPTER 63 ~

Susanna perched on the edge of the barge seat, her back straight, her eyes sparkling as she absorbed the Delaware River sights and smells. The sounds of flowing water, jumping fish, banks lined with cheering spectators, and sporadic cannon fire delighted her. She glanced sideways and smiled when her eyes caught Edmund's. He squeezed her hand and sat looking regal in his white, frilled shirt and brown, velvet breeches and waistcoat, as if he were escorting the prettiest maiden at the festivities.

Their flower-and-ribbon festooned barge on this balmy spring day in mid-May was one of many in the flotilla. Hundreds of boats of all shapes and sizes had assembled at three in the afternoon at Knight's Wharf, and three flatboats of musicians led the procession. Their gay music set the tone for the occasion.

When the barges passed the fort at Swede's Church south of the city, they eased to the bank and docked. Edmund held Susanna's gloved hand as he helped her ashore, and she squeaked in alarm as the vessel rocked with their shifting weight.

"The trip was exciting," she said, "but I'm glad to be back on land."

"You did well for your first boat ride."

"I can't imagine sailing across the ocean from England as you have done."

"This jaunt down the river indeed does not compare to weeks at sea. But I'm sure someday we'll travel to see the sights of Europe, perhaps on our honeymoon."

She flashed a smile at him. "That would be lovely."

Edmund held Susanna at arm's length and swirled his finger, motioning her to spin around. She performed a dainty pirouette. Her white silk gown formed a flowing rose with a wide pink sash at her waist. The sun glittered off the spangles on her sash, stockings, and shoes. Her headdress and veil, trimmed with silver lace, sparkled with pearls and more glitter.

"You are looking magnificent in that gown. Is it new?"

"Captain André designed all the ladies' gowns."

"I was fortunate to be invited to this Meschianza fête," said Edmund. "Although with General Howe's officers pulling out all the stops to honor his retirement and return to England, it seems half of Philadelphia is here."

"I'm sure your friendship with Captain André had something to do with it. And I am so lucky to be your guest."

"Who else could accompany me but my lovely fiancée?"

"All my friends from Mrs. Levering's squealed when the ticket arrived. They are anxious to hear my report about the gala when I get home."

Their gaze was drawn from the dock up an avenue of armed grenadiers standing at attention and backed by a row of cavalry.

Susanna pointed ahead. "Oh, what a grand house on the hill."

"That's the mansion of Joseph Wharton, the host of the party. He and I have had legal dealings several times. Just wait 'til you go inside."

Susanna and Edmund strolled with the other guests, chatting and speculating on the day's events. Shortly, they reached a lush green square lawn, lined with red-coated troops and dotted with pavilions of tents around the edges. A young boy dressed in a medieval costume escorted them to their seats.

The guests, over one thousand people, were eventually seated, and everyone waited in anxious anticipation. A hush fell over the group as the piercing sound of trumpets announced the arrival of seven knights resplendent in white and red silk who rode gray chargers. They circled the square and aligned themselves on one side. Soon more mounted knights arrived dressed in black and orange silk, and they took their place on the other side. The horsemen's squires armed the knights with lances, pistols, swords, and shields.

Susanna gasped. "Will there be a fight?"

Edmund shushed her. "Wait and observe," he whispered.

The groups saluted, then galloped toward each other with lances raised.

"They'll kill each other! I can't look." Susanna covered her eyes.

"It's just fantasy," Edmund said, pulling her hands down. "Keep watching."

The knights passed mid-field, feigning battle in the joust, but no one fell. Upon reaching their respective ends of the green, they discarded their lances and brandished swords. Riding again, they engaged in violent swordplay with their opponents. On their third encounter, pistol shots shattered the air as they passed. The Marshall of the Field announced, "This contest is declared a draw." The audience whooped and clapped their approval at the exploits of the brave contestants.

"That was thrilling. I've never seen anything like it," Susanna gushed.

"That's how they used to fight in King Arthur's day, hundreds of years ago," Edmund said.

The crowd exited, approached the mansion, and ascended a carpet-covered stairway leading into a grand hall that ended in a light and airy, mirrored grand ballroom. Musicians struck a lively tune, and everyone who had a partner joined the dance. Some guests visited the refreshment tables in the adjacent drawing rooms.

"May I compliment your dancing, Miss Sterling?" remarked Edmund as they whirled around the dance floor. "You are light as air and gracefully anticipate my every move."

"Thank you, Mr. Morris," Susanna countered. "Your strong arms give me no doubt where you will swoop me next."

After a few more turns around the ballroom, Susanna noted, "There seem to be a lot of men standing around without dancing partners."

"Unfortunately, many young ladies left the city when the British came to town."

"They are so eager to dance, with their toes tapping and heads bobbing in time with the music."

"They are envious of my delightful partner," he winked at her, "but I'm not giving you up for a moment."

The tune ended, and couples graciously bowed and curtsied to each other. "Let's get some punch, Edmund. All this excitement is making me thirsty."

He held her elbow and steered her to the refreshment table. While enjoying their drink, a tall, lean man in a British officer's uniform approached. A small ponytail hugged the nape of his neck, and his sparkling blue eyes and pleasant smile immediately disarmed her.

"John," exclaimed Edmund. "Let me introduce you to my fiancée. Miss Susanna Sterling, this is Captain John André."

Captain André bowed and lightly kissed the back of Susanna's hand. She curtsied and blushed. "Miss Sterling, I am delighted to make your acquaintance. Edmund tells me so much about you. Are you enjoying the Meschianza?"

"It's fabulous. I thought the knight's tournament was real since it was so artfully performed. This mansion is grand, and the decorations are stunning. I'm delighted Edmund asked me to come."

"We are pleased he invited such a lovely creature to grace our party. Do you know that Meschianza means 'medley' in Italian? We have planned a variety of activities we hope you will find surprising. You look quite lovely tonight. Do you like your dress?"

Susanna smiled and twirled around, billowing out the full skirt. "I think it's the prettiest, most flamboyant gown I have ever owned. You are a very talented designer, Captain André."

"It is easy to create a thing of beauty for beautiful ladies. I'm surprised I've not met you before tonight. Do you reside in the city?"

Edmund interrupted and possessively held Susanna's hand. "Miss Sterling recently came to live in Philadelphia. She's from a town called Hopewell, forty miles northwest of here. Her father is the ironmaster of a furnace there."

The music of the next song smothered further conversation. Edmund put down their glasses and began to move toward the dance floor. André grabbed Edmund's arm and said, "I say, Edmund. Would you mind if I danced one dance with your lady? If that meets her approval, of course?"

Edmund pursed his lips and looked at Susanna, who nodded demurely. "Just one, John," he said, handing her over. He looked at Susanna sternly. "I can't be without her too long."

"We'll return in a moment." André smiled and quickly swept her off into the crowd of dancers. Soon they were lost from Edmund's view toward the middle of the ballroom.

Dazzled by Captain André's nimble footwork on the dance floor, Susanna became breathless and exhilarated in his arms. She saw envious glances of other ladies as she passed them. Occasionally his hand strayed lower, and she thought she felt a little pinch on her backside. She wasn't sure, but when she looked at him quizzically, he smiled mischievously and winked. Her face reddened, but a giggle rose from her lips. She had never danced like this before.

When the music stopped, Susanna began to break away, but André firmly held her. "I must get back to Edmund," she protested weakly.

Without much pause, the music started again. "It's still one dance," André chided. "Edmund will understand." He whirled her away again.

Morris stood on the sidelines with arms crossed and fists clenched. A gentleman with whom Edmund had had dealings approached him. "Where is your lovely fiancée? Didn't she come with you today?"

"She's here, but she's dancing with André."

"You'll probably not see her the rest of the evening," he quipped. "You know how André is with the ladies."

"I catch glimpses of them periodically, so I know they're still dancing. I knew I shouldn't have let her go, but I had no choice. I know how André likes the ladies and the ladies like him, and now my Susanna is in his clutches."

"I think he respects you enough to return her unscathed."

"I hope so," Edmund groused.

Four dances later, André and Susanna made their way back to Edmund, who was chatting with some other men, appearing nonchalant. Susanna's face was shining with perspiration, and the broad grin on André's face showed he was enjoying himself. Edmund took Susanna from André's arm and forced a smile. "So, you finally decided to come back, eh?"

"Don't be upset with Miss Sterling," André admonished. "She's such a delight I couldn't be satisfied with just one dance. No harm is done."

Susanna was alarmed by Edmund's tone and the curl of his lip. She had seen him angry before, and his intense, quick temper scared her.

"Come on, Edmund," she cooed, running her hand up his arm and pulling him close. "I'm back, so let's dance."

Out on the floor, Edmund's dancing seemed clumsy compared to the flamboyant André's. He handled her more roughly than before, and she felt a tense rigidity in his shoulders. She chattered gaily to him and nuzzled his ear. "Don't be jealous, dear. You're the one I love." Gradually, he relaxed and loosened his grip.

At ten o'clock, the servants threw open the ballroom's windows and a loud boom outside startled everyone. The dancers flocked to the sills and were dazzled by magnificent fireworks. Over twenty different arrangements of rockets, each one more elaborate and beautiful than the last, filled the night sky. Some displays erupted low to the ground with bright bursts of light and loud, crackling sounds, while others showered flowing plumes of colored embers high in the sky. The crowd oohed and aahed with each burst and wondered how the next one could be better. At last, the explosions were so long and spectacular that the partygoers knew it had to be the end.

As everyone drifted back into the room, abuzz with the glorious sights they had just seen, large folding doors at the end of the ballroom opened. Chandeliers of candlelight hung from the ceiling, complemented by hundreds of tapers illuminating rows of dining tables set with sparkling china and crystal. The guests were seated and enjoyed a grand feast served by black slaves in Oriental dress adorned with silver bracelets and collars.

While the guests dined, dignitaries offered toast after toast—to the King's health, to the royal family's health, to General Howe's health, and to the success of the British army and navy. A blast of trumpets preceded each testimony, and a flourish of music followed.

After the banquet, the guests made their way back to the ballroom, where the dancing continued until four in the morning.

"Oh, Edmund, I'm exhausted," said Susanna. "Please, take me home. I can't dance another dance."

"Let's stay until dawn breaks over the river," he joked, as he pecked her neck in a half-drunken stupor.

"You can watch it break from the carriage ride home," she declared.

"All right, my dear, if you insist. Let's pay our compliments to the host."

After thanking the Whartons, they clambered into the next carriage waiting to transport people home. The night was chilly, and in the back of the open hack, Susanna started to shiver.

"Snuggle close to me," said Morris, holding her tightly. "I'll keep you warm."

She settled into his arms and began to doze, only to be awakened by his increasingly ardent kisses and roaming hands.

"Edmund," she murmured, "don't. The coachman will see."

"I don't care what he sees. He's paid to drive and mind his own business." The groping continued.

She played along, demurely kissing him. His tongue forced her mouth open. As his breathing became heavier, he pulled her hand to his crotch.

"Edmund, stop," she asserted, as she jerked her hand away.

He hissed, "You owe me, Susanna. I've treated you like a queen tonight, and I deserve payment." He grabbed her wrist, and when she resisted, he overpowered her and resumed his massage with her hand to the point of release.

Shocked and embarrassed, she sat stock still, hoping the coachman hadn't noticed. After a few minutes, Edmund sighed heavily, settled his head on her shoulder, and began to snore.

Susanna was relieved when they arrived at her boarding school. She disembarked, leaving the sleeping Edmund Morris to be taken home.

~ CHAPTER 64 ~

As Rachel entered the Charity School after being gone a few months, everything seemed different yet the same. The building appeared smaller, the halls narrower, the children bigger. She had pleaded with Miss Gardiner to let her return and assured her she would make no mention of the baby to the students. Miss Gardiner apologized for dismissing her so rudely and welcomed her return. Sarah took care of Little Nicky at home while Rachel resumed her duties.

The girls were all there, except Caty, and they seemed more grown-up, more mature. Harriet, the ringleader of the bullies who had been paddled for her misbehavior, welcomed Rachel with a big hug. Of all the students, Harriet was the most transformed. Instead of showing an unkempt, sullen demeanor, she now was clean, bright-eyed, and happy. After her initial greeting, Harriet and her friends ran off to play a quick game before school started.

"I'm glad to see you," commented a frazzled Miss Gardiner. "There's a lot of end-of-the-year work to complete, and I missed your help. Welcome back."

"It feels wonderful to be here," replied Rachel. "I can only come half days due to my obligations at home, but I'm willing to assist any way I can."

"The girls all asked about you. Did you hear the tragic news about Caty?"

"No, I wondered where she was. What happened?"

"Last week, her family's house caught fire. Caty, her younger sister, and mother did not survive. Her mother, returning from a trip to the market, saw the blaze and tried to save the children by going into the burning building. But she couldn't get to them and lost her own life too."

Rachel bit her lip to hold back tears. Caty had been one of her favorites, so small and delicate. *What a horrible way to die*, she thought. "How are the other students taking the news?"

"The first day or two after it happened, the girls cried easily and talked endlessly about the fire. But now we don't discuss it. The young are resilient, but they still take it hard when we find a book or something of hers that reminds us of her passing."

"Caty's family members must be devastated."

"Right now, they're trying to survive with no place to live. The school sent a small donation, but they need so much more. The deaths will hit them hard later when they've had a chance to sort out their immediate needs."

Rachel and Miss Gardiner fell silent a few moments, each lost in their thoughts of man's mortality and the cruelty of young lives tragically cut short.

Breaking the silence, Rachel inquired, "What do you need me to do first this morning?"

"Are you able to teach a math lesson about division to the older girls?"

"I can do that." She moved toward the chalkboard.

Miss Gardiner clapped her hands for attention. "Upper students, take your slates to the board. Miss Palsgrove will help you with your figures this morning."

The next several weeks were a flurry of activity. The pupils accepted Rachel's return as if she had never gone. A few asked her where she had been and why she wasn't staying the entire day, but Rachel dodged the questions with excuses.

On the last day of school, the girls alternated between tears at the goodbyes and joy that the term was over.

"Will ye be here next year, Miss Palsgrove?" asked Harriet.

"No, I'm going back to my family in Hopewell."

"Is that far from here?"

"It is several days away by carriage, but if I return to Philadelphia, I'll stop and see you. I'll miss everyone so much. Maybe we could write letters to each other."

"I would like that, miss. But I don't have any writing paper."

"I'll send Miss Gardiner some paper and stamps with my first letter, so anyone who wishes to write can do so."

"We will write for sure if ye do that, Miss Palsgrove."

Rachel hugged her. "I'll look forward to hearing from you."

Harriet smiled and ran to tell the other girls.

Later in the day, after the children were gone, Rachel sat down, drained from the day's emotional ups and downs. "Miss Palsgrove, please come to my office a minute before you leave," said the headmistress.

Rachel stepped into Miss Gardiner's office, where ledgers, books, and papers littered the desk. The headmistress moved some items aside, searching. "Oh, here it is," she said, extracting an envelope from underneath the pile. She handed it to Rachel. "Here's a letter of recommendation for your fine job during your time here."

Smiling, Rachel took the letter. "I'm grateful, Miss Gardiner. Under your guidance, I have learned so much about teaching. I appreciate the opportunity to work with you."

"You have a talent for education, young lady, and I hope you will further your career. Unfortunately, the Charity School and most other schools don't allow teachers who have children or are married. It is a poor policy because women should not be penalized for having families. I only accepted you back because our need is so great, and you are so enthusiastic."

"I will continue my teaching at Hopewell, if possible. I've enjoyed being here, but I miss my family. If I come back to Philadelphia, I'll visit, and I appreciate your praise for my abilities."

Miss Gardiner walked with her to the door. "I wish you good fortune with your future endeavors, Rachel."

~ CHAPTER 65 ~

Two days after the Meschianza, Captain Crammond and Edmund Morris met in the room at the back of the store. Morris was packing a small crate with his books and belongings. "I can't believe we're pulling out of Philadelphia," he complained to Crammond. "We've wasted a lot of time and effort here."

"I suppose it was a good place to spend the winter, and I enjoyed the plays and the dances, but I agree, our efforts to infiltrate and defeat the enemy here produced no results."

"Since General Howe's recall to England, General Clinton has reevaluated the merits of staying in the city. The French alliance with the rebels has changed everything."

"Yes, the troops are headed to New York City to defend against the French navy. With Howe's unsuccessful attempt to capture Lafayette the night of the Meschianza, and the Patriots' rejection of the Earl of Carlisle's peace commission offer, we now have no choice but to push north. As we speak, they're loading the heavy equipment on ships to meet us there. Where will you go, Edmund?"

"I can't stay here, but I don't want to go to New York. I have a bad feeling about this whole war, especially with the French involved. I'm taking my fiancée and moving west until we can escape to England."

"You shouldn't be so pessimistic. We'll defeat these rebels eventually."

"I hope you're right, Captain. I hope you're right."

～ CHAPTER 66 ～

Before dawn, a jailer came to the imprisoned men's cells and quietly turned his key in the locks. Most prisoners still slept, but a few wary individuals awoke. Jesse arose, tried the door, and found it unfastened.

He shook the shoulder of his companion, Charles, and whispered, "Wake up but be quiet about it. The cell door is unlocked."

"Unlocked?" queried Charles, rubbing the sleep out of his eyes and rotating his stiff shoulders and neck. "Why would it be unlocked?"

"Perhaps it's a trick. If we escape, the guards could shoot us."

"They are already killing us with starvation and cold," replied Charles. "Why waste the gunpowder to execute us with a bullet?"

"I wonder if any other cells are open." Moving to the front corner, they heard a low buzz of voices.

"Psst, Boyer," Jesse murmured. "Are you awake over there?"

"I'm awake. Did the guard unlock your door too?"

"He did. What do you think it means?"

"I'm baffled. Let me ask if the next door down is open too." Boyer returned in a few minutes. "They're all open."

By now, most of the men had awakened and muttered in apprehension. The leaders in Jesse's cell discussed their options. Flee or stay put? Send several volunteers out or exit en masse and overpower any guards?

One extremely gaunt man, Philip, spoke up. "I'll volunteer to go out and peek at what's happening. If I don't get out in the next day or two, I'll starve to death, so I have nothing to lose. A bullet would be a blessing."

"Do you promise to come back and tell us what's going on? If you don't return, we'll know there's a trap," Charles asked.

"I will," Philip said. "Tell the prisoners in the other cells what I'm doing so they don't follow."

Word passed to await Philip's safe return before leaving.

As Philip opened the iron bars, the men's voices hushed as they held their breath to see what would happen next.

The prisoner eased himself out, warily glancing left and right. The passage was empty. He slowly moved toward the nearest end, pressed against the wall, then disappeared. Within ten minutes, he was back, shuffling as fast as he could.

"No one is here!" he yelled. "All the guards are gone. The doors and gates are all unlocked. We're free!"

At those words, mass exodus ensued. Stronger men helped weaker ones to stand and exit the building while cautiously watching for signs of a trap. But there was none. No British soldiers were in sight, and the streets were deserted. The prisoners scattered in every direction. Three Patriot militiamen came around the corner into the street and rushed to them. "You're free," they yelled. "The British are gone. They pulled out completely. Philadelphia is ours again."

Jesse and some of his companions crossed to Southeast Square and collapsed exhausted on the lush, green grass. The scent of damp earth and blooming flowers smelled overwhelmingly sweet. The glorious sunrise to the east burst into a flood of colors, spewing streaks of golden sunlight. It was the best sight he had ever seen. *I'm free at last!*

By the light of day, Jesse noticed his fellow prisoners looked a sorry lot. Caked with dirt and sweat, their faces appeared almost black with just the whites of their eyes flashing. Their hair and beards were long and matted, and open sores peppered many faces, arms, and legs. Large patches of skin showed through the gaps in their ragged clothing that hung on their bony frames.

Charles clapped Jesse on the back. "I'll bet you're headed straight for that girl of yours, aren't you?"

"Yes, but I need a new set of clothes and a bath, and I don't have any money. Maybe Theuben Bailey at the dock would loan me some shillings."

Charles said, "You try him. I'm going home, but I don't even know if my wife will be there. She may have gone home to her mother since her last letter said she had no money to pay the rent." He rose to go. "Good luck."

The men slapped each other on the back and went their separate ways. Jesse started toward the docks.

When Theuben Bailey spied the ragged skeleton of a man approaching him, he shooed him away. "Begone! There are no hand-outs here. Get a job."

"Theuben," said Jesse. "I'm Jesse Quinter from Hopewell. I've just gotten out of jail."

"Jesse!" roared Theuben, as he picked him up and danced him around. "I didn't recognize you."

"And no wonder, I look terrible. Can you help me?"

"Of course. Come in, let's get you cleaned up and grab some food to eat."

Several hours later, Jesse, freshly bathed, newly clothed, and with a few coins in his pocket, sat with Theuben at Tun Tavern. The whole place was raucous, with everyone celebrating the departure of the British. Pints of ale flowed freely from the taps.

"I'm glad the Redcoats left," said Theuben. "No more interference and regulations from them. They combed through my shipments for contraband and delayed the departures. I can't imagine what you've been through, Jesse. Rachel said the conditions in jail were horrific."

"I'm lucky to have survived and grateful you gave Rachel information about the British soldiers' activities. Perhaps her messages will help win the war."

"She helped me greatly with my logbooks too. They never looked so orderly. I suppose you're anxious to see her."

"Now that I look presentable and have some food in my belly, I want to go."

"Let me know if I can help you further," said Theuben, clapping Jesse on the back.

As Jesse neared Mrs. Graydon's boardinghouse, his heart quickened at the thought of seeing Rachel again as a free man. He knocked on the door, and Andrew, who seemed a foot taller since Jesse had last seen him, answered the door. The young man invited him into the sitting room and disappeared down the hall to the kitchen. Jesse anxiously sat on the edge of his chair, impatient with the time it was taking to fetch Rachel.

"Hello, Jesse," the landlady said, drying her beefy hands on a dishtowel. "Isn't it a glorious day of freedom from those awful Brits? I've got my spare room back."

"The prison was a horrible place, but that's behind me now. Is Rachel here?"

"I'm sorry, she's not. She left yesterday for Hopewell on her horse. Her sister is gravely ill."

"I'm disappointed she's not here. Would you please tell her when she comes back that I'm staying at Tun Tavern? She knows where it is."

"I'll tell her just as soon as she returns." Mrs. Graydon patted him on the arm. "She'll be so glad you're out." Her eyes widened as she sniffed the air. "Goodness, my biscuits are burning!" She rushed toward the kitchen.

As Jesse pulled open the door to leave, a woman holding a baby nearly fell into the room from outside.

He grabbed her arm and the infant to steady them. "Excuse me," he apologized. "I didn't realize you were coming in."

Without a word, she gave him a haughty look and stormed up the steps.

~ CHAPTER 67 ~

At Tun's, Jesse sat at a table facing the window, watching for Rachel. Every minute ticking by seemed like years. The occasional old acquaintance from his hauling days or a former prison pal stopped by his table to chat and rejoice in the British departure, but his longing grew stronger with every passing moment. Every hour or so, he roamed a different part of the city looking for his cream horses, to no avail. He checked back at Tun's frequently in case she had arrived and was waiting. Would she ever come?

As he raised his half-full glass of ale to his lips, he spied her. In his haste to greet her, the drink spilled to the floor, but he was oblivious. Relief and joy washed over him like the rain of a sudden summer storm—cool, refreshing, exhilarating. Rachel rushed into his arms, and they held a tight embrace, oblivious to the other patrons' disapproving eyes on them.

Jesse said, "Rachel, sit down. You must be weary from your trip." She had dark circles under her eyes, and tears streamed down her cheeks.

"Jesse, I can't tell you how glad I am to see you. I'm so excited you're out of jail!" She caressed his hand. "I came as soon as I could. I'm sorry I was away when you called at Mrs. Graydon's." He mopped her face with his handkerchief. Rachel noted, "Oh, you look so thin. Your shoulder blades are poking the back of your shirt, and your hands are crisscrossed with blue veins."

"When I look in the mirror, I barely recognize myself. My skin is so white from the lack of sun that I look like a ghost, and my hair is thinner than before. I look ten years older, but I'm glad to be alive. Theuben loaned me money to get cleaned up when I got out of prison."

"I love you, no matter how you look." She smiled and squeezed his hand.

"How is your sister?"

Rachel's face clouded, and a new single tear threaded down her cheek. Her voice wavered. "I've cried so much for her that I thought I would never have another drop."

"Is she still ill?"

"She's dead," Rachel whispered, then broke into a sob.

"Dead? I'm so sorry." He squeezed her hands. "What happened?"

Rachel dried her tears again with the cloth and set her jaw, determined not to let emotion take her over. "Since Nate was gone to the woods so much, she moved back with Mother and Father when it was close to the time to deliver her baby. Her health had declined from being alone in the cold cabin so much this winter. She rallied in the last month, putting on some weight and being more cheerful. But when her birthing time came, something was wrong. She labored for hours and hours, and when the baby was finally born, the cord was so tightly wrapped around his neck he was dead. All that effort and the loss of another loved one was more than her heart could bear.

"By the time I arrived, she had lapsed into unconsciousness. Nate was falling to pieces, and he had so anticipated the arrival of the baby. I held her hand, stroked her hair, and told her how much I treasured her, but early in the morning, while I was sleeping in the chair in her room, she passed. I can't believe my sister and little brother are both gone. My parents and Nate are crushed. After the funeral, I heard the British had left Philadelphia, and I hurried here to be with you."

Jesse stroked her hand. "I'm speechless, Rachel. I don't know what I can say or do to comfort you."

"Your freedom is the best gift and comfort I can have." He saw her eyes soften as she gazed at his face.

"Your food and letters and that silly little rock in jail kept me sane and alive. I am forever indebted to you. I owe you my life."

"I wish I could have sent more."

"You did all you could, and I am grateful."

She smiled at him. "I would do it again in an instant, love."

They sat in silence for a few minutes. A barmaid with a rag came to wipe Jesse's spilled drink from the floor. "Can I serve you or your lady friend something, Jesse?"

He ordered new drinks and the daily special for them both. When the food came, Rachel picked around the edges.

"You need to eat. You're sad, but your sister wouldn't want you to become sick over this. We all have a limited time on Earth, and we can't predict when our Maker will call us home."

"You're right." She tried a small mouthful and chewed slowly, eventually swallowing. "Eating is hard. The food goes round and round, but I'll keep trying."

He let her take several more bites, enjoying the sight of her. She blushed when she saw him staring. "You are so beautiful. Where is your son? I'm anxious to meet him."

"Ah, Little Nicky." She smiled. "At first, I was unsure how to feel about him. The circumstances of his conception, how he interfered with my teaching plans at the Charity School, and the shame of not being married made loving him seem impossible. But as soon as he was born, I marveled at his beautiful blue eyes, his head of dark hair, and his tiny perfect fingers and toes. A feeling welled up inside me, more powerful than any I have ever felt before. It's like my love for you, Jesse, but also so different. You're strong and independent and my rock to rely on, and he's the opposite—weak and small and innocent, and I'm *his* rock. When I first laid eyes on him, I immediately thought of my poor brother, Nick. He has a warmth in his gentle, innocent eyes like Nick's. I can never replace my brother, but Little Nicky's personality reminds me so much of him." As she talked, her voice took on a different tone—softer, kinder, motherly. "Yes, there's not just me anymore. Little Nicky and I are a team. Is that all right with you?"

"I'm sure I'll love him as much as I adore you." He put down his fork. "I want to be with you and Little Nicky forever. It's all I thought about in prison. Will you marry me?"

"Yes, yes, I'm so happy you want to be with us! I can't wait to be a family."

They sat a few minutes, holding hands across the table, contemplating their future together and how their lives would change.

"When do I meet this wonderful baby?" Jesse asked.

"Sarah Brown, at Mrs. Graydon's, took care of him for me when I went back to Charity and watched him when I went to Hopewell. She's been a great friend through everything, and Little Nicky adores her."

"Why didn't you take him with you to Hopewell?"

"With Phebe so ill, I needed to get there fast, and I couldn't ride Missy with him along. I wasn't ready to explain to my parents that I have a child and add another burden to their woes. When I arrived in Philadelphia, I changed out of my riding clothes then came straight here. I didn't see Little Nicky or Sarah before I left. They probably were out."

"I might have seen Sarah and Little Nicky when I called for you at Mrs. Graydon's after jail. As I was leaving, they were coming in," Jesse said. "Once we're married, perhaps you won't need to tell everything to your parents. They'll assume he's my son."

"I hate keeping secrets from them, but you're right. There will be enough talk about him being born before we are married."

"Let's marry as soon as we can unless your heart wants a wedding at Hopewell."

"No, I want a small ceremony here. A big ceremony would draw more attention to us, and my parents need to mourn Phebe and her son. All that wedding fuss is nonsense anyway."

"Your presence with a new husband and little one of your own will help ease their grief."

She ate one more small bite. "I've eaten all I can, so let's go to Mrs. Graydon's. I'm excited to introduce him to you."

Jesse paid the bill, and they walked back to the boardinghouse hand-in-hand, stealing a kiss whenever no one was looking. The street was crowded with people because many families who fled during the British occupation were returning to the city.

At home, Rachel and Jesse burst into the kitchen, surprising Mrs. Graydon, who was clearing the dinner dishes.

"Mrs. Graydon," said Rachel, "I'm back. Are Sarah and Little Nicky upstairs?"

"No," said Mrs. Graydon. "Since Captain Crammond took his cow, they went out for milk and aren't back yet. I see you found your young man. He was mighty worried about you. How is your sister, dear?"

Rachel, Jesse, and Mrs. Graydon sat at the table while Rachel told the tragic news.

"I'm so sorry for you," sympathized Mrs. Graydon, laying a comforting hand on Rachel's. "Your family has endured such tragedy. First your brother's death and now your sister's. They'll be so excited to have you and Little Nicky back in their lives."

"And Jesse, too. We're getting married."

The landlady jumped up and hugged Rachel, then Jesse. "Congratulations to both of you! Even during a rainstorm, the clouds part, and a beautiful rainbow appears. You make a fine couple and will be good parents for Little Nicky. Now you go into the parlor and wait for Sarah and the baby. They'll be home soon."

~ CHAPTER 68 ~

But Sarah and Little Nicky didn't come home soon. After hours of waiting, Rachel was frantic. "Where can they be, Jesse?" she asked for the hundredth time as she peered out the parlor window.

"Perhaps they stopped somewhere to visit a friend. Sarah doesn't know you'd be home today. Try to be patient."

Another hour passed, and the front door opened. Rachel jumped to welcome Sarah, but it was Andrew Graydon.

"Andrew, were Sarah and Little Nicky on the street anywhere?"

"Aren't they home yet?"

Mrs. Graydon entered the parlor. "Andrew, when did you last see them?"

"This morning, they got into a carriage and headed out of town."

"A carriage?" asked Jesse. "Where would she obtain a carriage?"

"Oh, it wasn't hers. A man and woman were in the carriage when Sarah got in with the baby."

"Did you recognize the others?" the landlady quizzed.

"I only glanced at their backs as they left, but I think the man was Mr. Morris, who used to board here. I didn't know the woman, but she had blond curly hair and was wearing a plumed hat."

Mrs. Graydon said, "Andrew, if you saw Morris, you should have told me. He still owes me money."

Rachel gasped, "Mr. Morris! Are you sure, Andrew?"

"I wasn't sure it was him. That's why I didn't get you, Mother. They seemed to be in a hurry to leave and didn't look back."

Jesse said, "The lady could be Susanna Sterling."

"Andrew," said his mother, "go upstairs and check Sarah and Arthur Brown's room. Here's the key if no one answers." She fished it off a loop of keys in her pocket.

The young man bounded up the stairs two at a time and returned, breathless. "All their belongings are gone."

"Oh, no," Rachel cried.

"Andrew, see if Mr. Brown's horse is still in the barn. He came in late last night."

"Was his the black gelding with one white rear sock?"

"That's the one," said Rachel.

Jesse looked shocked. "What? I've been looking for such a horse. The man who robbed me at Berry's Inn had a mount like that."

"There are lots of horses fitting that description, Jesse. It could be a coincidence."

"Let's go." The men ran toward the back entrance.

They returned shortly. "Brown's horse is gone too."

Rachel now realized the awful truth. "Sarah stole Little Nicky!" she exclaimed. Feeling faint, she sank to the chair and held her head in her hands. Jesse knelt beside her.

"Don't worry. We'll find them."

"But how? We don't have any idea where they went. They left hours ago."

"It's too dark to go after them tonight, but let's go to Theuben Bailey's and ask his advice. We don't know what kind of trouble we may encounter once we find them."

Rachel pulled herself out of the chair, dried her tears, and clenched her jaw. Within an hour, they arrived at the shack at the dock. Jesse pounded on the door.

318 LINDA J. COLLINS

Startled, the dock man threw open the door. "Jesse, what's the matter?" He motioned them to come in, and his companion pushed back his chair from the table. "You nearly scared us to death." An upturned checkerboard lay on the floor, with checkers scattered everywhere.

Jesse spelled out their plight.

"Why would they take the child?" Theuben asked.

"Morris is a British spy and the father of Little Nicky," said Rachel. "He assaulted me when I first came to town, and later at his storefront, I slapped him. He hates me. I thwarted his plan to discover the cannon making at Hopewell, and he vowed to retaliate. Sarah, who I thought was my friend, has always wanted a child and has now taken mine. I'm not sure why they are together."

"Perhaps they are in league with each other and are making an escape since the British have abandoned Philadelphia," said Jesse.

"If so, I feel so betrayed by Sarah. How could she do this to me? I trusted her with my most precious possession, Little Nicky." She wrung her hands.

"If she was spying on you, that would explain how the soldiers knew when I would be in town with the cannon. She's responsible for my capture! We both have a score to settle," said Jesse. "How can we find them?"

Theuben's voice was firm. "You can't track them now. We'll start at first light. Let's look at my map and make a plan to trace them. People in the country will notice that carriage. But where can they be going?"

Theuben rooted in his cupboard, discarding bits of nautical equipment on the floor in his search for a map. He pulled down several rolls of paper from the back of the top shelf, briefly unrolled each, sometimes turning them which way round, and began to spread one out.

He unfurled a map of Philadelphia and the surrounding lands and placed lead weights on each corner to hold it flat.

"Where are we now?" asked Rachel, trying to orient herself to the dizzying array of streets and roads.

"We're here," pointed Theuben, placing a red checker on the drawing.

"They were last seen here, in front of Mrs. Graydon's." Jesse put another checker on the map. "Andrew said the carriage was headed out of town."

"Where do you think they might go?" Theuben quizzed.

Rachel replied, "Sarah once said her dream was to go west and buy a little farm and settle down. What roads exit Philadelphia in that direction?"

Theuben traced a road with his finger. "To go west, you have to cross the Schuylkill River at either the ferry at Gardiner's place or Suett's, a bit further north. The roads from both places branch off a short distance after that, the main ones being the road to Haverford or the road to Lancaster. Jesse, do you use either of those on your way to Hopewell?"

"I cross at Suett's, then travel the Lancaster Road until I reach Berry's Inn. Then I head northwest to Hopewell. But after either crossing, the first farm is David George's followed by Elisha George's place."

"If we go there," observed Rachel, "we could stop at each house and ask if they have seen the carriage. If not, we could try the next one, and if still no one has seen them, we could switch to the road to Haverford or the other road further south."

"Since you mentioned Lancaster Road, I remember Roy Dickinson, the man who robbed me at Berry's, said he lived in Lancaster. If Arthur Brown is the same person, they may be heading there. I propose we go toward Lancaster first."

"Sounds like a good plan to me," Theuben said. "What do you think, Rachel?"

"Let's try it," she said. "I'll be ready at dawn. We can travel faster on horseback than they can by carriage, so we might be able to catch up with them tomorrow if we start early."

Jesse asked, "Theuben, can you go along? I'm not sure what kind of trouble we might encounter."

~ CHAPTER 69 ~

Before the sun rose, the grim but determined Rachel, Jesse, and Theuben, left the shack. Missy and the horses borrowed from Caleb's stable were fresh, and in the cool morning air, they were eager to go. A light fog covered the ground.

"Theuben, I'm grateful you can come with us," said Jesse. "I'm not sure how many people we may have to deal with."

"I'm happy to help thwart any plan those traitorous villains are hatching. I hope to exact revenge not only for your suffering but also Rachel's. Imagine stealing a baby!"

They headed north from Philadelphia, crossing the Schuylkill River at Suett's Ferry, and at the intersection of Lancaster and Haverford Roads, they took the right fork toward Lancaster. About mid-morning, they pulled into David George's farmyard, where his wife was weeding her garden.

"Hello, Mrs. George," Jesse called as they dismounted.

"Greetings, Jesse. I haven't seen you or your wagon in quite a while. Where is your beautiful team of cream-colored horses?"

"It's a long story, but the British put me in prison and confiscated my animals."

"Ah." She shook her fist. "I'm glad to see those nasty, red-coated soldiers on their way. May they never come back around here. Thank the Lord you're free now. I suppose you're looking for that fine set of horses?"

"I would like to find them, but today we're searching for a carriage carrying a man, two women, and an infant. They possibly went by yesterday. Have you seen them?"

"I do remember it. It stopped here, and the woman asked if I had milk because the baby was crying. I gave them some, they watered their horse and then seemed in a hurry to be gone. Does that sound like them?"

"Yes, that's them," replied Rachel eagerly. "Did the child seem all right?"

"The baby quieted once given the milk."

Jesse said, "Did they continue on this road?"

"Yes. The blonde-haired woman whined and acted like she wanted to go back, but the man in charge was stern with her."

They remounted. "Thank you for the information, Mrs. George. You've been extremely helpful."

"Good luck finding them and your team," she declared, as they nudged their horses into a trot.

"I am relieved to know they are tending the baby," said Rachel. "Sarah always was caring with him."

As they neared Elisha George's farm, Jesse suggested, "Let's not stop here. There hasn't been any place for the carriage to turn off, and we're losing valuable time if we talk to everyone. Let's skip a few farms."

"That makes sense to me," agreed Rachel, as Theuben nodded his head.

Now that the sun was up, the day turned hot. "Let's stop a minute so I can shed my jacket," declared Rachel. Jesse held Missy while she pulled her arms out of the sleeves and tied the jacket to the saddle. Jesse and Theuben followed her lead, and the travelers rode on in their shirtsleeves. The road was dusty, and they sipped water from their canteens. The horses became lathered in sweat, and the riders' clothes stuck to their bodies from perspiration. After another two miles, they approached the Fisher farm. When they rode up, Mr.

322   LINDA J. COLLINS

Fisher was unhitching his team from the overloaded hay wagon in front of the barn.

"Have you seen a carriage pass this way? Maybe a day ago?"

"No, but I've been in my fields the last two days haying."

"Did your wife see anyone?" Rachel inquired. "Can we talk to her?"

"I doubt she saw anything. My son is deathly sick, and she's been nursing him day and night."

"We're sorry to hear about your child," said Rachel. "We won't bother you with our worries. I hope he gets better soon." The group rode off.

They stopped at the next farm, where the farmer's wife was hanging clothes on the line. The sheets were billowing in the breeze. She remembered seeing the carriage. "I didn't pay any attention to who was in it, but I noticed it because I was afraid the dust it kicked up would soil yesterday's laundry on the line. It was moving quite fast."

"Thanks." They urged their horses on.

Mid-afternoon, they pulled up under a stand of shade trees and watered the animals in the creek. "Don't let them drink too much," cautioned Rachel. "They're rather hot. Maybe we should rest them here awhile."

"I could use a respite too," complained Jesse, collapsing to the ground beside a broad oak tree. He wiped the sweat from his brow with his sleeve. "I'm not used to such riding." He stretched his legs. "And I'm especially not liking that saddle." Rachel could see him slightly trembling from the exertion.

"Me neither," added Theuben, wincing in pain.

Rachel dipped her kerchief in the spring, sat beside Jesse, and dabbed his forehead with the cool water. He gently rubbed her shoulder.

They enjoyed the shade and watched the horses happily cropping grass. Antsy to keep going, Rachel asked, "How much farther ahead do you think they are?"

Jesse said, "They are still quite a ways ahead if they kept going. We'll reach Berry's at the turnoff for the road to Hopewell in a few more miles. We can check the farm before Berry's, then the one on the Lancaster Road after the tavern to make sure they've gone that way."

"They wouldn't take the Hopewell Road, would they?" Theuben asked.

"Probably not, since they know we'll be looking for them."

Despite being bone-tired and hungry, they remounted. They had had nothing to eat after their early morning breakfast in Philadelphia.

Jesse eventually announced, "Here's the last house before we reach Berry's."

"I'll go ask," Rachel said. "You two can rest here." She turned the palomino down the short lane and gave her a sharp kick with her heels. Even Missy no longer wanted to trot.

Rachel came back, all smiles. "Yes, they remember them. They asked for milk again."

When they reached Berry's, they stopped for the night. Jimmy Berry gave Jesse a bone-crushing bear-hug after not seeing him for so long.

"No one by that description stopped here. I wouldn't forget a group like that."

"That must mean one thing," summarized Theuben. "Their first destination must not be far away, or they would have settled here. I can't think that bunch would camp out."

"Let's hope that's true," said Rachel. "We'll tend the horses, get a meal for ourselves, and turn in. It's been a long day."

~ CHAPTER 70 ~

After a quick, early breakfast, they saddled the horses and started again, continuing toward Lancaster. At the first farm, the farmer's wife recalled the vehicle passing late, two days ago.

Convinced they were on the correct road, Rachel, Jesse, and Theuben rode a few miles past several farms. When they stopped next, no one remembered a carriage. They rode on, and at the subsequent dwelling, no one had seen it either.

Theuben muttered, "There are only two possibilities. They either didn't come this way, or these last two farmers didn't notice them."

"Maybe it was dark when they passed by," suggested Rachel.

"This has to be the right road from the sighting of them at the house after Berry's," said Jesse. "Let's work our way back. I feel they're here somewhere close but well-hidden."

They turned the horses around. Two more farms back still yielded no carriage. "The next one back is where we stopped first this morning, so we know they were there. Somehow between this farm and that, they've vanished," said Jesse, exasperated.

"Perhaps we should turn around again," Rachel said.

"I think it's unlikely that two farms in a row toward Lancaster from here haven't seen them."

Theuben said, "Let's go back to the first house on this road where they were spotted and ride forward. We might see some carriage tracks or some other clue."

As they rode back to the first house, they discovered what they had missed the first time.

"Look," cried Rachel. "There's an overgrown lane."

"We must have ridden by it in the dark this morning."

"Is a house behind those trees?" asked Theuben. "The lane is so long I can't tell from here. If a house is there, it would be a perfect place for them to hide."

"Let's go." Rachel kicked Missy into a canter.

"Rachel, wait! Come back!" yelled Jesse. She reined in Missy with a sliding stop and returned reluctantly to the group. "If they're there, we can't barge in."

"Rachel, Jesse's right. We don't know how many they are."

Jesse said, "We don't want to jeopardize Little Nicky. Let's walk the horses slowly and see if they're there. Then we can plan how to deal with them. Remember, these are dangerous people."

On the verge of tears, Rachel admitted, "You're right, but I'm so anxious to get my baby back. I've already lost my brother and sister. I don't know how I'll go on if I lose Little Nicky too."

~ CHAPTER 71 ~

After locating a house and a dilapidated barn in a stand of oak trees a quarter mile down the lane, they waited for the cover of darkness. Had they discovered Morris's hiding place? The moonless night was pitch-dark. Rachel, Jesse, and Theuben crept through the woods to the rear of the barn and tied their horses. Stealthily, they circled to the front where the double barn doors stood open. They were ready to retreat at any sign of being discovered, listening for any noise inside the structure or farmhouse nearby.

Theuben whispered, "Let me peek around the corner to see who's there. Since they don't know me, if I'm spotted, I can pretend I'm a traveler on the road looking for water for my horse and a place to shelter for the night. You two stay here."

In a flash, Theuben hustled back, and they retreated to plan a strategy.

"Two men are harnessing Jesse's cream-colored horses to a wagon."

"My team!" hissed Jesse. "How did they get here?"

"Is that all you saw?" asked Rachel.

"I couldn't tell if anyone else was there. It's dark inside except for two lanterns hung on the main uprights of the barn."

"What do the men look like?" asked Rachel.

"One man is tall with black hair and mustache and dressed in city clothes. The other is shorter, about Jesse's height, but not as stocky."

"That sounds like Edmund Morris and Arthur Brown, Sarah's husband," said Rachel. "If Mr. Brown is here, probably Sarah and my baby are too."

Suddenly, they heard the cries of an infant.

"My Nicky! He's in there! I'd know his cry anywhere. I must go to him. He needs me!" She lunged forward, but Jesse held her arms tightly.

"We need a plan, or they'll escape," he whispered.

Raised voices came from the barn. "Sarah, keep that child quiet," admonished her husband.

"I'm trying, Roy, but he's hungry. He needs more milk. I'll try rocking him, and perhaps he'll go back to sleep."

Susanna's voice broke in. "I can't stand to hear the baby's cry. I'll ask if the farmer's wife has more milk." She headed toward the farmhouse.

"That's Susanna," Rachel said. "So, that has to be Morris in the barn. The carriage must be inside."

"Since she's going to the house, she won't get in our way," observed Jesse.

Theuben said, "There are only two men, Jesse. You take Arthur Brown, and I'll take Morris."

"No, I've got a score to settle with both men, but a bigger score with Morris," replied Jesse emphatically. "I'll take him."

"I understand. We'll go in together and confront them, but you take whichever man is closest. Rachel, come in behind us and find Sarah and reclaim your boy."

They crept to the edge of the doors and paused a moment until their eyes became accustomed to the dim light inside. Theuben looked at them, nodded his head, and they stormed inside.

Their sudden entrance startled the team, and the massive cream horses reared in their half-fastened harness. Arthur Brown held on to their heads, tried to quiet them, and then turned to face the disturbance.

328 LINDA J. COLLINS

"It seems we have company, Roy," said Morris coolly, stepping to one side, away from the unsettled animals.

"Roy Dickinson," proclaimed Jesse, "I see you not only stole my money but now you have my team too." He moved toward the thief.

"They aren't your team anymore, traitor," he snarled. "They're mine now. Confiscated in the name of the Crown."

Rachel hurried to where Sarah sat on bales of straw, vigorously rocking Little Nicky. "You took my baby, Sarah. Give him to me!" She reached for the squalling infant, but Sarah turned her back, keeping the child out of reach.

"Stay away from me, Rachel," Sarah warned.

"I thought you were my friend. Why are you doing this?" Rachel implored.

"I'm not your friend," Sarah shrieked over the baby's cries. "You don't want this baby. You're too busy with your books and studying to take care of him. I love him more than you. He thinks *I'm* his mother, not you."

"Why are you and your husband with this scoundrel, Morris?

Morris piped up. "Don't you see, Rachel? Mr. and Mrs. Brown, who I know as Mr. and Mrs. Roy Dickinson, are working with me. They agree that traitors need to be taught a lesson and lose everything they cherish."

Rachel confronted Sarah. "So, you're the one who betrayed Jesse to this spy?"

"I sold all your secrets to the British." Her voice was venomous.

Morris said, "Rachel, you seem to forget the child is mine too. I gave him to Sarah to take care of for me."

Jesse declared, "You don't want that baby. You stole him to get even with us."

"I had hoped you would still be in jail, Mr. Quinter, but your release forced us to act sooner. Now all of you will be going to jail as traitors, without the child, of course."

"Now that the British have left Philadelphia, *you* are the traitors. There's no way the two of you are taking us anywhere," threatened Theuben, moving toward Morris, while at the same time Jesse grabbed at Roy, who was still holding the horses.

Morris stepped back, reached into his breast coat pocket, and pulled out a pistol. As Theuben rushed him, the gun went off, the bullet striking Theuben in the shoulder, the impact throwing him to the ground. The loud gunfire in the close confines of the barn caused the panicked animals to lunge forward. Roy lost his grip on the harness and fell as the four-horse team and heavy wagon trampled him in their haste to exit the barn. Jesse had fallen, too, but he rolled as the horses and wagon narrowly missed him.

In the confusion, Morris took his opportunity to escape. Rachel and Jesse rushed to Theuben's side, fearing the worst. When they determined he wasn't mortally wounded, they dashed to the door to see Morris astride Missy, pounding down the road behind the stampeding team and wagon.

Sarah placed the baby on the straw and flew to her husband, who lay unconscious on the floor, his body a crumpled mass, blood pouring from his crushed head.

"I'll follow Morris," yelled Jesse, sprinting to his horse tethered behind the barn. "Rachel, take care of Theuben and Little Nicky."

"What's happening?" exclaimed Susanna as she and the farmer and his wife rushed into the barn. "We heard a gunshot. Rachel, what are you doing here with these men?"

"We're here to reclaim my baby and arrest these spies."

"*Your* baby? Sarah said he's hers. And no one here is a spy."

"Sarah kidnapped my baby, and she, Edmund Morris, and Roy Dickinson are British spies. Since the Redcoats left Philadelphia, they are trying to make their escape. They are the ones who tried to destroy Hopewell."

"They didn't try to hurt Hopewell. I don't know what you are talking about."

"I'll explain all that later," she said.

Rachel scooped up Little Nicky and cuddled him. Susanna gave her the bottle, and the baby began to suckle eagerly.

The farmer pulled Sarah away from Roy's broken body and felt for a pulse. "I'm sorry, ma'am, but he's dead."

Sarah burst into tears and collapsed to the floor, cradling Roy's bloody head and shaking his shoulder, willing him back to life to no avail.

After inspecting Theuben's wound, the farmer's wife helped him to his feet. "His shoulder's not too bad. The bullet went right through. Come to the house, and I'll put a dressing on it." The farmer, his wife, and Theuben haltingly made their way to the house.

"Rachel, tell me this instant what is going on. Where is Edmund?" Susanna demanded.

"Susanna, sit down, and I'll tell you everything. It's going to be quite a shock."

~ CHAPTER 72 ~

Hours later, in the darkness of the moonless night, Jesse returned to the farm on his horse, leading Missy. The body of Morris was draped face down over the palomino's saddle.

Rachel, who had been watching from the farmhouse window, ran to meet him. "Jesse, I'm so glad you're safe." She scowled at the body and noticed congealed blood covering Morris's forehead. "What happened? Is he dead?"

"Yes, he's dead. A few miles down the road, he turned Missy into the woods, thinking he would lose me or ambush me. But as Missy ran, she galloped under a low-hanging branch that hit Morris dead-on in the head. He never saw it coming until too late. I wouldn't have found him until first light, except I spotted Missy when she came out of the woods. I backtracked her trail and discovered him dead under the tree. It wasn't easy to load him on the saddle, but Missy was tired and stood still for me while I hoisted him on and tied him down with some grapevine."

"I can't say I'm sorry about his death after all his evil actions."

"How are Theuben and Little Nicky?"

"The bullet passed straight through Theuben's shoulder and didn't hit anything vital. The farmer's wife bandaged him and fashioned a sling for his arm. He'll be all right. The baby was just hungry and wet. They're both sleeping now."

"And what about Roy Dickenson?"

"He's dead. Sarah is heartbroken."

"I'm not sympathetic to any of them after what they put us through—your attack, the kidnapping, my imprisonment. They only wanted financial gain and to aid the enemy. They got what they deserved."

"I've been very naïve to trust everyone so much. I never thought my best friend would betray me as Sarah did. What will happen to her now?"

"We'll take her back to Philadelphia along with the bodies and turn her over as a spy. The Patriots will deal with her. Now that all the prisoners the British held in jail have been released, there's room for her there. That place is horrible."

"The farmer and I retrieved the team and wagon a short distance down the road. The horses were happily grazing in a field. He's been caring for them and had no idea they were stolen. We stabled them in the barn, then loaded Roy's body in the wagon. Let's put Morris with him so we can return to the city tomorrow."

They walked the horses toward the barn. Once inside, they unloaded the body, now starting to stiffen with rigor mortis, into the wagon, and covered both dead men with a tarp.

Jesse asked, "How did Susanna react to the news about Morris?"

"She was upset at first but gradually started remembering occasions when he had asked probing questions about her father's activities. She thought it strange at the time, but now it all makes sense. She realizes that he was manipulating her and didn't truly love her. Although disappointed she won't get her fancy society wedding in Philadelphia, she's glad to discover the truth. I also think she was discovering he was a scoundrel too. He told her they were taking a short ride in the carriage to drop Sarah and the baby off at Sarah's house, and by the time she realized that wasn't true, they were far from town, and he refused to take her back."

They put the horses in the stalls and tossed down some hay from the loft. Holding hands, they walked to the house with weary, shuffling steps.

In the farmhouse, Jesse sat down to a warm plate of beef stew over biscuits. As he savored each bite, he gazed longingly across the table at his fiancée. She grinned and blew him a kiss.

EPILOGUE

Rachel pulled the little wagon containing her precious cargo, Little Nicky, up the lane toward her parents' house. The autumn air was warm, and the trees were afire with glorious oranges, yellows, and reds. The mild temperatures of Indian summer were welcome before the weather turned cooler again and plunged toward winter. Having returned to Hopewell, she, Jesse, and the baby resided in the cabin Phebe and Nate had occupied. Although Rachel had never visited her sister there, she could sense the specter of her sister's presence at times. She was glad Phebe's suffering was over, but she still missed her dearly.

When she arrived at her destination, her mother eagerly greeted them at the door. "I was watching for you," Martha said. "It seems so long since I've seen you and my grandson."

"Mother, it's only been two days."

Her mother lifted the child from the wagon and settled him on her hip. "Have you taken off your socks again?" she cooed to Little Nicky. Rachel located the socks under the blanket in the wagon and helped put them on the baby's wiggling feet. Martha smothered the top of his head with gentle kisses until his chubby, little hands brushed her away. "I swear he gets heavier every day. Can you chat awhile before your lesson?"

"Not now, but when I return, we can talk."

"Plan on staying for supper tonight. Lewis and Jesse will be back from the furnace, and we can all eat together."

"Good. That relieves me of deciding what to prepare for dinner."

"Perhaps you should have paid more attention when we fixed meals when you were growing up." Her mother winked.

Rachel scowled, then conceded the point, patting her mother's arm. "You're right, as usual."

"Whose children are you teaching today?" Martha asked.

"First is Jacob Coggins, George Coggins's son. He loves science but hates writing and grammar, so I coax him into learning those subjects by writing about nature. Then I teach Patrick and Barbara Davis, the twins of the blacksmith, Valentine Davis. They're only six years old, so we're still working on the basics—the alphabet, counting, and the like, but they're extremely competitive and so eager. We're meeting in the Big House parlor until the school is built."

"I'm glad to see you're repaying the debt to the Sterlings for your room and board in the city even though it's difficult to both teach and care for Little Nicky."

"He's no problem, especially with a doting grandmother nearby. I look forward to teaching them. It keeps me challenged and feeling useful."

"An active youngster and new husband are usually sufficient challenges for a young woman," her mother observed.

"They do keep me busy."

"When did he last eat?"

"I fed him before I came, so he should be ready for a nap soon."

"You should get him on a stricter schedule, but I suppose mothers nowadays don't like the old ways." Anxious to be let down, the infant squirmed in her arms. "I'll play with him a little and wear him out a bit, first." She laughed as she resettled him on her other hip.

"He's trying to stand, so I think he'll be walking soon." Rachel turned. "I better go, or I'll be late."

As she walked toward the Big House, she crossed the bridge traversing French Creek and pondered how different her life had become since Little Nicky's rescue. Her former best friend, Sarah Brown, was in jail in Philadelphia for kidnapping and spying. Edmund Morris, her tormentor, was dead, as was Roy Dickinson.

After returning to the city with the bodies, accompanied by Sarah and Susanna, Jesse and Rachel pledged their love in a small marriage ceremony with Theuben and Mrs. Graydon as witnesses. A honeymoon night at Tun Tavern followed, then the couple packed Rachel's belongings into the wagon pulled by Jesse's cream horses for the return to Hopewell. She regretfully returned the last of her books to Francis Daymon at The Library Company and told him how grateful she was for his help. He praised her for her bravery in helping the Patriots' cause with her coded information.

She now could hardly believe her luck. She had a wonderful husband and a healthy child, she was back in the protective care of her precious parents, and she was fulfilling her teaching goals. She also was learning to take her mother's suggestions. Her mother meant well, and Rachel accepted many of her ideas, although she didn't always agree with them. The only black cloud came when she thought of her poor dead sister and little brother, who were not there to share her joy.

She stepped onto the wide veranda of the ironmaster's house, and Mrs. Sterling greeted her from her rocker. "Your first student, Jacob, just arrived and is in the parlor. I'm so glad you can teach these children who otherwise could not afford an education, Rachel."

"That was part of our arrangement, Mrs. Sterling, but even if it wasn't, I love teaching them. I'm so grateful for the opportunity you gave me to expand my knowledge in Philadelphia. Any letter from Susanna lately?"

"I received one yesterday. She's decided to stay on at Mrs. Levering's school. She thinks living here is too tedious. There's so much more for a young woman to do in the city, she says. I'm some-what envious of her there. I hope she gets married, like you."

"I'm sure she'll find a match. There are more opportunities to meet men there, although I ended up with a husband from Hopewell. The village is more my style of living."

"I doubt Susanna will ever move back. At least David still lives here. His father is teaching him everything about managing the furnace. At some point, it will all be his responsibility."

"It's a lot to learn, I imagine. Tell Susanna I said hello next time you write."

"I'll do that," said Mrs. Sterling. "Now, get on with your lessons, and if you need any supplies or books, let me know, and I'll order them."

"Thank you," said Rachel as she opened the screen door to the house.

She greeted Jacob and started his lesson.

After dinner that evening in the Palsgroves' keeping room, Jesse tried to hold Little Nicky on his lap. "Come here, you imp," he implored, as the child squirmed away and crawled towards his wooden ball.

"He's too interested in his toys," observed Lewis, as he rolled the ball that had escaped the child's grasp back to him.

Lewis said, "Jesse, do you like your new job at the furnace? Do you miss traveling?"

"I miss the fresh air and open spaces, but I won't miss the cold, snowy winter months. Now that I have a wife and son and new in-laws, I don't miss the hectic city life in Philadelphia at all. I've had my fill of that." He squeezed Rachel's hand as she sat on the settee beside him. "I like the new job, but there's so much to learn."

"You're a quick study, but it takes time for the procedures to become second nature. After a while, you'll discover you won't even think about all the steps to making good iron."

"I'm glad you have confidence in me," replied Jesse, "but now that we're again casting cannon and balls, I feel I have so much to learn."

"Since the British left Philadelphia, we can again support the Patriots' cause with munitions. Washington needs our help now more than ever since the war has resumed," said Lewis.

Martha added, "And we're so proud of Rachel's contribution of information to the General. I can hardly believe she took on such a dangerous task." Rachel beamed.

Lewis said, "We're so grateful you brought our daughter and grandson back to us safely. After the deaths we endured last year, we can't thank you enough. A job to keep you here is the least I could do for our family. We never felt close to Nate, and he's already moved on with a new wife."

Jack, the cat, interrupted by jumping onto Jesse's lap. "Oh, hello, Jack," he said, stroking the cat's soft fur and scratching under his chin. "I don't know whether you're here because you like me or you're escaping Little Nicky."

"I think both," joked Rachel, as the child crept over to Jesse and attempted to stand to reach Jack's twitching tail.

"What will you do with your team of horses, Jesse?" asked Martha.

"I'll continue to train them, but during the week when I'm busy at the furnace, I'm leasing them to Mr. Sterling to haul iron to town. They need to continue working, and in a pinch, I could drive the route if the new teamster becomes ill or injured."

"Rachel, will you be sending Missy back to Philadelphia for Susanna?" Lewis inquired.

"Susanna uses carriages around town, so Missy will stay here. I'll help Ben take care of her and exercise her to keep her in shape."

"Work, work, work," said Martha. "New husband, baby, a horse to tend, and new students to teach. I don't know how you will do it all."

The following Sunday after church, the family gathered at the little cemetery. A few parishioners milled around, musing over the gravestones of loved ones. The breeze rustled the dried leaves on the ground, and puffy, white clouds skidded majestically across the deep azure sky. Rachel laid chrysanthemums on the graves of Phebe, her stillborn son, and Nick. Little Nicky played on the ground in a pile of leaves, trying to catch them if they skittered beyond his reach. The family joined hands in silent prayer. After a moment, Little Nicky shattered the silence with a joyous shriek as he pulled himself up, holding onto the tombstone of Rachel's brother, Nick, and took his first tottering steps. They all laughed as Jesse scooped up his son, and they started home.

The End

AUTHOR'S NOTES

Dreams of Revolution uses various historic locations, people, and events that I depicted as accurately as possible. Some are fictional, and some are real.

Locations. The majority of locations are actual, and some still exist today.

Hopewell Furnace is located near Birdsboro in Berks County, Pennsylvania, and is a national historic site managed by the National Park Service, U.S. Department of the Interior. The furnace was active from 1771 to 1883 but subsequently fell into disrepair. In 1935 the U.S. government bought the property, and the Civilian Conservation Corps (CCC) stabilized five structures. Hopewell Furnace made 115 big guns for the Continental Navy and provided shot and shells to the army and navy throughout the Revolutionary War. The park and buildings are open to visitors. https://www.nps.gov/hofu/index.htm

For further reading, *Hopewell Village, The Dynamics of a Nineteenth Century Iron-Making Community* by Joseph E. Walker is an excellent, non-fiction work detailing all aspects of Hopewell Village (526 pages). *Hopewell Furnace National Historic Site, Official National Park Handbook, Handbook 124,* has excellent pictures and tells the history and operation of the furnace (98 pages). *Junior History Guide to Hopewell Furnace, National Historic Site,* is a 25-page booklet designed for young readers.

Berry's Tavern is known today as the King of Prussia Inn, located in King of Prussia, Pennsylvania. In 1975 it was listed on the U.S. National Register of Historic Places. Jimmy Berry ran Berry's Tavern beginning in 1774. It is not open to visitors. https://www.livingplaces.

com / PA / Montgomery_County / Upper_Merion_Township / King_
of_Prussia_Inn.html

Tun Tavern was established at Philadelphia's waterfront in 1685.
In 1732 the Masons first met there, and before the Revolutionary War
commenced, Washington, Jefferson, and the Continental Congress
met at the Tavern. The birthdate and birthplace of the United States
Marine Corps is considered by many to be on November 10, 1775,
at Tun Tavern. The Continental Congress ordered two battalions of
Marines to be recruited, and those men enlisted at the tavern. The
building no longer exists. https://en.wikipedia.org/wiki/Tun_Tavern

Charity School for Girls opened in 1753 for the education of children of the poor. An earlier Charity School was founded by George
Whitefield in 1741 but failed due to lack of financial support. The building which Whitefield started was incomplete, and in 1750 the property
was sold to the Trustees of Benjamin Franklin's College, Academy, and
Charitable Schools for Boys and Girls. In 1764 the school for girls was
moved to another location and was primarily funded by donations.
The buildings no longer exist. https://archives.upenn.edu/exhibits/
penn-history/18th-century/charity-school

The University, the brainchild of Benjamin Franklin, was char-
tered in 1755 and led by Provost William Smith, whose name I borrowed. Women were not admitted until 1878. It is now the University
of Pennsylvania (Penn). https://archives.upenn.edu/exhibits/
penn-history/brief-history

The Jail was built in 1773 and held prisoners in large rooms with
no effort to look after their well-being. The building was closed in
1835 and later demolished. https://philadelphiaencyclopedia.org/
archive/prisons-and-jails/

Carpenter's Hall was built in 1773 to demonstrate the carpentry
skills of the Carpenters' Company. Being the largest meeting place in
Philadelphia, the First Continental Congress met there in September
1774. The building still exists today and is open to visitors. www.
carpentershall.org

The Library Company was founded in 1731 by Benjamin Franklin and the Junto, a group of young men seeking to better themselves. The first rooms it occupied were on the second floor of the State House which is now Independence Hall. By 1741 there were 375 titles in the library and by 1770 there were 2,033 books and oddities. Having outgrown their space, the library moved in 1773 to the second floor of Carpenters' Hall. During the British occupation of Philadelphia in 1777-1778, wounded British soldiers were nursed on the first floor. The 'Wonder Room' housed many artifacts, including the ones mentioned in the story. The Library Company still exists and is now located at 1314 Locust St., Philadelphia, Pennsylvania. https://librarycompany.org/about-lcp/

Characters. The characters in *Dreams of Revolution* are predominantly fictional, but some are based on real people.

Francis Daymon, the librarian of The Library Company, was instrumental in coordinating meetings between Ben Franklin and the French, which led to French support for the war. An excellent book about his role is *The Spies at Carpenters' Hall A Blueprint for a Revolution* by Charles and Nancy Cook.

Marianne Davies, the glass armonica player, toured Europe where Mozart and Beethoven composed music for the instrument. https://www.fi.edu/history-resources/franklins-glass-armonica

Rachel Marks Graydon ran a boardinghouse for University students before a dormitory was constructed in 1765 on campus. I have borrowed her last name and boardinghouse for my story, but my characterization is not based on any history other than being a widow.

Captain John André was a British officer (he became a major in 1778) and head of the secret service. He was a flamboyant character with many talents, such as painting scenery and designing dresses for the Meschianza, the extravagant festival he planned. On October 2, 1780, he was hanged as a spy for assisting Benedict Arnold. https://www.thoughtco.com/major-john-andre-2360616

Jesse's Cream Horses are based on American Cream Draft horses, a rare draft horse breed with a golden coat, white mane and tail, and amber eyes. Although recognition of the breed only began in the early 1900s from a mare named 'Old Granny,' I took the liberty of using the breed during Jesse's time. https://en.wikipedia.org/wiki/American_Cream_Draft

Events. Descriptions of charcoal production, soap making, smallpox, Phebe's wedding, the Meschianza, the coding of secret messages to relay information to General Washington, and plays and dances during the British occupation of Philadelphia are depicted accurately.

American Charcoal Making, In the Era of the Cold-blast Furnace, is a pamphlet based on the recollections of Lafayette Houck, the last of the colliers of Hopewell.

The Reshaping of Everyday Life, 1790-1840 by Jack Larkin, details people's lifestyles and customs during the late 18th and early 19th century in America.